Dorothy McGuire:

The Final Chapter

Book 3

I0586576

Brian Reddish
©2017

Dorothy McGuire: The Final Chapter
© 2017 Brian Reddish

ISBN 978-0-9934887-7-1

Published by Caracal Books
United Kingdom
www.caracalent.uk

The internet addresses, email addresses and phone numbers in this book are accurate at the time of publication.

Cover photography:
Floral Pattern – www.allfreedownload.com/wedesignhot
Used under creative commons.
Woman – www.shutterstock.com/wrangler
Photo used for illustrative purposes only.

Dedication

This book is dedicated to:
Dr Greg Hibbins and Dawn Doyle
whose love, inspiration and dedicated work
behind the scenes has made this and other of my
books possible.

Preface

Book 3—The Final Episode includes the following:

- A brief inclusion of key events and characters from books 1 and 2 integrated within the story. These usually occur whenever the character is first mentioned in the book as it progresses.

- Further development of the persons Jennifer Townsend; Raymond Littleton and the complexities regarding his wife, Susan; and the two teenagers, Robert Templeman and Sarah Manning.

- The ultimate highlight—David and Dorothy!

There is a special emphasis upon the plights of disaffected youth who struggle to find purpose and identity in life. This is outlined in the person of Robert Templeman—otherwise known as *The Duke* from Book 2—who came out from the gangland culture of Damsonwood Estate and is soon challenged as he attempts to befriend Sarah Manning. The transformation from Robert's past to a new life following Jesus means he is now walking new terrain where things don't always go the way he pleases!

Sarah, faces her own challenges. Because of her easy-going, carefree lifestyle, she finds herself in serious trouble. The story outlines the essential need for friends of all ages to rally around young people in their difficulties providing non-judgmental attitudes, genuine love and care.

A second area of focus is on the circumstances surrounding Mary Osborne and the background of her divorce with Raymond Littleton. This aspect is new to Book 3 and gives an insight into the naïvetés and immaturity that can sometimes be found in the privileged society of the rich with its unrealistic, closed and separated world.

The long drama surrounding Raymond Littleton takes him into a valley of despair:

"…Raymond sank deeper and deeper into utter remorsefulness at the very thought of all he once had with the beautiful Mary and little Julia in their simple home. He would sacrifice all his wine bar antics and social lifestyle for this beauty that money could not buy!"

A whole list of other dramatic issues becomes alive throughout the book:

- The predicament of Maria Townsend who lives at home with her father, Alfred, whilst her mum, Jennifer, is living with her sister Betty.

- Jennifer Townsend's legalistic religious upbringing clashes with the beliefs of Dorothy.

- After all her struggles and heartache, can Mary find romance again?

Brian Reddish   June 2017

Chapter 1

Romance — Of a Sort!

A certain hall was almost empty, all the guests having gone home. A few people were walking in and out from the kitchen, cleaning here and tidying there; it had been a great time of celebrations! Now that the balloons and other decorations were taken down and chairs and tables stacked away, the place did look quite bare compared with how it had looked one hour previously! It was hard to realise that within these walls only a short while ago there had been such joyous laughter and fun! The children who had been playing in a corner of the room with Pastor John Peterson had all disappeared; tables each buzzing with light conversation had now become empty and quiet; a large group of young people who had been glued together chatting enthusiastically, choosing to stand rather than sit down, had taken their conversation elsewhere. In short, the engagement party of a certain young couple — if it was still acceptable to call them such who had not yet exceeded the age of thirty-two years — had been very acceptable and enjoyable and, as far as some were concerned, not before time! However, the two, whose day had been very special, were still around.

Far out of the way in a corner was a large settee turned around to face the wall. An observer would have heard conversation coming from that vicinity but would not have seen anyone. There was an explanation, however. The twosome occupying this convenient and comfortable piece of furniture were both slouched upon it next to one other in a lying posture, their bodies being at an angle of not many degrees above the horizontal with their feet resting upon chairs. Now, the gentleman loved to tease his betrothed whilst also conveying true sentiments to her. This enabled him as a man to speak many a mushy word or two which otherwise may have been mostly hidden and unspoken. Dorothy had grown wise to this form of behaviour from David but still liked it nevertheless.

"Dorothy McGuire, you are a most remarkable person, do you know?"

"Do go on, David; I am intrigued to hear what you are going to say next!"

"Are you really? Good! Well, the fact is, now that we have just become engaged, I have been thinking about a certain lady in a most serious manner, and I might add in a very grateful manner at that!"

"David Osborne! If you do not come to the point soon, I will…"

"I believe that when God brought this lady into the world, He blessed her in a most remarkable fashion for all to benefit. He has revealed within her and through her a love, integrity and beauty, so that I have to say it is

David Osborne who has been blessed in being the chief recipient of these wonderful virtues... and so, I would like to take this opportunity to thank this person for enriching my life with her embodiment of all these three!"

After all of that to-do, David leaned over slightly to kiss his betrothed who was quite amicable with everything, including the dramatization of her philosopher. However, she was never overly impressed with flattery at any time of the day, and therefore took the melodramatic words of David accordingly — that is to say, they were spread no more than thinly upon her heart and emotions — and indeed she could likewise give of the same in return but with an air of realistic pragmatism with it as opposed to airy-fairy sentiments.

"That is very lovely of you, David, to say such things about me, and I have to be grateful to have met such a fine, handsome, appreciable man as you, but... well, I also have to say a few things.

"Firstly, regarding integrity, I'm sure *that* is a matter of opinion. And as for beauty, well... is not beauty in the eye of the beholder? That, finally, leaves love. Now, that is the most special of all three, for God is love and love never fails. If, as you say, I have brought love, then that indeed is a compliment! Bless you, David, for that."

Once again, after all of that to-do, Dorothy leaned over slightly to kiss her betrothed who was also, like she a moment earlier, quite amicable with everything, including the dramatization of his philosopher.

Having said all, Dorothy continued, "There is one thing we both must come to grips with very early on, and that is this!

"A while ago, David, you told me something your father said to you regarding love when you had broken to him the news of our engagement—if you remember. Well, apparently, your father said that love will soon go out of the window when there is no bread upon the table!"

"Dorothy, he did indeed say that, but why go and spoil things when I was on a romantic roll just then? You had to quench it as if putting water upon the fire of my heart! You are, of course, speaking realistically in a most sensible manner and indeed so pointedly truthful too, but... be sure of this my lady—that I will always put my hands to work for you, and with the sweat of my brow ensure there is bread and a lot more besides upon the table!"

"I thank you for that blessed assurance, and I also will endeavour to do likewise you know, David. I mean, especially since my earnings are hee-hee... well, let us say no more upon that matter!"

"Do not fear to speak, my beloved, for you are my equal in all matters—if not more so at times—but I am convinced in my own mind to think, nevertheless, that God gave us giftings that complement one another and that these giftings are not all the same as one another's — do you agree? — but they are meant to work together in harmony."

"Absolutely! Or they would not complement as you say. Even so, your dad underlines a common misconception that love does nothing! On the contrary, love does everything possible for someone in an unselfish manner, yes? It is sacrificial, I suppose."

"Dorothy, you are speaking Scripture if you did but know it — *God manifested His love towards us in that while we were yet sinners, Christ died for us.*"

Unknown to the two philosophers, John had come out of the kitchen and peered around the room looking for two certain people, but had not seen them. Wandering across the barren floor towards a certain misplaced sofa, he stood still in his tracks having heard voices from that direction. As he approached it, he again stopped, recognising and overhearing the voice of David without seeing him in person. It had happened just at the point when David was quoting to Dorothy that particular passage of Scripture. Consequently, John, rather than proceed any further and interrupt their conversation, decided to return to the kitchen to speak with Miriam.

"Well, bless my soul, if David and Dorothy are not hidden away in the far corner of the room together. They appeared to be discussing Scriptures from the Bible; can you believe that? I just could not proceed any further and stop them. Interesting couple they are who can talk of such things anywhere and at any time!"

"Oh well, there you are," sighed Miriam, feeling unmoved and somewhat tired now and quite ready to go home.

"But this will not do; I am ready to go now. I don't know about you, John. So, what do you intend to do about our young couple then, may I ask?"

"It's a shame to disturb them," was John's immediate response, and after musing for a moment, he decided what to do. "I know! I'll just pop over to them and give them the keys; they can lock up after themselves."

Now, the young couple were having a brief interlude from talking to one another, and had instead become more involved with what by all accounts could be described as an intimate loving kiss and cuddle together, when suddenly David asked to be excused for just one moment.

"I need to visit the bathroom but won't be a minute." A gentle kiss upon the lips satisfied the lady in waiting as David got up to leave her for a while.

"See you soon!"

No sooner had David stood up and turned around, than he saw John approaching him holding a bunch of keys. David was taken somewhat by surprise at the sight of the silent figure marching robustly towards him, and as it happened, he was just a little grateful John had not come along a moment earlier!

"Oh, John! You made me jump!"

"Don't let me disturb you, David. You just carry on with what you are doing and don't come home until you are both ready. Just switch the lights off and lock up after, will you? Then drop the keys through the letter box. That will be okay."

"Yes... fine... will do."

David had stood somewhat spellbound for a moment in shock and surprise, but the occasion appeared to warrant it catching him unawares, and he rapidly became shaken back into reality by John's presence.

David would have felt a little embarrassed if John had observed him being romantically involved for a moment with Dorothy with a more intimate form of kissing. However, there was nothing untoward about the matter, other than that perhaps his chosen venue of privacy had turned out to be not so private after all, and therefore potentially inappropriate! David grew concerned. Outward appearances were just as important to him as actions themselves whenever under the eye of scrutiny, and the former, in this instance, could easily have lent itself towards embarrassment if nothing else. The fact was, David did not know the Petersons anywhere near as much as Dorothy did, she having lived with them now for some several months, and consequently, he was feeling apprehensive — if not a little remorseful — regarding that which he had permitted to occur. It could easily have led to an awkward situation. Whether his judgment was in error or otherwise was not the sole concern; the appearance of any inappropriateness was the issue! This was not an option David wished to entertain with his pastor and close friend! In any event or circumstance in life, there was acceptable kissing in public and that which was perhaps not so admissible — even in the case where the matrimonial knot had been tied between the two involved. At least, this was the feeling and conviction in their world of etiquette and propriety!

When David returned to Dorothy, both John and Miriam had gone.

"Well, Dorothy, I must say that was rather good timing, don't you? I mean me getting up and going to the bathroom and all at that precise moment just prior to John's arrival... a potentially embarrassing situation nearly happened just then, don't you think?"

"I would say, David, that you are right! John would have been just a little embarrassed observing us kissing just then. I think we must be more aware of what we do and where we do it; don't you think so, my dear?"

"Yes, I do believe so, Dorothy," replied David with some degree of remorse and regret, especially upon hearing once again his dearest's pointed outspokenness. "And it is good to hear your view upon the matter. I was just thinking the same, you know."

Now, David was in more fear and trepidation of the Petersons than Dorothy. He tended to be serious regarding the whole matter of concern regarding their conduct in public, strongly desiring to do the right and proper thing by his beloved Dorothy always. It did not follow, however, that David was being overly concerned — not in Dorothy's eyes! To her it amounted to integrity — well, at least perhaps in its initial developmental stages — and this was a most welcome trait of which she totally approved! Nevertheless, she thought there was no need to become too heavy about the matter, not now they were alone!

"We are indeed mere human mortals, David..." responded Dorothy, leaning over to give him another kiss, having now resorted to her lighter, less inhibited mood, and, importantly, having become satisfied by David's reaction and regret a moment earlier. "And I agree with you entirely, but... this is a private moment that we have now, I think!"

David glared at Dorothy warmly and cheekily upon hearing this forward, inviting comment, and decided to tease her in return!

"Dorothy McGuire, I do believe you are leading me astray!"

Dorothy gently kicked David in the shins, which had the effect of bringing their mutual discussion regarding kissing to an end.

"I must say, though," said David quite thoughtfully, "I was a little surprised by what he said to us both as he left; what do you feel?"

"Well, now you say it… yes, I was more than a little surprised too at his manner. There was an unusual casualness about his demeanour when he said, like… well… when he wanted us both to stay behind and—as he put it—carry on with what we were doing!" laughed Dorothy.

"I was on my way to the bathroom feeling a little taken by surprise. I cannot remember what he said—or what I said for that matter. I confess I missed that comment, but… still, I would have expected John to have waited for us; that's what I would have thought."

"John can be full of surprises, David. I guess we will never fully know exactly what was going through his mind. This is our day, and he didn't wish to disturb us, I suppose!"

Dorothy glanced at her watch, making a note of the time.

"Come now, it is time we were going anyway. Do you know where the light switches are?"

"Yes. If you go out the door, Dorothy, I will switch all the lights off and lock up."

Suddenly, the hall was in darkness, and David was in the process of closing the door behind him and locking up, whilst Dorothy waited outside as instructed. He stopped and turned to take one last glance at the empty hall, which was lit up only by the moonlight through a window, and thought to himself in a sentimental manner, *This is where we had our engagement celebration! This hall will always hold such fond memories that I will never forget!*

Dorothy's journey over the last year had been nothing short of incredible, if not miraculous in many ways. It had all begun with the lonely, isolated Dorothy suffering from severe depression. Things had been so different for her in those days. Her first major battle was learning how to control it, and with Miriam's advice, care and friendship with patient understanding, she had finally made some progress regarding that matter. And her newly found faith helped her beyond measure!

The next episode in her life was both good and bad; wonderful and yet a challenge for her. How would she cope with a relationship with a man like David Osborne, with whom she had fallen in love? This next learning curve had not entered the equation, until she had found herself attracted to him, and then the problem had sprung up as if out of hiding. It had proved far more delicate for Dorothy than the dilemma of depression, for it was related to and an offshoot of her being a victim of sexual childhood abuse, making it very personal and difficult to share with anyone. Nevertheless, a way seemed to have been made for her, instigated by invisible hands, when she discussed the matter first with Mary Osborne, then Miriam—and the outcome of their collective advice had led her in the direction of counselling, which had worked exceedingly well.

The real challenge then had been conveying all of this to David! This she had done one evening after arriving home from having a meal together. David had been so understanding and pleased that he had been told all the nitty, gritty details. It had impressed him and drawn him closer to his Dorothy, so that they had both promised to share everything together and be fully open with one another in the future. It was the very same evening that he had proposed to her! Dorothy and David now found themselves truly bonded by their mutual love, and the engagement celebration had now come and gone.

~~~~~~~~

Upon arriving home, Miriam immediately made herself a cup of tea and sat down in the lounge with her feet up, John following her not long afterwards.

"I've never seen so many young people, Miriam. I see that Robert Templeman managed to bring Sarah Manning, but he also brought three other young men who I've never seen before! How about that? I think David was pleased. He has more students for his karate class now, thanks to Robert.

"Who is Sarah Manning, John? I believe you know her."

"Why, yes. I met her at the *Chicken and Chips* restaurant in the precinct that time when I went to look after Robert, if you remember."

"Oh! My memory is failing me, dear. Can you elaborate upon the circumstances? I remember Dorothy meeting you there on one occasion. Was this the same one?"

"Can you remember, Miriam, when I telephoned you about Robert? It was my day off, and Ian McPherson had just phoned me to say he was concerned about Robert. Ian had said Robert was feeling a bit down in himself regarding this Sarah."

"Oh yes, I remember now. I suggested you go and see Robert and invite him over here for tea, since you were free and not doing anything special.

"So, how did you meet Sarah?

"Oh! She just came along and joined us as we sat outside the chip shop. Robert happened to see her; she works at a hair salon next door. She seemed a pleasant girl, and I do believe that Robert has a crush on her! He had been feeling down when she refused him on two fronts — going out on a date and coming to church with him!"

"My, oh my, young love, hey! Well, perhaps he was moving too fast, as they say; he needs to take his time if you ask me. What girl in the world would do the second if she were not interested in the first?"

"I completely agree, of course. I guess the lad is so used to getting his own way. Boys used to jump at his wish and commands in the gang world, but now things are different. Well, anyway… that's how I know Sarah, but now she has shown no interest in coming to church or going out with Robert, so we must see what develops between the two of them—if anything.

"The thing is that Sarah has bad memories of Robert when he was a gang leader called the Duke."

"The Duke! Goodness me! Don't tell me he was involved with robbery and drugs?"

"My dear Miriam, would it matter if he were involved previously? I can tell you he is a changed young man now, all thanks to Alfred Townsend who met him at his open-air event one time and befriended him. But Alfred tells me Robert never did drugs for fear of upsetting his late mother."

"Well, John, this Sarah came along to the celebration do with Robert… the Duke… whatever he is called, so things can't be that bad between the two of them; don't you think?"

"You're absolutely right; something is going on there. And from what I gather from

Robert, he does not intend to give up on her. He is behaving like a gentleman now, bless him! Still, that is their affair; who can say what is best for young people today? Perhaps, if it is meant, it might do him good—certainly it would be an improvement upon all his previous activities... settling down, I mean, with a nice girlfriend. All things in balance of course. He must do something; I can't hold that against him. We'll just have to see what pans out, as our Rebecca used to say!

"Just look at what Maria Townsend did with Ian McPherson when he was down and out on drugs! That was quite amazing—how she encouraged him to change his life and was there to help him do just that! Anyway, I'll have to tell you much more about Robert sometime, Miriam; things are very tough for him at home with his dad. Did you know the three boys Robert brought along with him today were all ex-members of his old gang?"

"That is quite amazing, John! I suppose... but oh, we do need to appoint a youth leader in the church! All this is getting out of my depth; the whole thought worries me. What are we to do with them all? And yet, I shouldn't say that, should I? But... well, it is all getting to be too much for me; forgive me, John, but it is! Alfred Townsend has completely revolutionised the church what with the miracle of his healed leg—and he, an alcoholic, turning to the Lord! But there again, John, this is exactly what you had predicted if I remember. You said things may change for the better in some quarters, namely among all the young people without exception, and probably all those who are born-again believers; but elsewhere, things could become worse. You said that God had done something wonderful and that the irony was that certain quarters thought it was not so wonderful!"

"You are quite right, Miriam. God is changing the structure of our church now, and we need to change along with it. But I have something in mind, my dear. Don't worry! God never intended us to do everything by ourselves. Look at poor old Moses! He got a bit flustered administering to all the people's needs, until God told him to appoint leaders over all the different tribes!"

John gave a little laugh, before continuing, "Isn't that what we have in our church... what you might call many different groups? There are the elderly, the young, the little ones, and the rest! Now, there are times when all the lot should be together in my opinion; it's when each group gets so big—then we must act! It is a good healthy thing, not a bad problem! We've got to find the Aarons and the like to help us!"

Chapter 2

Ministering Servants

As a waiter and waitress wait upon the needs of their customers and respond accordingly; as servants would wait upon their masters to do their bidding; so a minister, who is technically a servant, is available to respond to the needs of others. Just what occurs in practice regarding the latter is something else, but at least this is closer to the definition than perhaps what is sometimes displayed by those who bear such a title!

Waiting upon is nothing more than being ready and available. A flick of a hand and the waitress standing somewhere in a strategic position looking and observing what is happening upon the shop floor will come immediately to attend to whatever is required by her client. It's as if their wish is her command!

God desires waiters and waitresses. Indeed, *'As the eyes of servants look to the hand of their masters ... so our eyes look to the Lord our God. Those who wait on the Lord shall renew their strength...'*

Ministers of the Lord, in the real sense of the word, are to be found everywhere — not recognised by certain attire or position necessarily but by the actions and deeds that they unselfishly perform under the influence and guidance of the Holy Spirit. Alfred Townsend was such a person. He could be found within the town precinct, usually once each week, proclaiming his testimony and telling people of how he had been healed by the Lord.

Many people previously knew Alfred as a grumpy, old man who occasionally hobbled around the town supported by two crutches. Anyone who spoke to Alfred would be well and truly reminded or informed of his misfortune several years earlier with the wheel of a tractor. This accident had taken from him his livelihood as a farm worker, for which he had held bitter resentment for the Almighty. Alcohol had nearly been his ruin, but other costs had mounted in his life and circumstances. His wife, Jennifer Townsend, had moved away to live with her sister, leaving their eighteen-year-old daughter, Maria, the faithful ministering servant of her Lord, in the home alone with her father!

Two of God's ministering servants, hidden away from all limelight in the persons of Maria and Dorothy, worked endlessly to help Alfred; indeed, the far greater good in the world is based upon unhistorical and unknown acts of kindness, such as the deeds that were shown by these two ladies! When Maria herself became too embroiled within the work load and responsibilities of looking after her father—at the expense of her own life, including her studies—it was Dorothy who came to her rescue and organised home care and meals for Alfred. It followed that Maria and

Dorothy became the very best of friends, so much so that Maria could confide in her about any personal matter and receive the best and wisest counsel on offer. In Maria's own words, Dorothy was just great; 'awesome' was her description!

Maria was an up and coming Mother Teresa. As well as painlessly serving the needs of her father, she had brought Ian McPherson up and out of the miry pit of destruction. She had the hands and the willing, loving heart; God did the rest!

Given that a chief quality of a ministering servant is to do God's bidding in both His way and manner, it follows that it will ultimately bear fruit even if one does not see it happen personally. The beauty of God's servants is their utter devotion to obedience without seeking any personal acclaim or recognition. This is displayed and declared perfectly with that Psalm, *I delight to do your will, O my God, and your law is within my heart.*

This is what Maria had surely done in the case of Ian, though in her situation she saw it all happen before her very eyes! She had visited him one day in his plight after not seeing him for weeks. His frail, underweight figure, which had once been that of a healthy, clean, young lad whom she had known ever since she was a child, was now slumped upon a sofa in a sad state. It had been the drugs! Maria had been tempted to react in horror at the sight of him, but he had been past reproof. Instead she was moved with compassion and had spoken to him tenderly.

"From now on, Ian, I am going to help you get over this, okay? No more stuff from now on, alright?"

Ian had responded to Maria's loving care with tears! It had worked! Her strength and commitment in helping him had lit up a spark of encouragement within a hopeless situation and brought him hope, rather like a gentle breeze blowing upon a dying, smoking ember, restoring a flame of life once again.

It had taken well over a year for Ian to get back on track. With Maria's initial help and that of many others to follow, he had found a good job, started college and become the drummer in the church band, where, of course, Maria was the lead singer! In fact, Ian had not just got back to where he had been prior to drug taking; he had re-entered life and the world at a much higher level than before! He had learned the hard way of life's cruelty from unwise decisions and choices and now found himself re-united with his best friend, Maria, in a more mature frame of mind than previously.

Ian was working so well now in an apprenticeship. He drove his own car that had been a gift to him from his father upon his eighteenth birthday for doing so well. Yes, it was true to say that Ian was a new man, thanks to a dear ministering servant. Could it be said that it was a servant in the person of Maria Townsend sent to Ian by God that had helped bring about this restoration in his life? This would rarely be recognised by the world at large but would most certainly be understood by Heaven!

In the case of the once grumpy, old Alfred — well, he too was a changed man! The heroine was another one of God's ministers in the form of Dorothy McGuire, who had not been deterred by his obnoxious attitude to both God and man. Dorothy, being a close friend of his daughter, Maria, would visit Alfred on occasions — much to Maria's fright and horror, for she was afraid of her dad's behaviour and reaction in the presence of her friend.

Wisdom and integrity are often only manifest in dire problem situations when genuine thoughtfulness and unselfish concern are blended together with a personal knowledge and love of God together with His Word. Alfred needed this combination of love and firmness, and Dorothy gave it! He respected her from the start, especially after discovering what pain and anguish she had suffered herself from an abusive past and depression.

It had all happened one day when Dorothy had sat in his presence listening to all his bitterness towards God, blaming the Almighty for allowing his suffering. Dorothy had challenged him, saying, "God never promised you and me that there would be no suffering in life, but He did promise, however, to be with us through it."

Alfred had been challenged and lovingly admonished! There was no other way with him. Consequently, he had turned to God's Word to read about the suffering of Jesus, which had ultimately led him to act and respond to all he had read for himself.

There was no end to ministry of this nature — encouragement, help, words of blessing. They never became redundant or unnecessary; they were a lifelong necessary service.

Dorothy knew her calling, and that was to help others in the way God had helped her. But she was not exempt by any means from such ministry being directed towards herself. In the early days, it was Miriam who had befriended Dorothy as she lived alone with seemingly no help coming her way — from God or man!

What a grave misconception for one to think that initially a person needs to be morally good and upright, sound, with no problems at all before God can use them! Further, to presuppose there was a need to be well-accomplished academically or intellectually to be more suitably positioned and placed in life for God's service is equally untrue. Such ideas are unfounded in the good book, which declares exactly the opposite! The poor received Jesus gladly, relishing the prospect of being accounted worthy to follow Him. Jesus had compassion upon the sick and needy, desiring them to look up, believe and follow Him. The unlearned fishermen were also called to be His disciples, as were grave sinners! It is well known — but then so often seemingly forgotten — that God looks upon the heart of a person, knowing what potential lies within each one whom He created!

Dorothy McGuire had no doubts about her own vulnerability and weaknesses, but unknown to her, God saw great potential and inner strength which could move mountains! She knew only too well the hopelessness felt and brought on by depression, yet God was to prove to her that He was the God of the impossible! With God's service and ministry, He chooses the weak things of the world to confound the wise so that no one can boast saying, "It was I that did this, because I was good, clever, talented, rich, privileged or famous!"

Such qualities were never presented or even desired by the King of Kings and Lord of Lords, who on the contrary was despised and rejected of men, a man of sorrows fully acquainted with grief, and interestingly made Himself of no reputation! No, the listed attributes that men highly esteem have no bearing whatsoever in qualifying a person for God's Kingdom and service, though they may impress — having their glowing uses — in the eyes and opinions found in this world! Indeed, that which is highly esteemed amongst men is an abomination in the Lord's eyes, for it can easily bar the way of entry into His grace and forgiveness through a false sense of security and self-righteousness, believing that their accomplishments and position in this world increase their standing in the next! Whatever Dorothy thought about herself and her condition, she nevertheless cried out to God for His help, and eventually—after much persistence—found it! Having reached the end of herself, she discovered that God was waiting for her at that very point where she abandoned her own self and way of thinking and placed herself into the hands of the Lord!

Alfred had found this process in some ways much easier than Dorothy. In his case, he did not need to be convinced of his unworthiness and need! He had moaned and groaned for years; yet, he only needed a little of God's Word from Dorothy. A little was sufficient, that right word that completely transformed his life as he believed and acted upon it. Alfred latched onto a promise that became his favourite verse of Scripture, or as he put it, God's invitation to him personally—*He who comes to Me, I will never turn away.*

Once the understanding and enlightenment of the Holy Spirit had come upon him, speaking to him in a personal manner, he had realised an important truth: that God will forgive and receive you just as you are, if you believe in Him! Alfred believed this as if it were his last chance in the world to be saved!

Now, God was using Alfred in a most unprecedented manner! He had a way of reaching the neglected and downtrodden of the day, including the young, so that they were being drawn into the church and disrupting the status quo in the process. Through Alfred's testimony of healing and salvation, God was changing the concept of what it meant to serve Him — and this challenged the established church in the process!

Through a network of people, God moved upon the church, using one to help another and someone else in turn to help the one! This way people's needs were met. Prejudices, hurtful circumstances, wilful ignorance and unbelief were being addressed. Where just a little faith arose, there followed healing, restoration, salvation, as well as the building of friendships and relationships, strengthening one another. Out of this healthy environment were birthed ministries amongst ordinary people, all serving one another in love, considering the needs of others paramount to those of their own; God was working among them in life-changing power, yielding effective results. Even those from gangland territory, previously untouched, had been given by God!

Now, upon the horizon, were many other problem situations imminently waiting around the corner, all unknown yet, but waiting to surface nevertheless at some future time. Problems common to man—domestic quarrels, fighting, disaffected families yielding to separation and divorce, even dissentions within the church—are found wherever there is greed, selfishness, unruly attitudes and behaviour, disrespect, wilful ignorance and disobedience to one another, to family, to those in authority, and from such people, who not only know in their conscience God's disapproval and ultimate judgement upon doing such things, but also revel in their own audacity in doing them as if arrogantly displaying their abysmal behaviour with the declaration, "Where is God?"

God was preparing His army of ministering servants from within the church, servants who would take up the mission to reach such people. Sadly, they did not all come from the established resources within or necessarily from large churches where entertaining programmes kept many within a building and off the streets, but failed in making disciples and equipping them for the Divine commission to go out onto the streets! Instead, they came from a new generation of converted people, both young and old, who truly came out of the darkness of their own dismal circumstances, having been being born again into God's light for a purpose—to help others out of the same plight of which they too had been victims!

Chapter 3

After the Celebration Was Over

"Listen! That sounds like the door! That'll be Dorothy and David coming back. They have not been very long."

John peered through into the hallway, and sure enough, it was the two of them. "Well, you have not been long, David. Did you lock up behind you and post the keys?"

"Yes, we did, John." David took off his jacket and hung both his and Dorothy's in the hallway, whilst John walked back to Miriam, leaving the two to themselves.

"Help yourself to some of the leftovers in the kitchen if you are still peckish," he called as he walked away.

Shortly, the two came to join John and Miriam in the lounge, each with a cup of tea and a plate of cakes. Dorothy sat next to Miriam on the settee, and David seated himself upon the remaining easy chair opposite John. It was unusually quiet for a moment, as if each were waiting for someone else to speak; then David asked a question of John.

"We were both surprised that you and Miriam left so quickly, John."

"Ah well, Miriam was ready to go; weren't you, dear? And besides, we did not wish to disturb you. You both seemed quite engrossed in whatever you were talking about, so I suggested we left you alone to get on with it!"

Upon hearing this last comment from John, both David and Dorothy turned and looked at one another, just a little apprehensive and shaken by John's forthrightness regarding their personal conversation, and they wondered whether he had possibly heard any of it. David replied with a humorous tone but at the same time not without some curiosity. "Ah, so you heard what we were talking about then, John?"

The latter realised now that he was treading upon forbidden territory and tried his best to neutralise the situation without appearing to be deliberately eavesdropping. "Good gracious, David! No... well, not intentionally, but I did happen to overhear you say something."

At this David began to be concerned!

"As I approached you with the keys, I overheard you talking about a Bible verse... if you remember. That's all I actually heard; I can assure you."

Upon hearing John's last remark, David felt more at ease, and once again he and Dorothy turned and looked at one another, but this time with raucous laughter, all to the astonishment of John who was wondering just what was quite so funny. John had a good sense of humour and was very happy to have apparently been the cause of such laughter, even though he was oblivious to its cause.

"Well, clearly something is cracking you two up. What did I say that was so funny? If I may ask?"

For the third time, David and Dorothy looked at one another; only this time it was to decide who should take the lead in giving some sort of response to John. And this duty fell upon Dorothy. She tried hard to control another burst of laughter, then proceeded further in an unaccustomed manner of speech—coming from her that is—which seemed to fit the occasion perfectly.

"John! We had been talking… and yes, we did speak of a certain Bible verse, but the rest was… like… personal, private stuff, you know… and…"

It was now the turn of both John and Miriam to burst into laughter, the latter having been listening to the discourse thus far but without appearing to do so in any attentive manner.

"Whatever it may have been," added John humorously, "the subject of your conversation, that is, I assure you Miriam and I will most probably have done something similar ourselves, hey Miriam?" Now John was being liberal in his response, but Miriam was more conservative.

"Speak for yourself, John," replied Miriam in an austere manner that was a combination of both strictness and humour. "I dare to wonder what these two were getting up to, and here we both thought you were having… well… a mature conversation, and John said, 'Let them get on with it; we should not disturb them!' Just what we have both been privy to, I dare not think! Anyway, it is none of my business, so let us leave the matter at that."

Miriam was being both diplomatic and facetious, so that whatever was relevant regarding the matter it would have been addressed accordingly by her comments. In short, she covered herself for several different scenarios!

John decided it was now necessary to change the subject and congratulated them both on the occasion.

"We are both very pleased for you two, and I know of a certainty that my dear wife is one hundred percent with me upon this one, hey Miriam?"

"Absolutely!"

Miriam stood up to give Dorothy a hug, whilst a slightly more melancholic John could only regurgitate a sad thought he had just been musing over whilst observing the two ladies hugging one another.

"Soon, I imagine, we will lose another daughter from this house, I dare say!"

"Fear not, dear John," spoke Dorothy with affection. "If you will have me—the both of us, that is—we will still seek to invade this household upon Sundays in particular for some of my favourite pudding and custard and…"

"… and maybe one day there just might be

a need for babysitters!" added David. "At some time that is, but more likely the distant future!"

Dorothy rather liked what David had just said, despite feeling embarrassment! She thought it was nice and not too indicative of any particular time in the future when babysitting might be required, only that it was sometime in the future! That response she could handle comfortably.

"Before you arrived, David, Miriam and I were talking about the young people present this afternoon. I counted at least six or seven teenagers who were not part of our regular church families. Well, now you say that two of the three boys that Robert brought along with him were interested in coming along to your karate class; is that right? So, including Robert himself and Ian, that is four young men altogether!"

David nodded in agreement to John's arithmetic with pride and approval, whilst Miriam suddenly found herself not quite so concerned or overwhelmed about the numbers of young people coming into their midst as she had done recently. The thought of David possibly taking some of them under his wing gave her much-needed assurance, which she expressed to him with admiration and appreciation.

"That is excellent, David," added Miriam. "You could help those boys physically, socially and maybe spiritually, you know! The perfect combination, so necessary today."

"That is so true," commented Dorothy. "I

never thought about it in that way! What about that, David? Are you up to shepherding such a group?"

Before David could respond, it was John who came in quickly to endorse Dorothy's suggestion, leaving David wondering just whether he had any choice in the matter.

"Well, you are touching a very important topic there, Dorothy—that of guidance and leadership of our youth. Young men of that age need a role model, someone they will respect and yet who is young enough to involve himself... well... in their youthful activities, whatever they may be.

"That's interesting, John, what you said just now regarding role models," responded David. "I have observed Robert Templeman of late, since Alfred brought him into church and since he started attending karate along with Ian. Do you know that Robert speaks very respectfully of Alfred and woe betide any who should speak ill of him? He's kind of bonded with him in a way that is amazing coming from one so young... and Alfred being in his sixties, I guess.

"Listening to Robert the other evening in class—well, actually it was during break time— he told me that his father was never at home and that he did not get on well with him at all. To make matters worse, Robert's mother died about a year ago, which was very sad for he and his mum were close.

"Well, the point I'm getting at is this; Alfred seems to be a sort of role model to Robert as a fatherly figure, and he has a good relationship and rapport with him, something he does not get at home with his own father. What do you think?"

John rubbed his chin, giving some thought to David's observations.

"David, I appreciate what you are saying, and I'm not at all surprised by Robert's respect and attachment to Alfred, given his circumstances. I just don't know any more though what to think... You see, we are not used to having kids from disaffected homes, like Robert, in our church. Isn't it amazing that we always think that our own young people would naturally prefer a young leader? Well, this is the traditional way of doing things."

"John, that's what young people tend to prefer," added Miriam, "because young people like to do energetic things, don't they? That's why their leaders are who they are. Do you not agree?"

"Of course, of course," resigned John, grateful for that comment from his wife, which helped relinquish himself from such a responsibility, for David's mention of Alfred being a role model had set his own heart beating a little faster, it having pricked his conscience somewhat, imagining himself being considered for that role as well! John continued, "That will always be the case, I'm sure; but like I intimated before, the church is entering new territory, and I no longer intend to assume things should be done the way they have always been done! Let's plan, yes, and be practical of course, but let us also have an open mind too!

"You see, these kids are not the same as our church kids — if you'll forgive the phrase — for the simple reason that they have no parents within the church, and they have probably — like Robert — never stepped inside a church building before except on a school trip. That's what Robert told me about himself!

"Now, this is another point I wish to make, and I believe this to be very relevant regarding how we plan to help such young people in the future. When I spoke with Robert at the *Chicken and Chips* one afternoon... Yes, David, you are smiling, but this I believe is one way you can really get to know young people... Well, I discovered it was through their stomach; in fact, it's not a bad activity with anyone else for that matter, except maybe with those who are weight conscious. Anyway, Robert told me a lot of things about kids that come from the area around where he lives — I mean lots! I conclude that if we desire such young people to start coming to a church activity, they will need to be catered for. Again, I have an open mind, just like I said, regarding how we endeavour to do that.

"Robert told me they nearly all come from a background of clubbing, pubs and the like. Apparently, he asked Sarah out — she goes clubbing by the way — and at some point, he also invited her to church, but the lad got turned down on both accounts! I did have a word with him, telling him he must be patient and that you can't force people, you know.

"Now, Robert is not giving up, and what I noticed about him, even as we sat there eating chips... You remember the occasion, don't you, Dorothy? And you saw Sarah as well, for you dropped by and joined us, didn't you? Well, he was very kind and polite in his talking with Sarah... and so, you see, Sarah came along today — didn't she now? — so he must be doing something right!

"Well, this is the challenge! At some point, probably soon, I would like to see everyone who has contact with these kids in some way or another. There's you, David, with your karate; then there's Maria Townsend and Ian McPherson, who meet up with Robert a lot; then there's you, Dorothy — you know Maria so well. And we must not forget Alfred himself... why, he is the one who has started all of this conversation!

"Do you see what we have here? Just think about it for a minute... We have a wide range of people, all from different age groups, who make some sort of contact with this special group of young people!

"Interesting, I think, how God works! You see, God didn't necessarily propose youth groups — but that doesn't of course mean that we shouldn't have them, and I'm sure they probably existed, but there is no record of it as far as I can see — but He did create a body of believers with many different members and giftings. So, in a way, I should not be surprised if all kinds of people, irrespective of their age, influence the young.

"Well, you must excuse me for a moment; I need to go somewhere."

Miriam was quite taken aback and surprised by her husband's sudden zeal, knowledge and interest in the young people; it would appear to have started after eating that chicken and chips! Miriam added something of her own opinion upon the matter in her husband's absence, conceding just how easily you could get out of touch with youth from different generations now compared to previous years. Further, their traditional youth, what remained of them, all came from parents within the church, and therefore they were not typical, as mentioned by John, of the youth at large; they were merely the tip of the iceberg!

Miriam concluded thoughtfully, "I think we oldies can get too engrossed sometimes in just how to proceed in the church with certain matters like young people — probably because we get too preoccupied with all of our own problems so that we cannot see beyond them! There will never be an end to needs in the church, not until it has been snatched away in the rapture at that precise moment known only by God—and what a day that will be! Meanwhile, it is each one's calling to overcome this world and all it throws at us by living a life of faith and trust in God's Word. If we cannot grasp this, then I cannot see the church moving forward to fulfil the Divine mission to preach the Gospel to every creature. But I should not forget what Jesus Himself said, 'I will build My Church and the gates of hell shall not prevail against it!'"

Miriam was clearly reflecting upon years of experience. All those methods, programmes and ideas that had previously seemed good for a while, but now had gradually gone stale having run their course, seemingly not bearing fruit anymore. In the past, young people came to church, usually with their parents, and got involved in the band, socialising together—including outdoor activities and events where they shared God's Word in various ways. But then, they grew up and went to university or moved away to where some other church or organisation had an even younger, more vibrant atmosphere of their own.

"Sometimes, we think this is the trend we should follow, or that a different approach may be better than what we are doing now, as if we had been missing it all along, so we end up changing everything to suit a new modern idea. I'm not saying we should never change by any means. Sometimes we need to wake up to prejudices in the church that can so easily be directed against the noisy crowds of babies, children and young people whenever they interrupt our nice serene meetings… if you know what I mean… as if we would not take special care of them all. But at the end of the day, it is God who works and builds His House through His Gospel – and I might add, our faithfulness as well in ministering His Word from the top!"

Miriam's reflections were finalised by this conviction made to herself and most likely to all her audience, thus making way for contributions to follow from David.

"What I am observing," added David, "is this; you get most people coming to church with their own families, like you say, and occasionally others who are invited, like friends and such, but then there are people like Alfred who just felt compelled to come because God had obviously been working in his life. This does not seem to happen very often, I suppose; it's outside of the box so to speak, but of late, it has been happening quite a lot, don't you think? Someone must have been busy in the background, speaking to these young people who have been attending the church of late and who have no association with anyone other than the one they came with. Whoever they are, they have taken on this role of ministering to young people and befriending them. As a result, God is working in their lives, drawing them in! This is the only way, in my opinion, for the church and God's Kingdom to increase, don't you think?

"Why, I walked into church, too, just like Alfred — though I was only coming to collect Mary, and I did not come in until the end of the meeting! In my case, as soon as I entered, I felt a presence and just knew I had to get right with God! It was that real! I know Dorothy and John had both spoken to me previously and helped me a lot — along with others in the church — and I can tell you that it impacted me considerably. It was as if what they had told me had prepared me for later things that were to happen in my life — all quite unknown to me at the time. I know Dorothy had talked to Alfred as well, visiting and helping him in practical ways. What I am trying to illustrate here is that people have come into church as a direct result of someone speaking to them in some way.

"Look at Robert as well! He is a young man, and he did the same. Well, he came to church first with Alfred; didn't he? But then, after that, he came on his own. Do you remember one time when he could not stay for the whole meeting but had to leave early to let the dog out?" David laughed.

"Excellent! That to me is real, you know. It tells me a lot! He came on his own and left on his own! The driving force was not that he had friends in the church, because he didn't have any friends. He only knew Alfred, who was like his fatherly figure — and that was it! Bless him! I like Robert; the way he has come to the Lord does something to me, like I am witnessing the hand of God working in a person's life... well, that's the way I see it! He is a real inspiration to me at thirty-two years of age. I grew up going to church because I had to, and some good that did me, but then...," David suddenly pointed over to Dorothy, "I met this young lady!"

Dorothy smiled and held David's hand warmly. "Yes, and I met you too, David. Remember?"

"The first time I saw you, Dorothy, was when you gave a talk in church. You were so impressive!"

John entered the room at that instant and overheard the last words from David regarding Dorothy.

"Yes, I gather you *were* impressed with Dorothy, judging by the outcome of events, hey lad!"

"Indeed so, John; you are right once again. Dorothy was very impressive in many ways!"

"Well, all I can say to sum up is this," continued David. "I am relatively new to the life of our church, and I thank God I see some people taking the time to talk to others about their testimony of faith and go out of their way to challenge and bless!"

David was a young man who had been radically changed now that he had found that something special that only God can give a person — the reality of His presence — and he was developing a growing zeal for God, having tasted of the old wine but now thirsty for the new! He was concerned for people, who say they believe, to act upon their faith and help others who like himself had been bound in a form of religion but with no personal relationship — and without any real understanding or sense of God's presence! Interestingly, he perceived that people could still be religious whatever name was given to their particular church; he had become aware now that people could conform to a similar type of religious attitude to that he had himself previously held, irrespective of the church they attended; in short, those who were conditioned through familiarity with the structure and style of a meeting, whether it was formal or informal, evangelistic or otherwise, so that in either case, they were never moved in any way to be proactive or demonstrative in their faith but had become a people quite used to the church setup, even speaking the language from time to time so that according to David's observations, they could still be ultimately nothing more than religious in their habits — just as he had been for all those years!

David would be the first to admit what an arrogant and self-righteous person he had been in the past, thinking that he was right and that others were either wrong or extreme! Now it was as if scales had been removed from his eyes so that he could see and discern things that were real and based upon God's Word — or otherwise! His advice and opinion with young people was simply this:

It's the best life to have — knowing Jesus personally! Knowing God is alive and that you are serving Him!
He gives you a purpose in life and promises you a future!

Chapter 4

The Blue Moon

The west side of town was notorious for night life, especially amongst the young. It was here one could find the best restaurants, pubs, wine bars and night clubs.

The time was coming up to 10:00 pm one Saturday evening, and the air was still warm outside. Each building had its own unique noise emanating from within. There was an Italian restaurant with its doors ajar buzzing with a full house that evening, and numerous waiters were dashing to tables both within and without. Opposite this restaurant, on the other side of the road and just a little farther down, stood *The Red Lion*, where the noise was somewhat louder with raucous laughter, boisterous shouting, and loud music all intermingled together creating a typical lively pub atmosphere that would probably have been unheard of upon any other night of the week, but was just reserved for a Saturday.

Much farther down the street, where the lights grew dimmer and the noise quietened considerably, there were four teenage girls giggling as they walked together, having just left *The Red Lion*. One girl was wobbling from side to side, needing to be supported by two of the others as she trundled along; it was not clear whether her stilettos were responsible for her temporary

43

imbalance or whether it was as a result of just having come from the previous venue.

The girls were in full party mode, wearing glittering, dazzling clothes that were made using very little material! They were full of laughter as they crossed the road in the direction of some blue lights above what otherwise seemed a subdued, dark-looking building.

Upon reaching the other side of the road, a group of boys were also seemingly heading in the same direction as the company of girls — towards the blue flickering neon lights that revealed the large words, *Blue Moon*; underneath were the smaller words *Night Club*. As their two paths crossed just outside of the club entrance, one of the boys, who was clearly under the influence of drink, spoke across to the girls in a derogatory fashion, "Hiya, girls! Going for a good time then? We'll see yer right; hey boys?"

"Get outta here!" replied one of the girls, indignant at the belittling, uncomplimentary remark.

"Whoo!" reacted the same boy in response to the girl's abrupt reply; then he changed the tone of his unsavoury remarks and said, "Where's yer boyfriend then... the Duke, i'n it?"

"Why can't you jerks go and get a life... if you can, that is!" replied the same girl.

"I'll get you later for that, Sarah Manning!"

As soon as each group had gone through the entrance, they walked down a long, narrow, winding passageway leading to a large hall that had the appearance of a cavern hidden and tucked away underground. Here the whole place suddenly reverberated with sound and became alive! *Thud, thud, thud!* The dance beat of the music with its intense volume electrified the atmosphere. Inside were at least two hundred mostly young people, the majority seeming to be girls who were conspicuously dancing away in an uninhibited, sensual fashion, their body movements synchronised in unison with every beat and their arms raised high in the air.

The four girls pushed through the crowd of dancers, making their way towards the bar. There were some tables and chairs situated in one corner of the room where the lighting was more subdued. This area was positioned way back from the dance floor, and sitting together around one of the tables was a certain young couple, who unlike the majority were quiet and attentive with one another, having pleasant light conversation, seemingly oblivious to all the noise going on around them.

"Thank you for taking me out, Clive. I like it here. It's just a great atmosphere!"

"I'm only pleased you said yes, Hannah!
"Would you like a drink?"

"What are you going to have, Clive?"

"Me? Just a small beer probably; I'm driving! You have whatever you like though."

"Well, at Christmas my mum lets me have a Pina Colada cocktail… if that is okay?"

"No problem. You realise they contain nearly all fruit juice, don't you?"

"So! I like pineapple juice; so there!"

"That's fine — just wanted to tell you about the sugar content; that's all!"

Hannah had just turned eighteen, and Clive was her date that evening. They were very compatible as far as things go and grew up together in the same neighbourhood. Clive was a quiet-speaking, young man who was nineteen years of age, and he treated Hannah with much politeness and respect. This was Hannah's deciding factor in agreeing to come out with him the moment he asked her, for his looks she considered as average, but he was trustworthy and sensible with a kind, mature manner exceptionally uncommon for boys of his age.

Hannah's father's influence had altered her priorities and opinions regarding boys, and at an early age she had discovered that not all that glitters is gold! Her father was also a gentle, kind and caring person to her, and after all, girls judge all men against a good dad! Safety was the essence — and she trusted Clive.

He returned with their drinks, and after a while they took to the floor.

Four certain girls had reduced their numbers now to two, the others being occupied with dance partners. The remaining two sat upon high stools around the bar area, drinking excessively, when a recently familiar young man approached one of them.

"Look, just to say I'm sorry about the way I talked to yer outside; let me buy you a drink. What do yer say then?

The girl peered at the lad suspiciously, already feeling quite intoxicated, but her happy, carefree mood was about to make a choice.

"Well, what are yer drinking, before I change my mind?"

The girl slurred out the words, "Go on then. I'll have another gin and tonic."

Her friend, who sat nearby, casually reminded her to take it easy for she had drunk far too much already, but it was all to no avail. The young man's intentions were neither good nor honourable, and he arranged for the drink to be a double and appeared to discreetly place something inside it.

As it happened, Clive and Hannah were now dancing nearby, and Clive overheard the conversation between the girl and young man, observing his actions and manner, both of which caused Clive to be suspicious. He had recognised the girl as a close friend of someone he knew, a Robert Townsend.

"Hannah, I think something is going on; let's just sit down for a minute."

"What do you mean, Clive?" said an alarmed Hannah.

"I'm not sure, but look over there at that girl; I know who she is, and I'm sure that guy next to her is up to no good."

Within minutes of having her drink, the girl stood upright looking pale and staring blankly at her friend; she swayed from side to side, swirled around, then collapsed to the floor, vomiting as she fell. A scene developed with the second girl screaming and shouting at the culprit responsible, but he soon darted away, leaving in a hurry. People scuttled away from the surrounding area to another part of the dance floor, looking quite inconvenienced by the disturbance and not wishing to get involved.

"I think I'm going to phone Robert!" declared Clive. "He will be none too pleased."

"Look," said Hannah instinctively, "I'll go over to see if I can help the girl, okay?"

Hannah dashed over to the scene. She was familiar with some procedures as her mum was a nurse; meanwhile, a certain phone call was in progress.

"Robert, is that you...? This is Clive Johnson; how yer doin', mate?

"Hi, Clive. I'm good."

"Look! Where are you, Robert?"

"I'm with Ian McPherson and his girlfriend right now. Why? What's up, mate?"

"There is a problem over here at the *Blue Moon*; it's regarding Sarah Manning. I don't know whether you're interested to know this, but I think she's been spiked — she's just passed out on the floor!"

"I'll be there. Look after her, will yer? And you'd better phone an ambulance straight away."

Clive immediately did what Robert had requested and then went over to help Hannah.

Now, as it happened, the girl — Sarah Manning — had taken so much alcohol that the last drink was just too much, and this had caused her to instantly vomit. In this respect, there could be hope; whatever may have been placed in the drink would have been discarded along with it, but even so, there was still another problem; it was imperative to prevent Sarah from choking on her own vomit! Hannah knelt upon the floor next to Sarah and gently lifted her body onto one side in a recovery position to stop any choking. Sarah was writhing about in discomfort, but that was better, Hannah thought, than being totally unconscious.

"Clive, can you fetch some water for her?" Water would be good, if Sarah could take some; it would help bring up any more that was still down there and hydrate her as well.

Soon after Clive's phone call, Robert Templeman arrived with Ian, who had driven him over to the club; an anxious Maria came along too, being a close friend of Sarah.

Sarah was still lying upon the floor when Robert came over to her and knelt beside her alongside Hannah, taking hold of her hand. He knew a lot about victims of drugs and excess alcohol, though he himself had never been one of them.

Sarah's eyed rolled occasionally.

"Sarah! Sarah! It's me… Robert. Come on! Wake up; don't you go to sleep!

"Pass me that glass of ice water, will you please?" ordered Robert. "And fetch me some more."

Robert wiped Sarah's face with his handkerchief soaked in the ice-cold water, touching her forehead and cheeks and wiping away vomit; the freezing cold of the water helped revive her somewhat.

"Come on, Sarah! You're good; come on now!" Robert tried to think of everything, but the best had already been done; the ambulance had just arrived, and Sarah had vomited several times, mostly over him. She could stand up with the support of two paramedics, who checked her themselves on the spot, after which she was taken to the ambulance and then to hospital.

Robert stood up, soaked and dripping in water and vomit. He watched them leave, then turned to his friends, Clive and Hannah, thanking them for phoning him and looking out for Sarah.

"What shall we do now?" asked Ian, looking over at Robert.

"Look, you two; I'm going to go with Sarah in the ambulance," said Maria, still horrified and full of concern for her friend.

"Okay. That is good, Maria," added Robert. "If you will stay with her, we will join you later... Ian, can you take me home to get changed, and then we can both go to the hospital? What do you say?"

"Yeah, fine, but... what about you? You'll need to take that shirt off or something; just look at it! It's all messed up, man!"

Robert understood Ian's concern; it would not do Ian's car any good to have Robert sitting in it covered all over in smelly vomit, so when they had got out in the street, he obliged Ian and removed his shirt. Then, prior to getting into the car, he took his jeans off as well — after extracting his favourite belt and wallet from them. Then he threw both items of clothing into a nearby bin.

"Thanks, Ian; let's go!"

Hannah and Clive returned to their table and sat down again, both very quiet for a while. Hannah was clearly shocked.

"I'm sorry, Hannah... for bringing you here now. You must feel terrible, I'm sure."

"Don't be sorry, Clive," consoled Hannah reassuringly. "It's not your fault; you didn't know this would happen, did you? And besides... it's a good job we both came really, if you think about it! We would not have been able to help if it weren't for us being here! Why, you could have saved Sarah's life, yer know!"

Clive took hold of Hannah's outstretched hand and thanked her for her attitude and understanding.

"Well, I don't know about you, Hannah, but I've kinda had enough of this place; I'm ready for off."

"Yeah, me too; it's all a bit deflated now, sort a thing. Look around; everything has gone back to normal again, but I can't get it all out of my head… what happened!"

"If *normal* is the word, Hannah!" added Clive. "Who's next, you might ask!" Clive had a thought then.

"Anyway, how would you like it if we stopped off at the *Pizza Palace* on the way home?"

Hannah grinned at Clive. Her smile and unspoken answer were clearly a yes, so off they went.

Meanwhile, there was a bit of a practical situation awaiting Robert as Ian pulled up outside his home at the Damsonwood Tower block of flats.

"What are you goin' to do now, Robert?" asked Ian grinning.

"Now, that is a very good question! It's dark outside, so maybe no one will see me… Here goes!"

Robert ran across the courtyard to the lift and pressed number seven. Everything was good until he reached his floor; then, as the doors opened, he was greeted by three girls on their way out who made no little commotion!

"Wow! Robert Townsend! Forgotten something, have you? Phew! You smell!"

Robert pushed through them all and dashed away down the corridor.

"Can't stop, girls. Need to go to the hospital; it's Sarah Manning!"

The scenario was far too baffling to analyse, so the girls walked away shrieking with laughter, pondering amongst themselves and wondering whatever could be the problem with the girl called Sarah, and with equal intrigue, just what had happened to Robert for that matter!

He had not particularly planned to do so, but Robert thought it best that a quick shower would be the order of the day. The thought of the awakened Sarah in hospital smelling whatever the girls had just commented upon by the lift was not at all desirable to say the least.

Robert dressed himself for a Sunday in his best pair of jeans and posh brown leather jacket. His trainers were not too bad as they stood. Once again, he was about to see his beloved Sarah, though, as yet, his liking for her was not in any way reciprocated. But he was in hope that she was coming around to see him as a different person to the one she had once known as a gang leader. Sadly, it was not the ideal situation, having to visit Sarah in hospital, but he was only too pleased and willing to be there for her in any circumstance.

Ian hardly recognised the figure of Robert emerging from the building, looking so fresh and smart, and he couldn't help smiling. He knew in his mind what was going on; Robert had a sickness called *Sarah-itus*!

"Let's go, Ian. Thanks for waiting."

"Okay! Are you going somewhere special then?"

"Just drive!"

The streets were quiet at that time of night, and Ian could put his foot down on the accelerator more than usual. Approaching the outskirts of town, there was a garage that was open twenty-four hours, and Robert asked Ian to pull over so that he could get out and buy something.

Outside of the garage, within the foyer area, was a stall with logs and bags of charcoal and such, but also next to them were just three bunches of flowers left over from the day. Robert returned to the car, and now there were only two bunches of flowers remaining on show!

Soon, they arrived at their destination. Robert felt nervous. He was finding it hard to believe this was happening! He needed to remind himself repeatedly; he was going to visit Sarah in hospital! How was she going to be?

Passing via the reception, they were directed to get a lift to the third floor. The typical hospital smell and aroma gave him the shivers. The last time Robert had come to this place had been with his very poorly mother, and on that sad occasion, she had died! Consequently, the whole scenario brought sombre memories to his mind.

However, much water had passed under the bridge since that awful time. Since then, his life had turned around, and he was walking in a completely different direction. Having had an encounter with the Lord, all thanks to Alfred, he had more hope these days. Robert prayed silently as he walked down the hospital corridor, and somehow, he believed all would be well on this occasion compared to the last one!

They arrived at the ward, and in the far corner near to the window, they saw Sarah laying her head back upon several pillows and Maria sitting next to her bed. It looked as if Sarah was on a drip or something and being well looked after by a nurse who was taking her pulse. Ian followed Robert and walked over to the side of the bed where Maria was sat, whilst Robert went over to the other side, holding up the bunch of flowers.

Sarah looked as if she had been tearful, but upon observing her visitor coming towards her with the flowers, she struggled to hold back a few more.

"These flowers are for you," greeted Robert. "How are you feeling, Sarah?"

Sarah had given blood and urine samples already. Because she had remained mostly conscious throughout the ordeal, the nurse had said things were looking hopeful, but they were awaiting results to check for any substance that may have been used that could affect her liver function in particular, amongst other things. To all appearances, thus far, the signs were that she had been lucky.

Sarah had vomited much of what she had consumed that evening, which had been to her benefit, and under those circumstances, Robert was not going to raise an issue regarding his clothes! Apparently, both of Sarah's parents were away on holiday, so she thought it not expedient to inform them and spoil things if she was going to be alright. Maria had informed the nurse that she would stay with Sarah overnight if necessary.

Sarah started to feel remorseful and bad about herself in Roberts's presence and spoke with some concern to him.

"Were you at the club, Robert? I didn't see you there. I wished I had known that you were there; I blame myself now for not taking you up on your offer."

"No, Sarah; I was not there. Don't start upsetting yourself on my part. We are all here for you right now, and things are going to be fine. Okay?"

Sarah half smiled at Robert, looking at him with affection. It was the same old Robert, never getting cross or showing emotion and always sticking up for her, even after she had refused him in a café one time!

Sarah sighed thoughtfully, then being seemingly bewildered and oblivious about everything, enquired about herself, not having remembered very much about the evening. Her assertive manner, however, had not been mellowed by the experience—though she did speak somewhat more quietly than her normal self would have done.

"Well… like… just what happened to me, then? Will somebody tell me? How come you are all here? And for that matter, how did I get here?"

Robert looked over at Maria, and they smiled at one another. Clearly Sarah was oblivious of everything!

"Go on, Maria; you tell her what happened!" said Robert.

Robert considered it expedient that the two girls were left alone now, so he decided to depart for a while and take Ian along with him.

"I'll leave you two, if that's alright then. I'll come back later. I could do with a coffee now; how about you, Ian?"

"Yeah… me too!"

Ian had been prodded discreetly by Robert to make it clear to him that this was a command and not a request, so they went out together, leaving Maria to enlighten Sarah regarding the finer details of that evening, most of which had been reiterated to Maria by Hannah and Clive beforehand.

Robert and Ian sat drinking coffee, discussing the night's drama and giving attention to the possible identity of the lad that had done this to Sarah.

"Wait until the tests come back, Ian; then we'll know if she had her drink spiked. From what I gather, Sarah had drunk a lot already, and the barman said a young man asked him for a double gin and tonic for the lady. Let's face it — that alone could have floored her!"

Ian held his peace about the matter. He was aware just how Maria had been very upset that evening upon hearing the news about Sarah's situation at the *Blue Moon*.

As Ian was staring out of the café window on the ground floor of the hospital, he saw two familiar figures passing by.

"Robert, look over there at who's just walked past; it looks like Dorothy and David."

Robert jumped up from his chair, having recognised that it was indeed who Ian had said, and went out to meet them.

Both Dorothy and David looked serious, the former looking quite pale as they walked hurriedly along. Maria had phoned Dorothy from the club just as everything was happening and sent shock waves down the phone line to her friend!

"Hi there, David… Sarah is not too bad. We have just been talking to her, but decided to leave Maria alone with her for a while to have a chat about everything."

"Oh! Thank goodness!" Dorothy replied. "That is such a relief!"

"Ian is with me over in the café. It might be better to wait just a little while longer; then maybe we could all go in to see her. What do you say?"

"That will be fine, Robert," replied David, and the three of them went into the café together and sat down with Ian.

It took a good ten to fifteen minutes for Robert to explain to David and Dorothy everything that had happened that evening, starting with the phone call he had received from his friend, Clive, up to the ambulance taking Sarah away.

David patted Robert's shoulder warmly, showing much gratitude for what he had done and the initiative he had shown.

"Well done, Robert! You and Ian have done well! You could well have saved the day; it seems to me that Sarah Manning was in a precarious state, and you two probably saved her from far more serious things."

After everything had been told and shared, they decided to go in to see Sarah. She was still sitting up in her bed when Robert walked in followed by Ian. A few seconds behind them came Dorothy and David. Sarah could not believe her eyes as she saw how many visitors she had—five in total—all concerned and coming to visit her! The effect upon seeing so many people—most of whom she hardly knew—was too much to bear, and she burst out crying with joyous surprise and gratitude.

"Thank you, you guys; you are all awesome!"

Chapter 5

John Goes on a Mission

Sarah stayed in her hospital bed for a second night with Maria by her side. It was not possible for her to be released until her test results had come back, and that was not going to be before noon today, which was Monday.

Maria herself was fine; she had only missed one short lesson at college that morning, and with it being a tutorial, she would not lose out on any new work. She was hoping, however, to get into college for a 3:15pm lecture.

Meanwhile, Robert had quite a bit of phoning to do. Firstly, he informed Susie, the manager of the hair salon by the same name, that Sarah was in hospital having check-ups and could not come to work. The finer details he omitted to mention, except that Sarah had been unwell over the weekend.

After phoning Sarah's workplace, Robert went on to phone Pastor John, but it was Miriam who answered the phone.

"Robert, is that you? Tell me... how is Sarah Manning?

"Sarah should hopefully be out today," replied Robert. "After her test results are back."

"Dorothy told me last night what happened to Sarah! Goodness gracious! What a terrible thing! It's just as well that you were there… I hear that it was you who phoned the ambulance, Robert; is that right?"

"Well… no, it was not me, Mrs Peterson. It was Clive who phoned for the ambulance; he was there at the time."

"Clive? Who is Clive? Oh dear! I must have got things confused; it was very late. Perhaps you can tell me the details another time.

"Anyway… now, what was I going to say? Yes… Robert, is there anything that we can do to help? Does Sarah need picking up and taking home?"

"Well… Er… I'm not sure just what to do actually, Mrs Peterson. You see, both Sarah's parents are away on holiday now, and Maria needs to leave about 1:30pm today, so Sarah will be on her own after that — apart from me that is."

"Does that mean she will be going home all by herself and to an empty house then, Robert? Really! Well, that won't do; will it? You obviously need help, and I can only think of one thing, Robert — that's if Sarah is happy about it. I could send John around to pick you both up, and then you could come over to be with us. We can sort out what to do afterwards when Dorothy comes home; what do you think about that arrangement, Robert? Would you like to ask Sarah and see what she thinks?"

"Thank you very much, Mrs Peterson.

"Sarah knows John," added Robert. "She has met him before. I'm sure it will be okay, but

I'll just check with her now, if you like, and give you a phone."

Within ten minutes or so, Robert had left off speaking to Miriam, gone upstairs to inform Sarah of the proposal, then had returned downstairs again to relay Sarah's positive response to Miriam. She was happy to go ahead with the arrangement if it was no trouble, but being a little embarrassed about the whole situation, Sarah felt reassured to know that Robert would also be coming along with her for moral support — though that had been assumed by Miriam anyway. Everything was arranged! John would wait upon a phone call from Robert telling him when they were both ready; then he would drive over to collect them.

Miriam passed the information over to John, informing him that he was needed to go on a mission that day.

"Well, well!" exclaimed John. "So… I'm to get Robert again and bring him over here — and with Sarah too!

"Why, it seems that whenever Robert has a problem, dear, then I am your man!"

"What is that supposed to mean, dear husband? Enlighten me, if you will!"

"Well, actually, I remember a certain day not so long ago when Robert was suffering from the moody blues over Sarah Manning, and you asked me to resolve the matter. Remember?"

"Dear husband, if you would only speak to

me in English, then I might understand you!"

"Ha-ha! I thought that might confuse you, Miriam. Well, let me recapitulate upon the matter if you will allow me. It was my day off, and I was working in the garden when a panicky Ian McPherson phoned me, very concerned about Robert's well-being—for Sarah had apparently refused him on two accounts, which I will not bother to reiterate to you. Do you remember the occasion, dear wife?"

"Yes… sort of, I think. Was that when I asked you to go over to him and invite him here for dinner?"

"You have got it in one!

"Well, in the end it worked out very nicely," continued John, "because both Robert and I went for some chicken and chips—much to your disgust may I say—but I know you had my best intentions at heart, with cholesterol and all.... Excuse me. That was a joke, dear! And consequently, we in fact saw Sarah, and then Dorothy showed her face a little later as well."

"Ah yes, dear husband; I forgot about that. You get around, don't you?"

"Well, here I go again to get Robert. That was the point I was trying to make; that's all."

"After listening to all of that, what can I say, dear? You do a very good job, John! What could we do without you?

"The kids, I understand, do like you, yer know —
especially when you treat them out for chicken
and chips!"

"Really, who told you that?"

"Well, actually, if you really wish to know
everything, it was Dorothy who told me, after
that occasion you have so meticulously reminded
me of. She said how funny they thought you
were, because you ate a chip butty in their
presence!

"They like you, John; they thought it was
funny you being a pastor and all!" she chuckled.

"Thanks for that wonderful revelation; I
will cherish it forever!"

The telephone rang, and Miriam answered
it, thinking it could be Robert. But it was Dorothy
phoning from work, asking how Sarah was.

"Well, my dear, we are awaiting a call
from Robert to go and pick her up."

"Okay. Well, I've almost done here, so I
think I'll come home now to see Sarah. See you
later."

The phone rang again; this time it was
Robert, and they were ready to be picked up.

"John!" shouted Miriam.

"Okay. Robert is ready, I gather? Yes?"

"Indeed, he is."

"I'll be going then, dear. See you in a
while."

The Petersons had all kinds of people in
their home for a meal, though usually it was on a

Sunday after church. Such people on those occasions were often regular church members, unless—as in the case of Alfred Townsend, Robert Templeman and David Osborne—they were new to the church, and therefore, it was customary for the Petersons to invite such people home for dinner. Today was going to be a new experience for the Petersons by entertaining Robert and Sarah; Miriam had been interested in meeting Sarah, howbeit not under such unusual circumstances.

Robert was of a new breed, so to speak—a teenager who, having come off the street through Alfred's open-air witness, was fast becoming a fisher of men, inviting others along to church functions—the most recent being David and Dorothy's engagement, when he brought along three young men as well as Sarah.

Sarah did not attend the church; thus far she had refused to do so, but nevertheless was getting more and more attached to some of its younger members, namely Maria, Ian, and of late, Robert. She was a self-willed, independent person not easily persuaded to do anything she had a mind not to do — as Robert had discovered. Sarah was a bit of a mystery in a way. Maria had known her at school, but that was about it; none of the young people at church knew anything else about her.

Miriam had been baking an apple pie in the kitchen. Earlier that same morning, she had already prepared a cottage pie—with cheese on top of the mash at John's request— so that it could be warmed up in the evening. John had a liking for many other things, all of which were considered unhealthy in the present days, if consumed too often—items such as cheese, oven chips and egg and bacon. These would alarm Miriam who was very health conscious and insisted they be served no more than once per week! John tried to reassure his wife, however, that in his opinion it was too many sugary foods that were more potent to the body than fatty foods—and that protein was good for you anyway! They agreed to differ, but conceded that moderation was the key.

Three quarters of an hour had passed since Robert's phone call, when the sound of people could be heard entering in through the front door.

John came in first and the fresh smell of pie took him straight into the kitchen, followed by Sarah and then Robert.

"Well, I thought I'd make some apple pie for this evening; I hope you all like apple pie.

"Hello, Sarah! How nice to meet you!" chirped Miriam happily. "And Robert, well... I know you already. Please help them with their jackets, John, if you will... and perhaps they would like to sit down in the lounge. Can I get anyone a drink? Tea? Coffee?"

Everyone took tea, except Robert who preferred a cold drink.

Miriam had previously pondered what to say to Sarah without embarrassing her, whether she should mention the episode at the club or not. In the end, she decided that by not saying anything, it might seem a little odd and leave a tenseness hanging in the air. Sarah would expect someone to say something or other about it, though probably not too much. Consequently, Miriam decided upon a different strategy — to act normally, then at some stage enquire how Sarah was feeling.

"There you are. Tea is ready, and I've added some biscuits as well. Sarah, you go first.

"Well, Robert and Sarah, we are entertaining more young people in our house these days than we have ever done before."

"And I think that is a very acceptable sort of a change, my dear, if I may say so!" interrupted John, glancing over at Sarah as he said it and thus generating a half-smile from her in the process.

"Yes, I do agree," continued Miriam. "Both John and I want you to feel perfectly at home, Sarah… and Robert too, so please just relax. Dorothy will be home early this afternoon, so at some stage we can let you have a chat together on your own, and we will leave you for a bit of privacy."

"Yes indeed, yes indeed," added John almost reluctantly, for he loved nattering away with visitors — though, in Miriam's opinion, the feeling was not always mutual, and he should give way more in the conversation at times!

Now was the opportunity, thought Miriam, to break the ice with Sarah.

"Well, how are you feeling now, Sarah? What an ordeal it must have been for you!"

"I'm feeling fine, thank you; not too bad really, I suppose… but I'm not very hungry."

"Don't you worry about dinner then, Sarah, if you do not feel like having any. I can make something lighter for you if you wish. I know… we'll go in the kitchen together later, and you can tell me what you fancy. How about that?"

"Yeah, okay. But like a said, I'm fine really."

Miriam excused herself under the pretext of needing to do something in the kitchen and beckoned John to follow her without making it seem too obvious.

Upon arriving in the kitchen, Miriam whispered in John's ear, "Let's just leave the two of them together for a while. I get the feeling that Sarah is not up to too much talking with us just now."

John got the message and went into his study out of the way. He would find something or other to occupy himself, though it had to be said that he was just a little disappointed; he liked Robert and Sarah and loved talking to young people in general, but they all too often liked to be left alone and that was fair enough.

Robert also felt that Sarah was not herself, and even he was sensitive enough these days to appreciate just how she must be feeling, having been through all that she had experienced in the past two days. He imagined her feeling uncomfortable with herself in looking back at what she had done. He knew her only too well to be a girl who liked to be in full control, assertive and often quite tough; now, her pride would be hurt, and she would be ashamed of herself and probably feeling awkward, realising just what a spectacle she had made with so many people seeing her in an embarrassing situation at the club and then also at the hospital. Sarah perceived in her mind that adults would be judgmental about her behaviour in getting drunk and imagined being spoken of behind closed doors as an irresponsible girl! If this were to be the case in the household that she had found herself in — for she had nowhere else to go — then it would all be nothing new. She had no other choice about the matter really but to oblige and come to the Petersons!

Sarah had been labelled by her parents a wild daughter who would get herself into trouble one day; therefore, it was inevitable that she would do exactly as predicted. Such opinions — even if they may have appeared warranted — did not have a positive influence over her and indeed made her even more stubborn and rebellious! Young people in general, like Sarah, all too readily accept that if such adverse perceptions are held about them by their own parents, then undoubtedly, they must be true, so that they would often be tempted to behave accordingly to prove this! Yet, Sarah was desperate for a trusting relationship with her mother. As for her father — well, he didn't seem to care what she did! Daughters were often the father's favourite but not in that household; he had wanted a son, and that was the end of the story!

Robert glanced at Sarah with some concern, wondering how she was feeling. He could tell that she was not comfortable.

"Sarah, are you alright?" enquired Robert, knowing full well that she wasn't.

"Why are you asking me that question? If you had half noticed, you would have realised that I am not alright! Okay?"

"Okay, fine! So, what do you want to do then?"

"Just watch me! I've had enough! Okay? I'm going! I feel on edge all the time here."

"But they're nice people, Sarah!"

"To you, maybe, yes… but I feel odd in their presence. I don't know them… and well, they are church people, aren't they? Goodness knows what they really think of me!"

Sarah got up and reached for her coat, then made for the door.

"Please tell them I'm sorry, but I just had to go; I need to be by myself for a while."

"But, Sarah, where will you go? I can't just watch you go like this — not after what you have been through. Please… wait."

Sarah mellowed upon hearing Robert's remarks, realising he had genuine regard for her well-being and assured him she would be fine.

"Look, thanks for your concern; I will catch a bus and go over to see Maria. I'll be fine. Bye, Robert."

Sarah was about to close the door behind her, when she turned and looked towards Robert, observing a gloomy, dejected countenance. She did not particularly wish to sadden him or hurt him in anyway, so she went over to him and said, "Look, I really appreciate what you have done for me, Robert, yer know! Not many would have been there for me like you were. I am grateful, right!"

"Sarah…! Just… you take care… that's all!"

"I will."

Sarah went over to Robert and gave him a peck upon his cheek as an affectionate 'thank you.'

"See yer!" she replied. And then she was gone.

Robert stood up, trying to take it all in, but he knew Sarah was Sarah! She was obviously not used to adult company — that was very clear — at least not in a home setting like the Petersons, where she felt a stranger and very awkward because of who they were. Robert thought it would have been a good idea to bring Sarah back here; there hadn't been much of a choice at the time anyway as everyone else was occupied, but it was not to be. Sarah was angry with herself about everything and hence with others too! He decided very quickly to phone Ian and tell him what was happening.

"Don't you worry, Robert; I'm going over to see Maria later," said Ian to a very concerned Robert. "I could chat along with Alfred and let the two girls be together... I'll keep you in the loop."

Chapter 6

Alfred Entertains Sarah

The outcome of the previous drama was yet to unfold! Sarah was to see Maria soon, and more imminently, Robert was to face John and Miriam and explain to them somehow about Sarah's departure.

Meanwhile, Sarah had arrived at the door of a cottage that was quietly situated away from the main road in a rural area. She glanced at the surrounds decorating it, thinking to herself how very different it was compared to her own home in a traditional housing estate nearer town. There were flower pots situated either side of the door. Along the front edge of the cottage was a border with variegated flowering shrubs and taller plants. Overall, it was quite beautiful, she thought, with a warm and welcoming, friendly feel to it.

Sarah knocked upon the door, and soon a light came on in the hallway. It was Alfred who answered it at the request of his daughter who was having a shower, and sure enough, as he opened the door, he observed standing before him the young lady Maria had been expecting.

"You must be Sarah, yes? Welcome! I been instructed to sit yer down and look after yer whilst she's in the shower, so please come in and make yourself comfortable.

"Would yer like a drink? Or something to eat?"

Sarah was a little put out, desiring to see Maria and no one else. She had just left two adults behind, having felt conspicuous and uncomfortable in their presence, and now was faced with another; still, at least he was an old man. Reluctantly, she resigned herself to put up with the situation, hoping it would be of a short duration.

If the truth were to be known, Sarah was put out with herself and no one else. She had embarrassed herself, shamed herself and was disgusted with herself and needed no one else to rub it in! Though she was a strong-willed, independent girl, normally in control, this time she had let herself down, and her pride was showing it. What she had not prepared herself for, however, was the likes of Alfred and his unique, down-to-earth manner of communication!

Sarah did not give any answer to Alfred's request regarding having food or drink, but he had already put two and two together and made four; he had gathered something was not quite right, and with all his acquired experience of another certain teenage girl's moods and swings in the house, he was thoughtful enough about how he would talk to Sarah.

"Okay, so you don't seem to want a drink or anything to eat; that's fine. I'm feeling a bit peckish miself though, so I think I'll make some toast and butter."

Alfred walked away into the kitchen leaving Sarah somewhat gobsmacked! She joked and mocked within herself regarding Alfred's request, thinking to herself, *What a jerk we have here! Fancy asking me if I want any toast and butter, I ask you… like, how sad is that!*

Whilst Alfred was busy preparing toast in the kitchen, Maria came down the stairs wrapped in a towel and popped her head around to say hi to her friend.

"Sorry to keep you waiting, Sarah! I'll be about five minutes, okay? Why don't you ask Dad for a drink of something?"

After that, Maria shot upstairs again, leaving Sarah sighing to herself, *Not you as well! Oh, plea…se; just get a move on, Maria!*

Now as it happened, Sarah had not eaten all day because of her stomach's ordeal. She had felt completely out of sorts so that all her appetite had gone. The meal offered her at the Petersons was genuinely too much for her to face, and under the circumstances, it was perhaps only to be expected! Even so, it had to be said that Sarah rather liked the smell coming in from the kitchen at that precise moment. If there was anything she could stomach, it was some of that toast and butter — with a cup of tea!

Alfred came in and sat down then. He completely ignored his guest, refusing to make eye contact with her, and unreservedly started to crunch at his fresh toast with a drink of tea, deliberately making it obvious just how delicious it was.

"This is that special thick-sliced toaster bread; it stays soft inside, but the outside is a lovely and crispy golden brown... soft and crunchy. Yer have to get the heat right, yer know; toast it nice and fast on high. I always use unsalted butter; it tastes much nicer, I think!"

When he did look up at Sarah, he saw a gloomy face and a pair of eyes looking rather askance at him!

Alfred purposely ignored her again, then casually, half looking up, said, "Fancy some toast? There's plenty in there... if yer do."

No answer.

"Look, Sarah Madding, do yer wants some or don't yer? Yer look as if yer could eat half a loaf, if yer ask me!

"Manning! My name's Sarah Manning," she replied with disgust and growing contempt.

"Oh! Sorry, lass; its mi deaf ear on this side, yer know. Sarah Marning... I got it now."

Sarah held her head in utter disbelief and looked up to the ceiling, doing her utmost to prevent herself from screaming in dire frustration! *Oh! I do not need this*, she thought. *I give up!* Swallowing her pride, she decided to succumb to Alfred and all his bizarre antics and simply go along with him just as he was.

"Mr Townsend... go on then! If you insist! I would like some of that toast... and a cup of tea, please—not too strong. Is that alright? Can yer hear me, okay?"

Alfred got up, smiling to himself, but he was more than happy to oblige her. Upon returning with the food, Alfred sat there watching her eat like she had had nothing to eat in a month of Sundays, and before too long her plate was empty.

"More? Do yer want some more?"

Sarah had regained her appetite, and toast with butter was a good starter to get back into eating food! Her answer to Alfred's question was a definite yes, but rather than saying so, she simply nodded her head in approval. Alfred obliged her once again, returning with a second plate of toast. As Maria entered the room not long after, she straightaway noticed Sarah munching away.

"Oh, Dad, please can you make me some as well? Mm, I just love the smell of toast!"

"No problem—that's if there's any bread left; your guest takes a bit of feeding, yer know!"

It is often spoken of that the way to a man's heart is through his stomach, but after that evening in Alfred's lounge, another rendering was born. Clearly, Sarah suddenly found herself most amicable with Maria's father. Yes, she had initially thought him irritable and annoying, but she quickly realised he was harmless and knew he had her best interests at heart, so much so that she started to speak with him in her more usual manner, as if the old Sarah had suddenly found a new lease of life and strength having eaten some food.

Maria came and sat down, pondering what must have gone on in her absence between Sarah and her father, for Sarah seemed very settled and comfortable for a change.

"Thanks, Mr Townsend," spluttered Sarah in-between mouthfuls. "I really appreciate this, yer know. You're right; it is like... so delicious. I could keep on eating it forever! Please excuse my bad manners earlier; I've had a bad few days."

"Good for you, my girl; you're very welcome! Have some more if yer want."

"Yeah, Dad, and don't forget me please!" cried another voice.

A further trip into the kitchen proved necessary.

Sarah found herself being looked after in a most unlikely venue by a most unlikely person, and she relished it—well, for the time being at any rate! She was starving, and well, when you are drowning, you don't snuff your nose up at a floating plank! Such was her relaxed state now, that she instigated a conversation with Alfred.

"I reckon I know someone who knows you, Mr Townsend," spluttered Sarah whilst eating.

Alfred paused from munching his toast for a moment, then lifted his eyes gazing at Sarah inquiringly, "Oh yeah, and who would that be then?"

"Who are yer on about, Sarah?" interrupted Maria with interest, addressing her friend with similar curiosity to that of her father.

"His name is Robert... Robert Templeman," replied Sarah.

Now, unknown to Sarah, Alfred Townsend was very familiar with the boy in question. In fact, they were so close that Robert had confided in Alfred just about everything that was going on in his life, including those matters close to his heart regarding a certain girl he liked; and so, Alfred was not going to let on too much but chose rather just to go along with the flow of the ensuing conversation and see what materialised. However, it was necessary, he thought, to surreptitiously get his daughter's attention and convey some manner of body language—a sharp glance with a wink in his eyes—so as to inform Maria to go along with things for a while!

"Yeah, I know him," said Alfred. "He comes to our church! So, what do you know about him, Sarah?"

"I just know him; that's all. He talks to me a lot about you, yer know!"

"All good, I hope?"

"Is it true, Mr Townsend, that you used to be a ..." Sarah hesitated, glanced over towards Maria, then continued with the rest of what she was going to say, "...well, a cripple or something, Mr Townsend?"

"Yeah, I was; that's right. Did Robert tell yer that then?"

"Yeah, he did... so what happened to yer then, if yer don't mind me asking—only Robert said something about you getting healed an' all... like... by God or something?"

Sarah spoke in such a manner as to infer that it sounded a little too far-fetched, so clarification, as well as inquisitiveness, was the order of the day in her mind. This would be the first time she had ever known of such a thing—if, that is, it was true.

"Sarah... look at me, lass, and don't sound so surprised about what I'm goin' to tell yer, right. I was not able to walk without crutches for years—ever since I had a tractor accident. And then after a long time, this young lady that Maria knew came and spoke to me about Jesus, so I went to church. And He healed me there and then!

"It was Dorothy," added Maria, attempting to clarify the situation somewhat with Sarah regarding the young lady Alfred was talking about. "She was the one who came to our house, Sarah; that's the young lady Dad's on about. You met her at the hospital when she came with David to see yer, remember?"

"Wow! So it's true then! That's just what Robert told me, yer know. Well, I can't say as I don't believe you, 'cos I know a lady — a friend of my mum's — who says these things can happen. That must have been awesome, Mr Townsend… Where you there, Maria? When it happened?"

"Yeah, I was there — and David and Dorothy too."

Something was intriguing Alfred upon hearing what Maria had just mentioned, regarding Sarah having been in hospital, so he felt prompted to change the subject and to enquire about her well-being.

"Sarah… have you been poorly, lass? In hospital? What was the matter with yer?"

Alfred's manner of speaking to Sarah about her circumstances and going into hospital had been conveyed in a most earnest and genuine way, with no sense of inquisitiveness whatsoever, other than real concern. Therefore, Sarah felt something of Alfred's sincerity impacting her heart, and she was of a comfortable mind to tell him just what had really happened to her and why she had had to go into hospital. Sarah recounted to Alfred all the nitty-gritty details regarding how she had consumed too much drink and the dilemma that had occurred in the *Blue Moon* night club. It was the first time she had spoken about that occasion to anyone, and even Maria did not know everything about the circumstances regarding the events prior to her arriving on the scene along with Robert and Ian.

At that moment, there was a knock upon the door, which interrupted the proceedings temporarily as Maria went to let in a certain expected visitor, namely Ian.

"Hi there, Alfred... Hi, Sarah! Fancy seeing you here! How are you feeling now? You certainly look so much better than the last time I saw you!"

Sarah stood up to greet Ian with a hug. "Well, actually, I was just in the process of tellin' Alfred here all about it, before you arrived. Thanks for being there for me, Ian — both you and Maria; I really did appreciate that!"

Ian sat within the circle, making a foursome, and then joined in with the current conversation.

"Well, if you think about it, Sarah," added Ian, "you need to thank Clive as well. He was there all the time; he saw everything and phoned Robert, and it was then I drove all three of us over to the club."

"Oh! My! Yer jokin', right? Here I was thinking that Robert was there all the time! I can just about remember puking all over him! Did you say Clive was there? Is that Clive Melham?"

"Yep. He was there with his girlfriend, Hannah Johnson. He said they were dancing near the bar where you were standing — well, at the time you were standing — when he saw this guy get you a double gin and tonic, and he thought he saw him put something in it!"

"Sarah, what did they say at the hospital?" enquired Maria with concern, joining in with the conversation. "Did they tell you what was in it?

"They told me there was no sign of heavy drugs in my blood, just medication normally used for getting to sleep or something like that, yer know — sleeping pills, I think; I can't remember what she called it. Whatever it was, I had brought most of it up anyway. Thank God!"

"Where is Robert anyway?" enquired Ian. "I thought that you and he were going over to the Petersons today?"

The question was deliberately posed by Ian to observe Sarah's reaction. He was curious to know what she would say about the matter, for he knew first-hand from Robert's phone call about the scenario already and what had happened at the Petersons when Sarah had got up and left the house.

A sheepish-looking Sarah confessed all before the other three, astounding them with her forthrightness and honesty, hiding nothing from them. She elaborated just how she had not been comfortable in the house with people she did not know and had felt conspicuous, ashamed and needed some space.

"Well, I only hope yer been comfortable wi' me, lass!" added Alfred, feeling provoked in himself — being a stranger to Sarah — though inwardly he thought that she had now settled down in his company just fine.

"You're all right, Mr Townsend!" smiled Sarah. "But I'm a bit bothered now, yer know. What should I do about the mess I left behind me with Robert and them all? With me steaming out on everyone?" Sarah looked for advice from anyone with the hope of redeeming herself.

"Phone Robert to see how things are?" suggested Maria.

"Maybe I should phone Mrs Peterson first and apologise," said a remorseful Sarah.

Sarah turned and looked at Alfred, hoping for his advice, and the room went quiet for a moment with all eyes upon him waiting for his input.

"What do you think I should do, Mr Townsend?" asked Sarah with some degree of humility and growing respect.

"Now, there's a thing, Sarah! Well, I know Pastor John and his Missis very well; they are good people. I would imagine they are a bit worried about yer, whether you're safe and all that. That will be more important to them than anything else, don't yer think? I'm sure that's it! They won't be bothered about the meal or anything. I'll leave the rest to you, dear, to say what yer feel to. Over there on the sideboard is the telephone; take it in the kitchen, if yer wants to, and make that call."

"That's alright; I've got my mobile if you can give me their number please."

Maria obliged Sarah, who disappeared into the kitchen whilst the rest kept mostly quiet.

"I can't believe Sarah is doin' this, yer know!" whispered a surprised Maria.

"You can say that again!" added Ian. "What have you done to her, Alfred?"

"Me? Nothin'… just gave her some toast… that's all!" said Alfred, chuckling to himself.

"Shush… here she comes," said Maria, still whispering.

"Well! How did yer get on?" asked Maria inquisitively, whilst the rest listened intently to what was about to follow.

"Do you like waffles with jam and cream? Miriam said there's plenty of mixture made up if you would like to come over now and have some… that includes everyone!"

Chapter 7

All that Glitters is not Gold!

There is a saying to the effect that you should not judge a book by its cover, the implication being that though the outside may look extremely good and glossy, the inside may be quite different — in short, not very good at all!

It is interesting that God said something like this when Samuel was sent to anoint a son of Jesse to be king. Samuel's response was to look at the eldest and the tallest amongst them, but God had other ideas!

"...do not look at his appearance or at his physical stature... for the Lord does not see as man sees, for man looks at the outward appearance, but the Lord looks at the heart..."

In general, we can easily be deceived by outward appearances, just as Samuel was! An impressive person may not be so forthcoming after a while, when we get to know them warts and all!

Choosing the right person for a job is always going to be difficult, for you have a certain mandate of necessary requirements, and one endeavours to choose someone whom you hope has most of them! In fact, we are all in a sort of quandary sometimes regarding our judgement of the character that a person may have. It is never easy, and sometimes one's judgments are wrong! One illustration given by Jesus was a parallel between fruit and trees. You can easily recognise an orange tree simply because it bears oranges! You don't find thistles bearing sweet fruit like cherries! In other words, Jesus said,

"...do men gather grapes from thorn bushes or figs from thistles? A good tree bears good fruit, but a bad tree bears bad fruit...by their fruits shall you know them..."

Jesus was referring to false prophets who come in sheep's clothing! The outward appearance, like a sheep, is innocent and docile, but inwardly they are mean and callous like a ravenous wolf! However, the essence of truth outlined in this parallel can also apply to similar situations, namely understanding and knowing what a given person is really like!

Clearly, regarding relationships, it always remains good advice to observe a person over a period—if, that is, we have the inclination and patience to do so—and seek to ascertain what kind of fruit is produced in their character and life!

One could ask oneself, *How long does it take for a tree to bear its own fruit — to identify the kind of tree it is?*

There are other examples outside of relationships where certain good qualities are desirable and sought for, as is the case with some employers who sometimes may hire students during their vacation or offer part time work and finally give them the opportunity to work with them permanently. Why? Is it not because they have proved themselves as satisfactory over a period in the eyes of the employer and would therefore be considered an asset to the company and worth investing in?

When Dorothy had first met David Osborne, for example, she was immediately impressed by him! He was handsome, polite and kind, and said and did all the right things. He was employed at a good job, which was a bonus; so perhaps she considered that he could be an asset worth investing in!

Without the effects of natural chemistry, it is quite probable that few people would ever be attracted to one another, but unlike the birds and the bees, humans desire much more in life to satisfy their heart's desires—and these other necessities and requirements cannot be manifested instantly. Rather, like the analogy of the employer seeking to recruit the right person, Dorothy had needed to take things steadily, as indeed had David too, waiting to see how things developed between them; then perhaps, they had thought, there would come a point in time when a further decision of commitment could be made.

Everything went very well indeed with both until... well, until Dorothy's views and simple faith clashed with those of David's traditional religious background and upbringing, where a personal faith and relationship with God were non-existent! Consequently, a problem arose that could easily have ended matters between them, except that David's love for Dorothy was far greater and more important to him than what he later described as his dead, hypocritical religion. Therefore, David — having seen the true person of Dorothy and discovered what she was really like and, it could be said, having discovered what he was really like too — turned towards the Lord.

In Dorothy, he had seen some true, simple and genuine qualities of a child of God; and in himself, by comparison, only pretence and formality, with no real substance. This conviction had cut him through to the heart, in as much as he knew that in all his aspirations to live an honourable upright and good life, he could never make the grade and exhibit the authentic and genuine characteristics of Dorothy. David had recognised that he did not have what Dorothy had; when it came to God, they were like oil and water — they just did not mix together!

Only with a commonality where both were spiritually alive to the same thing, in short having a personal relationship with God and believing the Bible as it was written, could it truly work for them — and it had! Had David not recognised in Dorothy the kind of pure, unselfish fruit she bore, and equally, had he not admitted to the selfish and arrogant traits in his own life, he would have remained a victim of his own pride and self-righteousness; in other words, he would have been miserable thereafter, forever without Dorothy!

One could move on to the likes of Alfred Townsend and for that matter, Robert Templeman. Who would have recognised by looking at the front cover of these two books that they were anything other than depressing novels, or even, in both cases, horror stories? Certainly, they were not very good reading and certainly not a pleasurable romantic novel! Who could have believed that either of these two very different people with contrasting circumstances and ages could possibly turn out so changed for the better?

Alfred had been a bitter, resentful old man — a cripple and an alcoholic whose wife had moved out of the home because of his temper. Robert had been the leader of a notorious gang committed to violence and trouble, whose mother had died and whose father had abandoned the home, leaving him destitute and to his own devices! Yet both these were not changed for the better in a sort of moral turning over of a new leaf; they were radically altered towards God from deep within their heart in a loving, kind and selfless way, all because of experiencing living encounters with God. God does this sort of thing! He comes into ordinary people's lives — literally in the Person of the Holy Spirit—and changes them to do His will instead of their own!

It was this revelation to Pastor John one day that caused him to present a most challenging message to the church, where he emphasised a few Scriptures from the Bible that had been put away on the shelf and left there.

"For you see your calling brethren, that not many wise according to the flesh, not many mighty, not many noble are called.

But God has chosen the foolish things of the world to put to shame the wise, and God has chosen the weak things of the world to put to shame the things which are mighty;

And the base things of the world and the things which are despised God has chosen,

And the things which are not, to bring to nothing the things that are that no flesh should glory in His presence."

Pastor John had openly confessed to the congregation his own personal sentiments of late. *"Surely God has given me a new vision! He has brought Alfred into this church and then Robert! Who will be next?"*

No! We cannot judge a book by its cover! A seemingly good person can turn out to be not so good; likewise, a person perceived to be bad can ultimately become a child of God, demonstrating good works! It is only by their fruits that we can truly know a person. When Jesus told us that we should know them by their fruits, He also told us just what to look for – the fruit of the Spirit, namely love, joy, peace, kindness, goodness, faithfulness, and more!

~~~~~~

It was difficult for Sarah Manning to understand just what type of persons John and Miriam were. She had her own pre-conceived ideas that, being adults, they would be judgmental of her, especially in the light of the recent happenings of which she was not proud. Even her first encounter with Alfred had not been without some fear and reservation. Her first response to meeting Alfred at the door instead of Maria was one of dismay, and once again he was perceived as the enemy!

Oh! How delicate and hurt are the hearts and souls of so many people! And if only one could be sensitive enough to be aware and understand! How lonely and isolated must young persons feel when estranged from the adult world, seemingly left entirely to their own immature devices! When, like sheep without a shepherd, they feel isolated and on their own. Instead of love and care, they know only despair; instead of direction and guidance for their lives, they know and witness only argument and strife from those adults who should be showing them a better example.

It was Alfred's acute perception that had helped break through the wall of separation between himself and Sarah—and in his own unique style! He had sounded gruff, but had been kind; had sounded strict, but been loving! His firm, gruff comment was decisive and brought about a change in the atmosphere. *"…Look, do yer wants some or don't yer?"*

Why or how Sarah had responded to this brash-sounding comment from Alfred regarding the toast was not entirely clear, but its effect seemed to turn things around, and she yielded to his hospitality. Perhaps she saw within the coarseness of Alfred's manner a certain genuineness that prompted her to go ahead and take what was being offered. Did she feel ineffectual in her seemingly deliberate attempts to disturb or irritate Alfred's poise with her lack of propriety and good manners—for she had avoided speaking to him when he had asked her a question? And consequently, by not having received any form of correction from him—as would normally have been the case with an adult—did she warm somewhat? Perhaps out of respect, feeling a little guilty about her own attitude towards him, he being an old man and all?

The simplest explanation was of course that she was hungry, and nothing more needed to be said! Whatever the reason, the fact was that something had worked, and it had worked well!

The outcome was that Sarah no longer felt threatened in any way and felt completely reassured and accepted by Alfred; he was at ease with her, so why could she not reciprocate in like manner with him also?

As time progressed, things improved with Sarah in other ways too. Now that she felt comfortable and welcome in the home, she adopted a more mature attitude and was willing to phone Miriam to apologise for her earlier behaviour—much to the surprise of Maria and Ian!

Sarah had been taken by surprise regarding the outcome of her phone call with Miriam, and once again it was food that was the order of the day with her! First it had been toast and butter, and now it was waffles with jam and cream.

It remained to be seen just how Sarah would get on in the company of the Petersons upon this, her second visit to their home within the same day! This time, however, things looked a little more hopeful!

Chapter 8

Miriam Entertains Robert

Robert Templeman had been left in the lurch at the Petersons after Sarah's exit, feeling apprehensive about explaining matters to them.

"Mrs Peterson! Are you there?"

"Yes, Robert. What is it? Oh! Where is Sarah?" Miriam asked.

"That's what I wanted to talk to you about," said Robert. Miriam had just walked in from the kitchen, observing one figure and not two in the lounge as expected.

"Sarah was not feeling too good, Mrs Peterson, and really did not want any food. Then she had a headache and felt she needed to be alone and quiet for a while. I apologise, but really I had no idea this was how she felt."

"Well... there's a thing!" replied Miriam, seemingly unperturbed but not wishing to make Robert feel any more awkward than he already did. "Oh! Never mind, Robert; there'll be more dinner for us, yes?

"Has Sarah gone home then? Because we could have given her a lift?"

"No. She went around to Maria's house. They are good friends, and to be honest I think she has not fully got over what happened to her and needed some space."

"Well, don't you be overly concerned. It will

probably do her good to be over at Maria's. And besides, Alfred will be there too. Knowing him, he will cheer her up a bit—as well as Maria. He has a way with young people it seems... as you well know yourself, Robert; perhaps a few rough edges, but his heart is in the right place. So, what shall we do? It will be half an hour before dinner is ready... you are still staying, aren't you? You won't be doing a disappearing act as well, will you now?"

"No way, Mrs Peterson! Your dinner smells too good to miss! I don't often have a proper meal like meat and veg and gravy. Are you doing any Yorkshire pudding with it?"

"Most certainly, if you would like some. It'll be my pleasure," obliged Miriam, more than happy to hear that her guest was looking forward to her dinner and making a special request of his own as well. In fact, Miriam became quite delighted that at least someone was hungry and happy to eat of her cooking.

Miriam was enjoying Robert's company, having never had a son herself. She was amazed with his friendliness and respect. Having pondered her own negative reservations about him in her thinking not so long ago, she realised now just how wrong she had been.

Just to think that I, upon hearing of Robert being a gang leader in the past, was quite prejudiced against him, thinking erroneously that a leopard can't change its spots and neither could he... well, not without some Divine miracle! Yet, if that had been what he was in his past, a notorious gang leader — and according to John and Alfred, he was — then some miraculous change must have taken place. He certainly was grateful for his dinner, that's for sure! Shame upon me for thinking anything derogatory about this young man in my presence! What a lovely handsome young man he is!

"I tell you what, Robert. How about we sit down for a while, if you will? I would like to ask you a few questions about yourself. Don't worry; it won't be an interrogation or inquisition! I know how you met Alfred Townsend, but how is it you know Sarah Manning? Why, what a help you have been to her just recently!"

"Mrs Peterson, do you really want to know about me? Because my background wasn't very good for your ears, I'm afraid."

"Oh! Pardon me! My very first question is a bad one. Sorry, my dear; let's leave that one alone if it is a sensitive topic. But I can assure you that I am not easily shocked, you know! To be honest with you, Robert, I am so very happy for you to be here... and basically, I just wanted to know a little more about you.

"There! I am being straight and upfront with you. I do believe that is how many young people like you are these days; is that correct, Robert? If I really wish to listen to someone talk about themselves, then I must be prepared for everything and anything and never get surprised or alarmed!"

"You're right there, Mrs Peterson, and I will answer your question and be up front with you, since you are pressing me. It's okay, I suppose, to talk about when I first saw Sarah, but... well, you might just change your opinion of me. That's what I was thinking to myself, yer know. But here goes! I will describe to you exactly how I was and what I was.

"In gangland I was called The Duke, and we used to hang around the estate causing trouble, usually by fighting with other gangs over territory. My gang was different to all the others, because we didn't do drugs, yer know. Well, one afternoon me and two others decided to go into town to see what mischief we could do, when we saw two girls chatting to one another. One of them looked like a slapper by the way she was dressed, so I shouted across to her, saying insults and all that. That was Sarah! She was a tough nut and basically told me to get a life.

"Anyway, I turned on the other girl, who I recognised as Maria Townsend, and I gave her a lot of grief about her dad. It had gone around how he was supposed to have been healed, and... well... I just taunted her and said the whole thing was a farce. I poked fun at her and called her dad Alfred the Great—the great con-artist! Well, that provoked her big-time, so she ran at me, and I pushed her over backwards so that she went flying across the floor.

"Now, Ian McPherson came out of a nearby shop at that very moment and saw what was happening. The girls had been waiting for him outside, whilst he checked out new mobile deals. Well, I knew Ian at school as a wimp, but the way he came at me surprised me—and I ended up flying across the floor myself after he had put his knee into my face with his karate moves. He just knocked me flying actually! All my mates had disappeared, so I joined them!

"Well, that's when I first saw Sarah. Now yer know!"

"Goodness gracious me, Robert lad! You were a bit of a thug, weren't you?"

"Yeah, you could say that!"

Miriam had spoken in a light-hearted fashion upon hearing Robert's exposition, and he had replied to her with light humour as well; whatever he may have been in the past, it was no longer relevant now. There was one word, however, that Robert had spoken that Miriam had never heard of before, though it sounded like one used in a derogatory manner.

"Robert, what is a slapper?"

He smiled and answered hesitantly, "It can be used when a girl kinda flaunts herself with boys, but at its worst it means someone who like... sleeps around!"

"Oh dear! Well, the way I see it, Robert, is like this. All of us have done things in the past of which we are now ashamed—and that includes me and John. This I can assure you!" Miriam's expression was pronounced upon mentioning her husband's name so that the latter comment made Robert grin with surprise. Her body language seemed to suggest that John had a past!

"Do you know what the Bible says about that, Robert? It says, '*All have sinned and fallen short of God's standards.*' All means everyone! No one is by any means perfect, but it's when people acknowledge what they are and turn to God that wonderful changes can happen.

"It's only when you become a Christian and turn away completely from the old life and follow the new that you change for the better! So, don't you overly concern yourself about shocking me, Robert; it's what we do next that matters, not what we did before. If we have given our lives to Jesus and received Him as Lord and Saviour, then He forgives us—and that includes you, me and Pastor John! Forgive me for sounding a bit like a Bible-basher, but… basically, that's exactly what it says!

"What I see in you, Robert, is a young man who is completely different to the obnoxious one you have just described to me—if you don't mind me saying—and I am very blessed to hear your testimony of coming to the Lord. You are just the kind of person John and I love to see.

Unfortunately, much of the established church today has a sort of cultural past in that it appears to cater only for the so-called middle classes and traditionally-thinking, elderly people... God bless them. It is no wonder that young people like you are in small numbers within the established church, if at all. Why should that be, I ask, when the church should be full of sinners, young and old? In accordance with the Good Book, Jesus did not come to save those who considered themselves above reproach and righteous citizens. No, it says something very different indeed; it might even be considered by some as offensive—*Jesus Christ came into the world to save sinners!* Perhaps we should go and ask people who come out of church if they are a sinner saved by God's Grace! What a joke! Forgive me, Robert, but I get cynical in my old age!

"Now, you know David, don't you? David Osborne? Dorothy's fiancé? Well, ask him about what I have just been talking about. He will tell you how much he went to church in the past—in fact, ever since he can remember—but he said he never had a personal relationship with the Lord! Oh, yes... and he considered anyone who spoke about such things to be an oddball!"

Miriam finished with that last comment of hers and looked at her watch.

"Well, Robert, half an hour is up, and dinner should be ready and will need taking out of the oven. I think I heard the door a few minutes ago, so that was probably Dorothy coming in, I should imagine. Now all I need to do is go and disturb John in the study, so do excuse me for now."

Robert had been impressed, listening to Miriam's plain speaking, and thought through the gist of it in his mind.

Now that was cool! Who would have thought that Miriam would speak like that? Sarah misunderstood her, that's for sure, if she imagined being thought ill of by her!

To feel accepted was of immeasurable consolation to some people, and at that moment in time, Robert felt as if he were one of them! There was no way that Miriam would have been judgemental of Sarah. Robert also concluded in his own mind, *Only as a person truly understands what God is like, through knowing His Word and having a personal relationship with Him, can they fully appreciate how much He loves each one — whoever they are and without respect of persons — and that includes Sarah, despite what she has done!*

Miriam was a person who understood this. Sin was no longer the problem, not since the cross! The blood of Jesus Christ had paid the ransom required for all of mankind's sin! What remained now was for each person to come to God through Him and with repentance, if they would. And even then, it took God's love to draw them towards Him, just like Robert had experienced with Alfred's kindness! The only sin outstanding upon every person was the ultimate sin of not wanting to receive God's forgiveness and grace through Jesus Christ! What each person did with this knowledge of God's salvation would be the determining factor.

The difficulty for some people is simply this: they do not consider themselves quite as bad as others, and it would be beneath them to be considered on the same level as everyone else, if that included being equated with the vilest offender—though that is precisely the position God sees us in! God includes all under sin, not because of the wrong we have done, but because of what we are by our very nature. We are not sinners because we sin; we sin because we are sinners!

From the beginning of time—from Adam—our human natures became corrupted through one man's disobedience and rebellion, so that, rather like the genetic phenomenon whereby each child that is born into this world inherits something of its mum and dad, likewise and in a similar fashion, every baby is born with that same rebellious nature. It has been transferred throughout the whole human race! We do not teach babies how to stamp their feet and rebel against authority; they do it automatically. That is the reason why God includes all under sin and why the cross had to cover everyone. What an amazing salvation this is that anyone can now be reconciled to God through the blood of Jesus!

"In Him we have Redemption through His Blood!

This was and still is the amazing story! The price or ransom to be paid to secure our salvation was the blood of Jesus Christ. Because He had never once sinned — despite the devil's temptations — and, since He died an innocent death upon the cross, Christ had, if you like, accumulated through His death an infinite amount of redeeming power or buying power for God. And this is represented in His shed blood so that now God can legally receive and forgive any person that comes to Him through His Son!

It is true, therefore, for a child of God to say, "I have been purchased — or redeemed — by the precious blood of Christ! I am not my own! I have been bought with a price!'

This unique salvation is amplified when someone like Robert Templeman comes on the scene and accepts God's offer of grace and mercy! To many, he would seem like the kind of person that needs saving, and they would be right; however, so does everyone else! The fact is all must come the same way, for there is only one way — through Jesus Christ, just as He Himself said, *'I am the way the truth and the life. No one comes to the Father but by me!'*

What develops so often in reality is pride and prejudice. Pride, because we all must bow the knee, and prejudice, because we consider ourselves as good enough, perhaps even better than some!

The likes of Robert and Sarah were often discarded by the status quo as being teenagers who were beyond repair, no-hopers who deserve all they get! Fortunately, no one is ever considered undesirable or abandoned to the scrap heap by God!

It's when people think they are a cut above the rest that you can be made to feel rejected, thought Robert, *and yet, according to what Miriam said, God is not like that! Jesus came to save sinners!*

Alfred was right to be doing the open-air. I can see what he is doing now! thought Robert. *He is telling people what the Bible says Jesus has done for them, because most will not go to church — and, therefore, never hear it — and some might go to church and still not hear it!*

The truths from the Scriptures were already making impressions upon Robert, as he rolled them over and over in his mind and applied them to his young, simple way of thinking. His meditations, however, were suddenly interrupted by the bellowing voice of Miriam.

"John! Dorothy! Dinner is almost ready! Give it five minutes, and then I will be serving it."

Miriam's voice echoed up the stairs, and shortly afterwards, one could hear feet thudding down it as the two came in obedience, knowing full well that Miriam was always true to her word and that their dinner would be served upon the table whether they were sitting at it or not!

"Hi, Robert," said Dorothy to their guest. "Mm… something does smell nice; don't you think?"

"It certainly does," he replied, as they walked in to sit at the dinner table; the dinner was ready and so were they!

Chapter 9

Waffles for Pudding!

This was now the second time that Robert Templeman had sat at the Petersons' table for dinner. Prior to this, he could not ever remember sitting down for a meal in a home with others — not since his mother had died.

Robert was still fairly subdued about Sarah's recent escapade and disappearing act. He found himself alone again, in the sense that all the other young people in his life right now were together at the Townsend's home, and at that moment in time, he wished he were there with them too. Whilst he respected the warmth and friendship of all that were sitting around the dinner table and the wonderful meal served up by Mrs Peterson, he was now beginning to feel out of place.

After a while Robert was determined to text Ian to see how things were at his end, for as yet, Ian had not come back to him like he had said he would. Robert couldn't help wondering if Sarah had arrived safely at Maria's home and whether she was okay. Consequently, Robert excused himself to visit the bathroom to text the young man in question.

"Well, what would you all like for pudding then?" asked Miriam in Robert's absence. "I have got the usual fresh fruit with cream or yoghurt; that's the healthy option — well, with natural yoghurt that is — or... I *have* got some mixture made up to make waffles! What do you say?"

It was unanimous! "Waffles, please," agreed all enthusiastically without exception.

Miriam became distracted and went to answer the telephone in the other room, leaving the rest discussing what their favourite toppings were. It was hoped that Miriam, upon her return, might have in her kitchen cabinet some jam, golden syrup, maple syrup, lemon juice, ice cream, Nutella, a bottle of those continental cherries in gorgeous juice or simply thick double cream!

Miriam eventually came back into the room, followed closely by Robert, and all eyes were fixed upon her, hoping to hear what she would serve with the waffles. But they were taken by surprise due to an unexpected announcement. Turning towards a certain young man, she said, "Well, Robert, you'll never guess who that was. It was Sarah Manning! She is over at Alfred Townsend's house and seems in good spirits now, I'm pleased to say... But listen to this! Sarah apologised to me for leaving the house in the way she did, and... well, I've just invited her, Maria and Ian over here; I thought they would like some waffles too! Sarah has asked everyone, and they are all coming over!"

At that very moment, Robert received a text message from Ian informing him of the very same arrangement, and it went without saying how very pleased he was by the confirmation!

Dorothy went into the kitchen to help Miriam make up more waffle mixture, whilst John and Robert took responsibility to clear the table and wash up, then reset the table again with plates and cutlery.

"What are we having with the waffles, dear?" John asked. "Is there any cream or something?"

"Don't worry; all that is being sorted," retorted Miriam, just a little flustered, having been made aware of all the different requests for toppings. "But... I do need some maple syrup, and it would be nice to have a jar of cherries in juice. An oh! A bottle of Nutella would be good, too. I could do with someone going to go the shop for me... You wouldn't like to volunteer, John, would you?"

"No problem."

"Try the deli; that would be best."

"Okay," replied John, working in perfect unison with his wife. "Would you finish setting the table, Robert? And get some serviettes, please; waffles can be a bit messy. See you all soon... Ah! Here they come now; they didn't hang about!

"Good afternoon, ladies and gentlemen," declared John with great excitement. "Welcome to the waffle party! Miriam! Here they are! Just come through, all of you. I will see you soon."

The new arrivals entered the lounge area where Robert was seated, and Miriam cordially invited Sarah once again into her home, but without any reference whatsoever to previous occurrences that day. It was now being regarded as water under the bridge, especially since Miriam had received that most respectful, apologetic telephone call from Sarah, which had had the effect of clearing the air. She spoke to Sarah as if nothing untoward had happened that day — which of course was the truth anyway!

It had not been so long ago that Miriam had expressed no little concern over the young people with John or as she had put it, *'Oh, we do need to appoint a youth leader in the church; all this is getting out of my depth; the whole thought worries me ... what are we to do with them all?'*

Yet, she had taken a liking towards Robert when they had sat down together for a chat before dinner, having impressed him in the process with her forthright heart-to-heart talk. Further, Miriam had instigated a waffle party quite out of the blue, involving four of those young people with whom she had previously seemed to be getting out of her depth — and yet, she appeared very happy about entertaining the lot of them! John had originally spoken with concern about keeping all things open regarding the care of the latter group, which, he had said, was taking the church into unmapped territory, but today's event was perhaps a good start!

Maria had drifted away from the young group to sit next to Dorothy, leaving Sarah alone with the two boys. Sarah seemed quite unperturbed, however, and was busily consuming her fourth waffle. Robert and Ian were talking about karate, occasionally trying to bring Sarah into their conversation if they could – but she was fairly distracted by other things.

"Oh! These waffles are like, so delicious," Sarah spluttered, addressing the young men in a casual manner. "This Nutella is so awesome. I went for ice cream first, but I should have gone straight for this. Yummy! How's about you lot?"

"Yeah, I'm good too," replied Ian. "How many have you had, Robert?"

"This is my third one."

"This is my fourth. Hey, Sarah, we've been talking just now about new people for the karate club. Why don't you start karate lessons as well? Maria is coming!"

"Ian! Why would I want to do, like ka…ra…teee…, I ask yer?"

Sarah's response was intended to ridicule the whole idea of her doing karate, making it sound like something quite stupid and unrealistic, and she hoped to make it clear to them both that it was a no-go suggestion and they should drop the subject.

"It's cool, I tell yer! You should try it, Sarah; shouldn't she, Robert? It might help yer one day, for all you know."

"Well, it *did* help you with him; didn't it, Ian? Remember that time?" she laughed.

Sarah was pointing her finger towards Robert, referring to their fight in the high street when Ian had, on that occasion—now so boldly and audaciously brought up again by Sarah—come to the rescue of Maria whilst she was in the process of being attacked by Robert. In doing so, Ian had exercised clever karate skills that had saved the day! Sarah had also happened to be there, and she had observed everything.

"Well, you're right about that incident, Sarah, and I think Robert would agree too, hey. But now me and Robert are good mates, so why don't you come along?"

"When is it?" asked Sarah reluctantly, conceding that there was no way she could pursue that divisive line with the two of them any further, seeing as they now seemed to be bosom buddies!

"Tuesday night, 7 till 8. Are you up for it then?"

"I'll see," she replied.

Now, Robert was accustomed to hearing that kind of indecisive, non-committal response from Sarah, and it had caused him much grief by falsely raising his hopes and expectations when he had asked her out on one occasion, so this time he was determined to press her about the matter further.

"Sarah! That is your favourite line when asked to do anything. If you don't want to go, just say so; it's no skin off our nose if you don't wish to come. Hey, Ian?"

"Of course not, Sarah," replied Ian. "It's entirely your call whether you come or not. It's just like… well, I thought you might like to, that's all… 'cos Maria goes, see."

"Well, you'll have to excuse me," she replied with some resentment regarding the added pressure from the pair of them. "I need the bathroom." Sarah realised that the two boys, who happened also to be good friends, stuck together like glue and enough was enough for now!

"Whoops!" said Ian to Robert after Sarah had disappeared. "Looks like you pressed a button there or something, hey?"

"Let it drop now. It's up to her. Trust me, Ian; she won't come if she doesn't want to. Believe you me!"

"Well, like you said, why can't she just come out with it—yes or no? What is there to think about?"

"She does a lot of thinking, does Sarah! Like I said, Ian, forget it, and just leave her to decide by herself. Some girls are different to boys; we come straight out with things, but they have moods and all that… well, so I'm gathering! You should know, Ian, what I'm sayin'; we have to give 'em some slack at times."

Robert spoke from experience, but also with sufficient respect for Sarah to give her some space. There were some things best left alone, and clearly this was another one of them.

Maria saw Sarah returning from the bathroom and caught her attention.

"How yer doin', Sarah? I'm so full up now I could do with a walk! Do you fancy one?"

Sarah thought that a breath of fresh air would probably be a good idea, so she accepted the suggestion but at the same time felt a little uneasy about walking out again on Mrs Petersons' hospitality.

"Are you sure it will be alright for us to leave again so soon, Maria? This will be my second time in one day I'll have walked out!" Sarah whispered to Maria.

"Hey, don't worry, Sarah; it will be fine, I'm sure. I'll go and tell the boys what we're doing, okay?"

They were all about to leave for a walk when Sarah stopped in her tracks at the door, needing to do something else first. She wandered back, looking for Miriam, and found her washing up in the kitchen all by herself.

"Oh! Hello, Sarah. Are you alright, my dear? Can you believe this? I used up so much mixture for the waffles I have run out of flour! Did you enjoy them though?"

"Very much, Mrs Peterson—especially with Nutella. Thank you! The rest of them are just going for a walk, so I thought I'd join them, but... well, I wanted to tell you that's where I'm going too, if that's alright. I appreciate all you have done today, yer know; I'm sorry about earlier."

Miriam was moved within herself as she observed the young, lean figure of Sarah, standing there before her in the doorway, and just for a moment she imagined that it was her daughter, Rebecca! On occasions when she had got up to some prank or another, Rebecca would storm off into her room having been chastised about the matter; then, eventually, having calmed herself, she would come back down the stairs, stand there by the kitchen doorway as Sarah was doing, and talk to her mum in a contrite and regretful manner.

"Dear Sarah, you do not need to ask my permission to go for a walk. Bless you! Regarding earlier, you are free to enter this house when you please and leave it when you please, so don't ever be afraid to say so! I must confess, Sarah... just then you reminded me of my daughter, Rebecca, when she was about your age. How strange!"

"Where is your daughter now, Mrs Peterson?" enquired Sarah.

"Oh, she is married and lives in Bristol. She works in the hospital as a physiotherapist, and her husband is a doctor there, too... but we have no grandchildren yet!"

"I would like to talk to you sometime about her, if that is okay? I mean what she had to do to get her job, and... like, girly things she may have gone through, you know — growing up and all!"

"Yes, that would be absolutely fine, Sarah. Before you leave today, you can give me your phone number or email address so we can keep contact, then we will arrange a suitable time for you to come over. Is that okay? And you must come for tea as well!"

Sarah stood there motionless and just glanced at Miriam as if expecting something from her. Suddenly, Miriam's motherly instincts rose to the surface; she went over and gave Sarah a hug in like manner to what she would have done had it been her Rebecca!

"Has anyone seen Sarah?" sounded the voice of Maria nearby. "Oh! There you are!"

Maria stood back momentarily as she observed her friend embracing Miriam in the kitchen.

"Are you coming for a walk, Sarah?"

"Yeah, I'm coming. Bye, Mrs Peterson, and thanks again for everything."

Chapter 10

A Walk in the Park

The foursome crossed the road and entered a park. Initially the two boys and two girls walked together as a group, but as time passed Ian and Maria separated, holding hands, and went on ahead, leaving Sarah and Robert to their own devices.

"How did yer get on at Maria's house, Sarah?" enquired Robert.

"I was cheesed off, as yer know, and well... seeing Alfred there, like... in my face... I nearly blew a gasket! Maria was showering when I arrived, so I had to put up with him and his antics for a good while! Then... well, funny enough, things got better as time went on, and he asked me if I wanted some toast and butter. What a joke! He turned out better than I thought in the end and really seemed to care about me, and as that is not something I meet very often, I obliged and had some toast. Anyway, I went on and told him all what happened — about me getting drunk an' all, yer know — like yer would to yer grandad or something. And he never said how stupid I was or anything like that, which made a change. Anyways, how about you? What happened after I'd gone?"

"Well, when I saw Miriam, I told her you weren't feeling very well with a headache, and yer didn't want any food. Yer just needed some space to be alone and quiet, so she understood without any drama."

"Thanks for that, Robert; I appreciate yer coverin' for me."

"Yer know what, Sarah? You'll never believe this, but she wanted to talk to me and ask me questions."

"Oh my! What did she ask you, Robert?"

"She wanted to know how I knew you for starters, like... when did we first meet?"

"So? What did you say?"

"I told her the truth," laughed Robert. "I told her about when I threw a wobbly on the street and picked on you and Maria, and then all that went on after that—how I had a fight with Ian!"

"Why did you say all that to her? What was her reaction?"

"Ah, she was cool about everything. What about you, Sarah? I might ask the same. Why did you tell Alfred about getting drunk and all? Miriam was genuinely interested and wanted to talk, so I told her. She was alright too, actually; you would have been surprised to hear her. She was not like you thought—looking down on you, judging you for what you did. She ain't like that, and neither is John. They're alright for adults.

She said something like, "*Well, the way I see it, Robert, is like this; all of us have done things in the past of which we are now ashamed and that includes*

119

both myself and John… this I can assure you! It's what we do next that matters, not what we did before!"

"It made me wonder what John did when he was younger? Sounded to me like he had a past too, judging by what Miriam seemed to say."

"Actually, that sounds quite cool, yer know," added Sarah. "Well, so much for that, hey! We both seem to have got through that episode together okay at the end of the day! I appreciate yer sticking up for me; thanks."

"We? You said we got through that episode together! Hey! What's all this *we* and *together* business all of a sudden?" Robert replied bluntly and thoughtlessly.

Sarah just stared at Robert for a moment, not realising what she had just said, and rather than progress along the lines of being overly friendly or personal, she said, "Well, you know what I mean…"

"Sarah, if I ever knew what you meant, I would be a lot happier in myself than I am now."

"What are you on about, Robert, for goodness sake? Just because I might have used the word *we* back then? Get a grip, will yer!"

Robert stood to his feet and slowly walked away, seemingly disturbed by the way the conversation had deteriorated between himself and Sarah and realising he himself was not without blame by provoking Sarah in the first place. He had been getting increasingly frustrated with her for quite a while, and in his heart he just wanted clarification as to where they were going together – if anywhere!

"Hey, Robert; hang on, will yer please!" Sarah was none too chuffed by his manner or by his walking away from her, and so she ran after him. "Look, you're alright, Robert – as far as that goes, okay! But if you expect me to speak all mushy to yer and bow down to yer because you're the boy an' all, then it's not gonna happen, right! I've been trodden upon too much in the past. Whenever I've said nice friendly things to boys, it only makes them think I'm clingy, and I get it thrown back in my face. Then I'm made to seem too needy by being upset! It's a joke and not a very nice one. You never know whether the person has any real feelings for you!"

Sarah had become quite emotional suddenly. Robert walked back to her, forgetting about himself now, and resorted to being more concerned about how Sarah was feeling instead. He became remorseful for inadvertently hurting Sarah's feelings – an area in which he had much to learn. They both sat down once again on a nearby seat. Ian and Maria were completely out of sight by this time so that the two were quite alone. In a much quieter and mellow voice, Sarah continued, speaking of her feelings to Robert.

"The way I see it, Robert... it's like this. If you like someone, you don't tell them how you feel! Maybe I have just reacted too sensitively to people in the past. Perhaps I have allowed words spoken to hang in my head way past their sell-by date, but I've never known how the other person really feels, never known where I stand and been afraid to ask! What's more, we seem to live in a world now where people are afraid to feel anything genuine! Or at the very least, are afraid to show it! I am fed up with boys, fed up with just about everything out there!

"Another thing; I hate this modern-day hook-up culture where you get a text, right, and it says, *'Hey, Sarah! How about we hang out sometime?'*

"Nobody asks you to go out on a date anymore. It's, *'Oh, let's hang out!'* Everything is casual and made to appear thoughtless, and that's how it must stay. Even... even when you do stuff together, it makes no difference! *'Oh, I thought we were just hangin' out,'* is what you get thrown back at you. There comes a point in time when you want to know whether a boy has genuine feelings for you, so that you know where you are heading. Well, most girls I know think like that — as they get older especially — but as I say, they'll never show it; they are just too nervous and scared!"

Robert was stunned upon hearing all that Sarah had just said! It explained a lot regarding what he had previously considered to be her noncommittal attitude towards him in the past. Now he understood what was going on in Sarah's head! She was carrying so much baggage from previous experiences with boys and had been really hurting!

What could Robert say to her? What could he do to console her, given that all she had said tended to be true in many people's experiences! It was the new culture, one of no commitment, a casualness and carefreeness, void of all responsibility, that went too far, so that respect of the individual was side-lined and replaced by a selfish desire for fun and good times—all of which had reached new levels of indulgence way above that of previous generations. Sadly, it was usually at the expense of the girl's feelings and emotions, just as Sarah had vividly described. Her self-esteem and self-worth had suffered. She had nothing more to give once her ace card had been played, attempting to secure the boy of her dreams!

Yet, were there alternatives open to the patient person who would not allow their principles to be compromised? There were other shops to shop in!

Maria Townsend was a good example of a young teenager whose integrity had been tested and tried during her long-term friendship with Ian McPherson, and still she had guarded her behaviour with him and kept control. This was demonstrated after Ian was teased at college by his male peers for still being a virgin, but Maria would have none of it! Ian had been reprimanded by her for feeling embarrassed by this, and after seeing things in proper perspective, not only succumbed to her way of thinking but prided himself in having a girlfriend who was different and who preferred God's ways to those prevalent in the world! In such matters, it can sometimes be the girl who sways the power over the boy and not the reverse!

Ian and Maria had just about walked a complete circle in the park and were now visible over the brow of a hill some two hundred yards away in the distance. Robert glanced at Sarah with a new determination to examine his every motive from now onwards; she deserved that respect. In short, he had to watch his step!

It was a thoughtful moment for him, and he found himself thinking back and contemplating all that he had ever said to her, as well as examining his intentions at the time. He invited a light to shine upon him and decipher his true motives. He was a young man who, uncommonly, desired to think the right things as well as do them. Fortunately, he had not thought or behaved in the way Sarah had voiced regarding the selfish attitudes of other boys she had known. There was no occasion in the past that he could think of when he had thoughtlessly pursued Sarah purely for his own pleasure and not hers, for then he would now have been ashamed in the light of Sarah's heartfelt revelations to him. He would have felt guilty indeed! But no, Robert's conscience was clear, and he felt confident and exceedingly pleased in that respect. Sarah had highlighted the need for a sense of decency and respect of others, in this case girls; and given that Robert had chosen to walk the straight and narrow, it went without saying, as far as he was concerned, that you couldn't endeavour to do the second and ignore the first! It did not make sense to call himself a Christian and not walk differently to the way he had done before. People can be hurt by words, actions and deeds, so his faith had to be such that it changed him for the better!

Robert's comprehensions and convictions were beyond those of many his age who had been attending church perhaps for years, if not from childhood. He respected God so much that he knew God could not be fooled, or as he would say, messed around with! If you are following God, then you do just that—and do it wholeheartedly, else not at all! Robert's simple understanding and appreciation of God and His character was very real, and already there were developing signs, birthed within him, of a sure gifting from God—of which he himself was not aware! Clearly, his Divine perceptions and zeal—or what he would call common sense—had originated in his heart and not his head. Consequently, they could not have been developed through study or experience. In any case, he had not been around long enough to have developed such things!

Once again, Robert's growing integrity was manifest when he thought to himself that, as a child of God, you could not be piously devoted (or as he would say, twofaced) with God inside a church building on the one hand, then outside of the meeting do as you please! No, there had to be an inner change, as well as believing, or it wasn't real!

Even so, the pathway for all who would endeavour to follow God was the same — obedience and overcoming life's difficulties, not the least those from within as well as from without — and Robert's was no exception! Nothing yet had Robert ever heard spoken in a church meeting or house group that addressed these issues raised by Sarah regarding the dilemma in the contemporary hook-up culture out there in the real world, perhaps because they were unknown to church people; yet, he felt there were some aspects that were relevant for all to hear and that should be spoken of. There had to be some guidance regarding God's ways in these matters!

Even so, Robert just knew in his heart what was right or wrong, even if certain things had not been spelt out for him beforehand. He just had to ask himself what Jesus would do in each situation, and thereafter, he felt guided along a certain pathway that was quite different to that of his own! God makes it possible for anyone to do the right thing if they look to Him.

Ian and Maria drew close enough to converse with Robert and Sarah.

"Well, you two seem to have had a good walk then," said Ian with sarcastic humour when some fifteen yards away from the seat upon which Robert and Sarah sat.

"Hey, do us a favour, will yer?" replied Robert, taking no notice of Ian's remark. "Please tell Miriam we will be back in about another twenty minutes or so!"

"Okay, will do."

Sarah looked at Robert, somewhat amazed by his announcement.

"In twenty minutes?" she said, taken aback with some degree of surprise.

"Well, I just wondered whether you would like to walk with me around that wild looking woodland over there on that hill… if you wish, that is. Don't worry; I will look after you and take good care of yer, lass!"

Sarah understood this was a jovial Robert, attempting to be amicable and friendly with her, and so she decided to go along with his request without any fuss. She didn't have the heart to do otherwise by him!

"I'm surprised you even want to walk with me after hearing all that I just regurgitated in yer face! I thought I might have frightened you off!"

Equally, Robert understood this was a jovial Sarah, attempting to be amicable and friendly with him too, and he endeavoured to put her mind at rest by saying poetically, "I can assure you I wouldn't want to go for a walk… if I weren't attracted to a girl who can speak her mind and who I like all the more for doing so!"

Sarah's eyes gleamed at him like two sparkling stars!

Approaching the brow of the hill and woodland just mentioned could be seen the twosome, walking together hand in hand, slowly disappearing out of sight.

Chapter 11

Raymond and Susan Littleton

Few couples were ever left unscathed after divorce proceedings had been finalised, especially when one of the parties had remarried. The challenge that evolved within a certain dissolved family was surrounding a little girl who had been underestimated regarding what was dear to her young heart — her daddy! She was just turning three years of age and understood little about some things and much in others; just as a small rudder can turn the direction of a large boat, even in the turbulent seas of an ocean, so she of little stature influenced a new and different course to be chartered between her parents — against all odds — during the turbulent seas of their respective lives!

Raymond Littleton was in his early thirties and considered by most people outside of his immediate family as a respectable person with excellent social standing. He had worked successfully as an independent social worker for several years, enjoying his mission in life to help the elderly — a profession not particularly approved of by his wealthy parents who had other aspirations and hopes for him in the financial sector. It had to be said though that the opinions and thoughts of many close friends and family alike were simply this: Raymond was too vulnerable and easily succumbed to other people's views that persuaded and influenced his emotions — he had no decisive mind of his own — and in part, they were correct.

A closer look at the heart and person of Raymond revealed interesting findings to anyone who cared to know of them. To begin with, he was utterly gutted when both of his grandparents passed away, condemning himself for not spending enough time with them, and so he helped redeem himself by turning to a useful vocation in working with the elderly. Inevitably, as an Oxford graduate with public school education, he was ridiculed behind the scenes for selling out and wasting his opportunity to be a corporate banker.

As an only child, he had been wholly spoilt and consequently, not as mature as some of his age. He had no sense of lack — at least not in a material sense — but more practically, his judgements and expectations in life did not fit realistically into the real world now that he had left home. In short, his success in his work and society was not matched in his marriage to Susan Littleton — his second marriage at that.

He was a bit of an oddball, as well as a black sheep in the family! He did not fit in very well with his peers, for he never dressed down to wearing casual clothes such as jeans and T-shirt, he never went down to the pub, nor was he interested in football or cricket — though perhaps a little rugby caught his interest sometimes for he had some experience in that game from his public-school days. Instead, he always dressed suited and booted, though he often omitted the tie. He loved to dine out in expensive restaurants and hang out in wine bars. Most of his friends were from his old public school. In short, he was for all appearances a bit of a snob.

A good opinion of him was limited to those of the elderly generation, who tended to love his formal good sense of manners as he worked to help them! In the end, his actions in this direction spoke more to them than his elite-sounding accent and background. What he did was more important; that's what counted most of all to the residents in a care home that he regularly visited. In their view, he was a wonderful, kind and caring young man!

It was at this care home that he had met his first wife. Ironically, he had been attracted to one who was considered by his family as a mere mortal — Mary Osborne, the sister of Dorothy's fiancé, David. He had met Mary as she was visiting her late grandad. Mary, being quite innocent in appearance and very pretty, had appeared to Raymond as lonely and desperate one day as he had observed her sobbing by her grandfather's bed, whilst he was in transition from the earthly realm to the heavenly.

Raymond had scrutinised Mary from a distance and felt very sorry for her predicament;

the situation had reminded him of his own grandfather, so he had decided to ask Mary to come away with him for a meal to regain her strength with some sort of nourishment. That was how it had all started.

She had succumbed to his polite charm and hospitality very easily; he was after all such a handsome, well-bred and courteous gentleman. Raymond had been instantly besotted by her loving gaze. At one point, as Mary had been sitting by her grandfather's bedside, Raymond had done the unforgivable—he had physically placed his hand upon hers to comfort her—and as a consequence, had gazed into her large, affectionate brown eyes that were radiating genuine love and beauty! This action, together with Mary's sincere manner, her simplicity of nature and indeed her delicate soft hands, had done it! It was not too long before he had become irresistibly attached to her company.

Raymond considered Mary to be uncommonly pretty; she was to him the epitome of beauty, very rare and quite different to anyone else he had met before—though that was not too surprising as indeed all his friends and associates were from a secluded sector of life, the upper crust so to speak! Further, Mary had been to him a damsel in distress, and he couldn't bear to see such pain. Ironically, as far as appearances go, Mary had worn no make-up that day and had been plainly dressed, but Raymond had been completely oblivious of that, being absorbed in and awestruck by her person and nothing else. Raymond had seen much of the insincere posturing and glamour exhibited by so many ladies in his sphere of life. He could see through the tinsel and charm most women felt necessary and comfortable in, but when regarding Mary's appearance and attire, he had seen other things instead.

Indeed, as Mary had sat at her grandfather's bedside looking pale and in deep sorrow with seemingly nothing about her to particularly promote herself as anything special or beautiful to any man — though there was no desire upon her part to do so anyway — Raymond had seen beyond all outward appearances to nothing more than a beautiful countenance! Mary had been unconscious of her own self, her only concern completely and utterly regarding someone else — her grandad!

Raymond had seen her as the embodiment of a normal person from the real, non-superficial world and not a pretentious upper-class lady who considered herself above the majority. He, having never met anyone quite like her before — which was not that surprising for Mary never went to expensive restaurants or wine bars — had proposed to her and married her all within the space of two months. Raymond had assured Mary that he would look after her and take her away from all grief and pain; these had been his sentiments towards her.

Raymond's actions had caused significant conflict between him and his own family for having married beneath his station. He had been independent and headstrong, not deciphering or discerning between one station in life and another, for he had never known anything but his own unique and fortunate standing in life, which he considered as normal.

It had been later in their marriage, just a few months later in fact, when he had found himself very much incompatible with the normal, mundane things in life, where the demands placed upon him were all foreign and new. He had not been able to cook any kind of a meal, had not been accustomed to washing up and cleaning—for these had previously been the duties of domestic staff—and the whole idea of his going out with club acquaintances in society twice a week had brought no favourable response from his wife.

It had become clear things were not going to work, and then it had happened! Mary had fallen pregnant, to the horror of Raymond's parents who had immediately suggested and planned for an abortion in a remote private clinic. Mary would have none of it, and Raymond, not knowing what to think, had been wedged in the middle of two pressures—one coming from his parents on the one hand and another from Mary on the other.

Not desiring to make waves in the direction of where his bread was buttered — for he was sole heir to a great fortune — he had opted to lean in the direction of his parents rather than that of his own wife! This attitude of non-support for Mary had brought about irreconcilable differences between the two of them — a phenomenon common these days — and with it being a classic reason for divorce, it had taken no time to implement.

Raymond was now married to Susan. She had come from a similar background to Raymond, and they were, therefore, considered a good match. However, just like Raymond, she had been divorced, and both were in their second marriage. Susan usually got what she wanted, and what she possessed was not to be shared. Flexibility was virtually unknown in such cases and selfishness paramount. Consequently, through their marriage, Raymond now belonged to her and was not to be shared in any way with anyone else, especially his ex, Mary Osborne.

Susan Littleton was petite and of very slim stature, always elegantly dressed and full of airs and graces, in stark contrast to lesser mortals such as Mary Osborne whom she belittled constantly before her latest catch in the person of Raymond. It was beneath her to imagine how he could have married such a lowly person, given his own standing and status in life. Position and status were to her paramount; what else was there in life? You took what you could, provided it came with wealth and lavish living; love was a matter of chance and luck—nothing else!

Status and fortune with good prospects for the future were drilled into Susan from her childhood, and without exception, she had been meticulously instructed and groomed to steer clear of young and impetuous love and romance. Her mother had been her tutor throughout all her younger years, not unlike an Estella under the auspices of a Miss Havisham in *Great Expectations,* but with one exception perhaps—namely that Susan would not venture down the road of deliberately breaking the gentleman's heart just prior to a formal engagement, if he was approved of and possessed all the right qualifications—credentials, money and good social standing!

There was one aspect regarding any marriage of their daughter that was paramount to Susan's family, and that concerned any future offspring. It was vital and necessary for any children to come from a family of substance, well-placed within society and grandeur, and Susan placed this requirement alongside her own personal desires with equal ranking.

Raymond's folly in venturing under Susan's clutches could only be attributed to the parents' scheming on both sides. They had colluded together in an attempt at removing him from his current abysmal circumstances — as they thought of them — and restoring him to the rightful position and sphere where he belonged. Raymond's parents were like Susan's — very wealthy people and exceedingly well placed in society. Since their son's track record was that of being completely impulsive without due thought and consideration of others — that is, of their own desires and wishes — and since he clearly had no understanding or appreciation of protocol, they decided upon giving him a helping hand with the end justifying the means.

Raymond's parents, in collusion with those of Susan, arranged for a party with both their son and a certain, most eligible young lady to be present. It was not unlike a nineteenth-century ball, where prospective matches were to be made when new eligible young ladies were presented in court. The cunning craftiness of the two families — the main impetus originating from the mothers — paid off very well so that the twosome, with sufficient wine and the like, were to become attached one way or another!

The plan had been a success. Susan had secured her man with seductive words and flattery, prising a promise of commitment from him that very same evening. She had then stood up and informed everyone at the party of their decision to be married with a short engagement, announcing it to both sides of the family. There had been no turning back! Raymond had not gainsaid Susan's words nor shown any objection towards being married to her, and as soon as his divorce had gone through, it was all done and dusted; as planned, they had been quickly married.

Chapter 12

Raymond's Growing Dilemma

At a certain wine bar in town, a lone gentleman had been sitting outside for an hour or so, reflecting upon the morning's events. Adjacent to this venue was a café where a young mum was sitting at an outside table. She had a baby buggy, carrying two little babies, and the gentleman observed the situation next door to him with some interest.

By his reckoning, the little ones must have been about ten months old, and to all appearances seemed as though they could well be twins, a baby boy and a girl. The lady had been holding the baby boy in her arms, cuddling him, as he was unsettled and constantly grizzling, whilst his sister on the other hand remained in her pram, much more content than her brother. Occasionally, the little girl would turn aside and notice her mummy holding her brother. Her mouth could not speak, but her eyes said it all; she wanted to be held too and relayed this information back to her mummy with a similar grizzle to that of her brother. A single stroke of the head and a few consoling words, however, were all she received. But this action satisfied the baby girl, and she quickly became restored to her former state of peace and calm, as if her mission was accomplished having made her presence felt.

Even so, the girl's relative contentment was quite noticeable to the onlooker seated at the wine bar who was captured and intrigued at how different were the natures of the opposite sexes, even at so young an age. It seemed that even at such a young age and start in life, this was a typical sign of things that would always be true, both now and in the future, namely that the boys always seemed to need that reassurance and lots of loving cuddles, whereas the girls were more independent! That's how it seemed, and it was probably true!

Raymond Littleton imagined the home life of this quite attractive, young mum and pondered what it would be like. He imagined it would be the sort of pleasant atmosphere that was so very different to his own, though he readily knew only too well that his circumstances could have been similar at one time with at least one little baby girl at home—Julia—had he not walked away from her and her mummy. Remorseful guilt and utter dismay besieged his thoughts and mind, so he ordered yet another large chardonnay.

Despair following regret was an awful combination. Regret and self-pity were never short of memories! They rolled forth like oncoming waves on the seashore, then receded back again into the hidden closet of the soul, having deposited their debris on the sands of the mind. Raymond sank deeper and deeper into utter remorsefulness at the very thought of all he had once had with the beautiful Mary and little Julia in their simple home. He would sacrifice all his wine bar antics and social lifestyle for this beauty that money could not buy!

I could have done better than I did, came self-rebuke.

After a while, when Raymond had consumed well over his limit in wine, he observed the young lady leaving. By now, the scene before him was that of images spinning around in his vision with a sharpening of focus upon the young lady's features as she walked closer by, a phenomenon not uncommon in the intoxicated state. She smiled at Raymond, conscious that he was taking notice of her with her babies as they passed him. The baby boy, still in her mother's arms, had noticed the gentleman as the family party walked directly in front of him, and he waved at Raymond uttering a word that sounded just like '*da-da!*' Raymond waved back and received a warm, loving smile from the proud mother, as if to say, '*These are my two gorgeous babies! All the money in the world could not replace them!*'

Suddenly, all of Raymond's wealth seemed immaterial and worthless! It had often been said in Raymond's ear in the past, by well-wishers attempting to persuade him along his parents' desired course of action—namely to leave Mary and later marry Susan—that money could not buy you happiness but it certainly helped! At this moment in time, Raymond would have replied something to the effect, "Really? Well, I certainly am not happy, and money is not helping me one iota! I have none of the former and plenty of the latter!"

Something seemed to drop away from Raymond's heart that unfolded and released extreme anguish of spirit and soul with unbearable pain! What had he done? His Julia was now three years old or thereabouts — and so beautiful!

No sooner had the family party passed him by, disappearing out of sight, than he slumped upon the table, head in arms as if unable to carry the weight of his aching head upon his shoulders! What was the answer? Where could he go? What could he do to remedy this feeling of heaviness and void within his soul? To add further to his despondency, Raymond, being a very well-read person, recollected some words written a long time ago by another thoughtful person, words which were not welcome at that moment in time but protruded into his thoughts anyway. *Where was my heart to flee for refuge from my heart?*

That is me alright! thought Raymond.

Whither was I to fly where I would not follow? In what place should I not be prey to myself?

Raymond had been married to Susan for almost three years. They had no children of their own, for Susan did not wish to have her life burdened so early on in years. She was but a mere twenty-eight years of age, and she thought that far too young for the chains of family life to be shackled around her neck—though it had to be said that her father-in-law was none too pleased by her apparent feminist inclinations and what he considered to be an immature and selfish attitude. He, being much more conservative and old fashioned, would argue, *'What is the main purpose of marriage if not to bring forth offspring into this world and an heir to one's estate?'*

Ironically, Susan knew ladies who were in the process of going through divorce proceedings for exactly the opposite reasons to this, those who were in fact were desirous to start a family so as not to leave things too late, but their other halves disapproved!

Many times, Raymond would have a talk with his mother about his dismal marriage to Susan; after all, it was all her doing—at least that was how he saw it. This was Raymond's opinion, and he considered it to be the case, completely disregarding the fact that he was the one who had made the choices. But his mother had pressed her own agenda before him, knowing full well her son's weaknesses would manifest themselves and that he would yield to her wishes! Though he had spoken with his mother as before mentioned, he did not obtain from her any support, sympathy, reassurances or loving cuddles; the latter only applied to baby boys unfortunately!

Raymond was still musing over his sad state of affairs at the wine bar, and it should be said that he had managed to sit upright upon his seat in the process. He had had a terrible argument with Susan that morning, culminating in him storming out of the house and retreating to this, his regular venue of choice — but there was no real escape. He had made his bed, and now he must lie in it!

He began to replay through his mind once again his conversation with Susan earlier that morning. It had all started when Susan had confronted him regarding a visit he had made against her will to his ex-wife, Mary.

"Why do you find it so very necessary to resurrect that old chapter of your previous life, may I ask, by having to go over there and visit your ex-wife? Remember, you were the one who chose to leave her for me! Yes?"

"Yes indeed! And now I think seriously and regretfully about that decision every single day! Why I succumbed to coercion and manipulation from my mother... and probably yours as well I'm sure... and then being beguiled by you... It is all completely beneath me!"

"Ah! You poor soul! Having regrets now, are we?"

Raymond, determined to make his point without distraction, kept focused upon what he wished to say.

"Susan, I basically wanted to put it right with Mary, if you really wish to know. I wanted her to attend Julia's birthday party all along, and I told her straight that we had had disagreements upon the matter."

"You said what? How dare you tell another woman about our business and disagreements! You had no right at all, Raymond, to say such things, making me appear to be an awkward individual! How dare you! I will never forgive you for that... Mark my words!"

Susan was right! Raymond was out of order to disclose personal details to Mary as he had, but he had only perhaps unwisely said and done what many other unthinking men would have done, to speak about private matters without enough care, thought or consideration. Women were sensitive to such things, even if men were not.

"I am sorry, Susan. I should not have said all I said. Upon reflection, I agree with you; it was unwise, and I apologise. But if you could have only appreciated for one minute that Julia happens to be my daughter! And it was my desire that Mary should attend her own daughter's birthday party... But no, you would have none of it, and I couldn't understand why. Can you not see my reasoning behind that? Is there not an ounce of unselfishness in you? And thought for what is best for Julia?

"Think of it from my point of view for a change, will you? I thought it would be nice for her to have both her parents on that special occasion — her birthday party. After all, it *was* held in an outside public venue as opposed to our own home, where I agree it would have perhaps been a completely different matter. Mary had apparently been exceedingly poorly for some time, so I went to see her anyway, despite what you said, and pick up Julia from school to help her out at the same time. She had no one else!"

"You did this without consulting me? You knew full well my opinion on the matter, Raymond, and that I would be displeased with you going to see this... this Mary!"

Susan was in a huff and walked out of the room in exasperation. After a few minutes, she returned, holding a glass of wine in the air with a sense of superiority about her.

"Yes! I decided to go," asserted Raymond in a most unprecedented manner, for he had up until now never gainsaid Susan's opinion in any matter, not wishing to rock the boat. "I thought it unreasonable of you to stipulate such a thing!"

"Is that so? Well... I will not tolerate this deviousness, do you hear? I am your wife and deserve more respect than this kind of behaviour from you, Raymond! I have never ever been treated in such a manner in my whole life! How could you do this? What has become of you suddenly?"

Raymond just kept silent. He hated arguing with Susan and thought he had done very well over the last three years of marriage in composing himself upon such occasions when contention had surfaced between them—usually to do with Julia, Mary or both. Well, he had done well up until now that is.

He looked at Susan's countenance; she was most severe and seemed hardened, hurt and uncompromising. She had not finished yet with their current discourse; there was more to come, clearly still brewing in her mind.

"And just how did you know, may I ask, that your Mary was ill in the first place? Please answer me that... and truthfully if you will, Raymond! I am getting fed up with you more and more by the minute!"

Raymond was in the dock under her interrogation and was most subdued by this unrelenting pursuit of Susan's curiosity regarding his whereabouts of late and his dealings with his ex-wife. Susan was right; he had received information from a certain quarter regarding Mary's well-being, but it was a matter he would rather not have pursued with her, knowing full well what her reaction would be if she knew.

"Well? Tell me! How did you know that Mary had been ill? Who told you, may I ask?"

"Susan! For goodness sake! Is this some sort of inquisition? If you really wish to know, I happened to cross paths with her brother, David, downtown in a coffee house. I was on my office break. He told me about how Mary had been of late, suffering from depression — and very badly, I gather."

Raymond glanced down at the floor somewhat sheepishly, not wishing to proceed with any more details regarding his meeting with David, but Susan's sixth sense kicked in, picking up on her radar some other details that he was not disclosing.

"Are you sure that was all? What else happened? Was anyone else with him?"

Raymond reacted in horror, feeling the effect of Susan's interrogation deep within his conscience, wondering just where and how she managed to obtain this intuitive information! Why was he feeling guilty?

"Yes, there was someone else, seeing as you wish to know every jot and tittle! David invited me over to his table and introduced me to his girlfriend, Dorothy McGuire — though both are now engaged to be married. And yes, that was their engagement party I went to; okay?"

"And what is she like? This Dorothy McGuire? Is she very pretty?"

Raymond was nearly beside himself! He could not bear the conversation. Whatever he said to Susan, he knew his words would fall upon a critical, uncompromising mind. She was in that sort of a mood, digging up whatever she could to throw it back at him as spitefully as possible and with an envious jealousy that was like fiery judgment being unleashed.

Raymond decided to plunge into the deep end; at least the rest would hopefully be much shallower afterwards! He decided to tell Susan about Dorothy but with a deliberate and cynical twist entangled around his words.

"Now that is an interesting line of questioning, typical of a woman who constantly wishes to compare herself with the next one, just in case there was any possibility of a threat within her own territory!"

"So, she was pretty then; yes?"

"Pretty was not the word! She was that and very much so, but she displayed something more than just beauty; she spoke with much integrity and understanding."

Susan's countenance sobered somewhat upon hearing that; she could cope with the idea of Dorothy being beautiful — for many were — but integrity was a matter worth enquiring about and had an interesting sound about it.

"Okay, so what did you all talk about? I'm intrigued as to why you say she had integrity. Hmm… she must have said something to impress you, I think."

"Well, we talked formalities for a long while; then I asked David regarding his sister. I was very surprised to hear that Mary had had another serious bought of depression. *That* Susan was how I discovered Mary was ill. I had no idea before then, and I perceived that Dorothy was surprised about my ignorance regarding her condition. I gather she is very close to Mary — and Julia as well — and had met her a long time ago, even before she had met David in fact."

"So? Get to the point, Raymond; you are procrastinating. What else did she say to inspire your mind? She must have said more than that!"

Raymond had been debating just how much to disclose to Susan, for some words and thoughts spoken upon that occasion by Dorothy would no doubt provoke a reaction from her; this he was sure about. Though, in essence, there was no real reason for it; Dorothy had merely been stating the truth, he thought!

"Well, Dorothy must have already gathered from Mary that some things were not right in their home. It will have had something to do with the fact that I had invited Mary along to Julia's birthday party so that her hopes were raised, only to be deflated when I informed her that this was not going to be possible. Just what Dorothy knew about all of this and how much, I truly haven't a clue; only that whatever Mary knew I'm sure Dorothy would have been familiar with also.

"I thought that Dorothy said something that was interesting to hear regarding difficulties facing divorcees when there are children involved. Well, here comes the punchline you have been so eager to hear; Dorothy said that some things remain the same after a divorce where children like Julia are involved and never change. I will always be Julia's father, and Mary will always be her mummy. Therefore, perhaps it would be a good idea to put Julia's interests first, especially when there are moments of contention, to form the basis of compromise between the two parties concerned. Susan, Dorothy was merely advocating we both put aside our feelings about the matter just... *just for Julia's sake* — though she didn't mention us by name of course! She was speaking hypothetically about couples in general."

Susan could see some rationale in the suggestion and that it might work for some people, but it was not for her to entertain herself. It would have been just too much to see her husband's ex-wife amid everything.

"Well, it just seems to me that this Dorothy is poking her nose into things that do not concern her; that's easy for her to say, having had no children of her own and presumably having never been divorced! To then tell us to just put Julia first... then everything will be hunky dory!

"Oh! Raymond! How can you be beguiled by her? You are like a naïve little child. I would expect a husband of mine to at least have a mind of his own and not be taken in by such utter theoretical and idealistic rubbish! I would expect you to honour my opinion upon the whole matter... not hers!

"I have had quite enough of all of this! I'm going over to my friends for the day and probably won't be back until late; we're having a hen party."

Susan slammed the lounge door behind her and stormed off in a huff; then, a few seconds later, Raymond heard the front door slam too. Susan was gone.

Chapter 13

Two Good Samaritans

Somehow, despite his inebriated state, Raymond managed to get himself up from the wine bar and went wandering aimlessly down the high-street, wobbling from side to side in the process, occasionally holding himself upright with the aid of a lamp post or some building or other. He turned aside from the busy pedestrianised area and stumbled down a much quieter road to find a secluded place in an alley, where he could stand unseen and out of the way for a while and do what he had to do. It wasn't too long after that necessary but desperate task had been completed when he had to turn aside for a second time and for a different reason. Here, in a secluded spot, he vomited violently. Fortunately, he was a man who carried with him what was to many an unfashionable item called a handkerchief, which came in very useful on occasions like this — to wipe himself here and there just a little!

After this episode, Raymond staggered away headlong down a steep hill, partly walking and partly running, being unable to fully control his steps because of its sharp downhill gradient. His footsteps thumped hard against the road, increasing in speed as he went, and before long, he was running aimlessly and uncontrollably. By some miracle, he managed to stay upright until a perilous but inevitable situation arose. The levels of alcohol reaching his brain were having effect, and he completely blacked out, falling headlong into a stone wall on his right. One side of his face took the impact, brushing alongside the wall and causing instant widespread grazing with several lacerations and abrasions, each one bleeding. Despite all this, he was unconscious of any inflicted pain so that he just got up and carried on walking at a normal pace.

Raymond's mind was as if it were separated from his body. He envisaged a pathway that would lead him back to town by taking left turns whenever he came to a road junction, but he was in fact heading farther and farther away from his desired course and direction. Raymond stood momentarily still and gazed around him, trying to ascertain where he was, but it was no use whatsoever. The streets and houses around him were spinning like a Catherine Wheel in his vision; he was completely oblivious of where he was going and hadn't a clue of his whereabouts. Glaring faces of passers-by seemed to stare hideously at him, observing his condition and disfigured face; others crossed the road to avoid him. Unknown to Raymond, he was heading directly into a notorious gangland area called Damsonwood Estate!

Now, a well-known young man lived in the estate — none other than Robert Templeman — and as it happened, he was just about to be given a lift by his friend, Ian McPherson, who was taking him over to see Dorothy. Ever since Robert had started attending the church, she had promised to give him help and guidance regarding finding himself employment.

Ian was driving his red saloon, approaching Damsonwood Estate, when he swerved to avoid a drunk wandering out into the road. The scene was not particularly unusual — well, at least not around the area he was about to enter — and Ian thought little of it, except perhaps that the man was dressed in a suit rather like a gentleman, but he imagined him to be some posh business person who'd had a few too many at a work do.

Robert was waiting outside the tower block where he lived, observing the usual dismal and untidy state of affairs in the immediate surroundings. Cans and paper rubbish littered the vicinity where he stood; even household contents were dumped unusually close to the block! Surely the perpetrators could have walked a short distance away from the block of flats, where there was a nice hedge or something, and tipped their goods there — or better still, in some recycling depot! Robert walked a few steps away from the area onto the green and waited there; the smell of urine where he had been standing before had become too much.

Robert's father was still up to his old antics, spending all his benefits at the bookies, followed by his regular visit to *The Red Lion* and then arriving home drunk on most evenings. Recently, however, he had observed Robert's interest in going to church, and this had reminded him of his late wife, Catherine, who had upon several occasions desired to go to church herself — but he had refused to let her go. Even so, she would still be seen on occasion reading her Bible, which had made him bitter and angry. He would verbally abuse her by saying that his own father had made him attend church as a young lad, then afterwards, upon arriving home, had beaten the living daylights out of him for the smallest thing. It was probably a fact that Robert's father would be a tough nut to crack as far as getting him into church was concerned!

In the distance, just turning into the green, came the red saloon car belonging to Ian. He pulled over and wound his window down, shouting across to Robert in a joking but sarcastic manner, "Hey man, is this the recycling dump yard?"

Robert was not amused. "Okay, funny guy! You should live here and see what it's like. It would give yer an education!"

"You need to get out of here, man," was Ian's answer, attempting to console Robert's serious reply to his own humorous sarcasm.

"Yeah right! And how am I supposed to do that without a job? This is all I have in the world to stay in now. At least my mum lived here; and if she could stick it out, then so can I. The place reminds me of her, if nothing else; and besides, you know the saying, 'When you're drowning, yer don't snuff yer nose at a floating plank!'

"Come on then; take me to see Dorothy. She'll help me find work; I know she will."

"Jump in, Rob... Nice to see yer, mate. Sorry about what I said before; it must be tough living out here... I bet that's putting it mildly!"

Ian drove off, screeching his car tyres as he turned onto the road. He was a grateful young man at this moment in time, grateful that is to life and his circumstances, especially to his father for buying him a car. He had received it upon his eighteenth birthday for getting himself on track, having left his old life of drugs behind, and with the help of Maria having got rehabilitated, finding an apprentice job in IT, and now playing the drums in the church band. Robert was now his best mate, even though ironically their first meeting had been in a fight in the street! Stranger things may have happened before, but not very often!

There were some people at church who were still adjusting to these new, young recruits in their midst, but slowly they were getting there! The simple attitude and ways of this new generation were radically different to that of the rigid and sometimes lifeless old school, but that was a good thing, not a bad one. They talked about God as freely as if they were talking about their favourite football team.

The young lads from Damsonwood needed a purpose to redirect their energies, having come out of a gangland culture; and whatever buzz they had previously received, it was now being channelled down a new way. And it was Robert who had been largely instrumental in this! Their previous gang leader had turned to follow this new and different way — the way of the cross as some called it — and many followed him. If it was good enough for him, it was good enough for them. Purpose in life and identity was everything; it gave them something to live for. Now, it was to do good and help people instead of robbing and stealing from them. Jesus was showing them a new way of thinking and living; it was to follow Him by studying His Word and to look out for others as you would look out for yourself.

"*How wonderful are these lads!*" commented one lady. "*I feel much safer now than I used to before.*"

"*Let's see if it lasts!*" said her more conservative husband.

The red saloon had travelled only a few hundred yards down the road, running parallel with the green, when an incident close by attracted their attention.

"Wow! Just take a look over there, Robert; there's something happening. Someone is getting done over big-time."

"That's a mugging! I know those guys!" exclaimed Robert. "Quick! Pull over!"

Both young men dashed out of the car and ran towards the scene in the middle of the green. There was a gang of youths setting upon someone who was lying flat on the ground and being kicked by the assailants unmercifully.

"Right, Robert; this is what we do, okay? We get in there and split them up and do what is necessary without going over the top. Come on; let's do it!" Ian was the more experienced in karate and self-defence, so it was he who took responsibility for the situation and, hence, gave a rundown to his friend.

There were four young men assaulting the victim upon the ground with the clear intention of robbing him of anything of use to them. None of them had noticed Robert and Ian, however, until the moment they had both pounced upon the muggers, catching them completely by surprise. The four assailants were no match for the two 'karate kids' as they ploughed into them, bowling them over like skittles in a game of tenpin bowling. Robert retrieved the gentleman's wallet, wrist watch and mobile phone quite easily, for the attackers offered no resistance or retaliation, but instead ran away as fast as they could, dropping all that they had taken as they went. Robert, formally known as the Duke, had also taken up membership at David Osborne's karate club along with Ian, so that they were quite a formidable opposition to face—even when outnumbered two to one!

A slumped figure lay on the grass. Ian recognised him as the same drunken gentleman that he had swerved to miss on his way into Damsonwood Estate.

Robert turned the man over to observe who he might be. "He looks in a bad way, Ian. Just look at the side of his face! He seems to be out cold."

"I don't think so," added Ian. "He's as drunk as a lord! I saw this man stumbling along in the street; he could hardly stand up, and I only just managed to swerve and miss him. Actually, his face is a bit familiar, but I can't remember where I've seen him before."

Robert reached for his mobile, "I'll phone an ambulance and get him checked out."

Ian peered a little closer at the slumped figure, sprawled out on the grass, and then suddenly remembered where he might have seen him. "That's it! I'm sure this is the same man who was at David and Dorothy's engagement party. He was talking to David as if he knew him. Do you remember?"

"Not really; can't say as I do," said Robert. "Just check his wallet for any ID."

Ian pulled out a credit card showing the name R Littleton, and the contacts list on his phone yielded what looked like a personal home phone number against the name *Susan*. Ian scrolled down the list to see if he knew anyone, and to his great surprise, there was the phone number of a very well-known person — David Osborne!

"Get a load of this then, Rob! This guy knows David. Can you believe that? I'm sure now this is the same person who was at his celebration party!"

Within a short space of time, an ambulance had arrived, and Raymond was carefully transferred onto a stretcher and into the van. Ian and Robert had decided to follow on to the hospital, but Robert suggested certain things ought to be done to inform family and friends – and having kept the gentleman's mobile, he immediately started the process.

~~~~~~

Susan Littleton was at a friend's hen party. She was in company with three other ladies, each holding a glass of champagne and pre-occupied with raucous conversation, when suddenly her mobile inconveniently rang. She immediately rejected the call. Robert then tried to phone David Osborne next. He was out with Dorothy, driving back from Bath having done some shopping, and received Robert's phone call on his hands-free device.

"Hi there... Is that you, David? This is Robert."

"Yes. It is, Robert! Nice to hear you; is everything okay?" Robert had sounded quite formal and serious in his manner of speaking, and it had prompted David's immediate concern.

"To come straight to the point, there's a man on his way to hospital, having been mugged amongst other things, and his name is R. Littleton. I wondered if he were a friend of yours. Your name was on his phone."

"Oh dear... Yes, I do know him, Robert! Goodness me! How is he? Was he badly hurt at all?"

"Well, he didn't look too good to be honest. I'm not exactly sure what happened to him before he got mugged, but he could well have been drunk. Ian said he saw him` wandering in the streets not far from here looking as drunk as a lord; those where his words! That would have made him an easy and irresistible target around these parts. Anyway, he is being taken to Central Hospital, and Ian and I are going over there. I have the gentleman's mobile with me. I wondered if you might be able to tell others about him — friends and family... if you don't mind, that is."

"Yes, I will. I'd better contact his wife, Susan, first. Thanks for letting me know Robert.

Dorothy and I will drive straight over to the hospital and perhaps see you there."

"I've already phoned a Susan and left a message on her answer phone," replied Robert. "Maybe you could try phoning her again. See yer later, David. Bye for now."

Chapter 14

Susan Visits her Husband in Hospital

There was an upmarket hotel with a day spa treatment facility in town called *The Darlington*, and a certain function, commonly known as a hen party, was in progress.

The feature and theme of the party was one of pampering! Each participant could choose from a wide choice of treatments. They would all begin with a good swim, after which they could sit in the jacuzzi or sauna. Then, being fully relaxed, the next stage was a massage, including the very special option of a hot stone massage at no extra price! The final phase was a choice: a pedicure or a manicure, followed by a facial – carried out by a specialist aesthetician – or a hair trim and blow dry or restyle. It could only promise to be a very good hen party indeed for all the participants!

There were seven ladies present, all in their late twenties to early thirties, each one wearing a robe and slippers and sitting casually within a dedicated area that had a most quiet and peaceful ambience. A certain petite lady of very slim stature carried in a tray with champagne flutes and a bowl of strawberries. Judging by the response and the rapturous sound of the other six ladies, this interlude was most welcome. During the event that afternoon, the mobile phone belonging to the petite lady in question had rung several times, but upon inspection, she had not recognised the number. As it was not in her phone's contact list and no name had appeared on screen, she had simply ignored it, assuming it was some nuisance call at the other end.

After an hour or two, the magnificent seven moved into a restaurant area of the hotel, feeling quite hungry after their recent activities, and there they sat down for afternoon tea. The first menu was just for tea only and nothing else. It displayed numerous kinds to choose from and was accompanied by tiered sandwich and cake stands, which could be refilled as required.

By now much champagne had been consumed, and the petite lady in question stood up to announce a toast to the bride-to-be with the following, slurry words coming from her lips.

"Here's a toast, ladies... to our darling Charlotte! To a girl who knows how to have a party... or should I say... get sozzled!" she giggled. "And may she enjoy the new season ahead of her with that... hunky... gorgeous man of hers... and..."

At this point, the toast was interrupted by a burp from the speaker, who continued without batting an eye. "Oh, I could go on with the nitty-gritty details of what to expect and all that, but perhaps not, hey! Well, dear, may you be truly happy and... Whoops! I nearly lost my balance! Silly me... the day is not over yet!" She held her glass high for all to follow, intimating that there was plenty more yet to drink for everyone.

Raucous laughter followed, and the party continued to the next level until a certain mobile rang yet again.

"Susan darling, for goodness sake, answer that call!" shouted one of the party. "It just might be a secret admirer; then you would regret ignoring it.

"Or perhaps it could be Raymond, you know; perhaps he's missing you!" laughed Susan's friend mockingly.

Even Susan became irritated upon hearing sarcasm relating to her unhappy marriage relationship with her husband, and though it was true, she did not like it publicised in such a degrading manner before all her friends; it was like hanging out her dirty laundry for all to see!

"Okay, I'm going. Does that suit you? No need to get catty about it!" Susan walked out of the room, looking sheepishly at a certain lady as she left. Coming to a quiet area, she redialled the number that had come up on her phone.

"Hello. This is David Osborne."

"Who are you, may I ask?" enquired Susan. "I have received several calls from unknown numbers today; I hope it is nothing to do with insurance or double-glazed windows."

"Is that Susan Littleton?"

"It is indeed!"

"Oh! I'm sorry; this is not a nuisance call, I assure you. I must tell you that your husband, Raymond, has been taken to hospital. He was mugged on Damsonwood Green. I am the brother of Mary, Raymond's ex-wife. I'm sorry to have to tell you this news, but I thought you should know straightaway. I have tried to phone you three or four times as I wanted to speak to you personally."

"Oh! Dearie me; how shocking! Oh! How awful…" stammered Susan. "And how is he, may I ask?"

"He is under examination now, but he did come around upon arriving at the hospital and spoke to me. I think he should be fine, just badly bruised and grazed on one side of his face."

"Come around, did you say? Oh! My goodness! What on earth happened to him? Do you think I should come over? Would he like to see me, do you think?" Susan was in shock, and in a quandary as to what to do. This was a new experience for her. "I have… I have had a lot to drink and… well, I'm hardly dressed appropriately. You see… I am at a friend's hen party at *The Darlington*. Oh dear! What should I do?"

"Look, do not worry. I'm sure he would wish to see you. If I were you, I would get a taxi… or I could come over and collect you? If, that is, you feel up to it."

"Oh bother! I will come as I am by taxi. I take it you are at Central Hospital, yes? What is the ward?"

"MacMillan Ward."

"Okay. I will be there one way or another. Thank you for letting me know. I appreciate that."

"See you soon then, Susan. Take care."

Susan entered the lounge again. Everyone was still busy laughing, giggling and drinking. Her frame of mind had suddenly been transformed away from party mood to something far more serious. Of all things, she was suddenly confronted by that very same impertinent lady, who, being quite intoxicated, had spoken openly her derogatory comments about Susan's husband a moment earlier and now took it upon herself to continue even further upon seeing Susan's return. She was quite unperturbed and unrestrained, even though Susan had made her disapproval obvious before.

"Do tell us who it was, Susan; we are all dying to know. Was it your dear Raymond after all? Was he missing you, dear?"

Now Susan, upon hearing this, became deeply disturbed. Such comments had not only hurt her pride but had also touched her emotions; in such a state, she could be a formidable adversary.

Now, it could be construed that Susan may have gone along with the flow of sarcasm herself, regarding all that she had just heard said about her husband, and may have even contributed to it with her own causticness and contempt of him. After all, it was true—for a long time, she had appeared to her friends estranged and absent of all feeling for her husband; it was a well-known fact. However, Susan did not answer in response, but walked over to the lady whose defamatory remarks had provoked her beyond all control, gave her a fiery stony look in the process, then took hold of a partially full glass of champagne and hurled its contents in the lady's face!

"Wash your mouth out with this! I hate you! How dare you…! I will have you know that Raymond, whatever he may be, is a well-respected man in society, and way… way above your station in life! So don't you dare say such things about him in my presence ever again!"

The lady screamed out and went hysterical, "Oh! Look at my dress! You've just ruined my facial, and… Oh! My hair!" Apparently, several hours of pampering that day had suddenly come to no avail in the matter of one split second.

Susan quickly disappeared out the door and slammed it behind her, leaving all the ensuing commotion behind.

Could it be that Susan had feelings for her husband after all? The previous drama tended to point in that direction! Whatever the case, her reaction to hearing her husband being mocked had surprised everyone— including herself! Such was the complexity of this petite, beautifully elegant, highly strung lady's heart regarding her husband! Whatever happened between them, one thing remained loud and clear. Raymond was her husband. He belonged to her. He was all she had! The scene and its melodrama, performed for all to see and hear, had touched that delicate part of her heart and had trampled upon it. That place was out of bounds to everyone, except herself, and woe betide anyone who should trespass upon that sacred ground!

Meanwhile, David had delivered to Dorothy the news that Raymond's wife was on her way. David had had very little to do with Susan in the past; he had simply seen glimpses of her from time to time. It would be interesting, he thought, to meet her face to face.

Robert had originally intended to see Dorothy that day regarding employment opportunities at her work place and had been travelling with Ian to her home prior to the mugging incident on Damsonwood Green. Now, since they had both met up, howbeit under unplanned circumstances, and since they both had much time on their hands whilst Raymond was being checked out, they decided to leave David and Ian in the waiting room and have their consultation in a café at the hospital.

Meanwhile, a taxi cab had already collected a young lady from *The Darlington Hotel* and was now parked outside of her home with its engine running, waiting for her to return. There had been a change of plan. Susan was going to the hospital to visit her husband, and others were going to be there too, she realised.

It will not do to go as I am, she thought. *I shall need to get changed into something else.*

In fact, Susan's attire had dramatically changed from the loud, sparkling top and tight purple jeans she had previously worn into a more formal appearance. Neither her previous extrovert clothing nor any other low-key, informal dress was acceptable in the presence of this David Osborne, the brother of her husband's ex-wife. And goodness knew who else was going to be there with him; perhaps a lady! No, Susan had now dressed herself more elegantly, and though she had chosen an outfit with a touch of formality about it, it probably would not have been appropriate for every formal occasion, even so!

Susan had chosen from her extensive wardrobe a beige, A-line skirt that hung about three inches above her knee and a smart white cotton blouse. These complemented her long, straight, light brown hair, which was streaked with blond highlights. She also wore matching beige, chunky stilettos and carried a beige bag in her hand. Her overall appearance was quite unrecognisable to that of about ten minutes earlier, and with her facial and make-up from the spa, she did look rather stunning indeed. Even the taxi driver, upon seeing the lady approaching his taxi, had initially begun to apologise and say that it was already booked, but had quickly retracted his words upon recognising her!

~~~~~~

Dorothy had been talking a good half an hour with Robert in the hospital café. She asked Robert about his expectations and desires for employment, and then advised him of the appropriateness and whether they were realistic, manageable aspirations in relation to his limited experience and his qualifications.

"Robert, you will soon be nineteen years of age, so a free full-time course will soon be off the agenda. Would you be prepared to work and study day-release for at least a couple of years? Occasionally, my company offers limited apprenticeships that require you to do this."

It did not take Robert too much reflection regarding the offer at Dorothy's work; he considered it was time to commit himself and enter the real world of work. "That's what Ian does... IT. I wouldn't mind doing that, if it were doable that is," said Robert. "I don't have many qualifications, yer know."

"Look, Robert. Employers like people who are willing to work and learn on the job these days, those who will turn up on time and not take too many sick days. It's not about academic qualifications alone. Even graduates must be trained, especially when their number or writing skills are inadequate. This is the trend today, so you will not necessarily be disadvantaged on that front, but... you must be committed, Robert! If you get my drift?"

Robert grinned. He appreciated Dorothy's plain speaking; it reminded him of his mum. This was to be a major turning point in his life, if he were to follow through on any opportunity provided by Dorothy. Whilst she was in market research, Robert would look for an opening in IT, just like his friend.

"Thank you, Dorothy; I appreciate that. If an opening comes along and I get it, I will give it my best shot. My mum used to tell me to go for a trade or skill when looking for a job—and not just the money. Her words are coming back to me now! Don't worry, Dorothy; I will not let you down. I will tell Pastor John and Alfred what we are doing, yeah! They will pray for me to get the right job."

Having discussed and now concluded their discourse together, Robert and Dorothy got up to leave the café and made their way back to MacMillan Ward to see if Raymond was now free to receive visitors. The two caught a lift, walking behind a smartly dressed lady, and then pressed the button for the required floor. Being courteous and thoughtful, Robert asked the lady what floor she required, but it turned out to be the very same one he had pressed already.

Dorothy secretly admired the lady's appearance, thinking to herself that beige was a favourite colour of hers, too, and how lovely it looked on the stranger. The three got out of the lift and headed in the same direction towards MacMillan Ward, but the other lady disappeared, turning off into a nearby toilet facility. The seats where Ian and David had previously been sitting were now empty and that could mean only one thing; they had gone in to see Raymond. Upon reaching the door to the room, Dorothy observed the two of them chatting away to Raymond. She stood back with some degree of shock, having glanced at the patient; Raymond looked badly grazed and bruised. Not wishing to disturb or interrupt the three of them, who were in deep conversation together, and not desiring the room to be overcrowded by too many visitors, Dorothy decided she would come back later.

"Robert, you go in, and I will join you shortly; okay? Please tell them I won't be long."

As Dorothy turned around and left the cubicle, she walked directly into the path of the oncoming lady, dressed in beige and white, who was also heading to the very same place to visit Raymond. Dorothy thought it could only be one person—Raymond's wife, Susan Littleton!

Dorothy stopped and turned to gaze at the lady, a little inquisitive as to what her reaction would be in finding three male visitors with her husband. However, what followed came as a shock all-round. The lady, yet unseen by any of the gentlemen, took one look at Raymond's condition from the doorway and backtracked from the cubicle. She walked away in shock with a certain degree of growing hysteria, which was audible to Dorothy's ears.

"Oh my! What have they done to him? He looks so awful!"

Dorothy instinctively walked over to the lady, feeling the necessity to at least say something and offer her help.

"Hello. Are you Susan by any chance?" enquired Dorothy.

The lady looked aghast at the enquiring stranger, being taken by surprise for a second time in the space of a few seconds—firstly by the sight of her unrecognisable husband in a hospital bed and now by some lady she had never seen before who apparently knew her name!

"Yes, I am; and who are you, may I ask? Do I know you?"

"Forgive me. You do not know me. My name is Dorothy McGuire, and I couldn't help but be concerned upon hearing you just then. I gather you must be Raymond's wife.

"My fiancé, David Osborne, is visiting your husband; that's why I am here too. He knows him quite well, and one of the young men in there actually saw what happened in the park and phoned David. I can go and tell them you are here and ask them to leave so you can see your husband alone, if you wish. Just wait, will you? I will ask them to leave straightaway. It will not be a problem. They could come afterwards if necessary."

Dorothy's fleeting visit into the cubicle caught them all by surprise, especially Raymond who held her in high esteem after hearing certain counsel from her regarding his daughter Julia's well-being. Knowledge of this had now reached Susan's ears, having been prised out of Raymond during her recent interrogation!

"Raymond, I am so sorry about your misfortune. How are you? Your wife, Susan, is outside, waiting to see you at this moment. Perhaps you gentleman wouldn't mind leaving now. We could all come back later, if you like; that is… if Raymond feels up to it."

At this interruption and revelation from Dorothy regarding Raymond's wife, the two teenagers said that they ought to be leaving now anyway and said their goodbyes and departed. David and Dorothy also decided to leave but they promised to visit Raymond again the following day.

Now, upon leaving, David recognised Susan and greeted her cordially. She was quite curt with him, but thanked him nevertheless for all he had done.

"I can assure you it was none of my doing," replied David, as he felt obligated to inform Susan about a few things regarding her husband. "Those two young men who just left... they did everything. They rescued Raymond and called for an ambulance. Apparently, Raymond had my phone number on him, so one of the boys phoned me and told me what had happened. It was then that I phoned you, Susan."

"Thank you, David. I believe I need to thank those young men also at some point."

Before Susan left to see her husband, she glanced at Dorothy momentarily and actually made what appeared to all accounts to be a special thank you regarding Dorothy's thoughtfulness and kindness in speaking to her a moment ago. She then added a final thought-provoking word, just prior to leaving.

"I am sure I would like to meet you again, if you would care to do so, Dorothy. I have heard some interesting things about you from my Raymond recently! Thank you and goodbye."

Dorothy couldn't help but notice a certain foreboding manner about her features and final comment.

Just what could Susan be referring to? she thought.

Chapter 15

Susan and Raymond Talk!

Susan had plucked up her courage and the nerve to visit her husband so that, with the absence of all other visitors, she could now enter his cubicle to face him. Holding her breath as much as possible, she walked in, endeavouring to try her utmost to be nice; after all, he was looking quite dreadful in her opinion and given that their last words together had not been very amicable, she wasn't sure just how to proceed.

"Oh, Raymond! You poor thing. What an awful thing to have happened to you! Look at the bruising on your face... And oh! How on earth did you get that disgusting graze, dear? It looks as though you had a fight with a brick wall and lost," said Susan with a nervous laugh.

"I do beg your pardon, dear; that comment was not at all appropriate or called for, I'm sure. Still, you won't be able to go out for weeks. Really though, what happened? I can understand the bruising inflicted upon you by those disgusting Philistines from that diabolical area of town, but... that graze... It covers the whole side of your face; how did that happen? Really, please do tell me... if you will?"

And so, Susan broke the ice! Raymond was feeling quite at ease with her presence, and from there onwards, the conversion took the form of a much more open, informal manner to that of his previous visitors—after all, he and Susan were husband and wife.

"I thought you might just enquire about that, Susan. You are quite right in your thinking; I did have a fight with a brick wall it seems—and lost as well! You are able to see what others cannot perceive; you discern what others miss completely. But that is you, Susan. And being my wife—I believe you are my wife still, yes?—well, I'll tell you all!"

Susan gently tapped her husband on his arm upon hearing that cheeky comment of his, then quickly withdrew it just in case that region of his body should hurt him, for she herself could not bear pain and the whole thought of being in her husband's shoes at that moment in time was so abhorrent to her that if it were the case, then she would rather have curled herself up somewhere and wished to have died! Raymond's remark, though spoken with humour, was indicative of the instability of their marriage, for the opinions of many outsiders suggested they were both enduring such an uncivilised relationship that it was quite amazing for the knot between them to remain tied.

Raymond found it better, regarding any conversation with his wife, to lean towards frivolity, humour and sweet sarcasm; this she could take most readily. But to venture into any serious and meaningful talk proved too heavy for her! It was as if Susan had never progressed from her childish attitude into responsible maturity of behaviour and thinking; no, that was far too boring and unexciting! Rather, she lived in an unreal world and possessed sufficient wealth and means of her own — irrespective of her husband's fortune which was also materially substantial — to do so.

"Do not chastise me further, dearest loving wife of mine. If I tell you, will you promise not to do so?"

These words from her husband were far too generous, and that she well knew; therefore, he was either being funny or sarcastic, or he was out of his mind! Whatever the case, it required yet another tap on his arm; and seeing he had not flinched with her first tap, she felt more at liberty this time to give him the works with a full slap.

Susan could be equally funny and replied in kind, "Please get to the point, my dearest loving husband; else I will die of suspense and fear. You were about to tell me — if you haven't forgotten — how you were inflicted with those severe abrasions all over one side of your face, yes?"

Raymond decided to narrate the whole story to Susan regarding his activities and whereabouts that morning, starting from the moment she had walked out on him, slamming the door in no uncertain terms behind her as she stormed away to her hen party. He only hoped that she would have the patience to listen to him without getting too bored.

"You remember when we argued about various things? Of course, you do; it was only early this morning... So much seems to have happened since then, I must say. Well, after you left for your... your hen party or whatever... well, I went over to the *Princess Royal*, did I not? Feeling very sorry for myself, I sat outside for a good hour and a half consuming one and a half bottles of the best Chardonnay. There I was, drinking my blues away, when I saw this beautiful, young mother with her children. And I imagined just what it might be like to be happy like she was — even with two bundles of trouble!"

"Raymond, save me the gory details, if you will; you make me jealous when you describe another woman as beautiful! What about me, may I ask? Am I beautiful in your eyes?"

"Why should you care about what I think? You are beautiful in everyone else's eyes; are you not? What more could you possibly desire? Surely that alone should satisfy you? You know very well you don't love me, so why be jealous simply because I said I saw a beautiful lady?"

"Stop that talk, Raymond. I am what I am, and it may not occur to you — whatever your perceptions of me are — that... Well! I do have some feelings you know! But do go on; we are becoming diverted."

Raymond was not a little surprised by Susan's remarks. Was she on the verge of admitting some measure of affection for him? He had never heard her speak anything in the past to suggest that she had even the slightest inclination of thought or feeling towards him; this comment of hers was the nearest thing yet to anything of real substance that she had ever said. Even so, it was a pitiful shame, he thought, that she had not included the personal words — *for you* — when stating she had feelings; at least that would have made her statement more informative and intimate. But that was probably expecting too much from her, benevolence towards others not being her strongest point.

"Well, there is no easy way to say what followed, I'm afraid…"

"David, you didn't!"

" Didn't what?"

"You didn't speak or do anything untoward to… to this lady; did you?"

Susan's countenance changed dramatically to that of a pale colour, just as though she was having a panic attack.

"Good gracious, Susan! You can be so outlandishly paranoid and possessive, if you did but know it. I say one thing, and you always think another! Let me finish; will you?"

"The lady left, and that was it. I was about to say that what followed on — after my drinking binge, that is — was completely beneath me! I was so drunk... No, I became so paralytic that I blacked out, fell headlong and bashed myself uncontrollably against a wall!"

Susan sighed with much relief upon hearing this clarification from Raymond and held back her laughter — well, for as long as possible, that is — then out it came, raucous and uncontrolled. But her reaction came as no surprise to Raymond; he was used to it. She seemed to find everything about him funny!

"I should have known that you would find that somewhat hilarious," said Raymond remorsefully, but in his opinion he deserved all he got. He had done a stupid thing, and the clock could not be put back.

"Anyway," continued Susan, placing her small, soft, warm hand upon his, "I really am so sorry about what happened to you; really I am. But how come you went into Damsonwood Green? That was going out of your way surely?"

It suddenly occurred to Susan even before she finished speaking that her question was somewhat ludicrous given the drunken state he was in at the time, but it couldn't be retracted.

"Susan, I don't remember a single thing about it! I thought I was doubling back on myself, but in fact I was heading straight for that perilous district, where sure enough it happened! I was attacked and robbed, apparently by four young men. Fortunately, Robert and Ian — those two young men who were here a while ago — they apparently set into all four youths and rescued me," said Raymond with a chuckle. "Can you believe that? Mind you, they do attend David's karate classes!"

"Do you know those young people then? I find it quite strange that…well, you know… that they should just come on the scene to help you. Thank goodness they did, of course!" Susan had a point; few people would have got into a fight over a stranger.

"I first met them at Dorothy and David's engagement party, along with some other fine young people; fantastic lads they are! There is a story about how those two came together, you know, and are now the best of friends… but I really don't think you would be interested to hear that right now. Perhaps another time…

"Except to say that Robert was once a gang leader in that very same estate where I was set upon, but now he has changed for the better; and instead of robbing people, he and his gang actually go out of their way now to help them! Amazing turnaround, I know; but it is true! I should really like to tell you about them; the story is unbelievable and quite amazing!"

"You quite like your new clique of friends; don't you, Raymond? I can tell! I find it incredibly amusing — almost disconcerting in a sort of way — that you should have any inclination or the remotest pleasure in mixing with such… such… a manner of friends? They are rather outside of your station and sphere of life; are they not? I mean, young teenagers for goodness sake! And… well, then there's David Osborne, the brother of your ex-wife!

"I do confess, however, that I find that Dorothy rather interesting; she seems very bright and uncommonly attractive. And yet she dresses quite modestly and wears hardly any make-up! She, if anyone, could really blow people away with her looks."

"Susan, you are amazing. When a lady is – how shall I say? — really made-up in an outlandish, extrovert, blatant and conspicuous manner… all of that and more, a person who is clearly seeking attention… well, you are quick to criticise and judge in a most derogatory manner. But when someone like Dorothy comes on the scene, who as you say dresses more plainly — though in my opinion I think her dress sense is very womanly and naturally elegant — well, you still find criticism and negative comments! What is it with you ladies sometimes?"

Susan was quite unperturbed by Raymond's exasperation and observations as a man; in her opinion, there was an unwritten law and license for all women to hold onto such patterns of behaviour if they had a mind to do so, and she felt quite at ease not to provide him with the slightest explanation whatsoever in her defence.

"Raymond, you are entering territory forbidden to all men! This is a woman thing, I'd have you understand. Why, did you know that when a woman walks past a couple she straightaway observes the lady and weighs her up? And not, as you might think, the man. That's the way it is. Satisfied? That's how we women can be sometimes; we check upon the other lady to see if she is a possible threat!"

"Well, I suppose I should be grateful to you for being so honest and frank about it, but I confess, I am not really satisfied. Indeed, not at all! You have merely raised my curiosity and intrigue regarding women to a higher level of incomprehensible obscurity; in short, this is far too complicated for me to reason through. I give in!"

"Ha! Raymond, these are matters that do not concern you men, so… just shut up about it!"

Raymond was quite at ease with the conversation with Susan; it made a pleasant change, and ironically it seemed to have taken an adverse situation of being in hospital for it to have happened. The words Susan used in speaking to her husband sometimes were in themselves unquestionably blunt, abrupt and even offensive in part, but when judged in the spirit in which they were delivered, they did not suggest any real malice, antagonism or contention on her part; on the contrary, just as Raymond had stated, their dialogue together was a pleasant change, even if intermingled with the occasional outspokenness. And this mutual understanding was at least some positive trait in their relationship and understanding of one another that was not at all necessarily common or widespread with other married couples. Because of this absurd, unique phenomenon, which as just stated was amicable between the pair of them, Raymond tended to warm somewhat towards his wife.

"Do you wish to know something, Susan? You have been sitting here talking to me for nearly one hour, which must be a record! It is the longest I can ever remember that we have chatted together." He gave a wry chuckle. "Perhaps I should arrange to be in hospital more often in future!"

"Raymond! What a stupid thing to say! You are a prize jerk, I ask you!"

"Look! There you go again! Conversation followed by more conversation. In an odd sort of way, I quite like to hear you go on at me like you are doing. At least it is not malicious... like you were this morning, if I may say so; then you were like a Gestapo interrogator who spared me my teeth." Again, Raymond laughed at his words.

"Well! What did you expect? I was jealous about a certain lady talking to you, seemingly giving you advice when it was none of her business. What did you expect me to say? *'Oh, Raymond! That beautiful Dorothy has been giving you advice regarding our problems concerning Julia. Oh, how kind and thoughtful of her!'*

"Anyway, now that I have met her briefly, I have somewhat mellowed about that matter. Even I, you may be surprised to know, can tell when a person is sincere and not simply… well… trying it on!

"Raymond, I shall have to sit on the other side of the bed," said Susan, getting up to move around. "Do you mind? It means I can see more of the good side of your face. No offence intended! Have they said when you can come out?"

"I have to wait for further blood test results and the x-ray. The doctor must see those before I can be released. It should be sometime this evening, I would suppose… I certainly hope so.

"Thank you for coming to see me and for staying with me, Susan. Like I said before, I have never seen so much of you. And as stupid as this is — our meeting in such circumstances — I do find it rather pleasant being with you. In fact, I find… I find your company very special indeed; it's like I am getting to know the real Susan — and she is quite nice when she tries!"

"Oh, Raymond! You sound far too romantic for your own good, I fear," laughed Susan nervously. "I am a hurtful woman when it comes to romance, as you have discovered. Perhaps the tablets are affecting your better senses!"

"Whatever... I also realise that you forfeited your party today for me, yes? Now that was thoughtful of you, Susan. Indeed! Please, for goodness sake, accept my efforts at this moment to be kind and considerate to you, instead of brushing aside genuine sincerity from my heart all the time as though you were untouched by it or rejecting it, just like... well, just like water off a duck's back!"

For one moment, an uncanny silence filled the air, and Susan replied not a single word, as if dumbness had unexpectedly struck her, having heard these revealing, sincere and affectionate words from her husband for the very first time — words that had been forced upon her in a determined, uncompromising manner. As much as she had attempted to push them aside, it was of no use. Even though Susan had, from childhood, meticulously been instructed by her mother to steer clear of young, impetuous love and romance and instead pursue status and gain over all such inclinations, she now found herself unable to restrain her heart at this instant from certain feelings, which in the past she was so efficiently able to discard.

Even in marriage there had remained a hardness upon her heart that had evolved from having been so conditioned by her early years and schooling to reject all emotional situations; yet now something both new and strange had happened to her, so much so that she found herself succumbing to Raymond's feelings, expressed so tenderly, if only for the moment. She could not gainsay them anymore; further, she did not wish to!

Raymond, being quite oblivious of the inner turmoil that Susan had been experiencing, continued by changing the subject altogether.

"How did your function go today? Did you say it was a hen party? Was it good?"

Susan was in fact appreciating Raymond's gratitude towards her now more and more as her heart had altered for the better towards him. It was a pleasant change to be civil with one another, and if she were honest with herself, she was enjoying it! It had taken this adverse predicament to bring them together, and as it happened, she preferred to be sitting with her husband at this moment in time by a hospital bed than to be entertaining more of the same at the event she was supposed to be present at that evening.

"Do not be alarmed, Raymond, but it pleases me to be here right now too. I have a very good reason for saying that... no, I have at least two reasons. First, I am enjoying being quiet and alone with you; it's rather nice actually! There, I have told you my heart as well! Perhaps I am becoming just a little romantic, as you are. However, the rest of the day has been awful to be honest! A certain person at the hen party—drunk as a lord, she was... or should I say drunk as a lady—just got on my nerves with her snide comments, so much so that I… well, I baptised her in champagne — all over her recent facial!"

"I beg your pardon! What do you mean by that?"

"Well, what I mean is… I threw half a glass of champers into her face; that's what I mean! Only the contents, that is — not the glass itself!" Susan laughed at the memory.

"Oh, Susan! How could you have done such a thing, I ask you?" Upon hearing this last statement, Raymond couldn't help but grin, for he knew from experience what a short fuse Susan could have when provoked in any way!

"What was the provocation may I ask?"

"I cannot tell you; it was a woman's thing. But suffice to say she over-stepped the line regarding the sort of conversations and gossip we ladies have about our men folk!"

At that instant, there was an intrusion; the doctor was making his rounds now and approaching Raymond's cubicle.

"At last! The doctor is coming!" said Raymond with a hint of gleefulness about him. "Now I might be able to leave fairly soon, I hope!"

"Raymond, do you wish me to stay with you — or should I wait outside?" Susan's reaction was uneasy and cautious, not knowing Raymond's mind about this new scenario and only desiring for him to be at ease. Having never before been in a situation of this nature, she respected his need for privacy if he desired to have it. Raymond placed his hand upon hers and warmly invited her to stay.

"If you will, my dear, I would like you to stay, please." Much more took place within the atmosphere at that instant than mere words could tell, for of all things, at that moment, upon hearing her husband's reply, Susan blushed! Never had she been spoken to like that, not even by her husband, and never had he placed his hand upon hers in such a loving manner. At that moment, a sudden replay of all the gory, dismal details of their marriage up until that moment flashed through her mind in an instant of time, as these things can do.

Is this happening? she thought.

What her ears had just heard—and especially the manner in which she heard these words spoken—was most respectful, nice and unprecedented. She felt like a woman of importance to Raymond, one that he appeared to need! Susan experienced an inner witness and confirmation of feelings for her husband that she had never encountered before! They had not been that close in the past. Ever. Neither had they been that intimate in feeling. And certainly, they had never spoken and addressed one another with any such expression that contained the words '*my dear.*' That was the way they had been.

Raymond observed a twinkle of light shining from Susan's eyes, as she silently stared at him in a mesmerised, gooey fashion; and his own heart reciprocated as well, witnessing feelings for her in like manner to those she was radiating to him.

Words had not been spoken, but a communication had taken place nevertheless! It was a fairy-tale feeling to Susan; however, that would fizzle out over time like a sparkler on bonfire night.

Their mutual reverie was interrupted by an incoming doctor who announced his arrival so loudly that they both jumped at the sudden intrusion.

"Ah! Hello, Mr Osborne! How are you feeling now?"

"Very much better, thank you," replied Raymond in a submissive tone.

"Well, your x-rays have indicated slight fractures to the ribs on your right side, but you have not suffered anything untoward upon the head thankfully. I must confess that you were very lucky that those young men intervened when they did! The bruising is particularly severe upon and around your torso, but nothing that cannot heal over time.

"You must rest for a good while; it might be uncomfortable and quite stiff walking, but by taking things easy you should be just fine. You will find significant pain when breathing, I'm afraid, because of the fractures to your ribs, and you'll be tempted to simply take short breaths.

Even so, you must try periodically to slowly breath in very deeply as much as possible, then exhale. This way you will be ensuring the lungs totally expel all the air within them.

"Do you have any questions? Oh! And I nearly forgot to tell you; your blood alcohol levels were between 0.2% and 0.3% per volume, which is what caused you to black out when you did. Fortunately, you had vomited before arriving here. Of course, that is your body's way of coming to the rescue! Do take care in future how much alcohol you consume on any given occasion, okay."

"Am I allowed to leave now, Doctor?"

"Yes! Most certainly. I will arrange for a wheel chair if you wish. Perhaps you could get out of bed and try walking to see how you feel."

Raymond obeyed and ambled steadily around the room, then chose to decline the use of a wheel chair, declaring that with Susan's help he would be just fine.

The doctor left then. Susan looked paler than she had done prior to his visit and was visibly shaken. Having just then observed the severe bruising upon Raymond's body and the extent to which he had obviously been pummelled and kicked, she became subdued and upset by the thought of the whole horrific affair. To have had an accident or a fall was one thing — that could have been easier to cope with mentally — but to contemplate her husband being beaten up by people, kicked and hit... well, the whole scenario was hurtful and repulsive; how could civilised human beings behave in such a way?

"Oh, Raymond! It looked awful just now! I can't believe... it is incomprehensible that this actually happened to you — and all inflicted by other human beings!"

Susan once again looked at the injured side of his face, the one she had not cared to view before, and in doing so became overcome with emotion, bursting into tears. Raymond held her close to him.

"I tell you what; let me phone a taxi, and we can go home, Susan. I fancy something to eat now. Can you believe that? Don't you worry about me, dear; I am fine and only too happy to know I have you with me."

They walked from the cubicle into the corridor and made their way to the lift, with Susan supporting him as best as she could. Raymond stopped momentarily, as if to get his breath, then turned aside to Susan and repeated certain words again in gratitude to her.

"Thank you again for coming to be with me, Susan. You have been very brave. I know you dislike hospitals and the very thought of others being sick and in pain... but you came for me, and I am most grateful to you.

"Oh by the way, Susan, I do love your outfit; beige and white—wow! And matching chunky shoes too. Awesome!"

Susan looked up at her husband, for indeed he was a good six inches taller than she and briefly caught his eyes, acknowledging his appreciative and kind remarks. Raymond kissed her forehead in response, and continuing with his light-hearted humour said, "I fancy some brown bread and butter with chips and a cup of strong tea. What do you say?"

"At our home? Yes?" added Susan gleefully, wishing to clarify where exactly he wished to satisfy his sudden appetite for food.

"Absolutely! Then we can watch a movie or something together; what do you say, dearest?"

"That sounds nice; sitting curled up on the sofa, eating chips and watching a film. I think I could handle that, Raymond... on one condition though!"

"What would that be?"

"I get to choose the film!"

Chapter 16

The Press Arrives

It was a well-known fact that whilst Alfred Townsend resided in a two-bedroomed detached cottage, he both lived and slept in the lounge, which connected conveniently with the kitchen. At that precise moment, he was all by himself and could be seen busily cleaning the house in preparation for a special guest—a certain lady who was herself not too long ago the woman of this very house—and though this was currently not the case, Alfred hoped that one day soon she would return to that role once more.

Though cleaning a house is a common chore, it is worth some brief attention to observe and describe Alfred's unique methodology and manner of executing this task. Within a utilities cupboard was stored a modern electric cyclone sweeper, but this contraption was not being utilised. At the rear of the same cupboard was another much more antiquated sweeping device which was all of forty years old. Here stood a non-electrical device called a Eubank that had two cylindrical rollers embedded with brush's spiralling around each roller. By pushing the contraption over a carpet, the two brushed rollers collected dust and churned it into two collecting dust pans. Alfred often used the Eubank for quickness, but today? No, he was not using this old-fashioned device either. Instead, he had chosen to resort to a very basic method of sweeping, one that outlived them all; he was using a simple broom, one that had firm bristles!

After he had swept the carpet and kitchen floor, he used a dust pan and brush to collect the bits. These would suffice. Alfred's main concern was to sweep underneath the table, by the doorway and in the kitchen area; and this he did, concentrating upon these more pronounced dirty spots, after which he set about tidying up the room. He picked up newspapers that were strewn over the sofa, then put each page in sequential order and placed them tidily in a rack.

Shoes surrounded the vicinity of the doorway and needed to be put away somewhere out of sight; that is, his one pair of boots and Maria's three pairs of trainers and flats. Not being in possession of a designated shoe rack, Alfred simply opened a cupboard door, threw them all inside, and that was that.

Then, he checked the kitchen. Oh, dear! Maria always stacked the sink with dirty crockery and left it to be washed later. In other words, they would never get done. Alfred often told her off, but apparently, Ian did the same, as did Robert, so he concluded that it must have been a teenage thing and set about doing the dishes himself. His wife, Jennifer, had set a precedent of always doing the dishes after a meal, and Alfred was obedient to this directive of hers even when she was not around.

Alfred stood still for a moment and leaned against the mantel shelf, gazing around the room inspecting it. Everything looked good, until he removed his hand from off the shelf, that is!

Oh, dear! thought Alfred. *This cannot be overlooked today; this is terrible!*

He soon realised it had probably not been dusted and cleaned for months! So, Alfred took a damp kitchen cloth and wiped it down, then looked elsewhere to inspect other areas. After about a further ten minutes, he had cleaned yet more needy surfaces that had been in a similar state.

That should be good now, he thought. *Ah! There be one more thing Maria would do. Where is the air freshener?*

Not finding any spray, he resorted to using the one in the toilet, which was a nice lavender smell, hoping that this would suffice! This he sprayed here and there to take away the breakfast odours, for he had eaten fried bread and bacon. Now, interestingly, Alfred never grilled his bacon the healthy way. He used basic lard, which he usually found very difficult to purchase these days much to his dismay, and fried the bacon in the lard to release the tasty bacon fat. Afterwards, he fried his bread in the fat, and if there was any remaining, he poured it upon a plate and dipped his bread into it. Maria despaired whenever he requested this for breakfast, commenting upon the harmful effects lard would have upon his arteries, but he always replied in the same way.

"Don't get yourself in a twist, mi lass. I always had this kind a breakfast for work; it is fuel for the day, just like bread and dripping! Besides, I were reading t' other day how fat in yer arteries is from too much sugar, which turns into fat. So yer see, I don't reckon fat that yer eat goes to yer arteries, now then!"

Alfred had nearly completed his task of tidying up the house — or more to the truth, his living room — before his guest arrived, but then he thought of one more thing to do. *I should open a window; that would be good too*, he thought. *A change of air.*

Alfred's visitor was to be none other than his wife, Jennifer Townsend, who had been dropping in to see her husband quite regularly ever since that day she had interrupted him entertaining Maria and Dorothy one time. Alfred called to mind that interesting occasion when Dorothy had called to inform Maria and himself of her engagement to David. As she had been telling them the delightful news, Jennifer had arrived quite suddenly and unexpectedly, barging in upon their conversation. Right from the start, she had made her presence felt quite verbally and was most antagonistic towards Alfred, all of which had taken Dorothy by surprise. It was well known that the relationship between Alfred and Jennifer had been severely strained during those eighteen or so months when Alfred had had his alcohol problem, which had led to Jennifer moving out to live with her sister. But ever since a miraculous healing had occurred within that household, things had eventually turned around for the better for both.

Jennifer had been impressed by the way Dorothy had supported Alfred during those moments when she had been grilling and belittling him in her presence, but Maria had become so embarrassed listening to her mother's derogatory words to her father in the presence of her visiting friend that, ultimately, she could not bear to hear it all and went upstairs out of the way. Consequently, this support from Dorothy towards Alfred had led Jennifer to respect her and appreciate the positive influence she had with him—even though at the time she had not wished to show it.

Jennifer had been in another one of her weary moods over her husband prior to arriving, and meeting him face to face—with a visitor or not—had only brought to the surface resentment regarding all she had endured from him. What had proceeded from her mouth was payback of a sort. Unfortunately for Alfred, this payback of hers had been repeated whenever Jennifer had seen him!

Jennifer had been intrigued, however, to know more of how these changes had come about, especially regarding Alfred's sudden interest in attending church, though she, rather like Maria, still had to come to terms with this sudden change in Alfred—from a villain to a saint—for they had both suffered painfully at his hand for such a long time! Alfred had no option but to bare this reproach for a while. Time was of the essence; it would heal all wounds and it had!

~~~~~~

There came a knock upon the door, and Alfred answered it quickly—but to his surprise, it was not who he was expecting. Instead of his wife, Jennifer, there stood a smartly dressed gentleman who he remembered from a previous occasion when he had received a visit from that very same person.

"Hello, Mr Alfred Townsend! My name is Jerry Dickson; you may remember that I visited you several weeks ago regarding the matter of your alleged healing to your leg. I am interested in writing an article about it and wish to talk with you, if you would allow me to do so. I have been shown images of you... and a video taken by certain people who were present at the church meeting where the healing apparently took place. May I come in and hear your account of that day, sir? As I told you before, I am a reporter from the *Daily Herald* newspaper. We may choose to do an article upon the matter—if you agree, that is."

Now, Alfred had arranged to see the man that very same morning, but the occasion had been organised so that Jennifer would be present as well, as he did not wish to be alone. Jennifer, being his wife, was someone who obviously knew about his previous condition and could testify that he had indeed been a cripple. But as it happened, the gentleman had arrived before her.

"Come on in, young man, and sit yer down. I'm expecting mi wife soon, so you'll have to wait a bit, till she comes if yer don't mind. Can I get yer a cuppa tea... or coffee if yer prefer?"

"A tea would be fine, sir—white with no sugar. Thank you very much; that is kind of you."

Alfred, not being a man who ever found difficulties with conversation, entertained Mr Dickson for a good while, reiterating to him his life story from the age of fifteen years—that being the age when he had started work on the farm – and how, for thirty-seven years, he had still been in such employment until a certain dreaded accident had occurred with the wheel of a tractor.

Meanwhile, throughout this exposition from Alfred, Jerry's pen had moved continuously across his note pad, recording everything he heard from the old man throughout his discourse. After this episode of his life was exhausted, Alfred then went on to openly confess the next stage, namely his disgruntled state of mind and how he had been very bitter towards both God and man, blaming either one or the other as the need arose. Regarding man, he would insist that the tractor was too old so that it's brakes had not worked properly, but even worse in Alfred's reckoning was the matter regarding the Almighty—well, He could have prevented it if he had a mind to do so, but He hadn't!

Alfred was just coming to the third episode, regarding how Dorothy had spoken to him and challenged him concerning spiritual matters, when the door opened and in walked his wife, Jennifer. Then, following closely behind her, was an unexpected guest; it was none other than Dorothy!

"Well, bless my soul!" exclaimed Alfred in great surprise. "Why, yer brought the lady Dorothy with yer as well, Jennifer! I were just about to tell this gentleman about her an' all, when in she walks! What do yer reckon to that then, hey Jerry?"

Jerry hardly heard Alfred's comment, being particularly distracted by the entry of the younger of the two visitors who had immediately caught his attention!

"Alfred, what have you been saying behind our backs?" retorted Jennifer. "I happened to bump into your lady—as you put it—in the supermarket, so I asked her if she was free to join me. I do not know anything about the church or your healing, Alfred, but I do know all there is to know about you, my man!"

Alfred was, needless to say, delighted to see the extra visitor. "Well, I'm glad yer come as well, Dorothy. What mi wife don't know about church, you do, eh? And what you don't know about mi past, Jenny does," he laughed.

"Well, that kettle has not been long boiled, so you can have a drink with us too. This here is Jerry by the way, from the *Daily Herald*. He's come to see us about mi leg. You likes yer tea wi' no sugar, don't yer, Dorothy? And Jenny, well, you like yer tea black."

Alfred's etiquette was a far cry from satisfactory regarding his lack of propriety in introducing the gentleman from the press to his wife and Dorothy, but as it happened Jerry was quite happy to introduce himself. Having made a brief greeting towards Jennifer, he immediately redirected his salutations towards Dorothy; and whilst Jennifer left with Alfred for the kitchen to prepare tea, Jerry lost no time in addressing her. He stood up to greet her quite formally, then in a most polite and genteel fashion shook her hand.

"Dorothy, my name is Jerry Dickson; it is a pleasure to meet you. What, may I ask, is your connection with Mr Townsend? Are you familiar at all with the circumstances surrounding his... his so-called healing?"

Dorothy had been familiar with the enquiries from the press quite some time ago, but was intrigued to know just why it was all delayed, so to speak, from the time of Alfred's miracle up until now.

"Thank you, Mr Dickson. Yes, I am very familiar with the circumstances surrounding the matter that is clearly now of interest to you. I was present — and very close to the scene as it happens. It is also a pleasure to meet someone from the press — and not too soon, I would say — for Alfred had come to church that particular Sunday a few weeks ago for the very first time, and upon leaving the meeting, I do believe I observed you taking photographs of him. So, you were completely knowledgeable about the matter; were you not, Mr Dickson?"

"Your knowledge of my whereabouts is not incorrect. Yes, I was informed about a certain matter at a church, and the source showed me photos and videos that had actually been taken during the service."

"In which case, I do believe your apparent lack of response and delay in reporting the matter is even more intriguing upon hearing what you have just told me now regarding your familiarity with everything, including the independent evidence and eye-witness accounts. Surely if you had access to images of Alfred Townsend's healing so soon after the Sunday in question, I would have thought you should have been... well, shall we say, all the more interested and eager to get the story out. But clearly you were not, it seems."

"You are very perceptive, and your line of thinking is very accurate, I must say! You are quite correct, and I find I cannot be anything but honest with you about the whole matter. I was, shall we say, deliberately prevented from pursuing this case for a long while, until… well, until certain investigations had taken place.

There, I am concealing nothing, and I am endeavouring to be completely truthful and straight with you, Miss McGuire. You see, my boss is an agnostic, right? He would have none of it at the time—I mean, in me printing my story, which I considered to be of public interest—but he did ask me to research the man, Alfred Townsend, and find out whether he really had been a cripple or not. So, this is the reason, in part, as to why I am here. I finally persuaded my boss to allow me to run an article, and I wish to gather further information from the horse's mouth, so to speak.

There is a certain matter, if I may say, that would be most useful and which would add considerable weight to my story, and that is to have a doctor's opinion regarding Alfred's leg before and after the event in question… if you get my drift… and with some sort of written confirmation—you know, documented evidence that Alfred was indeed a cripple and that there is no logical explanation as to how he regained strength to walk again without the use of crutches. Without such a verification regarding these matters, there could be no credibility, I'm afraid, when put under the scrutiny of all the sceptics out there. This would simply be an opportunity for such people to discredit and ridicule the man, and having met Alfred and spoken to him just before you arrived, I should hate that to happen for I find him very sincere and a likeable chap."

"Jerry, I completely agree with you! Written documentation is a must, and I thank you for raising that very important consideration. I will bring this to the attention of Pastor John Peterson as well; I'm quite sure he would like to be informed about everything. Meanwhile, we should mention this to Alfred and see what he has to say."

Almost half an hour had elapsed when Jennifer came back into the room with the tea, followed by Alfred carrying a basket full of freshly made scones.

Dorothy loved the smell of home baking, and this exceeded all expectations. "Jennifer, what have you been up to?"

"Not I, Dorothy, but Alfred; he always was the baker in this house! Got it off his mum, he did. I suggested he make some of his special recipe scones; let's hope you are both hungry."

Jerry was both surprised and somewhat bewildered too.

"But how did you manage to make the scones so soon?" he asked in amazement. "Have you really just made them, Alfred? In so short a time?"

"I have that. Why, they only take twenty-five minutes from start to finish, yer know! These are my ma's recipe with a secret but common ingredient called bakin' powder; that's what it is! Everybody uses self-raisin' flour like, but they never think of addin' some bakin' powder to it. That makes them even lighter still. I then use butter or margarine. These are made with marg, which makes them light as well—after all, yer goin' to put butter on 'em anyway!"

Alfred, feeling quite proud of his achievement, endeavoured to be especially polite towards his guest, as well as to his dear Dorothy!

"Here, try one; will yer, Dorothy? And you too, sir. And tell me what yer think."

Alfred was correct; the scones were exceedingly light and delicious!

"Oh, Alfred," exclaimed Dorothy. "These are so delicious."

As for Jerry, he could hardly speak, being on his second already. "How do you manage it?" was all he could splutter.

"They are incredibly light," continued Dorothy. "So yummy, and with just butter on them, they taste excellent! Why is it whenever I make scones they always seem to come out heavy?"

"Nar, that is another secret I reckon. When I first made 'em with my ma watching me, she told me to go easy on the mixing. She said, 'Don't mix 'em up too much, else you'll kill it stone dead!' It goes against yer common sense maybe, but the more yer mix 'em, the heavier they come, I reckon! Anyway, tell me; are these scones light?"

"Indeed, they are, Mr Townsend!" spluttered Jerry.

"Incredibly so," added Dorothy.

Alfred, seeking to encourage his Dorothy and her attempts at baking, said, "No disrespect, Dorothy dear, but at least you have tried. I reckon lasses today don't care much about bakin' these days. I try to show our Maria whenever she ain't on her mobile or lying down on her bed with head phones on. I'm pleased yer like 'em anyway."

Now, the sole purpose of the visit from Jerry Dickson of the press finally got underway. He began by asking Alfred for a full account of things regarding his healing, so in his usual simple manner, Alfred told Jerry everything—why he had gone to church that Sunday morning, having never been inside one since going with his late mother; his experience in the meeting; and exactly what had happened. After a good forty minutes, the interview was almost over. Jerry commented that Alfred was fast becoming an expositor of the Word, and the latter said he put his developing abilities in that quarter down to speaking his testimony at his open-air in the town precinct once a week.

There was still, however, the very important and outstanding issue that had been discussed by Jerry and Dorothy prior to Alfred and Jennifer returning from the kitchen, and that was the necessity for documented evidence relating to Alfred's healing. Having presented this proposition to Alfred to try and obtain such evidence, both Jerry and Dorothy were very surprised to hear what he had to say in reply.

"Well, yer see, my last consultation at the hospital were about two weeks back, and certain things came out in the open, if yer know what I mean. My disability allowance had been stopped after the staff who visit me from social services saw me walkin' about, and this was reported to all kinds of people. Don't ask me who, but I tell yer, they soon stopped me allowance when they found out I could walk about wi' no crutches! They said that if I could walk into the kitchen and make meself a meal like and I could walk downtown, then I don't qualify for disability money - that were it. I put mi foot in it tellin' 'em God had healed me, see!

"Well, this led my consultant to thoroughly examine me at my last and final visit at the hospital, but he said he would have no option but to write that my leg was good. He said all the scars were there to prove I had mi accident before like, but mi leg was fine! That's what he said, and he apologised for having to declare it to whom it may concern. That were what he said."

Jerry Dickson had visited Alfred's home that day to obtain a good story; that was his job and profession. But he was himself rather sceptical of it all, right up to arriving at Alfred's door — though that was of no consequence to him if the end-product sold newspapers. However, upon hearing this account from Alfred regarding his losing special allowances and all the independent testimonies mentioned — the home visitors, social services, then finally the hospital consultant — well, this indeed gave much more credibility to his story! The evidence of change was there; people would be constrained to think and choose for themselves what they were to believe, but it was very clear in his opinion that in such a scenario, healing was a viable interpretation! Facts were in place, and one explanation of them was clearly Divine healing!

"Well, Mr Townsend, what you have just said certainly appears to shed new light upon your story; that is for sure! Now, all we need is the documented evidence to back all of that up, Alfred, and then I have... we have a story to print!"

Alfred got up from his chair and walked over to a sideboard, where he retrieved various envelopes from inside the drawer. "Here, take these; this letter is about losing my disability allowance, and here is a letter from the hospital consultant signing me off having examined mi leg. Will they do?"

Chapter 17

Jennifer Speaks with Dorothy

Jerry and Alfred had just left. Jerry was on a mission to complete his story for the Herald and was driving Alfred over to see Pastor John. He was interested to meet the person who had prayed for Alfred, and the opportunity to do so was now forthcoming.

Jennifer was now alone with Dorothy and eager to talk with her about herself, having been exceedingly interested in her person ever since that aforementioned occasion when Jennifer had chastised her husband in Dorothy's presence.

Why should Dorothy have been so interested in Alfred's cause? This had bothered Jennifer and, indeed, made her feel guilty when recalling all she had callously said to her husband on that occasion — so much so that she wished she could forget it had ever happened. But now the occasion presented itself — and not before time — when she could be at liberty to enquire of Dorothy regarding all those matters upon her heart.

"I understand from Maria that you have only been attending her church for a few months; so, what made you change and decide to go, if I may ask, Dorothy?"

"It was not the first time I had been to a church by any means," replied Dorothy, as Jennifer began her inquisition with a frank and pointed question. "But regarding Pastor John Petersons' church, which I now attend along with Maria and other friends of mine… Well, I happened to stumble upon it one morning quite by chance… or more likely by Divine Providence. I do believe it was of the Lord that this happened when it did!

"I had not been well at all Jennifer, for… for a very long time, and it would take too long to tell you all the details, except to say that I suffered from depression amongst other things. I was desperate at the time and had felt quite troubled within me; I was looking for some church to go to that might help me. I find it quite funny now upon reflection, but on that very same morning — prior to going in to Pastor John's church — I had started walking towards another church. But then, having heard the eerie organ music, I stood still in my tracks as if I was just about to walk into a brick wall; then I walked away with goose bumps all over me! I felt bad about it later, thinking he was probably a very accomplished organist, but primarily… it was not music that I was searching for — if you know what I mean!"

"Well, Dorothy, I am sorry to learn that you suffered from that dreaded sickness. I have had trouble, too, with the very same thing! But thankfully I am doing well now — touch wood! I was brought up to go to church, you know, as a child; you had to go whether you wanted to or not. But by the time I was thirteen, my first teenage birthday, I was no longer interested. Therefore, forgive me for saying this, but I do find it a little unusual that some people, especially those as young as you, should desire to go to church. I found it an ordeal and was glad to be free of it when I reached eighteen, I can tell you. I'm sure you can take religion too seriously, you know… in my opinion.

"I appreciate contemporary music as opposed to the organ music you talked about. That was quite funny by the way… when you described a moment ago how you felt upon hearing it. Yes, I'm sure lively music is more popular, because I would imagine it's very similar to other popular music you hear elsewhere. But be that as it may, I often read of so many religious fanatics out there today — nutters you know, luring young people away into bondage and chains, brainwashing them so that they believe bizarre teachings and end up doing weird things asked of them by their cult leaders who imagine themselves to be a cut above the rest spiritually or something like that.

"What I'm trying to say is this… well, I mean… there must be some sort of attraction for young people. Would you not agree? Otherwise, they would not come. That's probably why you turned away from the sound of the organ playing; it obviously did not attract you or compel you to enter. But was it perhaps the band and more palatable music in your church that got your attention when you first went? I am not knocking music, but something must draw people in, and then it's what follows on after that.

"Do you recollect, Dorothy, not so many years back, how a religious cult leader in America drew many people into a suicide pact—all in the name of God, I ask you! These people were not dumb nitwits either; some came from very rich, respectable families and were well educated, yet they still succumbed to this deceit and madness!

"You have your whole life in front of you, Dorothy. Why get involved in such serious and often morbid, joy-killing religion, I ask you? Obviously, there are those who will always be lovely church attendees; it's like they go to keep up with the status quo and be part of the accepted community..." Jennifer laughed then and continued, "I nearly said part of the furniture!"

She then continued, "You know who I mean, the over seventies and such like—those who I suppose were far more religiously minded than I was. I don't have a problem with that; I can see some going and that's it! But me? I didn't... full stop! Old people I can partly understand. They've seen a lot of life and suffering and need to pacify their minds, I suppose, and thinking about God can help them a lot. But the young? What is their problem?"

Dorothy gazed at Jennifer with much intrigue upon hearing all this. She was listening to someone who had lived a long time, someone who had seen much as a child and had experienced a hard time under a strict religious regime. What could Dorothy say to all of that?

"Oh, Jennifer! You are raising so much in what you are saying! Goodness me, I do not know all the answers! I do agree with you that there is so much deceit in the world — and all in the name of religion — and I can assure you that I do not wish to be included as one of them.

"What I try to do is this. I always seek to listen to what is being said; then I read the Bible for myself when I get home to sort of confirm it all. I confess that some things I have heard said on TV and elsewhere I find very suspicious, and when I follow these up by looking in my Bible, well… I just cannot see where they are getting it all from!

"I see where your train of thought is leading. How do you know what is good and what is bad out there? I can only say that the God of the Bible is surely much bigger than all this evil and deception that takes place. Like you just said yourself, these people are taught weird doctrines. But if they were to search their Bible — assuming they are supposed to be Christian, but I doubt that very much — they would be able to judge what is good and what is bad, for it is the Bible that is God's word to man and not the words coming from the preacher necessarily! When such awful happenings like you have mentioned do occur all in the name of religion, then I believe it is imperative to have a personal relationship with God through Jesus. If you are constantly listening to Him through His Word… not some church or individual… then He will guide you and protect you from error.

"Yes, we walk by faith; there is no question about that. And yes, we can be sincerely wrong about what we believe; no one is perfect and infallible. Yet I still believe if we want God and believe in His Son Jesus Christ, then He will correct us and teach us along the way, leading us into all truth. That is not my view, Jennifer; it is God's written Word!

"This may seem strange to you, but I find God speaks to me all the time by bringing His Word to mind; that's why it is so important to read the Bible every day for yourself. That way, He shows me the best direction to go regarding any matter. Jennifer, as I said a moment ago, I do not know all the answers, but I trust God to help and direct me as I go along; I cannot do it by myself… it's a personal relationship and walk!

"I think there is a devil, just like the Bible says, and he wants to confuse us as much as he can — especially through offering many religions — but Jesus said, '*I am the Way, the Truth and the Life; no one comes to the Father but by Me!*'

"Now, simple me believes that. It is not my opinion or view; it's what Jesus has said about Himself, so I accept it! I know Jesus loves me, so I trust what He says, and thus far He has never once failed me!

"Will you permit me to illustrate something to you, Jennifer? Do you have any money with you? A paper note?"

For a moment, Jennifer looked aghast at Dorothy, wondering how she could follow on the conversation with her after listening to all she had just stated! This request of Dorothy's was a diversion, she thought, so she happily reached into her purse and handed Dorothy a crisp twenty-pound note.

"Well now, Dorothy, if you are going to tell me that everything wrong out there is to do with money and power, stop there! Because I believe you!" laughed Jennifer.

"You are probably right, Jennifer. Absolutely! But that is not what I was going to say. Rather, I would like to pose a question about this particular twenty- pound note. Pardon me for resorting to pictures and comparisons in such a simple way, but I find they can help sometimes in presenting a problem or issue in a completely different fashion in order to make a point. My question is this; how do you know that this note is genuine currency?"

"Well, I'm sure there are watermarks," replied Jennifer, suddenly acquiring much more interest in this diversion following the initial surprise of the request. "Or something like that, amongst other things. That's what makes it genuine. Look, there's a picture of the queen's head. I do not know everything about it, but I know that if you lift the note up to the light, you will see things that you cannot see otherwise. Am I correct?"

"Yes, Jennifer. I couldn't agree more! You need to lift the note up to the light, then you can tell quite easily whether it is real or counterfeit – and so it is with other things, too, particularly with what we have just been talking about.

"In short, how we can discern truth and authenticity regarding a given matter whenever we hear of unusual or strange teachings and doctrines? When it comes to religion, I believe the Bible is God's Word, Jennifer—as I have already said—and that it is the genuine thing. It is the blueprint of every church that calls itself Christian, and it is on this that they should base their teaching. If we desire to know the truth about a given matter, then this is, in my opinion, the source to go to, right? It is rather like lifting the twenty-pound note up to the light—but in this case, it is the light of God's Word! It is the best way of discovering the truth about anything of controversy, especially regarding religion, which I reckon is mostly man-made or at the very least tainted and infiltrated with man's traditions.

"Sometimes the truths of the Word can even be blotted out and omitted so that it becomes too vague and obscure to see what was originally intended for you to see. For example, you must go a long way back to learn about the christening of a baby and how traditions brought this about, because, you see... there is no mention of this practice in the Bible! On the other hand, I once heard how a certain church denomination was abandoning the teaching on the blood of Christ — and yet the Bible is full of it!

"Now, regarding money, there are, I'm sure, many counterfeits out there, and some apparently only experts can recognise; but if there are counterfeits, then this proves to me that they must be counterfeiting something — that there exists the genuine article as well!

"I believe God is absolutely true and rock solid. If you like, He is the genuine article. Many make copies and use His name for their own evil devices, but He still has the highest power and authority! He never changes and is quite capable of preserving His Word of Truth for us all, despite everything. There is only one genuine article!

"I believe God has shown us Who that is in the Person of Jesus Christ. He is God's way, truth and life! The Bible says that in the last days — ever since the cross of Jesus, His death and resurrection — God has spoken to us through His Son. If we wish to know the absolute truth, then we need to focus only upon Jesus and leave the rest to Him!

"How do you get to have a personal relationship with God? Primarily, by confessing that you are a sinner — from birth — and receiving

Christ for yourself, turning away from your own selfish way to trust and follow Him as both your Lord and Saviour. I believe what the Bible says about this... that if we receive Him—that is the person of Jesus Christ and all He has done for us—we can become born of God, His children! Then, as we surrender our lives, desiring to trust in Him and obey Him, then—and only then—can we learn to discern good and evil, for He enlightens us by His Word. This is the only way it all works.

People often wish to know answers but are not willing to come God's way and surrender their whole lives to Him. You see, God's priority is not necessarily in giving us answers to everything! No, God loves us and desires us to be His children, and that is a completely different perspective to that of acquiring answers to everything. The fact is we would not understand everything anyway; we require His help and mind! Consequently, Jesus said you must be born again, and this—together with repentance—is what God requires as the basis for His forgiveness and new life. It is not easy! Being born again is literally starting out anew, but this time it's with God as your Heavenly Father. Every day you are learning about His ways, His thoughts... but the amazing thing is this; He is with you all the time to guide you and lead you!

"When I was about nineteen, Jennifer, I thought quite independently and a bit arrogantly, believing my own judgements on such matters to be just fine. I would believe what I wished to believe without any one trying to persuade me to do otherwise. I always knew best. Well, one morning, whilst in my mother's house, I observed her sitting in front of a warm coal fire, reading her Bible. I interrupted her, being quite put out, and confronted her about why she was reading a Bible.

"I said something to the effect of, '*Mum… if there is a God, then he ought to speak to you and you with Him. I find this going to church and wearing some nice hat and clothes and then coming home only to take them off… I do find this so hypocritical!*'

"Now, to my surprise, my mother, instead of perhaps getting cross with me and reproving me for speaking as I did, gazed at me quite warmly and smiled! I will never forget the way she looked at me at that moment; her eyes seemed to be shining lovingly, exhibiting no offence whatsoever! This was not what I had expected; it was just as if she understood what I was saying and knew that I had touched upon some important matter. She then went on to say, '*Yes, my dear, I quite agree with you. And we believe at our church that very same thing about God — what you have just said, that He should talk to you and you with Him!*'

"I understand more clearly now, these ten years or so down the line, what she meant. I have also lived a bit myself, and suffered somewhat as well. I believe my mum had a personal knowledge and understanding of God, or to be more specific, of Jesus and what He has done for all of us upon the cross. My mum went regularly to church, yes; but she did it for a different reason than what we were both describing. What you have said regarding your own experiences seemed to be mere religion and compulsion, but this was not the case with my mum. Further, I would not say that she was morbid or lacking in joy, like you seemed to attribute to such people who like to attend church! The faith she had was very personal to her; I could not gainsay it with any of my arguments and reasoning, but I was still not convinced in my own heart at that time. Nevertheless, I simply never brought up the subject with her again, realising it was pointless to do so."

"Well, Dorothy, perhaps I was a little hasty in my opinion and words; I can see where you are coming from… I think. I understand your parallel with my twenty-pound note — which I will now retrieve, thank you. And for all your sincerity and outspokenness in telling me about yourself and your mum — bless her, she sounded like a warm affectionate lady, I'm sure — you must understand where I am coming from too.

"My father was so strict on Sundays. We all had to go to church. There was no playing with games and toys. And I hated Sundays and religion. We said grace at the table and prayers in the evening — which could be fine, I suppose — but did he ever play with me? Did he ever hug me or kiss me? Was there ever any laughing and fun in the house? No, Dorothy. Forgive me for being suspicious about your religion before, but can you see why?

"My understanding of God was tainted by what I saw around me in the home, which was one of censorship and restrictions almost constantly; there was certainly no joy. It was as if living a holy life was to never laugh or smile, and well… following God meant no pleasures at all — especially on a Sunday. In fact, doing without seemed good, as if it were some sort of asceticism from which you gained spirituality through abstinence! I used to be told that you must deny yourself, but somehow, I don't think that interpretation was what Jesus had in mind!

"Further, my father had plenty of money to spare, but still he made Mum go without things; he was so mean to her! I always determined in my heart that I would never get too involved with religion after all that I saw of it in my home.

"Oh dear! What a miserable state of affairs it is that to think and feel about God in such a manner, especially in comparison to your wonderful endorsements of God and all! It cannot be right even now, I know… but I have carried those images and experiences with me all my life. I have had no incentive whatsoever to go to church, but I would like you to know that it has been refreshing and of help to me, Dorothy, to hear from you something more positive about what you believe. It has given me enlightenment regarding this born-again phenomenon you mentioned, because though such people are often criticised and ridiculed, they do at least seem to be happier as you yourself have clearly demonstrated. You certainly appear to have something we never had at church... and that's putting it mildly!

"In a way, I suppose, I am at that place where you were when you were eighteen; if there is a God — and I do believe there is — surely He cannot demand this lifestyle that I have known! He must be more personal, loving and kind than what I suffered! It all seemed too artificial, regimented and unreal to me as a child; it was sad and morbid...

"Sorry! I don't think He had anything whatsoever to do with all that superficial poppycock I had to endure! So, you see, Dorothy; there is so much that does not make sense to me."

Dorothy sat back in shock and disbelief, trying to digest the words coming out of Jennifer's mouth. They were legitimate and understandable reasons that she had expressed against all that was false, man-made and religious, but they were also bitter and resentful words revealing much hurt, pain and displeasure, so that she was disregarding and discrediting anything that was of a religious nature—so much so that even the good was automatically excluded with all the bad! She had tarred everything with the same brush and thrown the baby out with the bathwater so to speak! In Dorothy's eyes, Jennifer had shown very little response to Dorothy's words other than a polite recognition for speaking and sharing things that were obviously important to her. But as far as she herself was concerned, it had mostly been to no avail... just like water off a duck's back! Jennifer's mind was already made up, and she did not need to be disturbed with facts!

It did not follow, however, that Jennifer rejected all of Dorothy's words; it was simply the case that words alone were insufficient to change her mind's attitude about everything—even if they had been true. Her heart's damage was seemingly unrepairable, having been scorched and seared as with a hot iron by her childhood experiences. She had developed, over time, a crocodile-like skin, and it would take something very special to penetrate it and reach her heart!

Now, as it happened, her husband, Alfred Townsend, was a problem to her, but this problem did not concern his alcoholism for that had gone away now by some means or another! No, this concern of Jennifer's was more to do with his conversion to what she called brainwashed religion and his apparent healing! What was all of this about? It was imperative for her to get some sensible understanding about the whole matter, and this was a good opportunity in the presence of Dorothy to hopefully do so.

"Well, Dorothy, there is just one more thing I would value from you... your opinion regarding my husband. Just what do you make of it all? I mean this business about his leg. It seems to me it just got better by itself, I reckon; that's what I think... I mean, what else is there?"

"Jennifer, what happened to Alfred was not in the script or programme of a normal church experience, even though I believe God can and does heal people today. It was completely outside of the box! You see, no one was expecting this to happen—not even Alfred himself. He never asked about his leg at all when he came to church; his reason for coming, in his own words, was '*to get himself right with God—that were it!*'"

Dorothy laughed gently. "Forgive me, Jennifer, but I do love Alfred's simple way of saying things! He said that he had responded to the invitation of Jesus to come and meet with him... that's how he had considered it in his own mind! When I asked him what he meant by that, do you know what he told me? He said Maria had shown him some verses of Scripture, one of which was this: '*He that comes to me I will in no wise turn away!*'

"Alfred had interpreted this quite literally as an opportunity to come to Jesus without being rejected or condemned, seeing He had promised in that passage not to turn him away; otherwise, I think Alfred would have felt too bad about himself. He told me that he would never have dared to come — not after all his blaspheming and blaming God because of his bad leg! Now, what we see today is Alfred out there in the precinct downtown as a completely new man, full of purpose, standing in the open-air telling everyone passing by how God has healed him and forgiven him!

"Jennifer, if you are looking to me to tell you that it was all a hoax and that his leg was not healed but got better by itself, then I cannot possibly agree to that. I can tell you, however, what happened on that Sunday morning. I was seated in the front row, just a few seats away from Alfred. Pastor John asked him why he had come and if he wanted prayer. This is a normal procedure whenever people stand up at the front of the church, though this usually takes place right near the end of the service when people are free to leave — when the service is virtually over. Now Alfred told Pastor John what I have just told you, that he had come at the invitation of Jesus. Then he went on to say, *'Do you think that Jesus will forgive me for all I have done? I will serve Him forever with what life I have got left!'*

"I'm not sure exactly what followed, but Pastor explained a few things to him about God's forgiveness to all those who come to Him through His Son Jesus Christ. Then I remember seeing

Alfred quite overcome and weeping. Now, Pastor asked Alfred if he would like him to pray for him—again, this is normal practice—and Alfred agreed. Pastor John prayed for Alfred in the same manner he prayed with everyone else that had come forward, but in Alfred's case—to the shock and surprise of everyone—it was clear that God had something very special for Alfred. It was amazing to be there observing all that happened! The result was a manifestation of God's presence and power that I have never experienced before! It cannot be described in natural words.

"My fiancé, David, also came into the church at that precise moment to collect Mary his sister and witnessed it all. Such was the power and conviction of the Lord's presence in that meeting that David felt compelled to get himself right with God. David and I had been arguing about certain things the night before, and he told me afterwards how distraught and bad he had felt when going home—and the following morning as well—so much so that he couldn't get himself to come to church. Well, he walked into the church to pick up his sister and her child as I told you, for they had not come out of the building like almost everyone else. Upon entering the church, he walked right up to the front and asked for prayer for himself too!

"Now, Alfred had not asked for healing for his leg but to be forgiven by God; that was his reason for going to church that morning! As you very well know, Jennifer, Alfred was not a religious person at all. It was the first time he had been in a church apparently, since he had been taken as a child with his mother!

"Now you go and tell Alfred, Jennifer, that none of it was real or something of that nature and that his leg got better by itself! You know very well just how long he had been walking with the aid of a crutch. And further, as we have both seen, Alfred gave Jerry some letters of confirmation from the hospital stating that his leg is good and he therefore cannot continue receiving his disability allowance! Now, of course that is a shame, but I think Alfred would rather have the use of his leg.

"What do I personally think about everything, Jennifer? I think that God had a purpose for Alfred, and He has now equipped him to do it! Alfred needed to be able to walk to do God's will, so maybe God gave him his legs back to go and witness in the open-air! That is just my personal interpretation of Alfred's miracle; it fits!

"God has also demonstrated through Alfred that He is no respecter of persons and that whosoever comes to Him through His Son, He receives exactly in accordance with what the Bible says! Alfred took God at His Word and it worked, because God is faithful to His Word! Further, God always seems to be moved with compassion and pleased when a person comes to Him in faith—

and who is to say that Alfred did not show incredible faith that morning by coming in to church like he did! I am very moved in my spirit whenever I speak to him. His simple, child-like faith is wonderful and a testimony to everyone! He gets a lot of stick and abuse in the open-air meetings from all those who know what he was like before, but he is undeterred."

Jennifer was shaken by Dorothy's last words regarding Alfred and her opinion about it all. What she had heard from Dorothy was not falling upon good ground—well, not at that moment! No. Jennifer was challenged and convicted in her own self, and she was now ready to leave, being unable to respond positively to what she had heard.

Dorothy was oblivious of much of what she had shared with her that day; her speech had flowed like a playback recording of all that had occurred in church on that special morning, relaying it all to Jennifer's ears in an open and frank manner. It could not be gainsaid. It had happened. It was real. Whatever people chose to think or believe.

Jennifer excused herself and left shortly after Dorothy's discourse had ended, departing in a most sober and agitated mood. All her abhorrent memories from childhood had been regurgitated, and by speaking of them and sharing them openly, it had only served to defile her mind once again. She had found it all disconcerting to say the least, and whilst she had felt the indisputable impact regarding her husband's conversion and healing, it did not—it could not—penetrate the hardness of her own heart, for she had carried hurt and bitterness for many years.

All that Dorothy had said about Alfred may have been real, but it was not able to change her! It had not been her experience, but that of someone else! Miracles and testimonies by themselves could not impress Jennifer sufficiently to rethink her ways; they could never penetrate the hardness that had formed over time. The remorse, resentment and bitterness had set like lime scale, forming a hard shell upon the walls of her heart. Jennifer needed much more than this. She needed her own Damascus road experience—if that were ever to be forthcoming; only a personal encounter with God would suffice!

Chapter 18

Jennifer's Troubles and Woes

It was two days since Jennifer Townsend had visited Alfred's home for the interview with Jerry Dickson from the *Daily Herald*, and at this moment in time, she was to be found at home in her kitchen, about to ask her sister Betty what she would like for breakfast.

Of late — or to be more precise, ever since Jennifer had returned to the home of her sister, having spoken very much with a certain lady called Dorothy — she had not been at peace within herself. In her mind, it had not proved to be a desirable or beneficial conversation with Dorothy, having divulged so much to her about herself regarding her unhappy childhood. And having disclosed so much before another person, it felt as though everything had suddenly become alive again, and the effects were almost as devastating as those dreaded earlier years!

However, Jennifer had other troubles and woes that were still hanging around in her mind too! It was as if one problem had resuscitated another, so that all were hitting her quite hard at the current time. Well, they say troubles always come in twos or threes; or when it rains, it pours!

To add to her troubled memories from the distant past, Dorothy had illuminated her mind, during their long chat, with a different perspective regarding spiritual matters. Basically, she no longer felt justified in her condemnation of religious topics in the manner she had done in the past, for clearly there was the real thing—as Dorothy had pointed out—and then there was the legalistic way which she knew much about. She had tasted much of the latter, but the former…? This was all unknown territory that frightened her! Would her life need to change much if she were to embark upon such a road herself? And if so, what would it all entail? Of course, Jennifer had only experienced demanding rules, governing her behaviour—obligations that had to be adhered to. Consequently, she still only thought along those same negative lines, having known nothing else; in short, all she knew was the do's and don'ts!

Third, Alfred had made an impression upon her, which was also unsettling her! She had been sufficiently observant, as always, to notice how her husband had made considerable effort on her behalf to tidy up the house. It had made such an impact upon her that her reasons for living apart from him at her sister's home were becoming increasingly unjustified.

It was never the case that she did not love him. The only reason she had moved away was out of desperation and despair; she had needed a break, so to speak, or a place of refuge. Even so, she had intended to return home eventually, for her daughter's sake. But that had not materialised yet. As much as she felt bad about it all, the fact was she had all the peace and quiet one could dream of at her sister Betty's house; Betty had never been married and had lived all by herself. Consequently, Jennifer had procrastinated repeatedly.

It had been an ordeal living in that household before, and she had no longer been able to endure her husband's drunkenness and the verbal abuse he had doled out when he was in an intoxicated state, which had sadly been a daily occurrence. For her own sanity and protection—though Alfred had never once been physical with her - she had come to a decision, and this she followed through for better or for worse.

Circumstances were now very different, and all the above adverse criteria regarding her husband's behaviour were no longer seemingly relevant. Alfred had changed, not only from drunkenness to sobriety, but also from a sinner to a saint, having found, as she would say, religion. Could she cope, living with this new Alfred?

Things were fast becoming ironic to say the least! Jennifer was in such a tiz that morning. Wearing an apron and looking the part for preparing something to eat, she wandered in from the kitchen and ventured towards the dining area, where her sister, Betty, who had just finished putting her hair in rollers, was to be found sitting down on an old-fashioned solid rustic oak chair at a similarly styled kitchen table, as if in waiting for something to happen next. Preparing breakfast was a task taken in turns by the two of them. As it happened, on that morning, it was Jennifer's turn to do breakfast, and so Betty relished putting her order in, enjoying her day off from that chore.

"Well, Betty, what would you like for breakfast this morning?" enquired the would-be chef!

"The usual, I think, Jenny dear—some toasted sour dough bread with just butter on it... and of course, a cup of tea. No! I tell you what! Can you do me two slices of toast? Then on one slice, I'll have some of that almond nut butter I bought yesterday; I need a bit of protein."

They both preferred either sour dough or a light rye bread—and not just for breakfast but as a regular habit at any time of the day; it was so much lighter on the stomach, and when toasted and served with unsalted butter, it was so tasty that you did not need jam on it.

"Okay. I'll have the same as you," said Jennifer. "Except for the almond nut butter. Don't you think that almond nut butter is fatty for you, sister? I'm not sure just how healthy it is, you know."

"Ah! Well, I have researched it, and it does have a lot of fat, you're right... but it's that good fat, you know. What is it called? Mono saturates or something... Well, anyway, not the bad saturated fat. Mind you, it has lots of minerals as well — and like I said, it has protein. I need a bit of protein first thing; can't keep having eggs every morning. Oh! And Jenny dear, could you make up a pot of tea in the old way — tea leaves, not bags? I think that will be all, thank you; you are good to me ...

"And don't forget the tea cosy," she added with a laugh.

Jennifer took all this amicably, for the roles would be reversed the following day, and she could think ahead to exactly what she might get Betty to do on her behalf; that's how it was and it all worked so well. This way, they both had an opportunity to be innovative if they so desired — each hoping to sell to the other person some new thing to try — or to be traditional, just as they pleased. As it happened, Jennifer did try some almond nut butter! It had been so well promoted and recommended by her sister that she took her advice to heart then conceded afterwards that it was quite delicious.

Betty sat crunching at her toast, making sounds of satisfaction as she did so, and observed a quiet, subdued looking sister directly opposite her at the breakfast table.

"You seem a little quiet, Jenny dear; I do hope you didn't mind my finicky requests for tea and all."

"Goodness me! No, Betty! How could you

possibly think such a thing? It's exactly the way I prefer it myself, so you have nothing to fear. Actually, I have a few things on my mind now; that's all."

This comment of Jenny's was intended to provoke curiosity from her sister, to give Jenny opportunity to tell Betty about the things on her mind.

"Alright then, Jenny, tell me what's bothering you now; we always share things, don't we? I have noticed you a little down in the dumps of late... ever since you visited Alfred the other day in fact."

"Well, the thing is, he does seem to be getting on with his life these days," began Jennifer. "And I'm feeling a bit guilty, being here and not there if you know what I mean, at least for my Maria's sake. She says her dad is not the same old person he used to be and asks me if I will come home. There's no shouting and arguing, and he hasn't touched any drink for ages... In fact, according to Maria, he is all politeness and contriteness now; quite a new creature.

"As well as pressure on that front, there is something else. It's that Dorothy... Dorothy McGuire is her name."

"Who is *she*, may I ask, to be bothering you?" enquired Betty with some degree of surprise, being intrigued and very curious to know why her tough, resilient Jenny should be troubled.

"Now, Dorothy is not what you think, Betty. Were she a catty, old busy body putting her nose into other people's business or things of that nature, then I could handle that most easily, I assure you—and without getting the least bit bothered by it. But no, this young lady is a different kettle of fish; in fact, she is a most beautiful, elegant thing... and can you believe this? She is a church goer... But more than that, she is a born-again Christian!"

Betty instantly came to her conclusion. "Well, I'll be...! And I suppose she has influenced Alfred, yes? That's where he's got all of this from, I suppose."

"Yes, in a way; Alfred did say he had been impressed by something Dorothy had said to him one time and had been challenged by her, but it was also Maria who had something to do with it, I believe. Anyway, Dorothy and I had a long talk after Alfred had left with this newspaper man. They were going to visit Pastor John Peterson, you see. They all go to that church of his, not far from here in that modern building that doesn't look like a church; you know the one I mean?"

"Yes, I do," added Betty. "That's the same church where a couple I've met called Alice and Robert go. Mind you, they seem nice and live up the road with a little boy."

"Well, I ended up talking to Dorothy as I said," continued Jennifer. "And I'm afraid I gave her a bit of a spiel about our religious upbringing, you know... But for all that she never flinched or got the slightest bit agitated by any of my belittling remarks about church; she only gave me positive comments about her own faith and experiences — all of which, I have to say, sounded quite impressive! As far as that goes, I suppose! Now I just feel bad about everything; it's like it has all come back to haunt me years later, and I can't seem to shrug it off."

Jennifer had resigned herself to being honest and frank with Betty in this last statement, and stared down at the table quite thoughtfully as she recalled the whole episode she'd had with Dorothy. She could not fault Dorothy's authenticity and sincerity; she was not the same species as herself. Here was someone who seemed to genuinely enjoy church most enthusiastically! Consequently, Jennifer felt she had no option but to give Dorothy the benefit of the doubt and could only submit herself to the unquestionable fact that she was of a sound mind; she did not seem extreme — as she had originally thought — and for all intents and purposes, she appeared to be a woman of integrity with good common sense.

"Well, Jenny, I have always told you that you took Dad far too seriously in those days and let him get to you. But there again, you were the rebellious tomboy and kept riling him, instead of just shutting up and going with the flow. I did, and after a while, his words went right over my head, like water off a duck's plumage. But you…!

"Besides, I still go to church… Well, when I can. I do think it is necessary to do so and not do what you seem to have done, given up all together. Not everyone is like Dad by any means, so why throw out the baby with the bathwater by turning completely away from church altogether. I mean, who is being extreme now?"

"Oh! I think I envy you, dear sister. I wish I had your easy-going attitude to these things and had handled it in the same way you did. What a joke that would have been though!" she scoffed.

"Well, I think I'll wash up, then go downtown for an hour; it just might do me good and help get my head around things. A bit of window shopping, if nothing else, will be therapeutic, I'm sure."

Chapter 19

Downtown

Jennifer was subdued, staring thoughtfully out of the bus window as she travelled into town. Even though she took the very same bus several times each week so that it was a very familiar journey and enjoyable to her, this morning it was different. In contrast to other times, when her spirits were light and peaceable without a care in the world, today she was feeling rather low and troubled regarding recent matters previously mentioned, all of which were taking their toll.

A sore throat or headache were symptomatic of a developing cold or flu, and the one followed the other. In a similar way, it may sometimes be the case that stress and anxiety, if prolonged long enough, could develop into something more serious. Now, unfortunately, it was the case that Jennifer empathised and understood first-hand how Dorothy had felt with her previous condition of anxiety and depression, having experienced it all herself in the past!

At this moment in time, Jennifer recognised an all too familiar symptom; unpleasant waves of anxiety were once again sweeping through her body with their all too familiar feelings of torment. Jennifer knew the signs; she had to nip it in the bud. To combat it early on with a more positive outlook and frame of mind was essential, and this she well knew.

The recent developments and issues concerning Alfred, Dorothy, Maria and not least, herself, were the culprits so to speak. She was now feeling hopelessly ashamed of her life, with regret, guilt and a sense of being a complete failure. *Regret* and *blame* concerning her rebellious attitude towards her father, despite his hardness and totalitarian regime in their home, for if her sister Betty had managed to cope without scars, so perhaps should she have done. *Guilt* over leaving poor Maria to fend for herself!

Alfred had once been considered the bad guy, but now it had all reversed. She had no more reasons to legitimise or justify her decision to stay at her sister's house; now she was fast becoming the bad guy! How should she deal with this dilemma? What should she do? She wished to forget, or dismiss from her mind the pangs of guilt, but found it impossible to do so; they were like leaches clinging to her. All had come back to haunt her afresh and needed to be addressed.

To rub salt in the wound, Dorothy's challenges to her about God had served only to trouble her. Was it retribution, falling upon her like a day of reckoning? She was perfectly happy only three days hence, so why should she be suddenly burdened now? Moods outside of her control had resurged and lingered unwelcomely in her mind for too long, and having been left unchecked had developed further into something more prolonged and serious. What should normally be, upon a different occasion and under different circumstances, a relaxed and enjoyable time, taking a bus journey into town, was in fact a growing predicament with more than just a veneer of pain in all directions; embedded within her was a perplexity that seemed incapable of a simple solution!

Jennifer arrived in town and immediately took herself into *Max's* for a coffee, ordering a double espresso with a little hot milk on the side. Then, she did the unforgiveable and asked for a large chocolate brownie. A strong dose of caffeine, together with rash indulgence, could possibly do the trick... for a while! She looked towards the newspaper rack for a daily copy of something or other to occupy herself with, then retrieved two newspapers from it. Anything would suffice; she needed to distract her mind from other things. Had she kept up with the times in the technology department, there would have been plenty in the realm of social media to keep her busy, but she never had bought a smart phone or tablet.

Jennifer sat musing through the newspapers for a good half hour, but after looking through the first half dozen or so pages in each, she discarded them, having found nothing else of interest to her. She got up to walk over to the counter and request another coffee when she saw three young men entering the café, one of whom seemed familiar to her. The young man in question seemed to recognise Jennifer, and he walked over towards her.

"Hello, Mrs Townsend! What a surprise meeting you here! Can't say as I've ever seen you in *Max's* before. This is our hangout during college lunch times; I usually meet up with Maria, but she has an exam today."

The young man turned to his friends, beckoning them to carry on with what they were doing.

"Tell me, young man," enquired Jennifer, not without some curiosity. "I think I know you, but I'm not sure who you are... Please tell me. Where have I seen you before? You seem to know me and my daughter."

"Why, it's me! You know... Ian... Ian McPherson, Mrs Townsend... Maria's boy..."

Jennifer interrupted him suddenly, recollecting who he was; the young man standing before her was the boy she had known for many years, but now he was so grown up and different that she could hardly recognise him!

"Why, goodness me! If it isn't Ian! Oh! Please forgive me, young man. My, how you have changed! I knew there was something familiar about that face of yours, but, bless my soul, I would never have guessed it was you unless you had said. Look, I must not take you from your friends, but it is a nice surprise to see you again."

Now, Ian was feeling honoured at meeting his girlfriend's mother, and he stood as if stuck to the ground, feeling obliged to stay with her a little longer out of respect—especially as she had singled him out and seemed very pleased to meet him. Consequently, as he stood there motionless for a few seconds wondering how to proceed, Jennifer decided to ask of him, "Ian, please sit down for a moment if you wish... provided, that is, you don't mind joining an old lady in front of all your friends!" Jennifer paused and gave a wry chuckle.

"It is such a pleasure to see you... Why, you virtually grew up together with my Maria! Ever since play school! What are you doing now then, son?"

"Can I just get me a sandwich and a drink first, Mrs Townsend? I'll be back in a minute."

Upon returning, Ian sat down opposite Jennifer and proceeded to answer her.

"I have an apprenticeship working in IT. This will be my third year now. I have passed all my exams so far."

"Excellent! And you and Maria? Are you both still okay together then... I mean, goin' strong, as they say?"

"Absolutely, Mrs Townsend! We couldn't be better. I am very happy to be with Maria; I go to her church now, yer know... have been for a long time. And I play the drums; it's great!"

Jennifer was not without some further challenge upon hearing of Ian's interest in church; it seemed to be the topic of the moment, and now it had been raised once again by yet another young person. *Perhaps God wants to tell me something,* she thought, *in which case, He certainly lays it on thick.*

Consequently, Jennifer probed Ian a little further as to why he went to church, being such a very young man. To her surprise, he replied that church was for everyone, whatever your age.

"Why have you never heard Maria sing?" said Ian unhesitatingly and somewhat surprised, for unlike Jennifer, church was not a taboo subject to him, and his speech was as straight as an arrow with little restraint. Some people would talk about subjects such as depression and feel ashamed for doing so, but not young people; they spoke about it in the same way as they would if they had a bad back! Similarly, people would shy away from talking about God, feeling apprehensive, inhibited and nervous, but not young people; they spoke about it freely and openly without embarrassment or surprise. It had to be said that many in the new generation respected openness and directness more than ever, unlike the tight-lipped reserve of previous generations.

"She is awesome; you should come and hear her sometime! And Alfred comes regularly now! That was incredible, don't you think, Mrs Townsend? His leg getting healed? It was the most amazing thing I have ever seen in my whole life!"

Why did Jennifer feel at that moment the odd one out? What was this new world full of young people who were turning to God and religion? First Dorothy, then Alfred—and now this young man, Ian, along with her daughter Maria!

Why do I feel like I've got the wrong end of the stick about all of this? thought Jennifer. *Why do I get the feeling that I am the bad guy? They say, 'out of the mouths of babes and sucklings…'*

That was just how Jennifer felt upon hearing these comments from several young people. Then Jennifer realised, *Oh my! What I've just thought was a quote from the Bible!*

Ian ate his sandwich hungrily and gulped down his Coke; then seeing his friends about to head back to college, he decided to start moving himself and join them. "Well, I shall have to be going now, Mrs Townsend; nice seeing you."

"Just before you go, Ian… I'm curious about something. Those boys you are with? Tell me… do they go to church too?"

"Nar! Not them. Bye! See you!"

Ian walked away hurriedly to be with his mates, not wishing to get left behind, when suddenly, he stopped in his tracks with a burning thought running through his mind. Turning around, Ian walked back to Jennifer's table.

"Mrs Townsend, thank you for inviting me to sit with you just now. I appreciate that. If ever you want to go to church, Mrs Townsend, I can pick you up in my car. Just tell Maria to tell me. Oh! And by the way, Maria talks about you all the time and misses you. Well, I just thought it would be good to invite you; that's all. I know Maria would be pleased. Thanks! Bye!"

Soon Ian and his friends were gone, leaving Jennifer to regain control of her thoughts and emotions after hearing everything that had just been said to her. *What a sweet boy!* she thought.

Jennifer retrieved a handkerchief from her bag and gently dabbed each of her eyes. It was one of those elegant small squares of cotton with colourful embroidery around the edges that was at one time fashionable among all ladies, but nowadays was used only by a few.

It had been a blessing to hear the open outspokenness of Ian she thought. Within his words and sentiments she had observed a genuine love and concern for her daughter and, as it happened, a concern for her own well-being too. What a way to receive such a directive regarding church — and with provision of transport all thrown in! All thanks to a young man of about nineteen years of age!

What had become of this world she was now living in? How estranged she now felt from it. Yes, it had changed mostly for the worse, and yet—unknown to her—new things had developed of which she was oblivious until now, differences that had to be described, despite her misapprehensions regarding God and her hardness toward Him from childhood, as 'for the better' regarding at least some of the youth of the day. This young man had revealed to her something new, sincere and by all accounts what appeared to be most genuine in her reckoning.

She had considered the faith and commitment of her own daughter towards God and the church as a one-off, assuming Maria had moved in this direction because of troubles in the home. But, of late, circumstances had presented a different picture, almost a trend regarding some young people who clearly seemed to believe far more readily than she could ever have possibly imagined! And there she was stewing these years in her own grief! It was as if God had left the one and turned to the other—the young, those who would believe, accept and turn to Him with simplicity of heart and mind, not with a legalistic religious mindset but with a spirit of love and life!

Oh! The remorseful pain Jennifer felt at that instant alone in *Max's Café*! For a moment, she imagined herself as amongst the older generation in the wilderness for all those forty years! What a waste! Having been delivered out of Egypt by the hand of Moses, they could not and did not enter the promised land because of their unbelief; only their children did. That older generation had been called stubborn, stiff-necked and rebellious, failing to see, appreciate or believe that God was on their side, leading them into a new life without slavery. Instead, they longed for — even pined — to go back into Egypt to the old life!

What a joke! she now thought upon recollection of all this. *How stupid can one become?*

God had said that not one of those who came out of Egypt would enter the promised land — except two men, Joshua and Caleb! Those who entered were the children born in the wilderness during those forty years. It was the new generation that went forward then, and they seemed to be doing the same now thousands of years later! They believed what their parents would not; they inherited the promise and conquered the land before them!

Oh! I do not wish to be amongst the unbelieving carcasses that lie in the wilderness rotting! If it is possible... God, help me get rid of all this hurt I'm carrying, for certainly I cannot do it alone! I have been walking around in circles for far too long... in a wilderness of my own making. If there is still room for the likes of me, then I need to come out of this desert place. I cannot come as one of the young and vibrant... Only just as I am can I come!

Once again, Jennifer retrieved her handkerchief and dabbed her eyes with it. She needed to go. It had been an interesting occasion, meeting with young Ian, and what had followed in her thinking even more so. Her heart and soul seemed to have found a release she had never experienced before, as if an unseen hand of care and compassion had rested upon her, reminding her that there was a living God of clemency who was tender-hearted and merciful, ready and able to save anyone from their own version of the land of Egypt, which, in Jennifer's case, was her long and arduous rebellion and rejection. Now, she was reaping the bitter fruits of her prolonged choices; they were a hopeless sense of remorse and regret that were taking her nowhere... well, nowhere good.

Now, upon leaving the café, Jennifer turned to go into the Pound Saver shop, for she needed some washing up liquid, bleach and toilet freshener. This was the cheapest place to get them, and the money saved in buying these three items alone more than paid for the bus fare! Then, she walked into the precinct towards a shopping centre.

What a relief to be completely away from all the noisy traffic and fumes, she thought. This concept should have been thought of before; it was one modern idea that she liked very much. Wandering in here and there, mostly window shopping, chatting to old friends who were like minded as she, getting their bargains! What a pleasure this was!

After a good while she stopped and sniffed the air. *Ah yes! That is a whiff of a lovely familiar smell - fish and chips!*

Breakfast was a good three hours ago, she thought. *And after all, Jennifer,* she assured herself enthusiastically, *you shouldn't miss a meal; it is not good! This will suffice very nicely indeed!*

It was warm enough to sit outside at a table in the fresh air, and upon receiving her order that consisted of a small piece of haddock and chips with mushy peas, Jennifer relished the occasion, eating up every single chip and all the crispy fat that came with the fish. She did have one criticism, however; she thought the mushy peas were squashed processed peas, whereas in her childhood they would have been mashed dry peas that had been left to soak overnight.

But oh dear! Those days have truly gone now, I suppose; they would take far too long to prepare, I guess, and they just can't be bothered. What a shame; the taste is nowhere near as nice!

Once again Jennifer got up and moved on, feeling somewhat revived. Having paid her bill, leaving a generous tip for the waitress, she casually walked further down into the heart of the shopping area that led to a fountain feature in the open-air part of the precinct with seats surrounding it. This specific area was quite popular with buskers, because there was a large concentration of people sitting and relaxing, but upon drawing closer she instantly stopped in her tracks at the sight that met her eyes! Adjacent to the fountain was assembled a small group of people of all ages, listening to someone speaking in the open-air, and though she could not visibly make out the person at first, she recognised the voice.

Could it be…? Oh! My goodness, surely not! But upon further scrutiny, the truth became vividly clear; it was her husband! It was none other than Alfred preaching!

Jennifer went tense and flushed with shock, as if having a panic attack, then immediately looked for a seat somewhere close enough to hear but not be seen. She had been aware that Alfred spoke in the open-air one day each week, but upon which day this was she had had no idea—until now! Having found a whole free bench, she sat down within good sight and hearing, just slightly behind Alfred, and listened closely, curious to hear her husband. Sure enough, he was talking about Jesus alright, and Jennifer looked and listened for any possible reaction from the crowd. But there was nothing adverse that she noticed.

Another young man was present, bobbing around from place to place, then crouching down to take photographs. She recognised him to be a previous recent acquaintance of hers—Jerry Dickson from the *Daily Herald*, whom she had met with her husband and Dorothy, discussing in detail Alfred's healing.

After her initial shock and embarrassment upon witnessing her evangelist-preacher husband in action, Jennifer became filled with a sense of pride and admiration towards him for having the nerve and boldness to speak out like he was doing. He was fearlessly testifying of his previous, drunken life with a crippled leg, and how he had come to Jesus Who had both healed and forgiven him. And how now he felt God's call and commission to tell others about it!

Jennifer was mesmerised. What a change this was before her very eyes — her own husband preaching in the open-air! After a while, most people walked away, having received a tract handed to them by Alfred. But then, suddenly, a pretty young lady and a little girl walked over to converse with him, appearing to know him, for Alfred spoke to the little girl and referred to her as Julia. Jennifer turned up the hearing aid in her left ear and could just about hear every single word they were saying.

"Alfred, I thought I could hear you whilst shopping. It sounded great. Julia recognised you, too. She said, 'Look. There's grandad!' Oh dear! I'm afraid you remind her of David's father."

Jennifer was dumbfounded! *David! Grandad! Who on earth is David, I ask? And who is she?*

Jennifer's curiosity got the better of her, and noticing the lady about to leave, she was determined to talk with her and beckon her over as she passed by, if she could fathom some way of doing so.

As the lady and her child approached Jennifer's bench and were just about to walk past it, Jennifer boldly waved her hand, signalling her desire to speak with the lady.

"Excuse me, dear. Could I ask you something, if you wouldn't mind?"

"Yes, of course," replied the stranger, walking closer to where Jennifer was seated. Before Jennifer even began to say anything else, she spoke instead to the lovely little girl who must have been about three or four years old. "Oh! You do have a pretty little girl here," she said. "And what a pretty dress you are wearing! And what lovely shoes, too!"

"My daddy got me this bracelet for my birthday, and Mummy got me these shoes," replied the girl proudly, feeling quite at ease upon hearing Jennifer's friendly greeting.

Turning to the lady, Jennifer asked her a question in a more serious tone of voice compared with the manner in which she had just spoken with the little girl.

"Tell me; I couldn't help noticing you speaking with that man over there — the man who was preaching. What do you make of it all, may I ask? I am curious to know about him."

"Oh! That is Alfred Townsend. He is a most wonderful man, you know; we attend the same church. Have you not heard about him?

Why, that was the press just a while ago taking photos of him! They are going to write an article in the newspaper."

"What on earth for, may I ask? I mean, why should they wish to do that?" Jennifer was surreptitiously declaring her ignorance to ascertain independent opinions about everything. It seemed already that her Alfred had become a hero of some sorts, if not a spectacle, in the eyes of people in the church—and outside of it too!

"He is telling how God healed him, you know. Quite amazing it was! I was there at the time in church, actually, and witnessed it all."

"Really! You surprise me! Healing?"

The lady sat down next to Jennifer, gathering that she sounded sceptical about such things.

"Well, I can tell you that the man really was a cripple you know. A good friend of mine, a lady called Dorothy, knows his daughter… and she had visited him before in his home—that was well before he ever came to church—and I can tell you, he did have a bad leg. And I might add was very anti-God at that time!"

"Dorothy? I am familiar with someone by that name… I don't suppose her surname is McGuire, is it?" said Jennifer half seriously.

"Why yes, it is! Dorothy McGuire… do you know her too?" said the lady with much surprise.

Jennifer was flabbergasted by this turn of events.

"Good gracious! You mean to tell me you know Dorothy McGuire? Why, I was speaking to her only a few days ago! And who would you be, may I ask?"

"My name is Mary Osborne. Dorothy is probably my best friend. She is engaged to my brother, David."

"Oh my! What a small world this is! And I suppose you go to her church as well, do you? Don't tell me, along with my Maria … the whole lot of you! Well, bless my soul! Why do I suddenly feel like someone is trying to talk to me?" said Jennifer with a nervous half-laugh.

Mary laughed upon observing Jennifer's reaction, but one thing stuck out noticeably in what she had just said.

"Did you say *my Maria* just now? Are you…? Who are you, may I ask?"

"My name is Jennifer Townsend! Yes, indeed! Alfred is my husband."

Chapter 20

Maria's Encouragement

It hardly took a couple of days for the news regarding Mary's encounter with Jennifer to spread around like soft butter upon warm bread. Jennifer's observance of Alfred in the open-air, and on the same occasion the meeting she had had with Mary, became like a headline amongst certain close-knit friends, spreading like wild fire!

First, Mary phoned Dorothy, who in turn told Maria, and since Dorothy resided in the same household as the Petersons, it followed that Miriam Peterson would be the next recipient of the news of that which took place downtown. The effect upon Maria was quite remarkable. She became ecstatic upon receiving Dorothy's informative phone call and immediately conveyed to her father just how his presence at the open-air meeting had caused a stir in the unlikeliest of places. Her excitement spilled to overflowing as she relayed it all to him.

"Yes, Dad! Whilst you were there preaching in the precinct... Well, guess what? Mum was like sat close by listening to you!" she shrieked. "Awesome! Then, you know when Mary Osborne came along with her little Julia and they stopped to speak to you, right? Well, Mum saw you! I bet she wondered who on earth you were talking to. Later, after Mary left you...

well... Mum like grabbed her, didn't she, and started asking her questions about you! Dad! You're becoming a stirrer big time, did yer know?"

"Good gracious, lass! Slow down a bit, will yer?" Alfred had grown slightly pale after hearing his daughter's outburst and seemed to be disturbed by the impact and shock of knowing that his wife had been spying upon him.

"What! Do yer mean to tell me Jenny has been snooping on mi then? What's this about her talkin' behind mi back an' all to Mary?"

"Dad! Don't get in a tiz about it all."

Maria could sense her dad was becoming anxious; to her the whole situation was taken light-heartedly, even humorously, but clearly this was not reciprocated by Alfred.

"It's not what you're thinkin. Mum wasn't spyin' on yer, silly; she didn't even know you were there, did she? Mum had gone downtown, that's all, and happened to see you, right? Get it? I think Mum must have been curious to know who Mary was or something like that, and I gather she spoke with her. Anyway, you'll have to ask Mum about that yourself... or ask Mary when you see her at church. Please don't worry about it, Dad. Alright? Everything will be just fine; you'll see."

Maria had endeavoured to put her dad's mind at rest. She had not realised that her words would be received badly; in retrospect, this was the last thing she had wanted to do—cause him to panic. Her conciliatory efforts with Alfred at least appeared to have had some effect in diffusing the concern developing in his bewildered mind so that he became calmer upon hearing her explanation. Still, he had been shocked upon hearing Maria's news; and this had penetrated deeper within him than she possibly could have realised, leaving behind a mark, an impression that he could not get out of his head no matter how many consoling words Maria could have spoken. Alfred sat himself down and asked Maria if she didn't mind making him a coffee, for he had suddenly found the need to have one.

"Bless yer, lass; a strong cuppa would be lovely. I reckon I need a bit of caffeine in mi blood, havin' listened to you an' all. I were feeling good up to a moment ago; now I feel as if the stuffing has been knocked out of me! I can't believe all this is happenin', yer know. All I was doin' was standing out there in the open-air, minding mi own business!"

Whilst Maria was in the kitchen, Alfred was pondering thoughtfully to himself, reflecting upon all he had just heard. *What will Jennifer think about this? Will she be even more antagonistic towards me in the future?* Alfred had endeavoured to win his wife over in both words and deeds, trying his utmost to please her if he could, and now this had happened! It was like a blow to his stomach.

Maria came in with the coffee.

"Thanks for that, love. What else did Mary tell you about me then? What did Jennifer talk about?"

Poor Alfred was apprehensive about the whole episode; after all, it was his wife enquiring about him, and this alone had sent nervous reverberations down his spine. Her negative attitude towards her husband was still lingering in his mind, and now her opinion could well have worsened after observing him speaking in the precinct. Alfred thought her reaction may be severe, that she was probably thinking what a fool he was making of himself through all his open-air antics.

It was still uppermost in his mind as he recalled the time when Jennifer had visited him when Dorothy was present, and they had all had to listen to his wife's rude outburst and outspokenness. What a to-do that had turned out to be—so much so that Maria had gone upstairs out of the way!

Jennifer had made very clear her attitude and opinions—in the presence of Dorothy—and they were hardly good or edifying. They had been a sort of combination of dismal memories, associated with her legalistic religious upbringing, and blended in with Alfred's misdemeanours of life, which, when combined, were a toxic mixture indeed! Further, to add salt to the wound, Jennifer's mood had been volatile, caused by added stirrings of inner guilt regarding Maria. However, it had to be said that Jennifer had felt remorseful of late about everything, as if her day of reckoning were in progress—though whether this could lead to any reconciliation between the two parties was anyone's guess. It remained to be seen whether Jennifer's recent depressive moods of guilt and regret regarding her past behaviour were a sign of her mellowing to such an extent as to provide the basis upon which changes could happen between them. But her feelings were yet unknown to Alfred, and so to him circumstances were still raw and unhealed, leaving him in fear and trepidation.

Maria saw the anxiety upon her father's face and attempted to reassure him a second time that all would be well.

"Look, Dad, there is nothing to worry about! I'm sure Mary would have told me if she felt that there was a problem… okay?"

Alfred remained untouched by Maria's efforts to console him. As he sat in his chair, he bowed his head in deep thought so that Maria's affection was aroused as she observed his pitiful sight. She knelt on the floor to be next to him, then placed her arm around him and said in a gentle voice, "Don't worry, Dad; I keep tellin' you! Honestly, there is nothing you should be bothered about, yer know. Even if Mum should give you a bit of aggro—and I doubt that very much—you have not done anything wrong. You were still doing a good thing out there in the open-air… like God's work an' all, yeah? According to what I heard from Mary, Mum was interested in what you were saying and didn't wish to interrupt you. That's why she kept it a secret.

"She asked Mary what she thought, and Mary replied, saying only good things about you, like… she thought you were great speaking like you did in public. People need to hear about your leg and what God has done for you, Dad… and that's what you were doing, so don't forget that! At the end of the day, you were doing God's business like you've always told me, yeah? That's what you were doin'!"

Alfred looked up towards Maria in response to her kind, supportive words.

"Yer know what? You sounded just like Dorothy then… except she sounds posh."

"Gee thanks, Dad!"

"I reckon I hear what yer sayin'; even if mum did get a bit rattled, I were still doing God's work. But I hope yer right lass and that she were a bit interested, yer know! I get a lot of stick from some, and I would hate to think she were one of 'em!"

Alfred's contemplations were interrupted by another train of thought, having been diverted upon hearing Maria's words. This time he moved away from what his wife's opinion may or may not have been and thought of the Lord and what

He would say! As if by inspiration, something came to him as he thought about his Lord Who he believed had commissioned him to tell others. Maria was right! This, after all, was what he considered to be his Divinely appointed ministry of a sorts, having read one day in the Bible how that Jesus's last commission for His disciples was to go into all the world and preach the Gospel. From this new conjecture and perspective came light and illumination as Alfred began to see a different picture developing regarding the whole scenario.

Who knows? Maybe Jesus planned and purposed all this for Jenny's sake? Even if she disapproves, I will have to bear it!

Now, Alfred was a simple man and so was his manner in coming to this conclusion. The idea of a coincidence or that some random chance meeting of all parties concerned had occurred in the precinct was considered by him in a different light now that he had experienced the miraculous first hand in his own life. Perhaps the whole scenario was the inexplicable and marvellous hand of God; he dared not think otherwise just in case it was!

This redirection of his thoughts brought to him some release from his burden. Alfred's contemplation that the whole occasion was appointed by God — or certainly at the very least under His control — was of considerable consolation to him. In some cases — and with unbelieving people, perhaps — there would be a different conclusion about the whole matter. They would think it extreme, that his wife was right to be critical of him. To them, Alfred's opinion about himself doing God's work was merely unfounded and groundless; a sort of simple-mindedness prevalent amongst the uneducated, the religious, even the superstitious; a sort of simplicity for which there was no foundation in fact, and consequently, they would not hesitate to belittle opinions of this nature and scorn with distaste those who professed such interpretations.

With others, Alfred's opinion would at the very least be held with reserve, but never with outright dismissal. However, in many cases, where people had themselves experienced God personally in their own lives, Alfred's thinking would be most acceptable.

Maria had by now resorted to changing her posture and had sat down cross-legged upon the floor next to her father; the two were engaged in a heart to heart chat.

"Why are you so worried about what Mum thinks anyway, Dad? You were never bothered before. Can I ask you a question, Dad? Are you feeling bad in yourself suddenly because of..." Maria stopped short. She was about to mention her Mum by name but then hesitated, wondering whether to proceed with what she was about to say. As it was her own mother Maria was about to speak of — and to her mother's husband — she pondered whether it was the right thing or not to talk about such a personal topic. But then Alfred chirped in.

"Look, lass; spill it out. We don't keep things from one another in this house; do we? Just feel free to tell me what you're thinkin'."

"Dad, I was just wonderin', that's all…"

"Wonderin' what?"

"Are you feeling guilty, Dad — firstly because of your past and now this? Is that why you are afraid about how Mum feels? You don't wish to rub more salt in the wound so to speak by getting her even more upset with you. Is that it?"

Alfred rubbed his chin. There was so much included in that point raised by his daughter that would qualify him to feel guilty about many things — and certain aspects of his past were but some of them — so he wondered just what exactly Maria was specifically thinking of! Then he decided not to go down that road and retreated from enquiring any further. Instead he summed up all things diplomatically into one statement.

"You're on the right tracks, lass. Yes, as a matter of fact, I do find it hard to live with what I've done to Jenny — and you too for that matter. But I can't change anything. What's done is done! I keep wondering though whether yer mum will ever come around to forgivin' me… What do you think?"

"We are all different, Dad. I love you, Dad,

and so I forgive all your aggro from the past, but Mum… she has to do this for herself, I guess."

"I feel the time has come now," said Alfred with a distant look on his face as he stared out of the nearby window, seemingly deep in serious thought. "I think I need to see Jenny and have a good chat. We can't go on like this. It just doesn't seem the right thing anymore, yer know — she livin' there with your Auntie Betty and all."

"Well, why don't you arrange it then, Dad? You could see her now if you wanted to."

Maria's wish and prayer for her mum to come back to live within that household suddenly took on new light and hope; for the first time, she had heard her dad intimate that he would like her mum back! She was very excited.

Whilst Alfred resorted back to his melancholy state, once again staring into space, Maria thought of a way to help. She left the room momentarily and reached for her mobile to make a call.

"Hi, sweetie; it's me! Are you doin' anything right now?"

Apparently, judging by Maria's happy response, the recipient of the call seemed completely available and at her disposal.

"Okay… fine; then if you are free, would you come over and pick me up? I'll wait outside the house for you. See you soon. Bye!

"Dad! I'm just popping out for a while. I won't be long though. Will you be alright for half an hour?"

"I'll be just fine," replied Alfred.

Maria left quickly without any further to-do, and after closing the door, she stood outside to wait for her lift. She had waited less than ten minutes when a red saloon drove up. A young man got out of the vehicle and walked over to his girlfriend, who gave him a peck on the cheek.

"Hi, Ian. Thanks for coming. Would you mind taking me over to 49 Caledonian Road? It's just a bit past our church... on the left going out of town. Thanks; that would be great."

"Yep, no problem. I think I know who lives there. Is everything okay then?"

"I'll tell you on the way."

Chapter 21

Agapé Love

Two days later, the Petersons' home was running routinely, just like clockwork, each activity of the morning repetitive and predictable. John had concluded his meditation in the back garden, where he had spent some forty minutes giving thought to the Sunday morning message, and was now walking back towards the open door of the kitchen. Miriam was busy doing the usual Saturday morning chore, preparing a meal for the day. Today they were having Dorothy's favourite, which was a chicken curry, followed by apple pie. Miriam often did the donkey work of meal preparations first thing before life got busy during the daytime. In this way, she could warm them up later for dinner. Meanwhile, Dorothy had not yet ventured downstairs, for it was not quite time for her to do so.

As John approached the door of the kitchen, it was his habit to glance upwards at the rear of the house towards the upstairs bedroom that was at one time occupied by their daughter, Rebecca, but now belonged to Dorothy. The scene was like a replay of a video that captured similar events every week about this time.

As John reached the kitchen, there was a combination of two separate food odours filling the air. The first had already been prepared and was cooling in a hemispherical curry pot with its lid partially covering it, but the second was just coming out of the oven with its freshly baked aroma of pastry; indeed, it caught John's attention as usual, and without exception he would always comment, "What a wonderful smell that is, my dear… apple pie?" And Miriam would then go on to say, "Yes of course, dear husband… Dorothy's special!"

Suddenly, the footsteps of the aforementioned lady could be heard coming down the stairs, having been drawn to the kitchen like iron filings to a magnet. Her delightful morning greeting filled the otherwise still air with its pleasurable and cheerful sound!

"Oh! How wonderful! It's apple pie day once again…!" Dorothy leaned over to smell the pie, which was mesmerizingly pleasant to her.

What would normally follow sooner or later was John's statement towards their adopted daughter — of sorts — enquiring about her previous evening and how she had got on. Friday nights were always particularly special to Dorothy and David, as indeed perhaps with most young couples who were in love, and if anything of any significance was to happen at all, then it had to be on this specific evening. John undoubtedly took it for granted that Dorothy had seen David, so he spoke to her assuming this to be the case with several questions addressed to her all in one breath.

"And how did you get on last evening with David? All is well, I presume... Any date set as yet?"

"Good morning to you too, John!" replied Dorothy cheekily. "And what about you... and Miriam? Did you have a good evening, may I ask?"

Miriam chirped in with a chuckle, "So you see, John, you must give an account too sometimes, hey?"

"Well, of course," replied John cheerfully, thinking to himself that if one can be humorous, then so can two. "Well, we were just fine, Dorothy. After a delightfully romantic cup of English Breakfast tea with arrowroot biscuits, we sat down together. I read the weekend newspaper whilst Miriam did some knitting. How does that grab yer?"

Now, Dorothy could give as good as she got and still feeling light-hearted, decided to follow John's humour with some of her own.

"That speaks wonders to me, John. You know why? Because it shows me that when two people do love one other, then... well, they are quite content to simply sit quietly together enjoying each other's company without any razzmatazz at all necessary!"

"Too right, my dear," laughed Miriam. "Anyway... how are you, my dear? For we never know much about you between Sunday night and the following Saturday morning; such are the demands of work and life. If we are up late, you are out late as well. And if you do happen to stay in, well... we are often too tired and have an early night." Miriam laughed at the irony of this.

"Too true! Too true!" added John. "Well, you tell us only what you wish to tell us, my dear. But you must understand our excitement for you both — ever since your fairly recent engagement and... well... you know... what follows afterwards!"

John had two social qualities that were sometimes of a delicate and sensitive nature to some. First, he was outspoken and frank; second, he could be impertinent and irritatingly nosy, so that if ever the twain should meet he became provocative to even the mellowest of people! Miriam, sensing that her husband had stepped just a little out of bounds regarding Dorothy's private affairs, quickly intervened.

"John! You must not address Dorothy so! Today is her day off, and I am sure she does not wish to begin it by having an inquisition about her personal life first thing in the morning... if at any time!"

"No, no! Of course not," replied John, reacting spontaneously. "There I go again, stepping into forbidden territory. I will shut up!"

Dorothy could be gracious upon most occasions, and this was not an exception. Feeling the awkwardness or embarrassment that John must have been experiencing at that moment and with her not having been overly perturbed in any way regarding his prying remarks, which had been amplified and high-lighted by Miriam, she attempted to reassure him.

"I know you are only interested in the both of us, dear John, so please do not worry about anything you have just said. I am not so sensitive that I cannot deal with remarks of that nature. Why, I get them all of the time at work, so I can assure you I am quite used to it… and it certainly does not bother me one iota."

If Dorothy had tempered the atmosphere by what she had just said in response to John, she completely changed it next by being quite jovial about the whole matter. "But… nevertheless, since it seems you may be interested, you will be the first to know. Currently, a certain event is uppermost in both of our minds, but I cannot tell you how imminent it may or may not be…" she added with a laugh.

"Dorothy, you are too kind, but bless you for that!" Miriam, appreciating how nicely Dorothy had just responded, was also prompted herself to speak graciously in like manner. "And God bless you both for the future you share together!" Graciousness from one can birth further grace in another, and Dorothy had instigated just that!

After breakfast was over, the three were still sitting around the kitchen table drinking their tea—or in Dorothy's case, coffee. Conversation was light as they recollected the events of the past week, and then a certain topic resurfaced and became the next talking point.

"What about Alfred then?" began John. "Why, Mary told us how she met Jennifer Townsend downtown two days ago! And she had been listening to her husband in the open-air! I'm sure that will have interesting repercussions; what do you think?"

"Oh! That reminds me," said Dorothy suddenly, as a certain matter was triggered in her mind. "I hear from Maria that Jennifer is not at all well."

"Oh, is that so?" replied Miriam enquiringly.

"Yes. Maria went to visit her mum the other day, and she is feeling quite low in spirits. Apparently, Maria has never seen her like this before, and Jennifer — of all people — has asked if I could go and visit her today! I had completely forgotten all about it until just now when you jogged my memory, John... I switch off to everything on Saturday mornings.

"Maria phoned me yesterday afternoon at work; she seemed very concerned. The funny thing was that Maria and Ian had driven over to visit Jennifer the day before she was ill with the idea of setting up a meeting between her and Alfred! Alfred is also feeling down in the dumps, so they are both going through the wars at the moment!"

"Goodness me!" exclaimed Miriam. "When it rains, it pours! And just what is troubling Alfred, I wonder? This is most unlike him; he's usually a chirpy soul. Do you know what the matter is, Dorothy? And what you mean by Maria setting up a meeting between them both?"

"Ah, that is complicated, I'm afraid," continued Dorothy. "Maria told me about Alfred; she had a long chat with him. He is having a guilt trip about everything… like his past has come up before him afresh. He has been trying hard to make things right with Jennifer, and… well, he thinks that with her animosity towards God and religion, this episode will only make her feel worse towards him — you know… the situation where she saw him preaching in the open-air. He fears that the outcome may not be favourable."

"But the meeting between them both?" enquired Miriam. "The one you said that Maria was trying to set up? Tell me, was this in fact an attempt to bring reconciliation or something like that?"

"Yes, something like that, Miriam, but I'm not too sure. Well, Maria and Ian drove over to see Jennifer, like I said, and when they arrived at the door, Maria was met by her Auntie Betty who informed her that her mum was not well and had been in bed most of the day! Maria went up to see her, and the amazing thing was that Jennifer was also having a guilt trip… In her case it was about leaving her daughter and not showing enough compassion towards her husband, and ... Oh, it went on and on! And then, Maria said there was sobbing and tears all around; she seems to be far more depressed than Alfred!"

"Well, I don't think that is necessarily too bad a thing, you know — if you don't mind me saying so," added John, who had been listening meticulously to the whole scenario. "Sometimes it takes these things to happen before God can do anything."

"Explain yourself a little more, my dear, if you please," added Miriam, for his statement was too open ended and incomplete for her liking and required much more clarification before Dorothy's listening ears.

"Well, the only way for God to really bless and save us is through our submission and surrender to Him, and some will not do this without being taken to the lowest depths... That's the raw truth that I was trying to say, dear. God loves everyone more than they realise, and He is determined to provide opportunity for them to accept His salvation, even when they are not looking for it. That's what love does! Even in this situation... no, especially in this circumstance, where sickness or despair is involved. Who knows? There could well be present the hidden, invisible hand of God at work. Many people all too often ask the question why, if God is a God of love, he allows these things. But if the truth be known, it is *because* God loves us that He seeks to

draw each one into a relationship with Himself —
a relationship which will last not *just* for time here
and now, but for eternity.

"But if people shun that idea, perhaps God
has no other option but to allow circumstances to
deteriorate, so that when we eventually come to
the end of ourselves, we may just be prepared to
let go and come to God… That is what's at stake!
Dorothy, let us pray together before you go to see
Jennifer that God's will shall be done."

Dorothy did just that, and after praying
with both John and Miriam, she became quite
thoughtful about the whole concept of suffering
and God's involvement. Never before had the
thoughts and implications just raised by John
entered her head. *Did God allow some suffering for
a purpose?* It went without saying that there was
and always had been much pain and suffering in
the world. Dorothy went back in her thoughts to
the creation of all things and remembered many
words preached by John in the past, which were
suddenly foremost in her mind.

Sinful man chose to have his own way
right at the very beginning through exercising his
God-given right of freewill. Rather than obeying
God's Word and commandment, he succumbed
to the vile lies, temptation and beguilement of the
evil one, being deluded by his words and
surrendering to his will rather than that of the
Creator, so that he reaped what he had sowed —
all through that one action of disobedience.

Having made his choice, the whole of mankind became enslaved to a new master. Man's original sin of disobedience and rejection of God's Word was contagious, rather like a disease that is genetically transferred from parent to child, and so it became propagated and transferred from generation to generation through human nature, passed down throughout the whole human race!

It is often said, *'Like father like son,'* or *'They got if off their father or mother!'* It is indeed true that every child born, even though it is unique, has some resemblance to its parents in physical appearance, personality and temperament, as well as in many other complex ways. Every new-born child is born as a chip off the old block, with a hereditary nature from its parents and their parents before them, and so it goes back!

Satan knew that if he could get Adam to choose *his* way of thinking and give credibility to *his* words rather of God's, then allegiance would be attributed and transferred over to him! Adam's children would be under his own control and power.

Therefore, God requires our cooperation if we desire His help. He has secured for each and every one a way of escape from the judgement and condemnation we all came under because of Adam's choice—howbeit at a price! It is a tough decision, involving much struggle; there is a war between good and evil, battling for our very soul, all because of the unbelief and rebellion inherent in the fallen nature we were born with, and with which the enemy of our soul is reluctant to part. The only way for God to legally make His help freely available to every person was to heal the breach that we incurred through our disobedience, a gulf that separated us from His Grace. So, He sent His Son to do just that, to pay the price for our redemption and salvation by bearing all our sin, guilt and rebellion upon himself — the just for the unjust!

Ever since that moment at the very beginning, when man turned to go his own way, we became slaves to sin. Now that salvation has been purchased through the endless redeeming power obtained by God — not by money equivalent to the entire wealth of this world, but with the Blood of Christ — Satan's power has been broken! Even so, a personal surrender of self and will to God is necessary, through repentance, allowing Jesus to be both Lord and Saviour of our lives! Jesus is the only Person who can provide forgiveness and the promise of eternal life; no one else can! It was Jesus who died and paid the price — no one else!

If this is at stake — and indeed it is — then God's priority will not always be the same as ours. I'm quite sure God knows the right time for each one of us, the time when we will best respond to Him. He is longsuffering with each person until then. Only God's incredible agapé love can balance all this with the right time and place! Truly, in more ways than one, man is saved by a God of grace and by that alone; by a God who loves us and who is our only real friend — if we but knew it!

How does God manage it? How does He, knowing full well who and what we are by nature — a people who choose to live independently without Him with insatiable and sinful selfish appetites — draw us to Himself? Why choose a people who so often despise the very thought of His Name with contempt and arrogance, even though the truth is that we are the weakest and most helpless and vulnerable of all of God's creation upon this earth, always a mere step away from death every moment of every day, having no power or control over our lives — not even over a single hair upon our head!

There is an answer; God always has an answer! It can only be described by a word that is never used in literature, except when it is attributed to God Himself, for it is beyond human aspiration and ability to attain it! It is God's love — *agapé* love. An unselfish, unconditional quality of God involving His decision to save us! He will never give up and remains faithful and longsuffering towards us, because Jesus Christ died and rose again! Nothing or no one — not even Satan and all his fallen angels themselves — can prevent this! *He saves to the uttermost all those who come to God by Him!*

Chapter 22

God's Way

Dorothy was about to set out upon a mission to visit Jennifer Townsend, not knowing whether it would have eternal consequences. Given all she had just been pondering regarding the forbearance and foreknowledge of God, who was to say what this occasion would bring? Perhaps this was her time and opportunity.

As she walked down the high street, heading out of town on what would be a good twenty-minute journey, taking her past the church towards Caledonian Road, Dorothy was a little apprehensive about her forthcoming appointment with Jennifer

Her previous two conversations with Jennifer Townsend had both been fractious in nature. Right from the start Jennifer had made her presence felt quite verbally, and she had been most antagonistic towards Alfred, which had taken Dorothy by surprise. Maria had become so embarrassed on the first occasion upon hearing her mother's derogatory words to her father — and especially in the presence of her visiting friend — that ultimately, she could not bear to hear any more and had gone upstairs out of the way. Then, there was the second instance, when Dorothy had been alone with Jennifer and become bombarded by her questions, all of which were asked with negative intonation. Dorothy replayed them in her mind as she walked.

What made you change and decide to go to church, if I may ask, Dorothy? Don't you think you can take religion too seriously — especially for such a young person? You have your whole life in front of you; why get involved in such serious and often morbid, joy-killing religion, I ask you?

Dorothy had been taken by surprise at that time, having never before spoken to a mature lady who held such prejudices and low opinions of the church, so much so that Dorothy had expressed her own limitations quite openly to Jennifer.

Even so, Dorothy had underestimated herself and the impact and influence she was having upon Jennifer, despite the discomfort of the situation she found herself in; hence, the current situation had arisen, where it was Jennifer who had asked to see Dorothy — and not another! In fact, the truth was that Jennifer had been challenged by Dorothy's integrity in all she had said to her in the past, especially her view regarding Alfred's miracle and his faith in God. In her opinion, Dorothy seemed to have good common sense and authenticity and explained things as if she did believe sincerely in what she was saying; she was not fanatical in any obsessive way, and if anyone could advise her — and of necessity that person had to be a woman — then Dorothy was the one!

There was a nice florist on the way to Jennifer's home that always had an attractive parade of flowers outside the shop, and as Dorothy drew near, it immediately caught her eye. *That would be perfect!* she thought. Dorothy went inside and purchased a bunch of freesias, decorated with small light fern and a sprig of lily of the valley.

Within no time at all, Caledonian Road came into view at the next left turn ahead, and turning into it, Dorothy paused and prayed about the imminent meeting. Upon reaching number 49, Dorothy rang the bell, and it was Betty who answered the door.

"Hello! You must be Dorothy! Do come in, my dear, and let me take your coat. Oh! And do mind the step just ahead! That is one handicap of cottages, dear; nothing is straight or level, eh- eh! Do be careful, too, through the passageway, it is quite dark—but again that is normal in these places! Oh! It is so nice to have a visitor and such a beautiful one too. Please take a seat for a while, if you will."

Little appeared wrong with Betty. Her voice and mannerisms were as chirpy and spontaneous as the bird's dawn chorus just as the day was breaking through on a warm summer morning, and Dorothy immediately gathered by Betty's friendly easy manner that, just like the birds, their forthcoming conversation together would be just as energetic, easy and plentiful!

"Now, can I get you a drink to take upstairs with you? Tea?"

"Thank you," replied Dorothy courteously. "Tea would be fine... milk with no sugar, please."

"Oh, my dear," expressed Betty in a voice that had now taken on a more serious, ominous tone, though her light joviality could not be completely hidden even then. "Jennifer has not been at all well, you know... Oh, please relax, my dear, and make yourself at home for a moment whilst I get you your tea if you will; I won't be a minute... In fact, I have never seen her so down, not in a year of Sundays — never mind a month!"

"I am very sorry to hear that," said Dorothy with concern. "And what do you consider to be the problem, Betty? I thought she was quite well a few days back when we spoke together at Alfred's house. Has she gone down with something, do you think?"

"No, I don't think! It's not like that in my view, dear, though I stand to be corrected. No, in my opinion she's not sick in the body but in those places doctors can't easily heal! She's been... well, between you and me, Dorothy — and I feel I can share this with you because you are a good friend of the family from what I hear, so you will know about certain things, I'm sure — well... Jennifer, bless her, has been very troubled lately with her past coming to mind, invading her thoughts with fears like beasts let loose out of the dark dungeons and sent to torment her! There, I shall say no more! Maybe she will tell you herself, but don't say I told yer that, will you?"

Dorothy was vividly reminded of her own past horrors upon hearing this description from Betty and shivered with the impact. Nevertheless, Dorothy was well experienced and equipped to understand and help, if that were the case. The question was, what had brought it about so suddenly with poor Jennifer? It was time to find out.

"Is it alright for me to pop up and see Jennifer now?" enquired Dorothy, ready and eager to carry out the purpose of her visit, having been well primed beforehand—though she was determined not to be influenced by Betty's words but keep them in her heart.

"I'll check if it's alright for you to come up, dear; please wait just a moment…"

Dorothy could hear the clock ticking on the nearby mantle shelf, the room suddenly having been blessed with tranquil quietness for a few moments in Betty's absence. But then the silence was broken when Betty's face appeared again at the bottom of the stairs, "She's just woken up, dear, but she says you can come up!"

Upon reaching the bedroom, having navigated a dimly-lit, narrow, steep and winding stairway that creaked upon every step, Dorothy gently knocked upon the door, then entered the room to find Jennifer sitting up in her bed resting against several cushions and wearing a grubby white night-dress. Her countenance was pale, and her hair, being no longer held together in the usual bun, was strewn haphazardly and erratically so that her appearance was hardly recognisable as the same person entertained by Dorothy a few days previous. She resembled Miss Havisham of Dicken's fame, who forever lay in her bed in remorse; though, unlike her, Jennifer was not bemoaning the disappearance of her fiancé, but was troubled nevertheless! Despite this, Dorothy was surprised to hear Jennifer's lively greeting, and in this respect alone she was clearly the very same person whose assertive manner had not been diminished by a bed of sickness!

"Well, well, well… if it isn't Dorothy McGuire! How very nice of you, dear child, to come and visit an invalid in her bed of sorrow and morbid anguish!" she teased. "Sit down, my dear; do sit down. Why, your tall figure is making my neck stiff gazing up at you there!"

Dorothy smiled. She handed Jennifer her petite bunch of freesias, whose aroma had already been at work permeating the room.

"Bless my soul!" exclaimed Jennifer. "Now you do make me feel like a patient in a sick bed! But forgive me, that sounds ungrateful… Why, they are beautiful! And who told you that freesias were a favourite of mine?"

Jennifer's thoughts were often too quick upon her lips so that on occasions such as this she would correct herself accordingly, realising she had spoken in haste words that could be construed as being most unappreciative. Dorothy took it all in her stride; she was getting used to Jennifer's slight eccentricities and reminded herself of the purpose of her visit so as not to be diverted by unexpected comments.

Dorothy was attentive enough to observe that Jennifer's eyes looked heavy with strain and tiredness, despite her humour and apparent good spirits. With anxiety, Dorothy knew this was a typical symptom, one she was very familiar with. Indeed, the whole scenario reminded her of the many occasions she had felt the same, occasions when she could just not get herself out of her bed of languish and sorrow, being unable to face the day. In retrospect, she recalled how it was all to no avail, lazing like this; her sickness was no doubt not directly related to physical tiredness but probably of a mental nature brought on by something that was continually troubling her and would not relent. Consequently, Dorothy proceeded to ask Jennifer directly about herself.

"Jennifer, I'm sorry to see you're not well. Why, only the other day we were chatting away at Alfred's house; have you gone down with something?"

Jennifer looked at Dorothy seriously for a moment as if contemplating how she should respond to her question. She was aware of the trouble Dorothy had gone to in visiting her. It was most unparalleled, she thought, for a young person to call and see someone elderly these days — particularly someone who wasn't family or a close friend — and she knew further that Dorothy was not a person to be trifled with for very long with meaningless conversation; soon enough she would come to the point, and Jennifer considered it time to do so herself.

"My dear, Dorothy, I asked to see you in person for a reason you know. Ever since I first met you and learned just how much you had influenced and helped my Maria for good — and of late my husband too — I knew straightaway that you were a caring and responsible person who thought outside of herself, a quality very rare in the selfish world we live in, I'm sad to say. And with you being so very young…! Well… you put me to shame, my dear!"

Jennifer went on to speak openly and frankly with Dorothy and re-iterated once again similar words to those she had already spoken on the previous instance that they were together — howbeit, at that time and upon that occasion, it had been in a most condemnatory fashion and had included a venomous denouncement of her own specific religious upbringing.

She began by explaining her own childhood and continued right up to the present time. Dorothy was pleasantly surprised to hear everything said this time without sarcasm, remorse or criticism. Instead, Jennifer was far more penitent in her manner and far less judgemental in her attitude. She presented her discourse and life-reflections with humility and openness, not blaming every Tom, Dick or Harry for her troubles, and consequently, inevitably made herself vulnerable by confessing personal things that in theory could be used against her in an unscrupulous way. But being assured that her friend was not of that category and that Dorothy was a woman of substance and virtue who knew her Maker, and realising that confession was good for the soul, she proceeded to tell all — not just the circumstances surrounding her life, but also details and facts, even to the point of sharing some of her innermost feelings and guilt.

Dorothy was again reminded of her own situation at the time when she had first ventured into pastor John's church and had sat solemnly before Miriam, giving her an account of her own life. Now it was hard to believe that the current situation she found herself in was reversed; she was the one listening to another's life experiences — and someone much older than herself. It was not expedient, therefore, with such an age gap between Jennifer and Dorothy, for the former to share or disclose revelations about herself that were deemed to be too intimate or personal for Dorothy's young ears, so that she kept a wise balance between some nitty-gritty, personal details and all the feelings and emotions associated with them. However, the crucial part of Jennifer's disclosures, involving her guilt and regret towards both her daughter and husband, she did manage to unveil freely, for they were the culprits most relevant to the cause of her troubled state of mind—and these two alone had largely contributed to her current poorly condition. As a direct consequence of her willingness to address these issues by bringing them openly into the light, it proved to be beneficial to both parties.

Dorothy could empathise with Jennifer's situation regarding the difficulties she had confessed, being quite familiar with distress, due to her own childhood situation of abuse, despite this being a vastly different scenario when compared to Jennifer's situation. These two demons of guilt and regret were common factors in so many peoples' problems; they were without respect of persons and mercilessly clung to the soul like leaches from the miry swamp from which they came. Yes, in these two matters alone, Dorothy's own knowledge enabled her to be supportive and comforting, for she could testify of her own victorious experiences of being delivered from both!

"I confess, Jennifer, that in my own life I had to go through great torment and difficulties, too, before I came to know the Lord personally. And yet, ironically, whenever I do look back, even though it was as bad as it was, I see that all my problems were strangely beneficial, for ultimately, they brought me to a place where I could find God as my Saviour and friend! I agree it was very tough; it was not pain-free... I mean, I suffered quite dreadfully from depression and oh-so-much more as well.

"But I have recently come to realise that sometimes it takes a desperate situation in life for us to find Him! It's rather like He's standing there alongside each one of us all the time, but we don't bother to turn to Him until... well, until we *must* do so. Like it's our very last port of call, if you know what I mean. It does seem to take the unpleasant and adverse circumstances that we find ourselves embroiled in to persuade us to eventually look to Him and hope for His help and intervention. It's in times like these that we can see God for who He is — a Saviour who wishes to save and rescue us! His outstretched hand, reaching towards us in those unpleasant times and situations, requires only one simple response — to take hold of it!"

"Oh, dear Dorothy! I did not know you had suffered from depression, child!" cried Jennifer, having been taken by surprise at this disclosure and welcoming the opportunity to change the direction of the conversation.

"How awful! Are you alright now, my dear?"

"Thankfully... yes... I am," said Dorothy, intimating in her manner of reply that her suffering had indeed been a great ordeal, lasting over a long period. "Have you suffered in that way yourself, Jennifer?"

"Rarely, my dear. I experienced something the doctor called post-natal depression years back... you know, after Maria was born... and *that*, I can tell you, was horrible! But since then..."

Jennifer paused momentarily, looked Dorothy in the eyes and admitted, "Well, I have never ever had such an experience since then... until now that is! I must say that I'm currently feeling its pangs and waves in a similar ghastly way to then, and I know what has brought it on; like I told you earlier, I've been very worried and stricken with guilt of late about Alfred... and my daughter and..."

Jennifer became overcome with a spell of fleeting sorrow, exhibiting deep grief and pain in her countenance, so Dorothy remained quiet for a while and sought to remind herself what she would have done at such a time as this. She remembered very clearly how it was necessary to think about something positive — something, if possible, that could divert her attention and all the negative thoughts in her mind towards something or someone else. Anything would do.

It did occur to Dorothy that Alfred was himself unhappy with the very same circumstance of being estranged from his wife, and she wondered if Jennifer was aware of this.

Dorothy took a leap and decided to bring up that very point.

"Jennifer, I have to tell you that Alfred is quite upset himself and seems troubled. Did you know about that?"

"What do you mean, Dorothy? What is Alfred bothered about now, may I ask?"

Clearly, Dorothy thought, *I have hit a nerve.*

"Oh! Only that he said so; that's all."

"Come now, dear; you are holding out on me. He must have told you something as to why he was upset, though I find this all very hard to believe. You surprise me! Alfred never gets troubled about anything — other than his leg, that is. But well, I suppose it wasn't that... so what was it? Please tell me!"

Now, Jennifer was also holding some information back from Dorothy, quite deliberately, regarding her knowledge of her husband's disposition of late. Much had been communicated to her by Maria when she had purposely visited her mum as a mediator between her parents, attempting to set up a meeting between them to allow them to reconcile their differences. Upon this occasion, Maria had mentioned quite emphatically how Alfred desired to see Jennifer and was troubled about their separation.

Dorothy felt awkward upon hearing Jennifer's direct question and hesitated over just how to answer it.

"Jennifer, Alfred was quite remorseful it seemed about... Well, how can I say, for the matter is of a personal nature? But suffice it to say that it concerned you both, regarding... the domestic situation at home. I believe that was it... or something of that nature. I'm afraid I don't know actual details!"

"Yes, I must confess, dear, that Maria told me as much as well," admitted Jennifer. "I just wanted to hear your side of the story, too. Please forgive me, but both of you are saying the same thing, so it couldn't have been my Maria up to her tricks again! Well, I'll be! It seems we both really are bothered about the same thing, after all," laughed Jennifer.

Dorothy wasn't exactly sure what had happened just then, but one thing was for sure: Jennifer appeared to have a spark of light in her countenance from that moment on, and her depressed state seemed to take a turn for the better!

Now seemed a good time to leave, thought Dorothy, and she prepared to say goodbye. Just as she got up to depart, Jennifer called Dorothy to stay and asked her to please sit down again for a moment; there was something she wished to say to her before she left.

"Dorothy, before you go, I would just like to say how grateful I am that you took the trouble to come over. I am feeling so much better already; so, you see, you have been a tonic to me!"

Jennifer beckoned Dorothy over by her bedside to be close so that she could quietly whisper in her ear without anyone else—namely her sister—listening.

"What was it that led you to change and come to the Lord like you did? To me, it seems like you must have always been an upright sort of person. I appreciate you have suffered terribly in the past; who wouldn't have in those dreadful circumstances? I cannot imagine what it must have been like for you growing up with all of that hanging heavily upon you... But even so, for a person so young as you, what was it that caused you to change and believe in God?"

Dorothy smiled and welcomed Jennifer's forthright question; to be upfront, direct or outspoken was Dorothy's forte, and the opportunity enabled her to be herself in response.

Dorothy answered Jennifer in one short declaration, "Because I discovered that God loved me for who I was and desired all along for me to have a personal relationship with Him!"

"But it must have been a big commitment," replied Jennifer. "How did you manage all of that? Where did you get the faith to do such a thing? I would like you to tell me exactly what I should do if I wanted to get right with God—just suppose for one moment that I did. I have had religion up to here, but never anything like what you have!"

"You know, Jennifer, a person does not need a lot of faith; if you know God loves you, it is easy. But there is a way we all must come if we wish to get right with God. It is called God's way — not my way, but God's! You must receive Jesus for yourself, acknowledging that it was your sin that He took upon Himself when He died upon the cross so you don't have to face judgment for it yourself!

"I think many people find a problem with this because of their pride; they refuse this way and choose their own way, for example, by leaning upon their good works and assuring themselves they are just as good as the next person. This can never work! What God requires of us now is to believe this... that, yes, Jesus has paid the price, but more than that, to take and receive this gift of forgiveness for ourselves. This is coming God's way, and the Bible says there is no other way. In fact, Jesus Himself said, '*I am the Way, the Truth and the Life; no man comes to the Father except by Me!*'"

"Do you want to know something, Dorothy? We were never told anything remotely like what you have just said, not in my church! I was told we had to do this and not do that! There was none of all this love and forgiveness. To be accepted by God, you just had to live a good life.

"Are you sure, Dorothy? Pardon me, but it does sound too good to be true... like I don't have to do anything!"

"Jennifer, we have to believe and accept for ourselves God's Word — God's account of things! In a way, that is doing quite a lot, for we must agree to God's assessment of the situation as He sees it, when He says, *'It is by faith we are saved and not of works.'* Now, that involves realising there is nothing I can do to save myself! I can't do anything of myself to earn or merit God's favour!

"All the good works in the world can never save you before a holy God; there was no other way, Jennifer! The result of sinning against God was and still is death, so Jesus died for us, bearing upon Himself all our sin. This is literally the case; instead of each one of us dying and going to a lost eternity, Jesus took our place! That's how serious it is!

"You know that verse, Jennifer — John 3:16? I am sure you will have heard it. It says, *'For God so loved the world that He gave His only begotten Son that whosoever believes in Him should not perish but have eternal life!'*"

"Well, I am quite shell-shocked, you know!" replied Jennifer. "Had you told me all this a week ago, I would have been arrogant enough to laugh in your face with disbelief, but I have come to realise recently that you cannot trifle with God... and I believe He is telling me the time has come for me to come down a peg or two. Whatever it is, I just know inside of me that God is saying something to me, something I need to do; I cannot go on like this anymore. That's why I called you in, my dear Dorothy. I need someone to help me!

"Tell me, if all this is true—and, I might add, that I do understand now what you are telling me—I mean, it does makes sense to me, God saving those who cannot save themselves... Now, that is a God of love!

"It's those who think they are good enough and better than others that I can't stand! Why is it then, Dorothy? Why don't people come flooding in to get saved, and... like, take this gift that is free from God?"

"That is a good question worth meditating upon," sighed Dorothy. "Would you care to hear more if I read to you?"

Jennifer nodded her head in approval. No one had ever told her about such things before. Scriptures in the Bible were something you never heard spoken or talked about. Was it because religious people did not want you to hear these things? The statements of Jesus were so simple that ordinary people could understand them; the argument of differing interpretations was void in all these essential truths declared openly by Him. In His day, it was the common people who heard Him gladly; others, mostly religious leaders, had a problem with Him, for He was taking away their livelihood and changing everything.

Dorothy took out the New Testament she carried with her, turned in it to the book of John, chapter three, and read some pointed and challenging words.

"*'And this is the condemnation, that light has come into the world and men loved darkness rather than light because their deeds were evil.'*

"Jennifer, it seems that those who want the truth will turn to the Light, denying themselves and their pride, and will humbly believe and accept exactly what God says—just like a child! That's how it has been in every generation, and today is no different —it is God's Way!"

Chapter 23

The Valentine Card

A certain romantic day of the year was imminent. Whereas Dorothy, his betrothed, received the full works, David Osborne always visited his sister upon this occasion, presenting her either with a bunch of flowers or a special box of dainty homemade chocolates—not forgetting Julia, who received a tiny bouquet of flowers too. True, it was a ritual Mary had grown to expect from her brother each year—and an unusual one at that—but nevertheless, it was most agreeable. Mary never seemed to have the pleasure or excitement of receiving a card or flowers from anyone else on Valentine's day—not since Raymond had gone—so for this reason David stood in the gap to show his appreciation of Mary and demonstrate that she was still loved.

The special morning arrived! Mary collected the post, which still came at the traditional time of day—first thing in the morning. It was the usual large delivery of letters and pamphlets, which all too often were anything but real mail. However, today, upon inspection, one letter stood out conspicuously and immediately caught her attention, for it was pink! Mary's first thought was one of bemusement; it was most unlike David to post her a card, and indeed he had arranged to come over that very morning! Mary's heart trembled with excitement upon opening the letter, which revealed sure enough a beautiful Valentine's card.

Exhilaration hardly abated that morning as the tense but elated Mary mused over the signed initials scribbled down in such a way as to overlap one another, making it very difficult to decipher, and for the next half an hour she racked her brain, going through every eligible male she knew — all to no avail!

Mary remembered the occasions when the origin of her Valentine's card would have been predictable, when Raymond was on the scene in those happy years of their marriage. But that was then! In her heart, she wished the initials could have been R and L, but that would not do; Raymond was no longer hers! Despite all the hurt and pain suffered because of their marriage breakup, not least the impact upon her mental health, she still had feelings for her first and only love.

Mary heard the door to her apartment open and close, followed by the sound of her brother David's voice.

"Hi there, Mary; it's only me."

David entered the lounge and walked over to his sister, passing her a bunch of flowers and giving her a kiss upon her cheek. "Happy Valentine's Day, dear sis! Shall I make a coffee for us both? I'll put the kettle on anyway."

David marched into the kitchen, completely oblivious of the pink card standing upon the coffee table opposite where Mary was sitting — until, that is, when he returned with one Cappuccino and one Americano and sat down on the sofa next to Mary, and the card came into view.

"Mary! Is that what I think it is? My dear Mary, who is your secret admirer then?"

"I really haven't a clue to be honest, David. Look here; can you decipher these initials?"

Upon inspection, David resigned himself to defeat and gave up straightaway, declaring he had no idea what the initials were. "They are such squiggly letters, sis; I confess I haven't any inkling either. But surely you must have some idea... have you not?"

"No. None. It's a mystery!"

"Is it someone from Julia's school? What about church? There are a few I could think of there, I reckon."

Mary stared at her brother in astonishment and surprise. "David, if it were someone from school, then the person would surely be married ...or whatever. And if it is someone from church, then I confess they must be very obscure and elusive — that is all I can say. No, I don't think it can possibly be from anyone in church! Women can tell a look or a gaze, you know."

"Well, to change the subject, Mary... I bumped into Raymond Littleton yesterday, and he informs me that things seem to have gone back to how they were previously with Susan; after a good spell, they've started arguing again."

"That is not a particularly good subject to bring up, David! Not on this day! Anyway, what does that mean exactly? Like, after a good spell? What good spell was that, I might ask? Have they ever had such a thing?"

"Oh! You remember! After Raymond was mugged and Susan visited him in hospital, well… seemingly, they got on very well after that episode. Apparently, it brought them together – for a while, it seems. He told me that they became closer right there in the hospital ward, having talked together openly for the first time… but clearly that did not last very long!"

David began to realise that this subject regarding the life and times of Raymond and Susan Littleton was not altogether edifying or expedient for Mary. Raymond had realised he had needed someone to confide in when things began to deteriorate between himself and Susan, and the person he had chosen was David, being a man of similar age to himself. And since Raymond would always be the father of Julia, David respected Raymond for that reason only. Consequently, David regularly received updates and was knowledgeable of Raymond's domestic affairs, particularly whenever things got serious between him and his wife one way or another.

At this moment in time, David's thoughts and attention where redirected away from Raymond to Mary, having just felt her sensitivity regarding her ex-husband's marital affairs. Upon reflection of his sister's past, including all she had suffered because of Raymond, David suddenly felt unsavoury emotions resurrect within himself.

"What a stupid man! To think that he left you like that, dear Mary…"

David stopped short in what he was about to say. Mary's countenance sank at the sound of that subject again, her eyes gazing disdainfully at her brother as if to say, *Do you have to bring this up again?*

He knew it was a sore subject for her, if not a very delicate and sensitive one, and naturally so. Now, he wished he had not brought it up, and his visage showed his regret.

"Don't trouble yourself unduly about him, David. I realise that he confides in you; that's no fault of yours. In fact, I should hate it to be anyone else quite frankly."

"Mary, I cannot fully appreciate all that you have suffered because of him, and sometimes I can't believe it, you know… like… my remaining acquainted with him like I do, almost as though nothing had ever happened. I feel guilty about that Mary! It is not fair to you! Forgive me just now; it is so easy to forget things — the madness of it all — and I fail to fully appreciate how you must suffer every day, dear sister!"

Mary dabbed her full eyes with a tissue before continuing, "Like I said, David; please don't distress yourself. Julia loves him dearly; we must always remain amicable with him. As difficult as that is, it is the best for her! That's what your dear lady told me, David, if you remember.

"That was Dorothy's advice to Raymond that time you and she met him at *Max's Café*. That occasion seems to have changed things for the better; well, he at least listens and has started to think for himself for a change, so that is some progress, I suppose."

Mary resigned herself emotionally and remorsefully to her estranged situation with utter anguish of spirit, her soul crying out tearfully as she placed her hands upon her bowed face in despair.

"Raymond! Oh, how you have been so blind, weak and immature that you could not see that mother's treachery! Her deceitfulness in bringing you together with her daughter, Susan! How you have been beguiled and seduced by the charms of a rich and impetuous young lady. How you have been used like a pawn in a chess game to bring to fruition a so-called good match in society, so that in recklessly yielding to her mother's deception and scheming, you have now embarked upon and become embroiled in a loveless marriage! And I loved him so dearly, David!"

David comforted Mary in her moment of affliction and distressful reflections. Her own insight into her husband's misdemeanours and foolishness had only worked against her to amplify truths that she had observed and seen afar off, and all she could do now was to muse upon them with torment and sorrow so that her pain could not be soothed or mollified.

David sat next to his sister and held her close to him. Had she beheld his countenance at that instant, she would have observed a flow of tears running down her brother's cheeks as they streamed from his eyes.

"Mary, you are made of strong stuff! Somehow God will make a way for you; I know He will. You have kept your side of the bargain, and I will always be here for you… and Dorothy also! Even when we are married, we will look after you and our little princess."

Mary looked up at her brother with great consolation upon hearing his affectionate and kind words, and in doing so noticed his flushed, reddened eyes.

"My dear brother! Thank you so much for being here for me; I don't know what I would do without you. And I *will* take you up on that offer. When you and Dorothy are married—and it better not be too far away, or I will die of old age waiting for you — then I shall invite you both over to see me and Julia as often as you wish!"

Detecting a sense of relief and strength in his sister's voice, David became diverted and peered again in a dreamlike manner at the pink card standing on the coffee table, the wheels of his mind starting up again with curiosity as to who it could be from. In doing so, certain happenings came to mind that were thus far unknown to Mary, so David started to recount them to her.

"Do you know something, Mary? I hear from Dorothy that Jennifer Townsend may be contemplating a reconciliation with Alfred, much to the delight of Maria who partly helped instigate it."

"Oh! How amazing!" said Mary with delight, as if invigorated by the sound of pleasant news for a change. "And how did this all come about? Any ideas?"

"It seems to have been an accumulation of things," replied David. "And it all began after Jennifer saw Alfred speaking in the open-air one day purely by accident. To cut a long story short, Alfred became apprehensive about his wife watching him, and he perceived that it might have had a detrimental effect upon their relationship, seeing as she is so anti regarding anything to do with God or religion. Now, it turned out that Alfred's presuppositions about Jennifer's reaction were totally unjustified, and in fact, couldn't have been farther from the truth!

Instead of reacting adversely, Jennifer — to the contrary — was challenged by everything and enquired much from Dorothy about the Lord when she visited her the other day! What is going to happen next, only God knows."

"Oh! Dorothy has been at it again!" said Mary with pleasure. "I happened to be there, at the square, David, when this occurred. And I witnessed everything. I spoke to Alfred, and I spoke to Jennifer! Dorothy is amazing when it comes to challenging people about the Lord. I have a good feeling about everything, you know."

"Really, Mary! You didn't tell me about this."

"Oh, I had just been shopping with Julia, to get her some new shoes, when I saw Alfred and walked over to him." Mary laughed at the memory. "I had no choice, really; Julia recognised Alfred, saying she could see grandad. Alfred reminds Julia of Father!

"Anyway, there was another person there as well, a photographer, taking pictures of Alfred. He seemed a very nice young man and started talking to me, wishing to know who I was and how long I had known Alfred."

"Ah! That would have been Jerry Dickson from the *Daily Herald*; Dorothy met him at Alfred's when he came to visit him and gather information about his story. He is writing an article about Alfred, which should be out either this Thursday or next."

"Well, this Jerry Dickson seemed interested in Julia," continued Mary, "and rather cutely knelt to talk to her... Well, actually not so much to Julia, but rather to her cuddly teddy bear. Then, of all things, he asked her if she was going home now to Daddy! Of course, Julia came straight out with it, saying that Daddy does not live at home; he lives with Auntie Susan!"

"Oh dear!" exclaimed David. "Children always let the cat out of the bag like that!"

"Then, as I walked away, who should I see but Jennifer, sitting on a seat not too far away from Alfred? But Alfred knew nothing about it!"

"Amazing; quite amazing!" said David.

"Well, Mary; it won't do; I need to go to the shop now to pick up a few groceries on my way home. Then I have some work to catch up on tonight, which is rather important. So, I will see you again soon, dear sister. Any messages for Dorothy?"

"Yes, David. Can you ask her to come around sometime soon, if she is able?"

"Not a problem. I'll ask her now if you like. Dorothy knows I'm working tonight, so she could be free. Would that be okay? If she were to come over tonight?"

"Ask her to phone me, please. Either way, I can speak to her. Thanks."

"Bye! See you later."

"Bye, David. Thanks for the flowers and… well… you know… for everything."

~~~~~~

Upon receiving David's phone call and hearing what he had to say about Mary, Dorothy decided to call Mary back as requested and then drive over to see her.

The episode was not dissimilar to what had happened when David had arrived to see Mary. David had not told Dorothy about the Valentine's card, only that he had called to see Mary with a bunch of flowers, and she had been very upset about Raymond. Upon arrival, the first thing Dorothy saw was the large pink card standing upon the coffee table.

"Mary, what is this, may I ask?" enquired Dorothy with a cheeky tone to her voice.

"Oh! Not you as well, Dorothy! I've just been over this with David, and neither of us can think who it might be from. Here, have a look at the scribble and see what you can make of it."

Dorothy peered intently at it. "Well, he is not being entirely secretive, otherwise he wouldn't have written even this. Let us look very closely; he has overwritten one initial by another, that's for sure. Do you have a magnifying glass, Mary?"

"Oh, Dorothy! You sound a bit like Sherlock Holmes! Just a moment."

"Don't you have any idea, Mary, who it could be from?" enquired Dorothy.

"That's what David asked. And really, I haven't a clue."

"Think, my dear; think! It may not be a close acquaintance at all — perhaps a fleeting visit from someone. The postman? The milkman?" Dorothy laughed, relishing the mystery more than Mary, but slowly the latter responded with more eagerness and enthusiasm to try and solve it!

"Okay," responded Mary with much greater impetus and motivation. "The only time I could have met anyone at all would have been when taking Julia to nursery, going to the shops, or something like that… You see, I rarely go out at all, and then it is only downtown."

"Well, did you speak to any man on any of those occasions you mentioned? When did you last go downtown, Mary?"

Whilst Mary racked her brain, Sherlock began scrutinising the scribble with a magnifying glass just handed to her by Dr Watson.

"Actually… I went downtown fairly recently, come to think," recollected Mary.

"Well? Did you speak to anyone on that occasion? Did anyone give you the eye?"

"Oh, Dorothy! Ah! Wait… I did speak to a gentleman, you know! Quite a handsome one at that…"

"Go on!"

"Well, actually, I was with Julia, shopping, and we both saw Alfred speaking as he does. But there was someone else with him, a photographer. David told me his name. Just a moment, let me think…"

"Mm, Mary! That person would more than likely be a man I met recently called Jerry Dickson!"

"Why, yes, that's it! That's who David said it was too!"

Sherlock picked up the magnifying glass once again and analysed the scribble, deliberately looking for the initials J and D.

"Mary, what are the different ways of writing the letters J and D?"

At that moment, Mary was shaking nervously but took a pen and paper in response to Dorothy's directive and started writing.

"No!" said Dorothy emphatically. "There are squiggly ways of writing a capital J, and the same goes for a letter D."

Dorothy took the pen and wrote as she continued to speak. For example, you could write

$$J \text{ as } \mathcal{J} \text{ and } D \text{ as } \mathcal{D}$$

which, when superimposed gives what? Something almost illegible!"

"Oh, Dorothy," sighed Mary resignedly. "Can you see what I can see?"

"Yes, indeed!" replied Dorothy. "I do believe this is your admirer, Mary! It could well be... In fact, the more I look at it now, the more obvious it is! It definitely looks to me, Mary, like Jerry Dickson is your man!"

Chapter 24

Troubled and Searching Times

Raymond Littleton had slept upon the sofa that evening, whilst his wife Susan had had the king-sized bed all to herself. Her slim, petite frame did not lend itself to sleeping in such a large bed all by herself; she found it far too cold, and most of the night she had the electric blanket on a low setting to remedy this. On the other hand, there was no such luxury for the one who slept downstairs upon the sofa, and a sleepy figure still lay there, covered by a single blanket and several overcoats, all of which hardly sufficed to keep him warm.

That's how things were in that household at the current time. Ups and downs between the two of them came and receded everyday like the ebb and flow of a tidal river, and since the depth of love and feeling between the two parties was at its lowest, it was true to conclude that their relationship was in retreat—and accordingly, as with all low tides, much debris and rubbish became exposed and visible! It is said in such unfortunate predicaments that 'you have made your bed and must now lie in it'—but even this was a problem for Raymond!

Susan had resorted to her moods of dissatisfaction and boredom not long after Raymond's mugging dilemma had come and gone. For a while they had enjoyed one another's company, ironically with Raymond in a hospital bed and Susan sitting next to it. After Raymond's discharge, they had shared a most romantic evening at home, watching a movie together and consuming fish and chips—but it was all short lived. No sooner had the night ended and a new day dawned than they had resorted back to old habits.

An alarm sounded from Raymond's mobile. The time was 6:30 am. Most people slept deeply during the earlier hours of morning, and Raymond was no exception. He jumped out of a deep, dreamy sleep and managed to get himself up—though not without appreciable effort. In fact, the day ahead promised to be exciting; it was going to be different and challenging. After work that afternoon he would be attending an overnight conference where he was to give a presentation; he would be returning home on the following day, which was a Saturday.

On his way to work later that morning, Raymond desired to call in to see an old client of his who now resided in a care home for the elderly. This residency was largely a result of his painstaking, relentless efforts to instigate and acquire a placement there for her. Initially, the lady had been unsettled in her new home, but Raymond had made sure she had all she needed and of late things were more comfortable for her. The lady in question reminded him of his late grandmother with whom he had been very close, and though it was only an official requirement to visit her once a year, Raymond voluntarily went once a month.

Raymond's choice of occupation had been a sore point with his parents-in-law; to be more precise the animosity came from Susan's mother, whereas her father, preferring to agree amicably with his wife's desires and opinion rather than exerting himself to express his own judgment upon the matter, resorted to keeping his views quiet and hence preserving the peace! To him an occupation, if it were essential, was of negligible importance; name, position and social standing always spoke louder. Even so, Raymond had pursued his heart's desire to provide help and care for the elderly upon the death of both his grandparents on his father's side. As a senior social worker, he was in a good position to do this.

Upon arriving, all the residents were up and seated in readiness for breakfast in a rectangular TV lounge with comfortable easy-chairs situated around three sides and a large TV located along the fourth. Now, the lady that Raymond had come to visit was Nancy, and her usual chair in a corner of this lounge was currently vacant, so Raymond went to enquire of the nearest care worker as to her whereabouts. He thought it most likely that she was still being prepared to come down.

"Hello! Where is Nancy? Is she on her way down, do you know?"

The care worker was very young and hesitated to answer Raymond, but instead gave appearances of not knowing where the lady in question was. She turned and walked over to a senior and spoke to her about the matter.

A lady wearing a smart, distinguished blue uniform walked over to speak to Raymond in person, "Oh! Hello, Raymond. Have you come to visit Nancy?"

"Yes! Indeed, I have. How is she?" Curious to know whether anything could be wrong, he asked, "Is she not well?"

Speaking quite soberly and professionally the lady said, "Raymond, you obviously haven't heard, but Nancy passed away in the early hours of the morning, I'm afraid. She had been poorly since the last time you came and was slowly deteriorating. We were surprised that she went so quickly; it was quite sudden and unexpected."

The news of the sudden death of Nancy impacted Raymond inwardly, though in conversing with the senior staff member in the care home he manifested no emotion or sentiment and merely spoke with professional rhetoric that bore no resemblance to his deeper feelings.

"Oh! I see. I am so sorry to hear the sad news. Her sister has been informed, I suppose? Do you know who will look after everything for her?"

"Well, that is a good question, Raymond. I believe she had an insurance policy, which we are investigating right now, but I gather her sister will not be able to organise funerals and such since she is eighty-eight herself and in no state to do so!"

"I would appreciate it if you could keep me in the loop about when the funeral is," replied Raymond, revealing some concern. "And if there is anything I can do to help, just call me at work."

"Thank you, Raymond... We will keep you in the loop."

Raymond left the care home feeling very empty and sad. He turned around to glance at Nancy's room in passing, then breathed in deeply and carried on walking towards his car for the final part of his journey to work.

It was, of course, common place for at least one resident to pass away each week, and Nancy's number had finally come up! This statistic, however, was of no consolation; every person was just that, a person—and if one loved that individual, it was a different ball game altogether!

Raymond got into his car and immediately leaned over the steering wheel, resting his head in his folded arms as the reality of the sad news came home to him. The thought of never being able to see Nancy again came over him with anguish of spirit, so that, finally, emotion aroused within him uncontrollably, and a single teardrop emerged, trickling down his right cheek.

Raymond could not face going to work at that moment; he felt he just needed to call to see someone else first. *But it might not be possible. She may not be home. She may have already gone to nursery school!* he thought.

His impulsive desire was to visit his daughter, Julia, at all costs — as though it were his last opportunity on earth to do so. But all reasoning and rationality considered that idea to be inappropriate and irregular without any notice or previous arrangement — not the least because he no longer lived in that home! Wisdom and propriety were both absent, as were his fears regarding possible repercussions from elsewhere, all of which he considered irrelevant under the circumstances. An extra wave of disapproval by visiting his ex-marital home would be virtually negligible against the backdrop of the serious storms and tornadoes he was facing at home! Raymond, however, was not being rational; he was being erratic, disregarding all thought concerning anyone else. And so, he reached for his phone and made a call.

"Mary! It's me. Has Julia been taken to nursery yet?"

"Raymond! What? Why are you asking? No, Julia is still here with me; we are about to leave very soon. What is the matter, Raymond? Is everything okay?"

Mary's first reaction to the surprise call was that perhaps Raymond had been arguing with Susan and they had fallen out — yet again!

"I am basically okay," replied Raymond. "I was wondering if I could just pop over for a moment, if it's not too inconvenient. I realise it's a bit irregular, but I have just received some bad news. I will tell you about things later if... that is... you don't mind me dropping in. I just wanted to say hello to Julia; that's all."

"It's alright for you to come over, David; of course it is, but... it is a bit irregular like you said, isn't it? Anyway, you're welcome, provided it's okay at your end! Wait just one moment; I'll find out from someone if they desire to see you so unexpectedly...Ju-li-a! Would you like to see Daddy before you go to nursery?"

"Y-e-s!" came the cry through Raymond's mobile, indicating an answer in the affirmative.

"Okay! See you soon," Raymond replied.

~~~~~~~

When Raymond arrived, he entered the flat looking quite flustered and stressed, but then a little girl ran towards him with open arms, shouting his name, and that enabled him to forget about himself. He knelt, opening his arms to greet her, then lifted her up for a big cuddle and a kiss.

No sooner had he got inside than Raymond noticed a carafe half full of coffee and wondered whether to ask for a drink. *Or would that sound rude or too imposing?* he thought.

He needn't have worried. Mary, being quite observant of these things, couldn't help but notice his eyes peering in a certain direction, so she immediately asked Raymond if he would like a coffee. Upon reflection, Mary remembered that Raymond always liked a strong coffee first thing in the morning.

"Mary, you are so kind! Please forgive my impertinence in dropping in on you like this."

"Oh, Raymond! Sit yourself down, and I'll get you some coffee; I just need to warm it up in the microwave. You look quite tired; I don't know what you have been doing, but... you look very tired."

"Oh! Thank you for that," said a grateful Raymond, receiving his coffee. "You remember my longings for a drink first thing."

Raymond found himself very comfortable and at ease in Mary's presence and proceeded to open his heart a little to her.

"Well... actually, I am feeling a bit weary at the moment. I didn't sleep too well last night, but that's not the real cause. I have just heard some bad news this morning, and... well... I just needed to get away somewhere for a while."

"Bad news!" exclaimed Mary with a mixture of both shock and surprise. "What sort of bad news?"

"Oh! It's Nancy! She passed away this morning; that's all."

"Raymond, I'm so sorry to hear that, but — pardon me for asking — but who is...who was Nancy?"

"She was a client of mine, and I got her a placement in the care home. I used to visit her every month, you know. I became quite attached to her, really; she reminded me so much of Grandma, and we used to chat together for hours. But... everyone has to go sometime, I suppose!"

"Well, Raymond, she obviously meant a lot to you, and I'm sure she will have been very grateful for your care and all you did for her."

"Thank you for that, Mary. Like I said, I just needed to get away for a while and get my mind off things before heading off to a busy day at work. What better way, I thought, but to come and see Julia as you were so nearby — and, of course, to see you too, Mary. I am sorry to have delayed Julia in going to nursery; I really think I should get going."

"Oh! Sit down, Raymond. We are fine. Julia will miss her breakfast, but that is not a problem; she's already had toast and two Weet-a-bix!

"So... how are things with you, Raymond? I do hope your calling here like this will not cause trouble... you know... at home!"

"Oh! Mary, that would be the least of my problems even if it did; it would be like a drop in the ocean!

"Anyway… thank you so much. I have so enjoyed the coffee and… your company, but… it won't do; I must get going now."

Raymond stood up to go, but before leaving, he gave his daughter one final kiss and again thanked Mary for her hospitality.

"Bye, Mary; see you again. Bye, Julia. Have a nice day! Bye!"

As he walked towards the door, Raymond turned one more time to look at Mary and smiled warmly at her; nevertheless, even his smile could not conceal his countenance of melancholy. Just as he was about to continue again towards the door, he noticed a red card standing on the sideboard. It was a Valentine's card!

"Oh, Mary! A Valentine's card! Is this… is this yours? I guess it must be."

"It's mine, Raymond."

"I suppose you know who sent it; do you?" enquired Raymond.

"Well, I'm not too sure, but… I think I know who it is."

"Oh…well…" Raymond resigned himself, realising he couldn't press the situation any further. He tried to put on a brave face and make an acceptable if not indifferent reply upon hearing Mary's news, though it did not take much for a person to recognise that he was clearly jolted and inwardly saddened by the possible revelation that Mary could well be moving on with someone else.

He simply replied, "Good for you. Good for you, Mary... Goodbye."

Raymond walked towards his car, feeling sullen for a second time that morning as his heart began to sink again. However, upon this occasion, it felt far worse than the previous! If the first had been disturbing news, this latter revelation was a major devastation; if the first was a dismal affair, this was in comparison a tragedy of infinite proportions!

It was not proving to be a good day thus far for Raymond! Upon reaching his workplace, he was greeted by unexpected news that was both good and bad; the conference had been cancelled! Too many speakers where off ill, and it had been decided to postpone it until further notice. In some respects, Raymond was pleased with the change of plan; it meant there were no arduous preparations for him to do. This was useful, for already he was feeling tired and weary. The only drawback was that he had been looking forward to getting away from home — if only for a couple of days — but that was not to be.

The remainder of the day at work was an effort, with his mind preoccupied by two disconcerting events; uppermost in his thoughts was the matter of Mary and a certain someone unknown to him who seemed to have come upon the scene. *Will this lead to anything?* he wondered. *This thing with Mary and her admirer?*

Of course, it was none of his business; his opinion was irrelevant. But then why did he feel the way he did regarding the matter?

After work, he could not venture home straightaway. Susan was not expecting him. Instead, he walked towards town, and his first port of call was a Chinese restaurant. Upon ordering a meal and wine, he became irritable and dissatisfied with it. Why did the food seem so mediocre upon this occasion? Why did the wine taste like rubbish? The truth was he was conscious of these inadequacies only because there was nothing or no-one else to preoccupy him, for he was quite alone; any other time the situation would have been just fine. He considered that a second wine might do the trick, but then changed his mind and asked for a whole bottle instead.

The late afternoon soon became early evening, and as he became increasingly intoxicated, he developed a philosophical and thoughtful state of mind. He considered that to be alone in life was probably the worst scenario ever. It felt dreadful; it surely was not meant to be! Raymond recollected listening to Mary one evening reading a Bible story about Creation to Julia, and God had said that it was not good for man to be alone. *He's right there; that's for sure!*

thought Raymond, uttering the words under his breath.

Raymond realised only too well that he had played the fool in conceding to marry Susan—by yielding to her mother's scheming—and in short had simply been far too senseless regarding the whole affair! If the feelings of his heart were a reliable source—and increasingly he concluded within himself that they were—he had not just acted recklessly in his past actions, but he had turned away from a virtuous woman who was above all things faithful, loving and kind. And now he must bear the consequences of his own reckless and wayward behaviour by suffering from the aftermath of his error with torment and regret! The grass was not greener on the other side; the forbidden fruit did not taste nicer than that which he had had!

As Raymond sat there, alone in the restaurant drinking wine, his own heart told him a story loud and clear, and drink opened its door.

How stupid I was not to recognise this at the time! Yes, Mary is a very simple-minded person, with no great aspirations to be anything or go anywhere other than to keep her home and love her child and... as she would say, follow the Lord, but she is such a wonderful being of natural beauty and kindness that transcends and radiates through her simple dress and appearance something far more substantial and precious than skin deep make-overs! How I have been beguiled into thinking that position and status were so important! All that glitters is not gold! Now I would rather live in a modest dwelling with such a person as I once had than endure this horrible, loveless life of a superficial, self-consuming and lonely existence!

Oh, Lord, give me back the simple life I once had, instead of all this revelry. Better is a dry morsel with quietness than a house full of feasting with strife! I have made my bed... now I must dwell in it! Where can a man go to escape from his heart? Is there any hiding place where his heart will not follow? Oh! How painful is the realisation of what I have lost! It is more than I can bear!

Poor Raymond! By many, he would not be considered with such a generous sentiment as this, for it assumes he deserves pity for his current plight and state of mind, but life can reward rashness with troubles that must be borne; what a man sows that shall he reap! Instead, a more forthcoming and appropriate comment would probably be that he deserves all he has got for abandoning his lovely wife!

Raymond recalled a previous occasion, not too long ago, when he had consumed far too much wine, wallowed in a remote part of town in a drunken state, got mugged, and ended up in hospital, and realised this ought not to be repeated. In fear, he asked for the bill and set out to depart. Upon entering the cold, dark evening air, he seemed as if he were walking into a spin-dryer. He was dizzy, reeling helplessly, his head spinning round and round like a Catherine wheel. In desperation, he grabbed hold of a lamp-post, which by all appearances seemed to be moving directly towards him. Raymond hung on to it just in time and breathed in deeply so as not to pass out.

Recollections returned vividly to his mind of the previous time he had been in such a plight, but he calculated that this time it was not so severe. In truth, he had consumed the equivalent quantity of alcohol that evening as on the former occasion, but his susceptibility to its effects had increased somewhat with familiarity so that his body was more used to it!

Raymond was staggering along, keeping to the pavement quite well under the circumstances, when he felt a little nauseous. He moved himself away from the public eye to a nearby alley, where he vomited up much of what he had been drinking plus other things as well. Feeling substantially relieved, he stumbled forward at a steady pace and, surprisingly, managed to walk inconspicuously past the crowds.

He sat down upon a bench to wipe himself down and to make sure of his whereabouts. He was about one mile away from home by his calculations, but the walk, he imagined, would be beneficial for him and help sober him up before meeting Susan. Passing by a hotdog stall, the smell invited him to purchase a jumbo sausage in a bap with onions, ketchup and mustard, together with a can of Coke. He had suddenly obtained an appetite upon emptying his stomach and could think of no better way to satisfy that need than by indulging in some real food. One of Raymond's weaknesses was the smell of frying onions. The taste was superior to his previous, more expensive cuisine, as was demonstrated by the fact that it was utterly consumed — or rather decimated — in its entirety within the space of one minute.

Back on his journey home, having decided it would be too risky under the circumstances to consume another hot dog, he saw around him young people happily walking in the opposite direction, clearly looking forward to a Friday evening out. It was surprising to him, however, that they were mostly attractive girls with no partners! At least they were not alone but were in the company of others.

God help them find a good man who will treat them differently to how I treated a certain lady, thought Raymond, incriminating himself with this self-inflicted reproach, having felt a genuine compassion for the needs of others and realising the danger to society of men such as himself! Raymond tormented himself again with remorseful thoughts. *Oh! If only the tape of my life thus far could be edited and the errors of the past eradicated, destroyed and eliminated forever!*

Almost twenty-five minutes had elapsed when the view of his destination in the distance caused him to tremble. All the lights appeared to be switched on, both upstairs and downstairs, and upon approaching the house he could hear thumping music emanating from inside.

Surely not! he thought. *Susan usually goes out to party on Friday evenings… but that's when I am home!*

Raymond stood in his tracks for a moment. *I could do without this!* he thought.

Boldly he entered his dwelling—for indeed that's what it was; it was he who paid the mortgage! Upon opening the front door, a sight resembling a New Year's Eve party confronted his eyes. There was rowdy jesting and drinking, and some people were dancing. He waded through them, hardly being noticed; his presence was assumed to be that of another party-goer.

Where is she? thought Raymond. He restated his question, this time speaking it out aloud to some unknown lady nearby.

"Where is Susan?"

"Oh! Hello, darling! Where did you come from? I've not seen you before… Susan, my dear, is… I do believe upstairs, but… I'm so sorry… she is taken!" responded the lady with a laugh.

Raymond shot up the stairs, looking for his wife. Coming to their bedroom and finding it locked, he kicked the door several times until finally it burst open. The scene before him was an unbelievable sight to his horrified eyes! Turning around without saying a single word, Raymond proceeded back downstairs and went outside to make a phone call.

"David, it's me... Raymond. Can I stay at your place tonight?"

Chapter 25

Mary's Contemplations

Though it was quite late in the evening, it was by no means one well spent. This was a Friday night, and it was still young — well, for many that is. But not for a certain gentleman, standing alone under a street light, putting his mobile away in his pocket having just made a call. His day had been far too eventful, and now he was tired and weary.

Three woes had visited him that day. The first had brought dismay leading to despair, when the news of the one he had considered as his second grandmother, dear Nancy, had passed over to the other side.

The second woe had sounded like a trumpet heralding in his imminent judgment after his eyes caught sight of a Valentine's card in a home that had once been his abode, the effect of which had pierced his very soul with remorse and regret for ever leaving his pure innocent first love and wife. He had succumbed to the subtle cunning of a Delilah who cared for nothing but her own selfish pursuit of pleasure and dissipation, one who had lured him into her clutches for his wealth and standing in society, and in so doing had cut off whatever air of self-respect and uprightness he may have had, leaving him demoralised, destitute of all purpose—and all for being such a naïve, immature fool!

The third woe had driven the final nail in his coffin as he had witnessed his wife unashamedly in the bed of adultery before his very own eyes—and at his very own house during a weekend when he wasn't supposed to be there!

Out on the streets that evening, young people were moving downtown together in small groups of two or three, dressed in what would appear to be party gear. The occasional sound of spontaneous raucous laughter from some joke or another expressed by one to the rest of the troupe travelled through the air. The young man simply glared at them with envy that they at least had something to jest about!

He sat down upon a wall, waiting for his ride. He appeared troubled and deep in thought, holding his head sporadically in his hands. Then, he would stand up and walk a few steps away, only to return to his original posture upon the wall again.

Raymond Littleton had no appetite or desire to sleep in his own bed that night. Having just finished conversing over the phone with David Osborne, requesting his help, he now felt awkward and embarrassed by his actions. It had been the second embarrassing situation he had experienced that day, the first being his untimely visit to see his ex-wife and daughter in their home without notice and warning.

As it happened, David and Dorothy had called to visit Mary that evening, and at the exact instant that Raymond had phoned David, Mary had just been recounting the antics of her ex-spouse that morning to her two guests.

"Oh dear! You will not believe this," interrupted David. "That was Raymond just now; he's asking to stay at my house this evening."

"Oh! Goodness me!" exclaimed Mary. "There must be a problem of some sorts, though it's not too hard to imagine what it's about, I'm sure!"

"What was the reason, David? Did he give any?" enquired Dorothy.

"He didn't tell me all the details, just that there was a serious situation and he would explain later—though he did say he was okay. Look, ladies, I'd best go and get him and take him over to my place if that is okay with you all. I don't have much choice, do I? I think I'll settle him down, then come back here, Dorothy, to take you home; would that be all right?"

"W…ell. Okay then, Davy; you had better go, and… Well, see you later. Take care."

No sooner had David left than the two ladies continued with the same conversation that had been interrupted by Raymond's phone call.

"So…," Mary drew her breath and continued at the place where she had left off.

"Raymond came over about… just before nine o' clock, I think it was, and immediately went over to Julia and gave her a hug. Bless him!"

"Hmm… do you really mean that, my dear?" said Dorothy.

"Do I really mean what?"

"Well, your desire to bless such a person as Raymond! It was not that long ago when you didn't have a single pleasant word to say about him!"

Mary went on to explain her feelings about him regarding his situation. "I understand what you mean, Dorothy, but… of late, I've begun to think to myself quite differently about Raymond. If you'll allow me to explain…

"It's not that I like what he has done to me — most certainly not! Were I not who I am, I would surely say that what he did was unpardonable, and I would still be angry and bitter — perhaps like some others in my situation… the victim who has done nothing wrong!

"Of late, I have noticed many changes, you know… in Raymond — how he has behaved and spoken to me, how he has visited me even at the expense of infuriating Susan. He had no reason to do so, except… that he may have… perhaps… recognised where his bread was buttered…" chuckled Mary.

Now Dorothy, upon hearing Mary's comment, couldn't help but join her friend in hilarious laughter, though she was still curious about Mary's current light-hearted attitude concerning her assessment of the so-called new Raymond. Dorothy pressed ahead to find out more from Mary, seeking to ascertain her thoughts and whether she now felt differently about other things to do with Raymond as well.

"Oh, Mary! How is it you can laugh about such things? You are quite amazing — and funny too! But surely, if I have heard you correctly, do I gather you have forgiven Raymond for what he did?"

Mary pondered Dorothy's question deeply for a while before answering, as if searching her heart, looking for the truth somewhere amongst all the memories of hurt and trauma. Her health issues had now been healed, it was true; over much time and with help from many directions, her life had been restored again to normality. Financial changes had also come her way, improving domestic circumstances substantially, thanks to Raymond's recent unexpected insistence upon paying her far more money than he was required to. And yet, in all of this, his own home-life was degenerating.

"Dorothy, it is increasingly obvious to me that Raymond is not as mature and responsible as I originally thought him. He is more of a… a prize jerk! Forgive him…? What can I say? You ultimately know very well, Dorothy, the answer to that, for we are both like-minded about forgiveness, I am sure. Perhaps I am not like some people; I forgive him just as the Lord's prayer requires. You know? Where it says, *'Forgive us our trespasses as we forgive those that trespass against us.'*

"Yes, as hard as this is, of course I can forgive Raymond, because God has forgiven me. And, therefore, it takes the onus off my shoulders and releases me.

"But as for Raymond? He is now trying to do the right thing by me it seems… in his own way… though it is far too late, of course. But I believe he is going to have to forgive himself for all his foolishness and move forward in his life. He really looked anxious and a troubled man when I saw him this morning, I do have to say."

Mary stared thoughtfully, as if meditating upon her memories, all of which were water under the bridge now, but nevertheless had suddenly resurged into her mind once again with the current conversation, which had the effect of exposing deeper hidden feelings from her heart.

"What did he see out there, Dorothy? What was he thinking he would find? Was it like an illusion? You know, a perfect sort of utopia of happiness with Susan? Did he think of pursuing it to be self-gratified but find when he got there that the image had moved farther away from his grasp, disappearing somewhere else — that it was all a figment of his imagination, that it was not real, that it did not exist? And so, did he end up sacrificing whatever self-respect and integrity he once had and blow everything away upon the altar of his own foolish stupidity?

"Did you know, Dorothy, that behind it all was a conniving plot of returning Raymond to the aristocracy and elite status of his parents and Susan's family — to which he did not really, in spirit, ever belong? I don't know whether you knew this."

Tenseness filled the air at this point, and Dorothy drew closer to Mary and held her hand, perceiving she was becoming emotional.

Mary continued. "He did not know it, but in becoming a social worker, he had already opted out of the sphere in which he was born and become a lesser figure in their eyes. It was also an affront to their pride for Raymond to degrade himself by marrying a simple mortal such as I... so they decided to plot against me and secure Raymond back into their fold — via Susan of course. And sadly, they succeeded!"

Mary's tone of voice and expression had degenerated into that of a remorseful figure who felt slighted because of her perceived inferiority. Dorothy immediately sought to rectify her thinking about such matters as being totally and utterly untrue.

"Mary, do not be affronted in this way by them! If this is as true as you say it is, then they will one day bear the fruit of their actions and live to regret what they conspired together to do to you. I do not know of any other person with greater integrity of character and virtue as you, my dear. And you are a most wonderful and kind person! These attributes carry far more weight than their so-called elite society.

"So, please do not bemoan the opinions of such people who cannot see farther than their own prejudices and self–delusion! I mean... as if wealth and position in life have any bearing whatsoever upon the character and nature of a person! They certainly have no standing whatsoever before God Who judges all people without respect of persons!

"Susan is not all the glitter and gold that Raymond imagined. Far from it! Is he not a most unhappy man as you have just described a moment ago, and all because of leaving you and Julia? True, he has been chasing an illusion that did not exist, but now he is finally seeing the truth! What he saw was not real; what he had imagined was deception at its highest level... And yet, for all of that, it would not alter anything at all... not, that is, if you still loved him!"

Mary jolted herself out of her melancholic reverie upon hearing Dorothy's last statement and gazed at her friend with astonishment.

"You are in some respects quite perceptive, Dorothy, for indeed I have never hated Raymond for all he has done! That is the infliction of love upon us weak mortals. And despite everything, something of past feelings remains embedded in our soul like irreversible impressions set in stone, leaving an imprint that seemingly cannot ever be removed or erased! That kind of stain does not wash off easily; we must learn from our mistakes and grow from our misfortunes, but... they never leave us completely."

"Mary, if you will pardon my impertinence... I am impressed and admire what you are saying, but the person we are talking about has treated you in a grave manner — and you are the innocent party! This cannot be as simple or straightforward as you are making out, even if you did happen to have some feelings for Raymond. Or can it? At the end of the day, you have suffered so much because of him; surely you cannot exonerate him completely or so easily after all he has done to you?"

"I hear what you are saying, Dorothy... very well. I suppose the extent of my suffering was and still is to some extent directly related to how much I loved him; the more you love someone, the greater you become hurt, you know! Separation and divorce is never easy, no matter who is involved and no matter how one party has been ill-treated, abused or whatever. It will always be a hurtful wrench upon parting! Why? Who knows! In being married to someone and being intimate together, there is an imprint left behind of a love that never worked out... but a love nevertheless. Even the abused can still remain a slave to the abuser!"

"I think I understand something of what you are telling me, Mary; even now I feel so attached to David that he has become part of my very being... and yet, we have not been intimate together. Goodness knows what I will feel when we have! I can understand that there is a bond developing between us quite different from any other. Oh, Mary! How awful it must be for so many people in this same predicament of divorce and separation! I think of young people who sleep around for whatever reason, only to be slighted, discarded, and left abandoned. To the one, intimacy had little meaning, but to the other it was quite a different matter altogether — and that person is usually the girl!"

Mary deliberately chose to move away from this never-ending topic of conversation to a more light-hearted one.

"Well, dear Dorothy, I can tell listening to you that my brother already seems to be flesh of your flesh and bone of your bone; that is for sure!"

"Mary! What a way of putting it!"

Suddenly, the interrupting sound of a mobile phone filled the room.

"Dorothy! Is that your mobile or mine?"

"I think it is mine," replied Dorothy. "And it looks like it's David coming back. Hmm... I wonder how he got on?"

Chapter 26

A Surprise Visitor in Church

Circumstances had changed very much for the better in a certain dwelling where once there had been two occupants, but now three resided. Alfred found himself out-numbered again in his household with two ladies to contend with, but that did not trouble him one iota! One would bring him a cup of tea before breakfast, and the other would proceed to cook the meal for him.

So often in life troubles persist beyond comfort; where is the answer to remedy them? God seems almost reluctant to change things, no matter how much one prays about the situation, and He receives a lot of stick because of it – usually from those who never really think about Him until adverse occasions arise. This had been the situation for Maria, who had earnestly brought her parents' reconciliation before the Throne of Grace. But days had turned to weeks, weeks to months, and months to years without any answer.

Someone once said:

The mills of the Lord grind very slowly, but they grind exceedingly small; though with patience He stands waiting, with exactness grinds He all.
(Friedrich von Logau, 1624)

God is a refiner! He seeks the best, more-enduring solution, and not usually the quickest! With a refiner's fire, He purges our lives in His crucible in similitude to that of extracting the dross from silver and gold; He patiently works until impurities are gone—and we need to be aware and believe He knows best! It is not easy, and He calls upon our uttermost trust as we patiently wait for His timing. In one place, it is recorded, *'… and we know that all things work together for good to those who love God, to those who are called according to His purpose.'*

This is the dilemma faced by so many! Only those who love God and look to Him ardently, with unwavering trust, remain steadfast in that hope of seeing the end of their faith materialise—and that more often in a way totally different to what they expected! The fact is, God is in control all the time! He is the Creator who knows the end from the beginning, and if anyone perseveres with God, they will experience a solution in accordance with His Divine will and purpose.

Maria had a firm conviction in her spirit that her parents would eventually come back together again, and she prayed about the situation relentlessly—and ultimately had her reward.

As with most problems, people can desire quick solutions. A sudden headache is treated with paracetamol or ibuprofen, and provided it is taken early enough so has not to develop into a dreaded migraine, it usually works very well. A broken boiler or car is fixed immediately; this must be the case, for it is not possible to live without them. And so, the list goes on with innumerable requirements and demands, all of which have become indispensable to life. Yet, there are those things that we cannot fix so easily — things that are completely outside of our control — and seeing as we become accustomed to quick solutions, they become more unpleasant, wearing our patience and even our faith to the very limit.

The dilemma that Maria had faced was such a problem! It could not be remedied that easily or so it seemed, the setback being that nothing appeared to be happening to ease the situation, however she tried. She had desired something good to happen between her parents, but it had not seemed forthcoming. *Surely it is God's will for there to be a reconciliation; I cannot be praying amiss,* she had thought.

In the end, Maria had eased off with her continuous specific prayers, for she had grown weary — though not in her trust and conviction. She had decided to hand the matter over to God and leave it there, for the whole situation had led her to taking her eyes away from Him so that she had seen only the problem, which was not right. She had known that at the end of the day, she could not tell God what to do and when to do it, even if what she desired from Him was a good thing; she could, however, humble herself and trust in Him with all her heart—trust that He would do the right thing by her parents in His own way and in His own time, whatever the outcome! This was where her human will and desire had bowed in humility and surrendered to the sovereignty of God. To the will of God. To the perfect timing of God!

God has a thousand ways to answer our prayers; as it happens, we cannot be sure which one He will choose! Further, as it is impossible for us to foresee the future in the way God can, we can never be sure whether our request is legitimate and most desirable, given our limited knowledge and understanding of the situation. God has better plans than we can ever imagine—if we are prepared to be patient and trust Him and say, 'Not my will but Thine be done!'

A miracle had now occurred—but not in answer to Maria's specific prayers, for she could never have envisaged such a thing ever happening. God had touched, healed and saved her father, Alfred! Afterwards, there had come a short season when things had grown worse between her parents, and not better.

Jennifer, being very hardened towards God, had shown no great joy in her husband's Divine encounter on the Damascus road! She had been a victim in the past because of him. She was the one who had been mistreated by his violent behaviour. And yet it was the abuser that had received the blessing and not the abused! Oh, the unsearchable wisdom and knowledge of God; they are past finding out! But Maria, in the end, saw it all!

Her prayers had not been in vain, for in continuously coming close to God, she had understood at that point when her father had turned to the Lord what God was doing! She had seen the sinner come to repentance so that her self-righteous mother could follow on in his footsteps, and Jennifer had done just that — but not without a visit from Dorothy, who had inspired her to believe in the Lord for herself and not be so hard-hearted, thus preparing the way.

So, it was on this day, a Sunday, that Jennifer was to accompany her husband and daughter to church for the first time since she was a young girl. But unlike then, she was not going under duress or compulsion. Rather, having already met with her Saviour, she was now filled with joy and higher expectations, her eyes having been opened to perceive a truer understanding of what it meant to believe.

Alfred Townsend was currently preoccupied, looking out of the window for an expectant visitor who was to provide their lift to church that morning.

"Here comes Ian, drivin' that red saloon of his — and he's goin' too fast for my likin'," said Alfred as he peered through the curtain, gazing at an oncoming vehicle, unmistakably that of his potential son-in-law. Given that Alfred expected that Ian may well marry his daughter one day, Ian's character, integrity –and currently his safety — were of real concern to Alfred.

"Maria! Ian's here! Get yer clothes on and come down, lass. Right away! Yer been up there long enough gettin' ready; surely, you've done powdering your nose by nar!"

"Give her a break, Alfred," joined in Jennifer upon hearing her husband's remark, humorously but firmly adding her own thinking regarding the matter. "You have never understood — and I might add never will know — what it takes for a woman to get ready… especially a young one. And even more so, a young lady who is meeting up with her young man; so just be patient. Ian can sit down and wait for Maria; it's a woman's prerogative for men to wait for them."

"Argh! So be it — if it must be! We men can find plenty to talk about. We don't mind waiting; no problem!"

Ian McPherson knocked on the door, and being very familiar with the occupants and indeed they also with him, he felt quite at liberty to walk straight in to be confronted by Alfred who stood to greet him with a bear hug.

"Hey there, lad! It's good to see yer. She's just upstairs finishin' off, so yer better be prepared to sit down and wait for a while. Yer know by nar what it's like, eh? We got plenty of time before church anyways."

"Thanks, Mr Townsend."

Ian was always hesitant in conversation with his prospective father-in-law when they were alone together, for old memories died hard, and in times past — before Alfred's change for the better — he would chastise Ian with a gruff voice about some matter or another, usually regarding his daughter. Such memories resurged in poor Ian's mind once again, although he had known Alfred as long as he had known Maria — in fact, ever since she was a four-year-old and the two of them had played together in nursery.

One specific occasion always sprung to mind with Ian. It had been his eighteenth birthday to be precise, and he had received a special gift from his father — one that ran on four wheels. In fact, it was the very same red saloon he had just driven up in. On that occasion, Ian had called to pick Maria up to go ten-pin bowling. Alfred had answered the door, and being very protective of his daughter and her whereabouts, he had greeted Ian accordingly.

"Hello. It's you; is it? Where do you think you're takin' my daughter this time then?"

Something had happened to Ian upon that occasion that had permanently adhered within him; it resembled a sort of reverent fear which would serve the purpose, if ever it was required, to ensure he remained on the straight and narrow with Maria or suffer the consequences.

Within the space of fifteen minutes, the whole household was ready for church. Alfred and Ian had conversed together quite amicably whilst waiting for the ladies, who, in turn, had meticulously added the final touches to whatever they had decided to wear, having been in and out of each other's room upon several occasions seeking approval from the other about their attire. A different aroma filled the room as both Jennifer and Maria descended the stairs into the lounge to meet their respective men, and this had the desired effect of provoking complimentary greetings from each of them.

"You look nice, Maria," was the salutation from one young gentleman, and "Well, I'll be if that ain't our Jen going out somewhere!" was the welcome greeting from the other.

"Yes. Well, thank you, Alf, but I'm not going anywhere with you till you've cleaned the mud off your shoes. You ain't been on the farm now, so that's not an excuse!"

After a further five minutes of delay, they were finally ready to roll, and off they went with Alfred's footwear now looking impeccably shiny. Ian, feeling honoured and proud to chauffer everyone, scuttled ahead of the party to open the car door.

~~~~~~

Meanwhile, in another home not too far away, preparations had also reached their final stages, and David Osborne, together with his sister and her daughter, were likewise getting into a vehicle to go to church.

"I understand, Mary, that a surprise visitor will be attending church this morning for the very first time—one who will be of special interest to you."

"And just who told you that, David? Was it Dorothy, Maria or Miriam?"

"None of the above. It is to be a secret until you see the person for yourself. It is someone you are indeed acquainted with, but not to a great extent; you have met this person only once I believe."

Mary was excited about this mystery person, for she liked the suspense in meeting someone new, but still, nevertheless, pressed her brother for a clue.

"David! Why all this secrecy? All this concealment? Please, tell me who it is, if you will—or at least give me an inkling. I can hardly think of anyone whom I have only met once."

"Ah! That would spoil it for this person! It is to be a surprise! You will see soon enough—and I'm sure you'll be very pleased to see this person, okay?"

"Do you *know* who it is David?" pursued Mary like a dog with a bone, still not giving up on her search for information.

"Yes, my dear. I do indeed! And I can assure you that it is nothing to concern yourself over, so please be patient and wait and see."

Mary resigned herself to pursue the matter no further, knowing full well that her brother could be silent if he had a mind to be — even if she were a gestapo interrogator. She knew, therefore, that she stood no chance at all of gaining anything out of him.

David, together with his two passengers, arrived at the church well before Ian's red saloon, and consequently, they were all able to take vacant seats in the front row. These places usually filled up first, and already Dorothy, who had arrived earlier with the Petersons, was seated there next to Miriam. When Julia saw Dorothy, she left her mother and ran over to sit next to her. She insisted upon being next to Dorothy — and indeed near to the front as well to get a good view of her friends Maria and Ian as they played in the band, the former being the lead singer and the latter the drummer.

Mary would have sat next to Dorothy, but as the seats either side of her friend were taken, she sat next to her brother who was to Dorothy's left, whilst Julia was to Dorothy's right. Consequently, Mary could not talk discreetly with her friend about the surprise visitor, so instead peered around the growing congregation with both curiosity and excitement, searching for an individual who might fit the category — but there was no one yet.

The hall soon grew to full capacity, with people having to sit upon chairs in the aisles placed there by stewards. It became impossible for Mary's curiosity to proceed any further, and she resigned herself to waiting until the end of the service to discover this new person David had said would be of interest to her. The exciting news that David had conveyed to Mary diverted her attention upon several occasions during the ensuing meeting, until pastor John began to preach and she was taken up with his sermon.

Mary was spiritually mature for someone so relatively young and had encouraged and strengthened Dorothy upon many occasions regarding understanding the Scriptures. In return, Dorothy would reciprocate and pass on her own encouragement and revelations to comfort Mary during her difficult times of depression. They were unrelated upon this earth, but spiritually they were attached as sisters in the Lord, ministering to one another continuously like God's ministering angels. The beauty and success of their respective support one to the other was largely due to their practice of reading out God's Word. Spoken words of sympathy soon ran their course, as did advice, leaving nothing much more to be said to help ease difficult situations. By reading God's promises and words of comfort to one another, it provided a therapy that went above and beyond one's own self to have trust and hope in God.

Dorothy had progressed and moved on extensively since her turbulent past of illness and loneliness. She was now engaged to David, who was, of course, Mary's brother. Because of this close family tie, Mary was continually exposed to the daily romance filling the air, but sadly this romance never involved her — only her brother! Increasingly, whenever she was of a low disposition, Mary felt a growing sense of abandonment and loneliness, not having anything constructive happening in her own life. She was still very young and a beautiful woman. Outwardly, she was exceedingly eligible for progress in the relationship department with the appropriate person, but she felt like damaged goods left upon the shelf, and the thought of further romance and companionship seemed beyond her reach. Despite this up-to date assessment of a young lady who so often suffered with despondency regarding such matters, it was well known that she was a woman of substance with great integrity, a lady who was uncommonly and naturally beautiful.

This very same person suddenly stood to her feet. The meeting had now concluded, and a persistent little girl could be seen darting away from her seat and running over to her mummy with that all too familiar request, "Mummy! I need to do a wee!"

"Oh! Alright, my darling; come on then. Let's make our way through all these people and try to reach the toilets, shall we?"

Julia quickly took her mummy's hand and together they squeezed through the crowds, Mary going ahead, struggling painstakingly to get towards the rear of the building and hoping there would be no accident along the way! Many people acknowledged her as she asked to pass through, when suddenly Mary's eyes met those of a familiar young gentleman whose own blue eyes and bright, gleaming smile were directed straight towards her.

Mary was transfixed for a second wondering whether to say, *'Hello! Where have I seen you before?'* or *'Do I know you?'*

But then, she continued to move forward without speaking, attempting to recollect who this young man was, for at that moment it had not been opportune to pursue the matter — not with Julia's current pressing engagement. It was one of those instantaneous and unexpected moments, which would normally have been of no significance whatsoever, but upon this occasion, her dormant emotions had been revived by his appearance, for the young man was indeed most handsome.

Upon returning into the hall with her mission successfully accomplished, Mary walked with tunnel vision, hoping to avoid a second encounter with the gentleman. But it was no use.

He had already made a beeline for her with the intention of making himself known.

"Excuse me! I believe I know you. It's Mary, isn't it? And this is Julia, I do believe."

The gentleman was full of airs and graces, conversing in a confident, light-hearted manner; and then, desiring to carry on the dialogue with the youngest of the two ladies, he knelt to have good eye contact with her and spoke charmingly with no qualms or embarrassment.

"Hello there, I remember seeing you and your mummy downtown. You were talking to… now, who was it? Ah yes! You were talking to your grandad, Alfred, I think… And I commented on what a lovely pink dress you were wearing! Remember? And you had a cuddly teddy bear."

Julia smiled. "Yes! I remember you; you were taking pictures of Grandad," she said with a giggle.

It suddenly dawned upon the older of the two ladies who the gentleman was, and Mary blushed momentarily as his antics on Valentine's Day rose to the forefront of her mind! Mary and the gentleman conversed for several minutes; Mary could not get away if she tried. Then, finally, the gentleman departed, leaving Mary glued to the spot, gazing at the floor with a smile and deep in thought. Now, as it happened, Dorothy had been seeking Mary out, wondering just where she had disappeared to, when suddenly she saw her.

"Mary! Where have you been? I have been searching all over for you, and... well, you missed seeing the surprise visitor after all that!"

"No, Dorothy; I did not miss him at all. I saw him just now. Why didn't you tell me he would be here this morning?"

Dorothy was puzzled. "Seen him? Who are you talking about Mary?"

"Your surprise visitor of course. He approached me, and you'll never guess what..."

"Mary, the surprise visitor was Jennifer Townsend, who came to church this morning for the very first time with Alfred and Maria, but they have gone now. Who are you referring to?"

Mary looked at Dorothy and burst into spontaneous laughter.

"Dorothy! He was here! Jerry Dickson in person! You remember? Those initials, J D... and a certain Valentine's card?"

Now, Dorothy was most perceptive and observant, noticing a certain hint of glee in Mary's countenance. She sensed there was further information and enlightenment yet to be heard from her friend's lips!

"Mary! What have you done?"

"Mm! He asked if he could see me tomorrow after I drop Julia off at school. If we could go out for a coffee together."

"Well...? What did you say to him?"

"Yes!"

Chapter 27

Rendezvous at *Max's Cafe*

A few days had passed since the events and confusions at church associated with the surprise visitor, and Dorothy happened to be seated alone in *Max's Café*, having finished work early that day.

It was a pleasant day. The days were getting warmer and staying light for longer. Blue sky was more prevalent than the blustery, rainy days during the long and seemingly endless wintry period that usually started at the beginning of November and lasted until the end of April! Sometimes one could be blessed with cold, frosty mornings followed by sunny, cloudless skies during the day, but the winter that had just passed had been most unsettled and miserable, with no such seasonal beauty to behold.

The aforementioned six-month wintry period had finally ended, and Dorothy stared out the open café door. A comfortable and mild breeze blew through it, and Dorothy observed sparrows darting around at the entrance after crumbs of food. There was a shortbread biscuit in a wrapper that had come with her latté, and this she unwrapped; then, observing a waitress nearby clearing an adjacent table, Dorothy called to inform her about her proposed intentions.

"Hi there! Would you mind if I litter your doorway with some more crumbs for the birds? I'm sure they will eat everything clean in a few moments."

"Not at all; please go ahead. They are getting very bold, aren't they? Sometimes the birds come inside, you know, right up to the tables. No one seems to mind, however. It looks like you have found a free table just in time; it's almost time for the lunchtime stampede. The students come in floods about this time of day for their snacks and drinks."

"Yes. I'm waiting to see two students myself as a matter of fact," replied Dorothy. "This is a favourite place of mine; I come in here often — two or three times a week in fact — with friends. I like the ambience... as well as the coffee. But there is also a very special memory I treasure about the place! You were probably not working here at the time, but a long while ago I bought a stranger a coffee in here, and since then she has become my very best friend. Can you believe that? Well, best friend apart from my fiancé, that is! In fact, I invited her to sit with me at this very same round table."

"Ah! That's nice! Shows you what a coffee can do, hey. Hmm, did you say fiancé just then?"

"Yes! And this is even more incredible," continued Dorothy, quite eager to share another matter with the waitress. "The lady that I bought the coffee for… well, she happens to be my fiancé's sister!"

"Good gracious! Now that was an important coffee you bought that day, hey? Have you fixed a date then… for the wedding day?"

Dorothy was taken by surprise and put on the spot by what was a natural and obvious question. Both she and David had initially agreed not to set a date for their wedding, owing to a certain mitigating factor, namely the completion and success of Dorothy's counselling. This, they knew, was crucial to her own personal readiness for intimacy, though friends had been told that they both had much to prepare and that the wedding would most likely take place after six months—but not later than a year's time.

All this had been said and done some five months previous, making the waitress's curiosity in raising her question regarding a date for the wedding very applicable in its timing. Dorothy replied diplomatically that a specific date for the wedding was pending due to certain preparations that needed to be put in place.

Thereafter, it was true to say that this important occasion occupied Dorothy's mind considerably, and she realised that it was now time for friends and acquaintances to be brought up to speed and informed of the latest information at the earliest opportunity, for nothing more had been disclosed. Dorothy was excited! She felt good and decided to phone

David there and then about releasing their news to Maria.

My counselling sessions have now finished, she thought to herself. *What prevents me now from sharing things with others, given that we have both talked about the matter and made interim arrangements already?*

Dorothy's eyes gleamed with unprecedented joy as she placed her mobile back upon the coffee table; David was over the moon at the prospect of going public and only insisted that he likewise be at liberty to announce things. Regarding protocol, David suggested telling his father and sister during his lunchbreak that day, and perhaps Dorothy could reciprocate with Miriam and John, as well as Maria — after which, it was over to the highways and byways!

Suddenly, the waitress was in great demand by an influx of students entering *Max's Café*, and, consequently, she quickly brought her conversation with Dorothy to an end, wishing her the very best for the future and the forthcoming happy event. Meanwhile, Dorothy looked out for her two friends within the incoming bustling crowd of young people, and spotting Maria, she called across to her.

"Maria! Hello there!"

Maria Townsend always bounced with energy and enthusiasm, especially in Dorothy's company, and this occasion was to be no exception. She bubbled with life, excitement and energy.

That's the way she was; Maria Townsend was a fountain of joy, a tonic for the down-hearted with her delightful constitution and abundantly happy charisma, a girl who usually took the centre stage without even realising or being aware of her powerful, contagious dynamics upon those in her presence. Further, she had that typical mannerism of a young person that was often seen and observed in her generation in that she spoke forthrightly and openly without any qualms or hesitations. In short, she was a most delightful young lady, easy to get on with and whose directness only served to add to her appealing nature.

Maria's outgoing nature and confidence had not diminished throughout her demanding experiences in looking after her father. Having taken upon herself the role of caring for him during his cantankerous years, she had adapted two of her qualities to perfection, namely her assertiveness with her father and the gracious humility she displayed, which together diffused Alfred's harshness and kept him in place. It had been an arduous task looking after Alfred. Maria's unfailing attitude, however, seemed to have spread a warmth of love and affection whatever state he was in, rather like soft butter upon bread. It had had the effect of diffusing the grizzly animosity that he had generally thrown at her, smoothing and easing the situation time after time. Maria had not been deterred! She had never grown discouraged and, therefore, had not been detracted from her mission by all his antics.

Now, as Maria entered the café, her boyfriend, Ian McPherson, was following close behind, so she left him in the queue to buy the drinks and goodies, then darted over to Dorothy to give her a hug. If Mary Osborne was Dorothy's best friend with the one obvious exception, then Maria came a close second. They had known one another right from the beginning, when Dorothy had first attended the church and Maria had casually introduced herself, being exceedingly pleased to find a new young lady in church whom she could befriend. They had soon begun meeting up and before long had become the best of friends, trusting and confiding in one other about everything.

After their greetings and hugs had ended, Maria observed Dorothy's countenance and immediately noticed that she was looking particularly exuberant, with a spark in her eyes, as if excited about something. She sat close to Dorothy and whispered in her ear, "And what are you so happy about, Dorothy? Got any good news to tell me?"

"Oh! I was looking out for you; I'm always happy to see you... well, usually!" replied Dorothy humorously.

"I just thought you seemed happy about something, that's all," added Maria with accurate perception. "And anyway, I am happy too. Ian's taking me out for a meal tonight!"

Maria stared curiously at Dorothy's facial expression once again, and it was obvious she did have something to tell! Some bursting news was imminent upon her lips, and there was only one course of action to take.

"Dorothy! Come on; spill the beans! What is it?"

Upon such occasions as these, when certain important news was about to be announced, it was never the right thing to procrastinate and delay, but rather to just come straight out with it so that one could maximise the surprise. This strategy was in fact adopted by Dorothy.

"Maria! David and I have arranged our wedding date! It is to be the second Saturday in June — in about six weeks' time — and we would both like you to be a bridesmaid, if you please."

"Wow! Wonderful news! You are soooo cheeky and sly, Dorothy McGuire! I knew you had something brewing. And yes please! I would love to be a bridesmaid… That's sounds not too far away though; shall you get it all sorted by then?"

"Don't worry; David has been busy preparing just about everything for ages — all except the special particulars, like bridesmaids, and other stuff that he is leaving for me to do!" This subject alone was addressed in fine detail, for Maria questioned every aspect about the colour and style of the bridesmaid outfits and asked how many there would be. Then there was the question of Dorothy's wedding dress and what design she was going for. In fact, all those matters associated with a wedding that were of interest to ladies and especially the bride were addressed ardently and enthusiastically, until a certain interruption occurred.

Ian finally arrived with the food and drink, but after observing Dorothy and Maria deeply involved with what by all accounts was clearly a girly conversation and not wishing to interrupt them, he decided to drop the food and drink off for Maria, then excused himself to sit at a nearby table and join his friend, Robert Templeman.

Dorothy continued. "Julia will of course be a bridesmaid, and… well, I wanted to ask you; what do you think of the idea of asking Robert's girlfriend, Sarah Manning? She has just started coming to church now after such a long time of being out there on the periphery, and I would like to take this opportunity to welcome her. What do you think? Would she be interested and up to it in your view? I know it's my choice ultimately, but you know Sarah very well and your opinion would be appreciated."

"Well, that's interesting, Dot… and I would say it's very thoughtful of you, yer know.

You are right about her. For a long time, she was reserved and sort of worried about us lot at church; yer know what I mean."

"I guess she was apprehensive about coming and mixing, I suppose, not knowing anyone," added Dorothy.

"Yer, that's right. She was never a church-goer before, but she has stopped her night club antics, mainly because of Robert's influence upon her after that escapade at *The Blue Moon*. Sarah has certainly started to trust Robert these days. He's been a good encouragement to her... Can you believe that coming from him? But really, Robert is a nice guy now.

"I think Sarah realises there is another life out there and has mellowed a lot compared to how she used to be. To be honest, Dot, I'm not sure how she might react, yer know. But there's no harm in askin' her."

"Okay, leave that one with me... Back to the dress! I'm thinking of wearing a long, elegant, slim-fitting dress," said Dorothy. "And not the large, bell-shaped type. As for my hair... what do you think? Curls? Partly up and plaited at the back? Or all of it up? I know my hair is wavy; do you think straighteners might work and give it the chic, sophisticated look?"

"Dot, if you want my opinion, I think you would look beautiful with curls. Honestly!"

"Really, do you think so? I wasn't too sure how they would look on me."

"Definitely! Don't worry about that one, Dot. Take my word for it; you will look absolutely gorgeous with loose curls!

"Where will you have the wedding reception? Have you got that sorted?"

"Yep, we have indeed. We're thinking of going to *The Darlington Hotel*... you know the one that has a spa. But also, it has so much space for children to play, and the grounds are wonderful at the rear; they drop down a gentle hill into long grass and woodland. The kids will love it."

"Awesome! You're going to have a hen party, I hope!" said Maria with a giggle.

"Probably... but I shall have to think about that one," replied Dorothy, smiling at Maria with some degree of thoughtfulness.

Maria eventually started into her lunch; then, after a short interlude, having consumed several large mouthfuls of her sausage bap and having drunk a gulp of Coke, she changed the subject. With all the excitement regarding Dorothy's news, she had completely forgotten to tell her about her own.

"What's this I hear about Mary then? Is it all true... like, is she goin' out with that newspaper guy? What's his name?"

"Jerry Dickson! Yes, I do believe she is, Maria," replied Dorothy, knowing very little about the circumstances other than what Mary had said to her after church.

"Hey! Talkin' about newspapers," continued Maria, quickly changing the subject yet again. "Have you read the *Daily Herald* this week? There's a write-up about Dad in it!"

Dorothy stared at Maria in a mesmerised fashion, completely captured by her friend's natural exhibition of spontaneous hilarity as she simultaneously spoke and ate at the same time.

"Maria! You are a most wonderful, genuine person; do you know that?"

"What! What do you mean...*genuine*? What on earth are you on about, Dot? Did you hear what I just said? About Dad and all? I think it's awesome, yer know... my dad on the front page. Wow!"

Realising that she had just been musing in a different realm to that of Maria, who was oblivious of all she had been thinking, Dorothy moved back again into reality.

"Yes! Yes! I did hear you, Maria. Have you got a copy of the Herald with you by any chance?"

"Yep! Look at that! Dad is on the front page... And see, there's another picture here inside with Mary and Julia in it. It says, *Local Healed Cripple Is Preaching on the Streets!*"

Dorothy was diverted for a while as she read the newspaper article.

At last something had been published, she thought, *and not before time.*

Dorothy had been instrumental in reproaching the very person of Jerry Dickson when he had visited Alfred to interview him at his home. In Dorothy's view, he had procrastinated and failed to report the amazing miracle in the first place, especially given that he had been present at the church and had witnessed Alfred walking out of it unaided. At least now it had finally happened, and overall, given that it was supposed to be an unbiased report, it was not too bad in Dorothy's opinion. It did at least draw attention to the fact that something unexplainable had happened and that Alfred himself was now publicising it abroad in the precinct every Tuesday, testifying in the open-air of how God had healed him.

"That is quite something, Maria," said Dorothy, fully endorsing the article with her approval. "Hmm! I do wonder if the lady in that picture had something to do with drawing Mr Dickson in like a fish on a line?"

"What? You mean Mary? How's that?" questioned Maria. "Oh! I get your drift, Dorothy... at least I reckon so! Do you think he liked her all along and so gave a good report in his newspaper? Is that what you're sayin'?"

"Not exactly that, Maria! I was thinking about something else. But who knows? Perhaps it could have pushed him a little more to write favourably about Alfred, especially to include the Scriptures he has quoted! I'm sure he didn't have to say that, but he has done, even though it is a secular newspaper. I'm sure he must have known that would please Mary... And now he has asked Mary out, and she has accepted!"

"Well, I for one am pleased for her," replied Maria emphatically. "She is a big girl who is well capable of looking after herself, and at least he came to church to see her, so he must be keen I would say."

"Hmm... maybe... anyway," said Dorothy cautiously, not displeased with her friend's comments, but as always careful not to overstate her own opinion upon the matter. "I agree too, Maria; Mary certainly does deserve a break. She has been out on her own — bless her — for several years; she has suffered a lot, and that I know only too well!"

"Anyway, Dot... that is fantastic news about the wedding!" exclaimed Maria as yet again she changed the subject abruptly. "I'm getting so excited!

"Whoops! I do need to go soon; my lecture starts in fifteen minutes. You'll have to excuse me now, Dot," said Maria. "I'll just get Ian."

"Maria, before you go, please would you ask Robert over there if he can see me for a minute... if he is not rushing off himself, that is? There is something I would like to ask him."

"Okay. Will do."

As Maria and Ian left *Max's Café*, saying their final farewells to Dorothy, Robert

Templeman followed close behind them, stopping to sit at the same table as Dorothy.

Robert was casually but smartly dressed, with a clean-cut finish to his attire. His jeans were a distinct, uniform light blue as opposed to the popular type worn by many of his contemporaries that usually displayed variations of a sort of blue colour, ranging from very pale and worn-looking around the knees to pale, torn and creased elsewhere — as though they were several years old and worn and grubby, though they were in fact quite new.

Robert's stylish jeans were held up by a smart brown leather belt with a golden buckle, and he wore a matching brown pair of narrow leather shoes and not the predictable trainers. Underneath a brown leather jacket — which had been a favourite of his late mother's — he did wear a conventional T-shirt, and around his neck hung a small crucifix on a silver chain, which had been a present to him from Sarah Manning.

His jacket had been promoted to being special, ever since Maria had commented how nice it looked when he had first attended church; before then he had considered it to be too posh. His friends and associates at college never commented adversely about his conspicuously different dress code; they were too afraid to do so, having previously been informed about his formidable reputation. Instead, they gave him respect, though some — those who never knew of his past—would by coincidence call him *The Duke,* being ignorant and oblivious that this name had been his title in gangland. Robert, however, never let on about it and took it as a complimentary remark instead.

It was true to say that Robert had never been the same since that occasion when he first met Alfred Townsend in a café upon a very rainy, but nevertheless memorable day several months earlier, when he had run out of the house from his father after a violent argument over loud music and made his way in the pouring rain into town. It was there that Robert had observed the old man preaching in the precinct about Jesus. Hearing this had brought back memories of his dying mother's words when she had also told him the same. Afterwards, both he and Alfred had sat together in a café speaking to one another in a personal manner.

Robert had been miraculously converted to the Lord in a most remarkable and emotional fashion. Sitting there in the café, sodden and utterly drenched from the rain, Robert—who had given much abusive rhetoric to Alfred that morning—had without being chastised finally succumbed and become overcome by Alfred's kind and encouraging words, for though Alfred had seemed such an old, insignificant man, yet he had spoken openly, sincerely, and firmly to Robert as though he really cared. Above all, Alfred had invited Robert to trust in Jesus and yield his life to Him. Unknowingly, Alfred had used the very same words as Robert's mother, Catherine, saying that Jesus would look after him! This seemingly coincidental reminder from Alfred about Robert's mother's dying words had melted his heart and reduced him to tears.

Robert now sat opposite Dorothy and politely addressed her, "Hello, Miss Dorothy! How are you?"

"I'm very well, Robert, but do call me Dorothy. And yourself?"

"Excellent! I want to thank you for helping me get a job at your work. It's really going well, thanks to you."

"And you too! I get feedback from time to time… all very good, I might add!" encouraged Dorothy.

"Well, Robert," she continued. "David and I would like to convey some good news…! We are getting married in the middle of June, and …well, how would you feel if we asked you to be best man?"

"What? Me? Are you sure? I don't know what to say…"

"Just think about it, Robert. Then, let us know soon. It's okay if you would rather not, but it was David's suggestion. Apparently, you two get on very well since you started attending his karate class. By the way, congratulations! I believe David is entering you for a 1st-dan black-belt!"

"Yes, you're right; Mr Osborne is very good to me. I mean, he helps me no end—and not just with karate. Last weekend he showed me how to do spreadsheets by entering formulae and then how to import them into my word processing document."

"Oh! Wow, Robert! Heavy stuff, hey? Yet it becomes straightforward once you have done it and get used to it. I used to find spreadsheets difficult at the beginning, because I was never very good at Algebra, but now I see some point in it… I suppose. Excellent, Robert! I am so pleased you are getting on at work, and it seems you are handling your studies well, too."

"Thank you, Dorothy. Life is like… so different these days, thanks to you guys. I would say it all changed after meeting Alfred in the precinct and he pointed me—shall we say he pointed me in the right direction?—and prayed with me in a café! Everything is going good.

"Then, I met you, Dorothy. Remember when we were having fish and chips with Pastor John and Sarah during her lunch break, and you joined us? I really can't believe what's goin' on, yer know. It's like a dream or something, and… I just want to thank you, Dorothy, for all you've done for me—especially getting me a job!"

Robert had developed a solemn tone in his voice whilst reminiscing about past events with Dorothy and was full of gratitude and appreciation. Dorothy smiled warmly. It was very true; Robert had come a long way from being *The Duke* in gangland, terrorising the local neighbourhood. He was now a most sincere and likeable young man, whose direction in life had been completely changed around for the better!

"Well, I'm glad I saw you sitting over there, Robert. I had arranged to see Maria, and we had a long girly chat together. In fact, Robert, I wanted to ask you something else before you leave. David and I would like to invite you over to his flat one evening to talk about a few things; would that be okay? And we could have a few eats and a drink together."

"That would be good, thanks. Is it for anything special?"

"Ah! That is a secret for the moment, Robert. Nothing bad, of course, but… Well, you will see; it's a surprise!

"May I ask you something else? How are you and Sarah getting on together — if that is not prying or nosy of me?"

"No, not at all. We are getting on very well — extremely well in fact! We are officially going out since last Sunday."

"Congratulations, Robert! I am so pleased to hear that news. I do like Sarah. Well then, would you both be able to come to David's? What do you think? There is something we need to ask both of you, and it would be nice if you were together."

"I will ask her first. On what evening would that be?"

"We were thinking of Friday… about 7:00 pm if that is okay with you both?"

"I'm almost sure it will be fine, but I'll text you after I see her. Actually, I'm off to meet Sarah now, so… I'll see you later. Bye."

Chapter 28

David and Dorothy Entertain Two Guests

It was late Friday afternoon, the day when Robert and Sarah had been invited to visit David and Dorothy, and the latter had just left work and was walking in the direction of David's flat. Dorothy looked very smart, even in her work clothes; she was wearing a brown skirt with complementing jacket and a pair of brown sling-back heels of a 'mere' three inches. Even so, she could be seen walking quite briskly over the pavement; this type of shoe provided her with that extra support at work and enabled her to move around quite quickly. The rhythmic sound of her heels upon the pavement suddenly ceased as Dorothy impulsively turned aside and entered a grocery store to get a few goodies for that evening.

David was already home and preparing a coffee with some rock cakes, a speciality that went down well with every visitor — especially when freshly baked. Dorothy had asked David in the past if he would make this kind of cake as they contained little sugar, but had stressed that using butter was fine by her. Decisions about diet and health seemed to change with the wind, and now the emphasis and flavour of the month was to cut back upon sugar, eat small portions of carbs with plenty of vegetables and protein; this, Dorothy had read about, and she assured David it would be good for him, too, so they both ardently took it to heart — at least for the moment!

Upon arrival, Dorothy could smell the inviting aroma of fresh baking just coming out of the oven, and she enquired of David how long she had to wait before trying one.

"Just give it a few minutes... if you can wait that long, Dorothy. Or be very careful and have one now if you wish." Dorothy chose the latter and sat down at the kitchen table, gently sipping her hot latte and even more carefully biting at the rock cake.

"So, what sort of a day have you had today, David? Anything interesting?"

"Well, not so much at work, dear, but I had an illuminating conversation with my sister this lunchtime."

"Really! How is Mary? Any romance in the air with Jerry Dickson?"

"Ah, you have hit the nail on the head. She has been out with him twice since last Sunday, and... it's difficult to know from her whether she is serious about him or not. I am a little concerned about her — being her brother and all. If you were to speak to her yourself, you might gather more information than I did. But I have to confess, I haven't seen her so lively and happy in a long time. I do hope she knows what she is doing. Jerry seems a respectable man, but apart from that, little is known of him, so just what his intentions are... who knows?"

"Ah! David, you are her caring, protective brother."

Dorothy was impressed by David's affection for his sister, and his display of brotherly concern had simultaneously stirred her own emotions. She perched herself upon his knee, placing one arm around his neck, then tenderly held his head with her other hand and kissed his cheek. David reciprocated by placing both his arms around her waist, drawing her closer to him. He gazed into her eyes, rubbed noses and kissed her most affectionately.

Whilst Dorothy's action had been a welcome surprise, David marvelled to himself in many ways. *How she has progressed*, he thought.

When he had first met Dorothy and understood her situation, it would not have been possible for her at that time to have instigated such a display of lovingkindness towards him; but now she was clearly confident and able to initiate such an action, expressing her feelings in a manner that would have been unheard of then.

"I shall eagerly look forward to my next little chat with Mary," said Dorothy in response to David's suggestion that she ought to speak with her. "And hopefully, not before too long. I can then give you my picture of things. Perhaps I could see Mary tomorrow... we'll see.

"Mm, would you share another cake with me, David? They are so nice."

Dorothy cut another cake into two pieces as she was speaking and gave him one half so that David had little choice in the matter.

"I wouldn't be overly concerned about Mary, my dear; who knows, this sort of thing could do her a world of good... don't you think? She has suffered and been alone for such a long time now — some two and a half years. She is young and very attractive, and some time or another this sort of thing will happen. We just pray for the right person; that's all.

"I try to put myself in her shoes. She must have felt unwanted and rejected after Raymond walked out on her; how dreadful that must have been! Now, suddenly and unexpectedly, Jerry comes on the scene giving her attention, putting her in the spotlight and making her feel wanted again! I think I can understand where she is coming from, and I pray she will not get hurt in any way. Why, all the attention will flatter her I'm sure! And as you say, he seems a respectable man and very handsome too. He *is* humorous... and seems very nice."

"Really? And that is your opinion of him, is it? And yet you know nothing about him?"

David had responded solemnly, but in a slightly irritated manner, as he gazed at Dorothy. He manifested a hint of envy at hearing her assessment of Jerry. Dorothy retracted from talking about him then, even though she felt there had been nothing untoward in what she had said.

"Well, I confess I am only judging the outward circumstances and appearance, David. My dear, Jerry is after all a likeable young man who went into church to see her... That, I suppose must count for something! Though, of course, even then you cannot really tell for sure.

"I met him by chance at Alfred's house and confess I did find him to be polite, well-spoken, and funny at times. Perhaps he was a little full of himself as well... But Mary would relish the attention he has shown her — sending her flowers and a Valentine's card! And, after all, the point is... she is in her late twenties, and he is about thirty-two. Well? What can you say?"

David could understand Dorothy's logic, but he was still apprehensive upon hearing her speak so frankly and outspokenly with such complimentary language about a man other than himself. And further, the effect this man seemed to be having upon his sister was of utmost concern to him.

"I can only suppose your comments and analysis of the situation, Dorothy, are typical of those within a ladies' forum, my dear. But as for me... Well, I cannot particularly make any constructive remarks like yourself — except that you are probably right about the whole matter. I do confess, Dorothy; I find the whole situation somewhat distressing!"

This he conceded in a dejected manner, feeling quite out of depth about this side of his sister's personality, regarding her feelings for other men. However, in truth, David was being protective of Mary, and Dorothy's outspoken description of Jerry had the effect of provoking a hint of jealousy at the same time, so what came out of his mouth next took Dorothy somewhat by surprise.

"I do hope your adulations of this man do not suggest he is a contagious sort of person, winning you over too!"

It would probably not be advisable for a man to pay too many compliments to another woman in front of his lady, unless perhaps the two had been well acquainted for at least forty-odd years, but when the circumstances are reversed, the lady can sometimes feel more at liberty to express her opinion freely about a man! Certainly, this was the case with Dorothy, and she did not think anything of it either! Even so, Dorothy instantly responded to her fiancé's growing desperation, having finally realised the effect it was all having upon him! She immediately brought consolation to him.

"Ha! Davy boy," — this she called David whenever in a playful mood — "you are such a sweetie, my dear love! Fancy being jealous over him! But … I do think that is rather nice."

She sat once again upon his knee, made herself comfortable, gently held his head with both of her warm, soft hands, and told him convincingly all he wanted to hear. Suddenly, a distinct knock upon the door disturbed the two of them with a start. Dorothy jumped up and quickly tidied her hair and dress, then suggested David do likewise before he went to answer the door to let Robert and Sarah in.

"Hi, Robert! Hello, Sarah! Do come in. Thanks for coming tonight, guys. You're in for a treat, too — if, that is, you like rock cakes! Give me your coats and go through... Dorothy is in there."

The ladies hugged one another, but Robert shook Dorothy's hand, for he was not comfortable with that form of greeting — except with the young lady who had accompanied him.

Upon entering David's flat, Sarah looked around from corner to corner, eyeing everything with interest and was quite impressed with its décor and intrigued to see more.

"Would it be possible to have a look around your flat? I am pretty interested in some sort of a place myself."

"Come with me, Sarah," said Dorothy, jumping up from her chair. "I will show you around. We'll leave the men by themselves for a little while — as long as they don't eat all the rock cakes!"

Robert sat down next to David at the table, whilst the two ladies disappeared upstairs.

"I think it is a women's thing, Robert," grinned David, turning to his guest to make conversation. "Whenever a lady enters a new place, they always like to be shown around it!"

"No. Actually, Mr Osborne, Sarah is lookin' out for a place of her own; that's why she wanted to have a look round. But I reckon this'll be a bit too expensive for her."

"Oh! Really? Why is Sarah wishing to move out, Robert?" David asked with curiosity, not without some concern about the idea.

"Oh, it's her parents—especially her mum. She doesn't get on very well with them. She is just not happy at home. I can't say much more, but Sarah is looking for a place."

"Well, Robert, after Dorothy and I are married, there will be a vacant place at Pastor John's you know. You could always ask them if they would take her in… if, that is, Sarah would be interested in that set up."

"Thanks for that, Mr Osborne," replied Robert with gratitude. "I can mention it to her and see what she says."

"Do bear in mind though, Robert, that it is only a thought; John and Miriam might not wish for anyone else after Dorothy has left. But if Sarah would be interested in the idea, then let us know and I'm sure Dorothy will put feelers out."

David gazed downwards at the table, contemplating further conversation after that enlightenment about Sarah had run its course, for Robert was not yet forthcoming in talking about himself with one much older than himself.

"You know, Robert, I hear from Dorothy how well you have settled in at her workplace.

That is so good, for I must say from my own experience in the office that young people sometimes find the whole process of work quite… shall we say… challenging."

"How's that then, Mr Osborne?"

"Not everyone is like this — please understand me — but one young man who started a few weeks ago… well, he just wouldn't be told what to do and got quite stroppy. The only way we got around it was to get his peers to talk to him about not arriving in late and that worked. Now he is fine."

"I can relate to that myself, yer know, but after talking with Alfred, I started thinking seriously about the way I was going. When he told me about the Lord, it changed my whole attitude. This lad at your work thought a bit like I did before. Most lads in my gang couldn't be told anything by an adult without giving plenty of lip back! There was a lad called Joe… Well, his dad always laced into him whenever he came home, probably because he was late or he'd left his room untidy or something like that. And his dad would hit him. That's how it is in the real world out there; some people don't know anything about the sort of homes many come from."

David placed his hand upon Robert's shoulder, assuring him that he believed in young people and wanted to be there for them to help in whatever way he could — and that was the reason he had opened his karate club up to youth.

"You are an inspiration, Robert; I learn a lot from you, and I know the people respect you a lot at the club. I want you to know I appreciate that, and I like it that you are here right now having a chat with me and getting on with your life in such a positive way. Nice one, Robert!"

Feet were heard coming down the stairs, and the ladies were back.

"You were a long time up there, both of you!" commented David.

"Ah! We were having a lady's chat; weren't we, Sarah?" replied Dorothy. "Now, let's sit down together and have a rock cake. Come sit down next to me, Sarah. I'll get you a plate, then you can help yourself. They have not long come out of the oven... David made them, and they are actually good; I can assure you!"

"Hmm! Typical, Robert, isn't it?" David added upon hearing the last comment from Dorothy. "It still seems that we men are considered second best to women when it comes to baking. What do you think?"

"Now *that* I wouldn't know anything about, Mr Osborne," replied Robert, sounding diplomatic, though he was in fact speaking honestly. "I reckon the most important thing is that they taste good, whoever makes 'em... And yep, they taste good to me!"

Robert had followed Sarah in helping himself to a cake, and after consuming it quickly, he was eyeing the plate for another. Dorothy, noticing Robert's countenance, gathered he was perhaps too embarrassed to ask for one more, not wishing to appear greedy. So, she, against etiquette, took another cake and placed it on his plate. Robert did not argue but simply grinned back at her with appreciation. No sooner had the two young guests finished off the cakes, than Dorothy decided to get straight to the purpose of the occasion.

"Well, Sarah and Robert, we wanted to ask you both something. And well, we are soooo hoping you will say yes... But we must ask you, nevertheless, and you must also tell us plainly how you would feel about our proposal." Dorothy looked up towards David and requested he continue. "Please would you carry on, my dear, and tell them."

A delighted David gleamed at the two visitors and did just that.

"Sarah, both Dorothy and I would like you to be a bridesmaid at our wedding... and Robert, have you thought any more about being our best man since Dorothy last mentioned it to you?"

Sarah's countenance was over-awed for a moment, looking in similitude to that of a humbled, shy child who had just been given a wonderful gift or complimented on achieving some great accomplishment. She gazed into Dorothy's eyes and uttered her response, hardly believing her ears.

"I would love to be a bridesmaid, Dorothy…but are you sure? I can't quite believe that you would possibly choose me, yer know! You've only known me such a short time, and… there are so many others you could choose!"

"Sarah, to have you as one of my bridesmaids would be a great privilege and blessing to us both. Time is not the essence. We have grown to love you dearly as a good friend; you are a very special person. Maria and Julia would join you as bridesmaids, too!"

Sarah could not help herself and instantly became tearful upon hearing Dorothy's warm and kind words; her response was positively confirmed as she kissed and hugged Dorothy.

"And how about you, Robert?" continued David. "Are you okay with your role as my best man?"

"It will be my honour, Mr Osborne; thank you very much."

"That settles it then," said Dorothy excitedly. "We are thrilled to have you both as a couple taking a part in our wedding—indeed, a handsome couple too, I might add!"

A keen observer would have noticed that some degree of emotion also overtook Robert momentarily, but it soon became hidden away. He, just like Sarah, had been overwhelmed in being singled out for such an important role at a wedding—and not just any wedding, but that of David and Dorothy, two special people who were exceedingly popular and highly regarded; people who, in their eyes, could easily have chosen a bridesmaid and best man from so many others, but instead they had preferred and chosen them.

From that time forward, a bond of mutual respect and trust for both David and Dorothy was birthed deep in their young hearts. Both Sarah and Robert had felt accepted, and, furthermore, they had felt wanted!

Chapter 29

The Hen Party

A special event prior to a certain woman's up and coming wedding had finally arrived — and in no time at all. It was being held at *The Darlington*, and the special function — commonly known as a hen party — was in progress.

Five ladies were attending the get-together — Dorothy, Mary, Maria, Sarah, and Hannah. Now Hannah Johnson, as she was called, was a special acquaintance of Sarah. They had become friends ever since Hannah had come to Sarah's rescue during the *Blue Moon* escapade some time ago. Hannah and her date, Clive Melham, who had been conveniently situated at a table close to the scene, had witnessed Sarah collapsing under the influence of drink, amongst other things, and had rescued the injured party from her own pool of vomit prior to the arrival of an ambulance.

The party was loud and lively! Having arrived in the spa section after a swim, the girls embraced the exhilarating delights of the jacuzzi and sauna, after which they entered a specially designated area with a most quiet and peaceful ambience. Wearing robes and slippers, they relaxed casually over a healthy, cold, fruit-mix drink. The area was not exclusively set aside for their use. Another party had also passed through the stages previously mentioned and was now entering the very same zone.

Sarah looked very hot, wrapped in her robe, as she sat prostrate on an easy chair; her cheeks were flushed like two red peaches. She was gently drying her long, wet hair, whilst drinking a glass of fruit juice, when she suddenly exclaimed with great appreciation, "This drink is like… awesome!"

"Wow!" added Maria in full agreement. "Any more where that came from?"

"Stay there," said Mary, "and I'll get some more. Would anyone else like another juice?"

"Yes please!" was the response from all directions, at which Maria got up deciding that she should be the one to help Mary, having set everyone else off.

There was a bar area with the ready-made drinks placed upon trays; one held the fruit juice and the other a sparkling bubbly. As the two of them arrived, a petite, young lady was just turning around rather quickly, carrying two glasses of bubbly, and bumped straight into Mary.

"Oh dear! How clumsy of me!" said the lady. "But you came upon me very suddenly; don't you think?"

"I do apologise," replied Mary profusely. "That was my fault; let me get you two more glasses."

"Do not concern yourself; I can manage very well, thank you," replied the lady curtly.

Mary had been genuinely apologetic, but she had to be quick to restrain Maria, whose adverse reaction to the rude lady was brewing quickly. Upon hearing the woman's arrogant reply, Mary responded simply, saying, "Excuse my interference; it was kindly meant."

At this the lady turned sideways, looked askance at Mary; she scowled at Mary and then turned away in contempt. Moments later, an unexpected — and quite unrelated — incident occurred.

A stranger — another lady of similar age to the first (that is, probably in her late twenties) — went over to the first and purposely knocked her two glasses of bubbly all over her.

"Well, Susan Littleton! Now is payback time! That's for throwing bubbly all over me the last time we were here... and ruining my fresh makeover. Remember?"

"Oh!" exclaimed the sodden lady, drenched in bubbly for the second time in as many minutes. She lashed out in rage, her hand slapping the other with a cracking smack on her face. Scuffling broke out upon the floor, the two screeching and pulling one another's hair, fighting like wild cats.

Sarah shot up off her lounge bed, discarding a hair dryer in the process — and almost her robe as well — and instinctively ran over to help the underdog of the twosome, whoever that turned out to be. As it was, she gave assistance to the lady addressed as Susan Littleton who lay upon the floor with the other person on top of her.

Meanwhile, Mary had run over to the frantic scene and was pulling the second lady away from Susan and helping her get up from the floor. Sarah stood between them with her arms raised, preventing round two, and after shouting at the second lady, succeeded in persuading her to leave. This she did, but not without dispersing abuse at her victim in the process.

Now, Mary was not without compassion as she helped Susan up from the floor. She spoke to a member of staff who had come to the scene, assuring him that all was fine. Susan was bleeding slightly on one cheek due to a scratch, so Mary took out a tissue to dab it and then drew her to one side, finding a quiet area away from the others to sit Susan down to recuperate.

"Well, Susan! This is certainly an unusual way for us to meet," said Mary. Having recognised Susan Littleton from the beginning, she was now attempting to forget about earlier happenings and bring some humour to the situation.

Susan burst out laughing. "Even after what I said to you back then, you can still show pity like the Good Samaritan! I knew who you were all the time, you know. Well, I appreciate your offer of help this time. Forgive my arrogance before and the way I spoke to you; I confess, upon reflection, that it was beneath me, especially since it was you."

"Susan, you needed help, and I would have offered it to anyone. Would you like a drink of something? If so, I'll get one for you. A coffee? Or maybe you would like a shot of brandy?"

"Funny, funny! I've had enough to drink, thank you. And I am feeling okay — under the circumstances. But a strong Americano would be good, thanks."

Mary walked over to Dorothy to apologise for leaving the party and in the process reminded her who the lady was, just in case she had not recognised Susan.

"How dreadful!" responded Dorothy. "Yes, Mary, I immediately recognised who she was as well. Still, Susan does get herself into mischievous situations… very often, I believe!"

"Who *is* that?" whispered Sarah to Dorothy after Mary had gone to get Susan a coffee from the bar.

"The lady is called Susan; she is the wife of Raymond Littleton, Mary's ex-husband!"

"Oh!" exclaimed Sarah with amazement. "That's incredible! And there Mary is, helpin' her out as well. Wow! I'm not so sure I would have done what Mary did, if it were me; I'd probably end up pouring another glass over her head." Sarah broke into laughter at the thought.

The three girls were left to chat amongst themselves for a while as Dorothy decided to walk over to Susan and say hello, for they were after all acquainted with one another. The last time Dorothy had met Susan was when they had both been visiting Raymond in hospital after his mugging in the park on Damsonwood Green.

Susan saw Dorothy approaching and cordially invited her to join them.

"Dorothy McGuire, I presume!" said Susan happily, being quite pleased to see her again, having been impressed with her at their last meeting together.

Continuing within the context instigated by Susan, Dorothy replied, "...and you must be Dr Livingstone! What a dreadful situation back there, Susan! Are you alright?"

"Ah! I've felt worse... the stupid woman! Still, perhaps I had it coming sooner or later, I suppose," said Susan resignedly in admission to a previous occasion that had been relevant to the current happenings.

"Oh dear! And what did you do previously then, Susan? I'm afraid you will have to tell all now you have intrigued us," replied Dorothy.

"Well... I did hurl a glass of drink in her face, I suppose..."

"What?" replied Dorothy, bursting into laughter. "You did what?"

"Yes well... she had it coming, you know. We were all at a hen party a few weeks ago, and she was speaking sarcastically about me when my mobile kept on ringing. I didn't bother to answer it—well, not straight away, I didn't. She spoke out, in front of everyone, belittling me and said something like, '*Oh, Susan darling! For goodness sake answer that call; it just might be a secret admirer and then you would regret it. Perhaps it's Raymond you know; perhaps he's missing you!*'"

"Forgive me, Mary, for talking so about Raymond in your presence, but... I did not take it too kindly, being showed up in company—even about Raymond—and... well, I just lost it and told her to wash her mouth out with *this*, throwing the contents of a glass of champers into her face and all over her make-up!" Susan laughed at the memory. "Actually, it turned out, Dorothy, that the person on the phone was—would you believe?—your David! He was trying to contact me to inform me of Raymond's terrible mugging and that he had been taken to hospital."

In the meantime, the other three girls of the party had suddenly stopped their girly talk to look up in amusement, being distracted by the raucous laughter coming from the others, and they could only surmise amongst themselves what was happening.

Meanwhile, Susan got up, preparing to leave. In doing so, a casual but interesting comment regarding Raymond popped out of her mouth, which came as a shock to both Mary and Dorothy.

"Of course, you will know, Mary, that things have not worked out between me and Raymond, but… it was always you he loved and never me! Still, that's how the cookie crumbles as they say. I'm afraid I was led to marry for other reasons and certainly not romantic love, so I deserve all I get I suppose. I know that will sound horrendous and obnoxious to your ears — both of you — but that's the way it is where I come from. Raymond was far too good-natured for me anyway; I never really deserved him.

"Well, I must get out of these wet clothes and be moving on. There, you see, I have told you my heart… for what it's worth. But I have said what I have said and that's it. Thank you, Mary, for your help; I did not warrant it, which only exemplifies the sort of person you are — in short, a far better person than I am."

Susan was gone, and Dorothy and Mary just stared at one another other aghast.

"That was enlightening, Mary, to say the least!" commented Dorothy.

"I'm not sure whether to laugh or cry now to be honest, Dorothy! Hearing her talk like that so blatantly, and… well, in such a casual, carefree manner about herself and Raymond. Well, it's beyond belief! I just don't know what to think!

Mary frowned, scratching her forehead nervously. "And what is more, she came across as genuine in all she said, as though she was openly speaking the truth—well, from her viewpoint that is."

It was quite clear to Dorothy that Mary really had been shaken by Susan's outspoken revelations, so Dorothy decided to console her as best as she could.

"I think, Mary dear, that Susan lives in a different world to you and me; I would not let her opinions disturb you any. The irony is, as you say yourself, that she was genuinely being honest with us, or so it seemed. Listen, after we have finished here, let's go over to your place and have a good natter. What do you say, Mary?"

"Oh! Dorothy, I'm so sorry to put a damper on your celebrations; let's have our meal now and enjoy the rest of a most wonderful occasion. Then, afterwards... you're on, Dorothy!"

Chapter 30

Further Revelations

Emotional conflicts can all too easily become a battlefield of the mind. The right course of action is never straightforward, especially when under stress, and this was precisely the dilemma facing Mary Osborne after recent revelations had been made plain and clear to her by none other than Susan Littleton!

Susan's recent outspoken words and her candour in the manner she had said them had surprised Mary, catching her off guard; her comments — though flippantly spoken with a carefree and casual brashness, which was Susan's trait in every way — had shaken Mary. Susan's motive for speaking out openly, disclosing personal information as she did, was not clear. Why peg her dirty washing out upon the line for all to see? Why confess her loveless marriage with Raymond before the ears of Mary and Dorothy, divulging such personal matters about herself, knowing full well that in doing so she was only incriminating herself?

Further, Susan had openly confessed private matters, touching upon her background and sphere of society with all the demands and importance of social standing, wealth, and position that come with it — requirements that apparently pressurised her into marrying a man who possessed such credentials, a man whose qualifications had been approved of and seconded by her parents. This had led her into making a marital choice that was potentially doomed before it had even begun.

One could only assume, therefore, that, when looked upon in this light, the whole matter of a soon-to-be-dissolved marriage was a triviality with Susan—and one she felt unperturbed about.

That's the way the cookie crumbles. Mary remembered Susan's words clearly.

I suppose you cannot expect miracles when you marry under such credentials and for such reasons! she thought

Susan, of late, would surely have observed in Mary a different kind of person to herself, particularly during those moments when they had met in peculiar circumstances at the bar in *The Darlington.* While Susan's actions had led to a distasteful and unpleasant confrontation, Mary's response had been to demonstrate an act of kindness and intervention. This she had admirably displayed when coming to Susan's rescue after the incident and subsequent commotion, even though Susan had previously spoken to her in a very rude and abrupt fashion.

Perhaps this was why Susan had mellowed and become more amicable towards Mary—even to the point of complimenting her, if that's what it was, by admitting it was Mary

Raymond loved and not herself! Susan had not hardened towards Mary throughout all this, for an envious or jealous woman would have responded more callously; instead, she had relaxed to the point being cordial — and even sociable — with Mary.

Mary was not of the same mind as Susan, or from her sphere of society, but for a brief moment it appeared a sort of reconciliation took place between the two, as if it were long overdue. Whether these sentiments were a true reflection of how Susan was thinking towards Mary was not clear, but a bitter, harsh woman would not have said what she had, and Mary was taken aback by her words, being left in shock and in a quandary about her own feelings ever since!

Over a long arduous period following her divorce, Mary had battled with serious depression. The upheaval in her life that she had been thrust into — and through no fault of her own — had taken its toll; though, finally, with the help of her brother and Dorothy, she had dealt with it and put it all behind her. All had been laid to rest — until now that is!

In part, it was true to say that Mary's morale and self-esteem had received a new and welcome boost of life since going out with Jerry. A woman is normally pleased to know that she is loved, whether she reciprocates the feeling or not. However, had she been in the same circumstances and frame of mind to that of a few weeks earlier—that is, before ever having associated herself with that certain gentleman—Mary would have more than likely dealt with the situation regarding Susan's revelations about Raymond's true affections in a far better way. But now things were different. She was involved with another man. This created a complication, a rift, much like a disturbance upon a calm lake causing ripples; her emotions were being pulled in two different directions. Which way should she go? The appearance of Jerry Dickson upon the scene had indeed changed everything; she had been progressing favourably in this new relationship—in short, Mary was finally moving on and enjoying herself!

The confusion and struggle uppermost in Mary's mind was concerning the right course of action to take. It all centred around one question—namely, what were her feelings towards Jerry? Did she love him? Would she feel any differently now towards Raymond, having heard Susan's declaration—assuming it were true—that he loved her more than Susan? Would that make any difference to her? Did she still have feelings towards Raymond hidden deep within her?

Mary would always defer coming to a decision regarding important matters, including small things, until having prayed about them first to obtain in all good conscience an appropriate direction to take. *If unsure about anything, don't do it*, was her motto.

This current trial, suddenly thrust in her pathway, was an emotional one of the worst kind — one which she had never encountered the likes of before — and it was emerging into a full-blooded time of testing, challenging her deep within the core of her inner being. What should she do? What would the right thing to do be?

A close, trusted friend such as Dorothy was the ideal person for Mary to share any personal thoughts and intricate feelings with; that is, if she were at ease and ready to do so. And the opportunity was forthcoming, having been conveniently instigated already by Dorothy who had discerned the situation during their meal at the hen party. Dorothy had realised that Mary had looked pensive and may have been wishing to talk about certain matters, given what Susan had just relayed.

Dorothy and Mary had recently arrived at Mary's flat after leaving *The Darlington*. Dorothy was lying upon a sofa, resting her head upon a cushion, whilst Mary had taken to the kitchen to prepare drinks for them both. The air was filled with the aroma of freshly-made coffee, and whilst food was not of interest to either party — enough having been consumed already — a coffee was definitely the order of the day!

Both parties were feeling very relaxed, if not a little tired, the sauna, jacuzzi and swimming activities—amongst other things—having taken their toll.

Dorothy's mind flicked through the events of her hen party as she lay gazing upwards at the ceiling in meditation. It had been nice, she thought, for Sarah to have come along with Maria. For a long while Sarah had been standing on the periphery of her circle of friends, as if contemplating whether she should enter or, indeed, whether she was welcome to do so. Her inhibitions had not been well-founded or in fact warranted; Sarah was well-liked by all. Miriam had also taken a liking to the girl at the Petersons' waffle party, for although Sarah had stormed out of the house leaving Robert alone to face their host, she had returned a different creature later that same day, seemingly changed for the better following her dialogue with Alfred.

Mary entered the lounge with two mugs of strong coffee as ordered, and upon noticing Dorothy's posture—for she was sprawled flat out upon the sofa—she commented, "Well, Dorothy, you are never backwards in making yourself at home these days, and that is exactly how I like to see you. In the early days of our acquaintance you were—what shall we say?—more prim and proper! It would have been quite beneath you to do such a thing in public. But now you are a member of the family, so to speak... well, almost!"

"Thank you, Mary. I think that is a compliment, though I am not really in the public eye, am I? Just yours! Anyway, thanks for the coffee."

Mary sat down on the carpet, close to Dorothy, leaning her back against the edge of the sofa in a relaxed but thoughtful posture and quietly sipped her coffee. After a moment or two of complete quietness, Mary started the conversation with a more solemn tone of voice.

"I cannot get over the incident with Susan back there, Dorothy. She said some interesting things; don't you think? I mean… like, personal stuff! What was all that about?"

"I think that for the first-time, Mary, I really saw Susan for who she is, you know."

"And just what would that be?"

"Artificial. Completely unnatural! She was unmoved, untouched about the prospect of divorcing Raymond, as if nothing disturbed her at all. She gave the impression of taking it all in her stride, like it meant very little to her, which I find strange. She showed no remorse, no anger or animosity, and… well, she even kind of complimented you in the process, I would say."

"Oh! Dorothy, was that how you interpreted it? I take it you are referring to Susan's remark about Raymond's… shall we say his apparent affections towards me, rather than her. What a joke that is!" laughed Mary wryly before continuing.

"I really do not think that was very fitting of her to give such a flippant excuse, given she drew him into her trap in the first place. And he ended up marrying her! She may have been playing the fool, behaving in an artificial way as you say, but what was Raymond doing throughout all this? No, she acted selfishly with her own interests at heart with no care in the world about how she was affecting others... breaking up a family!

"And me? She couldn't have cared less about me! She was absolutely thoughtless and uncaring, showing no interest in anyone or anything other than herself!

"And as for Raymond! He was naïve and beguiled by all her artificial charms... Yes, artificial is a good choice of word, Dorothy. But he couldn't see her for who she was — as false as eyelashes, as they say. And then he comes crawling back like a drenched beetle coming in out of the rain, having found the grass is not greener on the other side and says he loves me more than her! You mean to tell me, Dorothy, that that is a compliment! More like a slap in the face, I would say. I am the last resort!"

Mary sat, face buried in her hands, shaking and weeping under the impact of her emotional outburst, so Dorothy jumped up off the sofa and joined Mary on the floor, holding her in her arms to console her. Mary wept bitterly, with obvious anguish of soul, as deep hurt resurfaced to torment her all over again.

Betrayal by Raymond was a frequently occurring traumatic experience for Mary. Being divorced from him may have separated them physically, but it had not — nor could not — detach her from unfaithfulness's tormenting pangs and distress, making her susceptible to disturbing emotional flooding for years! Susan's so-called compliment had triggered an overflow of emotions by reminding her of all she had been through.

The stark reality was that Mary's grief and pain had only partially resurfaced. Dorothy, at that moment as she held Mary close, could never see or know exactly how her dear friend felt in its entirety; at best, she could only vividly recognise all the hurt she was experiencing by the number of tears that were flowing! Even so, it had to be said that, having suffered extreme depression herself for several years, Dorothy could empathise in part with the experience of unbearable mental anguish. Ironically, Dorothy's abusive past had wrought similar afflictions on her, despite the contrasting circumstances. Both had caused guilt and shame, arising from a sense of failure. Both exhibited excessive strain, low esteem, a fear of the future and perpetual anxiety, leading to depression.

Little more could be said for a while. Mary had just one option; she needed to get a grip of herself, as she had upon countless similar occasions, and move on as best she could. Despite Dorothy having mentioned Susan's comment regarding the place of Raymond's true affections, thereby triggering the emotional eruption that had followed, Mary appreciated Dorothy's companionship. She needed opportunities such as these to release her feelings. As they say, a problem shared is a problem halved.

Dorothy could well recall how she would sit upon her sofa alone in her flat and be in the very same predicament as Mary was right now — weeping profusely and having no hope or solution to the way she was feeling. It had been a most horrible episode in her life, and upon reflection, she wondered just how she had managed to cope in those days! Even so, Dorothy had to admit that it was during those times of hardship that she had come to a living and personal relationship with the Lord. Though her problems had not left her instantly, she had discovered an encouragement that had gradually taken her forward in a positive direction. Indeed, many other problems had needed to surface over time and be faced if she were to fully overcome her past, not least the overcoming of the effects of her child abuse and its impact upon her relationship with David.

Now it was Mary in need of encouragement. Susan's words, re-spoken this time by Dorothy by way of recollection, had had the detrimental effect of regurgitating all Mary's bad experiences over the last three years, the duration of time spent separated from Raymond.

At least Dorothy had triggered Mary's true feelings — for better or for worse — and now Mary, having regained her composure, began to open her heart once again, this time in a calm and peaceable manner, the worst of the storm having passed.

"Forgive me, Dorothy, but it all came back to me just then, you know. Thanks for bearing with me. I feel a lot better after getting all that off my chest."

Dorothy did not respond straightaway but continued to console Mary by stroking her head. She then spoke softly to pacify Mary.

"I understand a little, Mary, of what you must be going through. Please do not be concerned about me; I am here for you."

"Of course, I do have another problem, you know, Dorothy — one I have not shared with you... It's to do with Jerry."

Suddenly, Mary found a new lease of energy. Now, there was more to follow, and she seemed encouraged to bring it out into the light. Now was a good time, she thought, whilst words were flowing and easy to find and able to be expressed openly. Dorothy sensed the re-ignited spark in Mary and became chirpier herself.

"Go on then, Mary; share it with me. But first... how about a chocolate truffle? I brought some back with me from the Darlington."

"Cheeky girl! Yes please!"

"How about another coffee with that chocolate?" asked Dorothy. "Coffee and chocolate go so well together!"

"You're on! Thanks, Dorothy!

"Fancy you of all people, taking chocolates away like that! I would have thought such a thing beneath you — so glad you did, mind!"

"Here! Have one and tell me what you think," replied Dorothy, handing Mary a small box containing six truffles, seemingly deaf to her jovial comments.

"Mm! Dorothy! These are like... *so* delicious, you know! They are sort of a thick dark chocolate, powdered with cocoa, and they have a delicious dark soft centre!"

As she finished her truffle, Mary began to tell Dorothy her story. "Well, Dorothy, it's like this. Ever since receiving that Valentine's card awhile back... Remember? With those initials J.D. which were so vague to read until you cracked it?

Well, I felt... shall we say... flattered that such a young, eligible, handsome man should be interested in me, you know!

"Okay...," said Dorothy in a cheeky tone, having gathered where the conversation was heading. "Do go on."

"Well, you know yourself what happened next; he popped up at church the following Sunday morning and asked me out, didn't he? And ever since then, he has not stopped pampering me in one way or another. Well, it was great fun to begin with and, I confess, most enjoyable. I mean… like being taken out for the first time in years, having flowers delivered… It was like a new lease of life, and my depression has completely gone!"

"That will be the positive endorphins released in your body, my dear," replied Dorothy, speaking like a biochemist. "It happens when you are exhilarated and anxiety free! It's like a tonic, having something to live for — or someone!"

"Yes, I suppose. But… what happens next? Being elated is good, but it doesn't follow that I should go down that road with Jerry. If that's all I am feeling! Like he was some kind of medication!"

Dorothy burst out laughing at this. "Mary, you are funny, and yet the matter is of course serious; is it not? So, what are you going to do next, may I ask?"

It was that famous question that always appears after a certain duration in a friendship, and only one's heart can determine a right response.

"Dorothy! This will sound very selfish of me, I know, but I am going to tell you some deep, meaningful stuff. Okay? So, bear with me! The thought of going to the next level with him petrifies me! It's like walking towards a brick wall; I just don't want to go there, you know. I'm too scared!

"A long time ago, I listened to you, Dorothy, when you opened up to me one day about your own fears and all that. You shared with me the prospect of having a relationship and said that, having experienced abuse—well in my case that word would be replaced by betrayal or infidelity— can cause a problem. As you progress in another relationship with a man, you tend to hold a part of yourself back to avoid future pain. While there's a part of us that longs to be connected to a special person, taking that risk seems next to impossible, if you know what I mean!

"Well, that's how I feel now with Jerry. Having been betrayed by a man once before... You know. Once bitten, twice shy!"

"Yes, Mary; I think I know where you are coming from. But, ultimately, I had to confront those fears or lose your brother, and knowing how I felt about him, I persevered—even to the point of getting counselling."

"That's just it, Dorothy! Now you have hit the nail upon the head. I suppose my real dilemma is... do I love Jerry?"

Chapter 31

A Lost Man is Found

Raymond's divorce proceedings had advanced rapidly, he himself having been the petitioner. The respondent, Susan, had complied with the matrimonial court order on the mutually-agreed and non-explicit grounds of unreasonable behaviour and had therefore presented no opposition to the process. It seemed her casual attitude and outspoken remarks about the break-up of her marriage to Mary and Dorothy at *The Darlington* were not flippant or exaggerated comments after all, but had proved to be true to the letter.

The well-dressed figure of Raymond was just leaving the premises of a certain prominent solicitor's office in town early one warm and sunny morning, just a week or so after the discourse between Mary and Dorothy had taken place, and he could be seen carrying a large brown envelope under his arm. Raymond was wearing a suit as usual, with a white shirt and tie. No sooner had he left the previously mentioned office, than he loosened his tie and opened the top button of his designer shirt, obviously finding it too cumbersome in the balmy warm air and needing some immediate ventilation. Having traversed no more than a few steps, he then took off his jacket and threw it over his right shoulder.

His countenance was very serious, his gaze focused towards the ground as if he were a man with many pressing matters upon his mind.

Very early that very same morning, as Raymond had set out to work, he had walked — as was his habit — past a certain house that constantly filled his mind with fond memories. To his horror, he had observed a handsome young gentleman entering that property, the door having been opened to him by an attractive young lady — one who now appeared even more beautiful to him of late — and peeking behind said lady was a little girl. The scene displayed before his eyes had proved too much to bear; he had diverted his journey to work and had headed straight towards an Off Licence, having previously phoned in sick.

Quite spontaneously, Raymond turned aside to rest upon a nearby seat, which was in the shade, his body-language indicating that his legs were just as physically heavy as his mind; he then drew from his pocket a bottle recently purchased from the liquor store. He stared at the bottle for a while, contemplating its contents, as if undecided and hesitant about what to do next. Having removed the top from the bottle, instead of putting it to his lips, he poured its contents upon the floor, stood up, then turned and threw the bottle over a wall into a canal, continuing his walk towards the precinct in town.

I have made my bed and now I must lie in it! thought Raymond, deciding to inflict upon himself harsh judgement rather than drown his sorrows. He had once tried the latter, but now knew it did not work.

I have been stupid and thoughtless and deserve to suffer. Still, I cannot stand the thought of that man seeing Mary. And to contemplate him touching her! It is too much to bear.

As it happened, Raymond was fairly close to one of his clients who resided in a care home and decided to go a little out of his way to pop in and see her. He thought this would prove a useful distraction and help him to avoid wallowing in his own mire of regret and remorse; helping another person at least had the benefit of also helping him in the process by thinking about someone else's needs instead of dwelling upon his own.

Raymond rang the doorbell and waited for what seemed ages until a care worker finally came along and tapped in a code on the combination lock to let him in. Security was imperative—not just to prevent intruders coming in, but to ensure none of the clients went out. There was usually at least one 'street-walker' resident at any given time, and this ensured their safety; for, sadly, if the patient suffered from short term memory loss and wandered outside, this person would inevitably not be able to remember the way back home.

Upon entering, a staff nurse—who was distinguished from other workers by wearing blue—immediately recognised Raymond.

"Hello, Mr Littleton. I'm just making a cuppa; would you like one?"

"Thank you, no. I have just come to visit Myrtle. How is she today?"

"A live wire as usual. If it weren't for her legs, she would be everywhere! She's not long gone back to her room... didn't eat a lot of her dinner. Here, if you're going up there, would you mind taking her some tea? That would be great; thanks."

Raymond unbolted a stair gate and proceeded up to the first floor. There were always staff members around, changing bedding, cleaning toilets and generally caring for the needs of everyone. Myrtle's door was left ajar, so Raymond knocked and entered straight into her room. It was a narrow, rectangular room with a single bed and minimal furniture. The window sill was full of various flowers and well-wishing cards, but there was an absence of any photographs. There was a reason for this, however. Myrtle had never married and was the only daughter of a vicar who, together with his wife, had passed away a good twelve years earlier so that she was very much alone in the world with no-one to look after her, having now become incapacitated in both her legs.

Myrtle was entrenched in a book and was somewhat startled by Raymond's entry. Staff would normally speak out their presence upon entering the room, but Raymond had not done this. However, it only took a glance from Myrtle to observe who had entered the room; recognising Raymond straightaway, she welcomed her visitor warmly.

"Bless you, Mr Littleton. You have come to see me again… and so soon after the last visit. I wasn't expecting you today. Is that large envelope you are carrying for me by any chance?"

"No, Myrtle."

"Ah! And he's brought me a cuppa as well! Any biscuits?"

"No, but I can fetch you some. What kind would you like?"

"Arrowroots. I like arrowroots, please. Thank you so much. And could you get me another carton of milk, dear? The green top. This is too strong for me; who gave it to you?"

"The staff nurse as I came in. I brought it up for you at her request."

"Oh! That will be Grace; she's on today. Well, don't tell her I thought it was too strong; she's kind to me that one. I don't want to sound ungrateful to the hands that feed me, you know."

Raymond couldn't help smiling as he went downstairs, reflecting upon Myrtles mannerisms. *This is the beauty and attraction of social work,* he thought, *especially with the elderly.*

It was not widely known by others in his profession that he had put aside a prospective career in the stock exchange, desiring to work in this vocation instead, despite a loss in salary of at least one hundred thousand pounds a year! However, Raymond was a unique character who had loved his grandparents more than his own 'closer' family; and, therefore, it was in their memory he had pursued and dedicated himself to this kind of work—much to the dismay of his parents.

Raymond's footsteps were heard once again entering Myrtle's room. "Here you are, Myrtle. Two green-top cartons of milk and some arrowroot biscuits just as you ordered."

"Thank you, dear. Well, what brings you here again so soon, young man? How are things going?"

"Well, I have seen better days, but let's not talk about me. How about you? How are you feeling, Myrtle?"

"Well, I am quite happy here now—thanks to you for getting me a reading lamp and permission to stay up late sometimes. I cannot complain, you know. I must be grateful; a lot of the other residents just sleep all day—but not me! I like to be about the place. There's nothing wrong with me, you see… it's just my legs. I can't get about without a wheelchair.

"I wish I could get to go downtown sometime and have a look in the shops. Then there's *Max's Café*; I miss seeing young people a lot, what with being a headmistress at a school all my life. Ah! They are a lovely generation, you know; they make me feel happy to see them laughing—and all the girls wearing their tight leggings and all…" Myrtle's voice trailed off with a chuckle.

"Well, I can take you out one day a week, I'm sure. How about now?"

"Oh! Bless you, Mr Littleton! But I can't go today; I'm having my hair cut later, and then my chiropodist is coming to do my nails… Let's go some other time, though.

"Anyway, I am ranting on and on; how about you? What are your troubles? You said you have seen better days; talk to me about them. I love a little natter—or as we ladies say, a chinwag! You never know; perhaps I've been through whatever it is you are experiencing."

"Well, I doubt that very much," replied Raymond apprehensively.

"How do you know if you don't tell me about it?"

"Because, Myrtle… you have never been married."

"Oh! I see. Well, maybe not, but I've been round long enough to have known plenty of people who have been!"

Raymond produced the large envelope he was carrying and held it out before Myrtle.

"Myrtle, you asked about this brown envelope; it is for my wife, Susan, and contains various forms to do with our divorce proceedings. So now you know."

"Oh! What a shame! Now I am sorry to hear that."

"You may be, Myrtle, but I have to say that I am not! There is no other option after... well, after I caught her in the very act... you know!"

Raymond proceeded to tell Myrtle everything, starting from the very beginning, including how he had foolishly left Mary and soon after married Susan, something he would regret for the rest of his life. Myrtle listened attentively, showing no surprise nor judgement towards either party, but when Raymond had finished speaking, he was surprised to hear what she had to say.

"Raymond, my parents were believers in the Good Book. Indeed, my father was a vicar for forty years, so what I'm going to say to you very simply is this: the rest is up to you. I believe in repentance and forgiveness, followed on by a new life and a new start. If you have done wrong — and who hasn't? — you need to face up to that and do the right thing. What you should do is get yourself right with God first; that we all must do eventually, if we know what's good for us. Are you willing to do that?"

Raymond looked at his client in astonishment.

"You really are old-school; aren't you, Myrtle?" said Raymond, aghast at her directness and personal challenge towards him.

"I am, and 'old-school' is exactly what you need! Look, it's up to you, but if you do what I am saying... nay, what God commands... your life will never be the same. You'll see."

"Well, I thank you for that, Myrtle. I'm sure your advice is good, but... how does it relate to my situation?"

Myrtle went on to give Raymond a concise Bible study with even more personal challenges, and at one point, when she told him that Jesus had died personally for all his sins, he felt uneasy and overawed, asking her to stop.

Being told he was a sinner may have been the truth, but it cut him to the core so that he began to shake nervously. Was he confronting his real self for the very first time and somehow facing his Maker? It certainly felt as much! And yet the words he had listened to had come from a mere old lady! Even so, there was no escaping it; the words could have been coming straight from God Himself, as though a light was shining directly upon him, so that the more he tried to shrug it off, the greater his guilt seemed to be.

"Myrtle! I feel I need to get myself right with God somehow; what should I do?"

The following few moments were solemn and sincere as Myrtle, with her same boldness, told him what the Bible said he should do.

"Believe on the Lord Jesus Christ, and you shall be saved. If we confess our sins, He is faithful and just to forgive us our sins and to cleanse us from all unrighteousness. To as many as received Him—Jesus—to them He gave the right to become children of God.

"Now, God will know it, Raymond, if you are truly repentant and believe in your heart these words from the Bible. You should read them out now for yourself, Raymond… and then let's pray together—first you and then me. Are you up to this?"

Like a child, Raymond said he was ready and then followed Myrtle's instructions, reading out loud the words from Myrtle's Bible, which had been placed before him. He felt a release of his burdens, like weights dropping off him, as he confessed he was a sinner needing God's help and forgiveness. Finally, he finished his prayer by adding of his own accord, "I give my life to you, Lord. Please direct me from now onwards to do your will above my own. Amen."

"Now, Jesus promises never to leave you or forsake you, Raymond," added Myrtle. "You are His child now, so put Him first and read His Word, and He will come to you. You will know exactly what I mean as you continue to trust Him. So now, take care; I will pray for you. Come and tell me how you are getting on next week, if you will.

"Oh, and by the way... when you go out there, you may at some point feel stupid about what you have just done—even to the point of doubting it as being real. Well, just disregard all of that; it's just the devil having a go. Just think of what you have read and speak it out, then he will go away; he can't stand God's Word, you know—not when you speak it believing!"

"Thank you, Myrtle. I think I should go now; I feel the need to go and tell someone what has just happened."

Raymond got up and left the care home, then continued walking in the same direction as he was going before. Upon reaching the precinct, he saw an old man standing in the square preaching. He had heard much about this person when he had recently stayed overnight with David. This was Alfred Townsend!

Raymond immediately walked over to him, being neither afraid nor embarrassed, and asked to speak with him. No sooner had he told Alfred what he had done than Alfred spoke out to the passing crowd of people, making Raymond's heart jump!

"This man 'ere has just not long ago made a decision. He tells me he needed to get himself right with God. Is that so?" asked Alfred, looking directly at Raymond.

"That is true," said Raymond.

"Do you want to tell 'em why yer done that? Here... just tell 'em the truth of what yer did."

Raymond spoke out in a contrite manner, and yet he was fearless before a growing crowd of people who could sense the authenticity and sincerity of the words he spoke. His simplicity was contagious, for he did not come across as a religious person but as someone who had recently had a personal experience — one who had just met with God! Even the mockers — and there were always a few — stood speechless and could not gainsay Raymond's words and personal testimony of what he had just experienced; instead, they turned away and left, confounded and feeling guilty.

"All I can say is that I was feeling very bad about wrong things I had done in my life, but after believing and accepting certain words from the Bible that an old lady read out to me and which I then read out loud for myself, something happened inside of me. I feel completely forgiven now, like I've been released out of prison. And a great load — all my guilt and wrong-doing — just fell off me! I feel as light as a feather!"

Alfred went over to Raymond and shook his hand. At this, many in the crowd began to realise that the whole thing had not been staged but was real! One man walked out from the crowd and asked more of Raymond, and then several others followed in his steps. Suddenly, something special was happening! There was an unseen presence and power urging people to come forward, as they experienced a compulsion—just like Raymond had—to get right with God! Little had been preached or said, but what had been spoken had penetrated the hearts of the people—so much so that after being prayed for by Alfred, they wept openly, thanking God for His forgiveness.

Those who remained in the crowd stood speechless, watching the scene before them with great interest having never witnessed such a thing before. The reverence and respect was unprecedented. It was not as if they were in a church or religious place—for many would only associate the presence of God within such a building. No, this sight was displayed in the open-air, on the cobbled stones of the precinct at the centre of town, so that if anyone did have such a perception of God being limited to a church, they would have been gob-smacked by what they now witnessed before their own eyes.

Raymond stood back and gazed at the spectacle. He knew he couldn't have caused this to happen! His own words had been simple and hardly eloquent. Something had seemingly been released or triggered into being, and clearly God was involved in it! Human scrutiny and natural reasoning were both irrelevant; the fact was people had heard God's Word, both through Alfred and then unusually in the form of his own testimony. And God had turned up! The scene had confirmed in his own heart—if he had had any doubts at all previously—that what he himself had done at Myrtle's bedside was responsible; it was real and true! From that time forward, all doubts were completely vanquished forever from his mind. He had turned in simple faith and trust to God's Word, howbeit having been led there by an old lady, and had experienced something he would never ever forget!

Unknown to both Alfred and Raymond, a gentleman could be seen rushing from a nearby building, which housed the *Daily Herald*, and he headed straight towards them to take photographs. Alfred saw the man first and recognised him as the same gentleman who had taken pictures of him on several occasions before; consequently, he was not taken by surprise by the man's presence at all.

However, as Raymond turned to face the newspaper reporter, his face sent a shock-wave running down Raymond's spine! Raymond was momentarily transfixed as he recognised the man as the very same person he had observed entering Mary Osborne's house that morning; it was none other than Jerry Dickson himself, the mysterious gentleman who had been lurking around Mary, having surreptitiously sent her a Valentine's card, and who was now seeing her more publicly!

Chapter 32

A Surprise Encounter

The observation of outward appearances can be extremely deceptive, and rarely do they convey the truth about a person or circumstance to a curious onlooker! In such cases, especially when there is ambiguity, any speculation or attempt to accurately understand the situation can lead to erroneous conclusions, convincing the observer that his judgement is correct. Such entrapments and confusions were to catch Raymond Littleton unawares that morning. His perception of Jerry Dickson was that Jerry was considered to be the definition of a gentleman, but more of his attributes were soon to be revealed.

Of late, it had to be said that Raymond had developed a sense of jealous possessiveness towards his ex-wife, due largely to seeing her going out with another man—even though he himself had taken the liberty to go out with (and marry!) another woman. He was genuinely suffering remorse and shame, learning the hard way just the sort of person he had been to treat Mary the way he had. Circumstances had proved to his immature, naïve mind that the grass was not greener on the other side, and his errors in all accounts were substantially great indeed.

Raymond was so distressed, now that his marriage to Susan was virtually over, that he hated himself, and seeing Jerry on the scene was like rubbing salt in a wound! Any selfish sorrow and shame such as this — even if it were sincere — would surely need to be borne. The Divine law — *What a man sows, that shall he reap* — escapes no one, as if insisting, in at least some measure, that we all must bear the yoke of our infidelities.

Whatever the complexities and turmoil troubling Raymond's heart, he now had an opportunity to face up to them, for Jerry Dickson was currently standing right in front of him! For better or for worse, Raymond now had an occasion thrust before him — seemingly from out of nowhere — whereby he could at least confront reality by facing up to circumstances as they were.

Alfred was oblivious of all that was running through Raymond's mind, and he cheerfully introduced Raymond to the new arrival on the scene, the crowds now slowly diminishing from the vicinity.

"This 'ere is a young man called Jerry Dickson from the newspaper. He often comes out 'ere to take photos of me, yer know. But it seems he's taken a likin' to you now as well, eh? Jerry, this is Mr Raymond Littleton."

Alfred went on to inform Jerry about the situation that had arisen with Raymond's arrival and how the latter had not long before experienced God's forgiveness for himself.

"I tell yer, Jerry sir, yer should have been 'ere ten minutes ago to see what happened after Raymond 'ere had finished speakin'. I've never witnessed anything like it before! People were comin' to be prayed for as if they were bein' pulled out by invisible hands and seemed to know God would forgive 'em if they turned to Him! Awesome, I tell yer! If yer wants a good story for yer paper, Jerry, write that down!"

Raymond began to feel uncomfortable in the presence of the young man whom he had witnessed that very morning entering Mary's house; nevertheless, he acknowledged Alfred's statement about him and his vivid description of events. Raymond confirmed them as true, then went on to inform the reporter of further details concerning the role of Myrtle during his visit to the care home, prior to arriving at the precinct.

Jerry then left the two of them for a moment and walked over to some people still standing nearby to enquire of them what had happened. As a good reporter, he needed statements from eye-witnesses to verify all that had taken place if his story were to be credible and interesting, and this is what he sought.

Upon returning, Jerry approached Raymond and spoke to him directly.

"I do believe I may know who you are, Mr Littleton. Can we sit down and talk? If you don't mind, that is."

At this, Alfred walked away to let the two gentlemen have some privacy, thinking to himself that Jerry would probably wish to question Mr Littleton further.

"Fine! I do believe I know who you are as well, Mr Dickson. I think it would be most expedient to talk—and not before time I would say."

Jerry, upon hearing the change in Raymond's tone and manner, gathered exactly what he was referring to, and finding a seat nearby, they both sat down. The atmosphere was tense and volatile; it felt as though it would take little to ignite it.

"I realise you must know, Mr Littleton, that I have been going out with Mary Osborne, who I understand is your ex-wife. Well, I hope you appreciate that the decision to date one another was mutual between Mary and myself, and it is therefore, of course, a private matter between the two of us."

Raymond was caught unawares by Jerry's assertiveness and the formal, legalistic stance that he had taken. Gathering that the ensuing conversation could easily become argumentative and problematic, he considered it expedient to refrain from manifesting any objections about Jerry's relationship with Mary or revealing any personal feelings about this 'private matter' so as not to cause any negative repercussions from certain quarters.

Reluctantly, he took a deep breath and tried to talk amicably as far as was possible, for he was aware that Raymond would undoubtedly end up relaying the whole conversation back to Mary, and bad impressions would make the end even worse than the beginning. Even so, being agreeable about a matter he found hard to approve of in the first place was going to be difficult; so, as a compromise, Raymond quickly formulated in his own mind that to be as cordial and blameless as possible was the best option — even if it did not reflect his true feelings. Certainly, Mary would be more impressed by this approach, if it ever reached her ears.

"I fully appreciate the situation, and you are right; it is of course yours and Mary's private business. I was just interested and, I confess, curious to know... Well, how is Mary these days? Is she well?"

Jerry stared at Raymond with curiosity for a moment, as if taken by surprise, for he had anticipated an argumentative conversation to follow their initial greeting. But he assured himself that he had heard correctly and that his ears were not deceiving him and that just perhaps Raymond had been brought to his senses by the manner and tone with which he had assertively spoken to him.

Raymond's plan worked; Jerry's attitude towards Raymond mellowed, and he dropped his guard and began to speak openly about his relationship with Mary, no longer feeling any adverse threat from his counterpart, who clearly appeared to have resigned himself to the situation more amicably than was his first impression.

"Well, I would say that Mary has been very happy… up until now that is. And she certainly has confessed to having enjoyed herself."

"Excellent, I am pleased to know of her well-being and that she is happy; that is the most important thing. And, of course, I am glad that Julia has a man around as well; it's more like a family atmosphere for her."

Raymond could hardly believe his own words at that instant; his reference to Julia had made his heart cringe within him! Yet, ironically, he knew it was the right and unselfish thing to say. Indeed, the happiness of both Mary and Julia was paramount.

Jerry was impressed by Raymond's attitude and felt at ease to enquire of him regarding his own personal circumstances, for he had heard from Mary in passing that things were not going so well in his marriage.

"I'm sorry to learn about your situation, Raymond; I understand that things are not working out for you with your marriage — pardon me for saying so. Is this true, old chap?"

"Ah! Indeed, you could say that! I realise now that it is far too late, of course. I have made a grave mistake in doing… Well, what can I say… in leaving a genuine person and marrying someone entirely superficial! What a fool I have been! But, as they say, you cannot cry over spilt milk, can you?"

"Why! Do I gather then that you have regrets in ever leaving Mary in the first place?"

Raymond glanced at Jerry seriously.

"I do indeed, looking back. But Mary hates me for it, and things will never be the same again. I have nailed the lid upon my coffin as far as that goes; that's for sure!"

Jerry condescendingly patted Raymond upon the back in a patronizing fashion without any real feeling or concern, but inwardly he revelled in his triumph over securing Mary for himself.

"Hard luck, my man! But I'm certain you will have another lady soon. Of that I am very sure! Why, you have wealth and position; that is an attractive virtue in itself, hey!"

Raymond turned and looked Jerry in the eye, then restrained himself somewhat before replying, "Thank you, Jerry, but I fear those qualities are greatly over-rated and do not lend themselves to true affection, if they alone are considered to be the means of bringing about a happy marriage. Rather, they divert one from those essentials that matter most of all in a good relationship... Need I elaborate?"

Jerry, not desiring to listen to any of those 'essentials that matter most,' shied away from the prospect, the truth being that he felt uncomfortable as to whether he himself would qualify in any of them!

"No! Not at all. Look... I perceive I have enquired about very personal matters, and I apologise for being impertinent in asking about your private affairs. Please forgive me."

Raymond thought this reply from Jerry very interesting, especially since it was he who had asked to be enlightened regarding Raymond's downfall, as if relishing Raymond's predicament now that he had acquired Mary's affections himself. Further, Raymond was curious and suspicious, wondering whether the man really was that sincere; a genuine person, in his thinking, would have been less frivolous in his choice of words towards Raymond, and this had registered a sour note. He did, however, tend to judge people in the light of his own personality and character and expect the same in return from others; but this was hardly ever reciprocated with equal sensitivity and gentleness of heart, so effectively he was probably expecting far too much from Jerry.

Finally, Jerry stood to his feet, about to leave. He was feeling much happier and congratulated himself upon his success after the

the discourse with Raymond, inwardly reassuring himself that there would never be any threat from that direction in the future.

Raymond, however, was feeling all the worse. This unexpected turn of events and good fortune in meeting with Raymond had turned out to be most amicable in Jerry's opinion; it had not degenerated into anything he had pre-supposed might happen, and he felt he had the upper hand. Consequently, Jerry was feeling quite elated and self-confident and felt sufficiently benevolent to leave Raymond with a charitable gesture — albeit one with a sting in its tail!

"I shall endeavour to get this article processed and out in the Herald by next week, Raymond, my friend — incorporating your interesting testimony into Alfred Townsend's monthly slot. I must leave now. I am visiting a certain lady, you know! Bye!"

This last remark from Jerry was very much below the belt, but Raymond gritted his teeth and bore it bravely.

Not long afterwards, he said goodbye to Alfred, thanking him for his words of encouragement. Walking on, he didn't make it very far from the precinct before feeling the need to sit down, yet again feeling the sudden weight and burden upon his mind. Raymond sat there upon a bench musing over everything; his encounter that afternoon with Jerry Dickson had left him feeling demoralised.

How can Mary tolerate such a man? he thought to himself. It was none of his business, however, and he was powerless to intervene. But the fact was he had seen more of the real Jerry in the space of thirty minutes than Mary ever could.

He had always considered the man to be a reputable sort of gentleman, but now he thought differently. How deceived he had been! Having observed the outward appearance, it had proved to be extremely misleading and deceptive; it had certainly not conveyed the whole truth about Jerry. A smart, good-looking man who was suited and booted. Yes, he was all of that, but obviously, this did not make him a gentleman or a nice person! This sense of hopelessness added more sadness to gloom. Raymond continued mulling over his dire predicament and all the dreaded repercussions of his past errors that were now materialising and falling upon him.

As he plunged further into despair, he thought of his old way of escape — alcohol! For a moment, he nearly succumbed to it, but then cast that old remedy aside for the second time that day. What could he do next? In contrition and sorrow, Raymond yielded to his inner emotions and shed a few tears, holding his head with anguish of spirit. But as he did so, a calmness came over him; it was completely contrary to his state of mind, for there was nothing to warrant him feeling at all tranquil at that moment in time. Yet a peace seemed to be overshadowing his pain with comfort, endeavouring to turn him away from all his negative commiserations and nullifying their effect.

This interruption in Raymond's thinking caused him to reflect upon his personal actions and prayers that day with Myrtle, and for the first time, he began to think about God in the context of his own needy situation. Myrtle had prayed in a serious and personal way for Raymond and had asked him to do likewise for himself. God, she had told him, was interested and concerned about the lives of the individual — especially, Raymond's own situation and circumstances.

In the past, Raymond had shunned such a thing, but now it was different. When you are drowning, you don't turn away from a floating plank; when in a desperate state, you listen and receive help wherever it comes from. Raymond was desperate!

Now his very own words, those he had prayed out aloud, were coming back to him. Could it be that God had listened to his prayers perhaps and remembered to help him in his time of need?

Myrtle was right; part of him began to question it all. Things had just gone from bad to worse! He called to mind the words of Jesus that he had not long before read out aloud and saw that the choice was very simple.

Do I believe these Words or not? Irrespective of how I feel right now?

"I will believe God's Word!" he said out loud, and immediately Raymond felt stronger for asserting his declaration — to himself, yes; but also for all out there to hear as well!

Raymond was relieved to have made this commitment to God, and it comforted his mind. At least he was on the right side for a change, doing the correct thing — and probably not before time. He needed help and direction and was now willing to receive it!

Was this peaceful, reassuring experience he had just experienced some manifestation of the presence of God? It felt weird! Raymond, being unfamiliar with anything regarding God, church or religion could only make sense of it if he discarded his own reasoning and believed everything in a simple, childlike manner. He humbled himself at the thought of his coming to God in a such living way and yielded himself to Him.

Raymond was subdued, and part of him thought shamefully that it all had to come to this! A battle raged through his mind — from a different angle this time to that of only a moment ago, one of ridicule and delusion.

But uppermost stood out the fact that he had experienced something that he could never forget even if he tried, for it had been real! Against all reasoning, he'd had an encounter with God, and that was it. The remainder was now up to him!

Raymond had a new sense of hope and purpose, having just crossed two hurdles that had challenged his faith; he could not alter the past, but somehow he had received the impetus to walk in faith, believing God was with him and that a new direction was set before him. There were good people out there that he knew, people such as David and Dorothy; they would advise him, especially since they were people of faith in God themselves.

Raymond could not help but consider the incredible situation. Was it really possible to have some sort of relationship with God birthed within him? His initial response to such an idea had been that of wishful thinking and not reality. *Who am I, amongst so many in this universe, that God should come to me?*

Despite this, Raymond's inner spirit challenged him to believe it to be true!

He was not the first person to marvel at such a notion regarding the personal mindfulness between God and man; one person in the distant past had expressed similar amazement and wonder when he had said in the Psalms,

"When I consider Your Heavens,
the work of Your fingers,
the moon and the stars which You have ordained,
what is man that You are mindful of him…?"

Raymond could not fathom the overwhelming sense of peace and assurance he was experiencing since repenting of his sinful life and calling out for God's forgiveness and help!

He stood up and started to make the forty-minute journey towards home. Without speaking audible words, he prayed that God might help him to face all that was about to happen in his life; for, indeed, under his arm was the large brown envelope he had been carrying ever since leaving the solicitor's office in town. Now, though somewhat crinkled, it needed to be delivered; its contents would terminate his current relationship with Susan forever, bringing about in an official capacity their divorce.

Whilst Raymond was making progress with growing confidence in his prayers, petitions and requests, he especially asked for God's help to overcome his hurt regarding Mary who was clearly moving on with a man he barely trusted.

The way ahead was still going to be difficult, but Raymond took consolation in believing that, whatever the future had in store, at least he was no longer alone but had a new friend to walk with.

Chapter 33

Mary Has Three Unexpected Visitors

Alfred Townsend returned home from the precinct that day exceptionally happy about the mornings events, and he couldn't wait to inform Jennifer about what had happened.

"Jenny! Are you there?" shouted Alfred upon entering the house, only to find that his wife was not in the living room. "Yer never seen anything like it, Jenny!"

Alfred heard voices coming from the kitchen, so he made his way in that direction. But upon opening the door he saw, to his surprise, three ladies sitting around the table immersed in deep conversation. His wife and Maria were entertaining Dorothy in what sounded like wedding talk.

"Whoops! Pardon mi, ladies," said Alfred apologetically. "I didn't know you were having a meetin'."

Maria turned to respond to her father. "Hi, Dad! We're talking about Dorothy's wedding; it's not long to go now, hey Dorothy!" Maria had turned to look at the bride-to-be, smiling as she made her comment.

"Oh! Well, I'd better be leavin' you all alone then," said Alfred politely. "And I'll tell yer later, Jenny, what happened this morning."

"Oh no, you don't! Tell us what it is you've

been up to, Alfred. We've finished; haven't we girls? Well, for now that is."

Suddenly, Alfred had an audience as the three peered at him, waiting expectantly to hear what he had to say; if Alfred was excited about something, then it was going to be interesting. Dorothy pulled a chair aside for him and poured him a cup of tea whilst pushing a plate of biscuits in his direction.

"Thank yer, my dear."

Alfred shuffled in the narrow chair, trying to get comfortable, for his rotund frame rendered the chair most inappropriate to accommodate him. Then, he prolonged the suspense further, taking a gulp of tea as if it were a pewter of ale, before finally addressing the group.

"Ah! Dorothy, you will be very interested to hear this, you will!" he chuckled.

Dorothy looked at Alfred, mesmerised with a concoction of shock, surprise and blushing, whilst quietly waiting in suspense for Alfred to speak.

"There were this Raymond Littleton… you know, Mary's ex. Nar you ain't goin' to believe this—what I'm about to tell yer. None of yer! Well, he comes over to me whilst I'm speakin' in my little corner of the precinct… yer know, where I always stand. And guess what he told me?"

"I wouldn't have a clue, my dear," replied his wife, attempting to break the suspense. "But I know you are about to tell us all; so go on!"

"Well, let me tell yer somat else first. Apparently, Raymond had just come out of a care home where he had been visiting one of his patients—he's a social worker, yer know. I think her name were Myrtle, and she told him about the Lord. Well, bless me if he didn't get down to pray with her himself, and I believe he accepted the Lord whilst at it. What do yer reckon to that?

"But that's not all! After he comes out of the care home, he straight walks over to me askin' to talk, then tells me all about what he'd done."

"Good gracious, Alf!" exclaimed Jennifer. "Are you serious? Are you sure it was this... this man who was once married to Mary that you're talking about? Now don't get it wrong, husband; this is serious stuff!"

"Upon my word, it were him alright. He told me his name; he said he were a social worker and had just visited Myrtle—you know her; don't yer, lass?"

"Well, bless my cotton socks!" exclaimed Jennifer in disbelief. "I remember you, Dorothy, telling me about him and how he had treated Mary badly, leaving her for some flighty woman! Seems to me Myrtle Skinner ate him alive. She's a battle-axe, she is. Didn't half used to get on my nerves, she did—always talkin' about the Lord, saying you must repent of your sins and get right with the Almighty. But that were all before... well, before I had a change of heart and saw things differently for myself.

"Good for her, I say; she's got another sinner into heaven—another notch on her belt now—even whilst she was sat on her bed!"

"Well, that weren't all, yer know. I asked Raymond to tell everyone in the crowd what he'd done, and bless me he did an' all!"

Dorothy was astonished. "Alfred! Do you mean to say that Raymond actually spoke out to the crowd?"

"Yes, Dorothy; that's exactly what he did."

"About God?"

"Hi! He did an' all; very proud of him I were! The crowd seemed quite taken aback when they realised he were not jokin', and some people came out to be prayed for feelin' convicted! Then Jerry Dickson comes along to take his pictures again as usual, and he took one of both of us."

"What! Do you mean to say that Jerry Dickson was there too?" Dorothy was by this time becoming more and more amazed by the events Alfred was replaying.

"And what did Raymond say to Jerry Dickson?" enquired Dorothy curiously.

"Nothing special, dear. They did sit down on a bench together for a while and talked, but I don't know what about.

"I got the feelin' Raymond were a bit troubled about somethin'; he looked anxious like somat were botherin' him… But then he thanked me for helpin' him and walked off."

Dorothy stood up. "I think I should tell someone about this news," she said, immediately leaving the room to make a phone call to Mary.

~~~~~~

Meanwhile, the lone figure of Raymond Littleton could be seen sat in a café some thirty minutes' journey away from the place where he had left Alfred — who by that time had reached home to share all the news. Having felt the need for some sustenance, Raymond had decided to stop and have a sandwich and coffee, spending the good part of an hour there simply thinking about things. In an odd sort of way, Raymond seemed to be relishing the freedom he was about to enter. He had, in all good conscience, sought to reconcile his situation with Susan — and this despite the blatant infidelity on her part, exhibiting her antics before his very eyes — and yet to no avail! Susan was determined to move on; she was not remorseful, only sorry she had been caught out in the act — this she felt awkward about. She had suggested an arrangement whereby they could carry on as they were, with him living his life and she hers, but Raymond was not into such a licentious scheme.

The day was very pleasant, with a warm breeze and broken cloudy sky. Raymond was enjoying being alone for a while; it was a pleasant change, and he could think freely and clearly. He was happy with himself for doing the right thing. It felt good — like he was now addressing his life sensibly for a change and not drinking away his blues. Raymond contemplated his previous social life with much thought. One thing was particularly bothering him. Why had he found it necessary to go out with his friends to the wine bar, engaging in fruitless revelry simply to binge-drink and get drunk?

I reckon this was all a matter of social obligation and of being afraid to say otherwise! Surely, if I do not wish to go along with them, I should say so without fear! I now feel free to make genuine choices. Forget the lot of them!

Raymond suddenly recollected how he had once said he would sacrifice all his wine bar antics and social lifestyle for a beauty that money could not buy; at the time he had been thinking of none other than Mary.

The world was yet to see this new Raymond Littleton. Some would be pleased; others would not. Though only a babe in Christ, knowing hardly anything about the Bible, Raymond had a zealous spirit born in him as is so often the case with new converts who have suddenly seen how wrong they have been about God all along and have realised that every person needs to get right with Him!

He had understood something clearly — God forgives you through the cross. This illumination had been like a torchlight shining inside of him, and now he saw it so very clearly! He finally understood what Mary had often spoken about when attempting to explain to him her own personal experience with God. She had called it being born again, but at the time he had ridiculed her! This was now a matter he knew must be resolved and made good as soon as was possible. There was a sense of urgency about Raymond and a determination to put such concerns right. Much work was to be done, but first he had to deliver the brown envelope he had been carrying around for most of the day. And then maybe he would call upon Mary afterwards, before venturing home.

It is time to leave now, he thought, downing the last of his coffee. *Time waits for no man; why do tomorrow what can be done today?*

He left the café, leaving a tip on the table; then, after walking about two hundred yards, he took a turn down a quiet road and headed in the direction of the large residence looming up before him called Chesterton Park. It stood secluded from the public eye by a high wall which circumscribed its extensive grounds. This he followed round for about a hundred yards until finally he approached two very large wrought-iron gates which were locked. He pressed the buzzer system, which though silent to him, was heard by a porter inside who came out to enquire regarding his request. However, upon recognising Raymond standing there, he cordially greeted him.

"Good day to you, Mr Littleton. And how are you, sir?"

"I am as well as could be expected, Charles, but I need to see Susan; is she in at all?"

"Yes indeed; please come in, sir. I will ring for her, and if you would care to wait in the drawing room, I'll tell her you are there. You do not need me to show you the way, do you sir?" added Charles with a soft laugh.

Clearly Susan was having a shower or something, imagined Raymond, for she was in no hurry to see him. After about ten minutes, she arrived, dressed up to go out and looking like a film celebrity about to attend a preview in Leicester Square.

"Dear Raymond, it is you! What is the nature of your visit, may I ask?"

Raymond held out the envelope. "This. You requested I deliver it to you in person... remember?"

"Of course, of course. Here, let me sign it straightaway; no sense in procrastinating, is there?"

Susan perched herself down as carefully as she could so as not to unduly crease her garments; then, taking a letter opener, she carefully sliced open the envelope and skimmed through its contents. After a few seconds, she placed the paperwork upon the table and called for Charles to bring her a pen, quickly signing in the appropriate place that had been highlighted by the solicitor, before handing the document to Charles.

"Ensure this is posted today; will you, Charles?"

"Yes, indeed madam. I will see to it right away."

Susan was expressionless! How she was feeling at that moment Raymond could not fathom, but she had been efficient and clinical about what was really a sensitive matter — the end of their marriage. Raymond gazed down towards the floor pondering what he could possibly say next, when suddenly Susan burst forth before he could say anything.

"Raymond, I wish you well! Now, if you'll excuse me, I must be going. I am expecting a taxi at any moment, so please forgive me if I say goodbye to you now.

"Charles! Please show Mr Littleton to the door; he is about to go… Goodbye, Raymond!"

Charles escorted Raymond to the wrought iron gates where he had greeted him earlier and addressed his old friend before he left, not knowing if or when he might see him again.

"Mr Littleton, this is a sad moment for me, sir, and I am very sorry to see you go… but I'm quite sure you are making your decision after much thought and consideration. I do wish you well, sir, and hope to see you again perhaps... if that is at all possible."

"Thank you, Charles; that is very kind of you. I will miss you too, my man."

The two shook hands, and after Charles had returned to the house, Raymond turned to observe the residence of the family of his ex-wife one last time.

As the two gates began to remotely close together, they revealed large elegant golden letters within the design which read *Chesterton Park*. The scene before his eyes represented the end of a season; the gates were not the only thing being closed, but a period of almost three years of married life to Susan also—three years which he would rather forget had ever happened. It had been a mistake—a grave error—and yet God was there to help and direct him along a different pathway if he so chose. And he did! Raymond turned away and headed for a certain young lady's dwelling, intent on carrying out his next mission.

~~~~~~

Dorothy, after making her phone call to Mary, informing her of the surprising news regarding Raymond's experience in town, had become troubled about her friend's current situation. She had overheard Mary, in the background, arguing with someone else in the room—and the voice of the other party was clearly that of a man. Dorothy pondered just what to do and finally decided she would drive over there under the pretext of paying Mary a social visit, and in doing so ascertain her well-being.

Now, as Dorothy was returning into the room to Jennifer and Maria, she observed that they were engrossed in a deep and meaningful conversation, discussing together the appropriate age and circumstances for young people to marry — in short having a mother to daughter natter — so she excused herself from their company and left them alone. It appeared that Maria was clearly having matrimonial aspirations inspired by the previous conversation associated with Dorothy's own forthcoming wedding, and therefore they should not be disturbed. Within seconds, Dorothy had grabbed her jacket and keys, jumped into her red sports car and was gone.

So, as it happened, Dorothy was heading towards Mary's house from one direction, and Raymond was walking towards the very same place from another. Now, Raymond was only a good one to two hundred yards away from his destination, whilst Dorothy was more like half a mile away, but their differing speeds and respective distances of travel brought about an amazing convergence of the two at the steps of Mary's dwelling, for they both arrived at the same time!

Now, the approach to the front door was via two sets of four steps separated by a space, as if designed for one to stop for a breather — or, in Mary's case, to temporarily pause with Julia in her push-chair whenever returning home encumbered with bags of shopping.

Dorothy got out of her car, and after automatically locking it, turned to meet the familiar oncoming figure of Raymond.

"Raymond, is that you?" she said in great surprise.

"Dorothy McGuire!" he uttered with astonishment. "Are you visiting Mary as well?"

No sooner had they met face to face, than both were taken aback in shock and horror at what followed next. The front door suddenly burst open revealing a man arguing with Mary, raising his voice in a rage whilst Mary in vain kept asking him to leave. The offender turned and came into full view of the two onlookers, gazing up at him aghast. There, standing before them at the top of the stairs, was the culprit; it was none other than Jerry Dickson!

Chapter 34

Raymond's Reconciliatory Words

Raymond's mind reflected back to when he had been talking with Jerry at the precinct in town an hour or two earlier. He recalled how Jerry had left him with that stinging sarcastic comment. *I must leave now... I am visiting a certain lady, you know!*

Raymond had realised there could only be one person that Jerry was referring to — Mary Osborne! However, it was very clear things had not gone as expected for Jerry. As Raymond was peering up the steps leading to Mary's front door, his eyes fixed upon the two of them quarrelling with one another. He was not at all displeased by the turn of events; as unpleasant as they were and as ghastly as the situation was, things were obviously not going well for Jerry — and whether his own feelings at that moment were right or wrong, Raymond somehow felt pleased with the situation!

Dorothy, however, had turned pale with shock and alarm at the sight of them arguing, and she cowered away from the steps where Jerry would have to descend, desiring to stay well away from him!

Jerry turned to look down the steps at the two spectators and sarcastically commented aloud for all to hear, "Oh! We seem to have an audience! Well, I'll be going and good riddance!"

Now, Raymond had refrained from moving away like Dorothy and stood fixed to the spot on the steps, waiting to confront the approaching Jerry face to face.

"Have you seen enough?" remarked Jerry in a derisive manner as he eye-balled Raymond.

"Yes! As a matter of fact, I have seen quite enough," replied Raymond curtly. "Sufficient to realise you are not the gentleman you exhibit yourself to be, my man!"

"Ha- ha! Is that not the pot calling the kettle black coming from you?"

"Some people are ashamed of their errors, but not you it seems!" replied Raymond in disgust at Jerry's impertinence.

"Ooh! You really have seen the light; haven't you? Well, you might as well join this club here," he said, referring to Mary. "And for that matter your acquaintance standing down over there. You will all get on just fine together, I'm sure!"

Now, Dorothy had boldly moved up a few steps towards Raymond and held him back, restraining him by the arm, sensing that things could easily get out of control. This she did before there was any chance of Raymond reacting to Jerry's provocation and the ridicule that he had unashamedly hurled at Mary especially. It was not clear what Raymond would have said or done in that instant had Dorothy not intervened, but it was very possible that she had saved him from behaviour he would have lived to regret later.

Jerry was gone. Dorothy ran up the rest of the steps to Mary, who was emotional and disturbed by the events. The two were going inside when Mary turned to beckon Raymond to join them as well; he followed them indoors, but, feeling awkward under the circumstances, he suggested that he ought to leave them to be alone.

"Raymond! Don't be silly," replied Mary in a welcoming tone, already feeling relieved by the intervention of her two visitors. "Please, come indoors and sit down for a while, if you will; I wish to hear from you exactly what happened downtown today."

Suddenly Raymond felt encouraged. At least someone was interested in what had happened to him, and of all people Mary was a person who would understand — and, for that matter, Dorothy too.

Raymond went into the kitchen to make coffee for everyone; it was familiar ground, and he knew where everything was. Meanwhile he overheard the two ladies talking together.

"What happened back there, Mary?" enquired Dorothy immediately after they had sat down together upon the sofa.

"Well, I invited Jerry over this morning; I

said I wanted to talk to him about something important and left it at that. In fact, I wanted to speak to him about ending our relationship, you know.

You remember our last chat together, Dorothy — well, maybe you do and maybe you don't — but you were telling me about your difficulties in the past... about men in general. And I was telling you about how I felt having a relationship with someone else — that person being Jerry — and how difficult it was to move on, you know... having been betrayed by a man once before. You know. Once bitten, twice shy! Well, in the end I confronted my real dilemma like you said and asked myself, 'Do I love Jerry?' I realised I didn't, and... well, I decided to end it!"

Raymond decided to make a move now from the kitchen and bring in the coffee, thinking most of the personal chat between the two of them was over. What he had overheard had encouraged him even more; there was no lasting threat from Jerry — and seemingly there never had been, he thought.

"Coffee is ready!" Raymond shouted, heralding his entry into the room, expecting the conversation to be immediately altered with his incoming presence — or so he thought until Mary went on again without inhibition or concern, though it was quite possible she deliberately wished him to hear what she was about to say next.

"Dorothy! I tell you! The man would not hear it!" continued Mary. "He just flipped, you know! He would not accept it; then he tried to control the situation by denouncing me with a guilt trip for leading him astray—not as though we had done anything, mind…"

Raymond breathed a sigh of relief upon hearing this last declaration from Mary.

"In the end, I got cross and insisted he leave. That's when I got your phone call, Dorothy. And you thought to come along when you did—thank God!—and Raymond too!"

Mary looked across towards the man in question and smiled with gratitude. "The presence of another man on the scene was necessary. Thank you, Raymond, for being there."

"Oh yes," agreed Dorothy, looking towards him. "I don't know if I could have handled him on my own… amazing we both met at the same time; don't you think?"

"Yes, I think so too," replied Raymond, happy to have been of any assistance. "I had met him earlier downtown."

Mary was intrigued and amazed all in one about the news she had heard over the phone from Dorothy regarding Raymond's experiences in town and was dying to enquire of him to tell her everything; she thought now was the time.

"Raymond, I hear certain things have happened to you today. Alfred relayed some news to everyone when he arrived back home from the open-air, and Dorothy here phoned me to let me know. What have you been doing, Raymond? Is it true that you have been speaking in the open-air with Alfred?"

"Yes! Yes, I did! I have had an interesting and eventful day thus far... in short, I have prayed and made a decision to follow the Lord. You will understand that can happen without mocking me or thinking I have been silly!"

Mary's eyes watered upon hearing her ex-husband speak so earnestly; the news was unbelievable to her ears. The sound of his mellow voice and manner Mary understood very well to be authentic and sincere. She looked over towards Dorothy and could contain herself no longer; moving towards Raymond, she surprised both him and herself by hugging him, feeling over-joyed with his news.

"Raymond Littleton! You will have to tell me every nitty-gritty detail, if you please! This is amazing! Wait... let me get another strong coffee first, then you can carry on."

Dorothy smiled at Raymond as Mary dashed away into the kitchen; her behaviour and forthrightness was so typical of her. It was a trait of hers, a warm and friendly but outspoken manner she possessed that identified her uniquely as the person she was — one blessed with a most sincere, kindly and wonderful disposition.

Upon returning, Mary sat down upon the sofa next to Dorothy, holding her coffee between both hands; then, having crossed her legs and shuffled somewhat to find a relaxed, comfortable posture, she said to Raymond, "Carry on!"

Mary had asked to hear *every nitty-gritty detail* of his adventures, and Raymond therefore felt free to convey all that had happened that day.

"I left the house very early this morning and walking past... your house, I saw a certain man — whose name I will not mention — enter in. I confess, I was disturbed to see him. I hope you don't mind me saying this, Mary, as it clearly was none of my business... but I never did like him. I just felt I could not go into work, so I decided to phone and tell them I would... well, I made an excuse, saying that I would do a visit which at the time was untrue. But in fact, that's what materialised in the end — and just as well it did!

"I had arranged to call at the solicitors in town to collect a certain legal document which Susan wanted me to deliver to her in person; she couldn't bear the thought of it going astray in the post, I suppose. Then as I was about to...

"Oh! I forgot... I'd visited an Off Licence before, and as I was in the process of opening the bottle, I decided against it and poured it all away."

At this, Mary responded in a gentle, non-condemnatory tone of voice, "Raymond! What were you thinking?"

"I'm giving you the finer details, just like you asked."

Mary was listening intently to Raymond, focusing upon his every word and facial expressions throughout. It didn't take long for her to realise, by following the dots, that he must have been feeling down with himself about his carryings on.

"I was close to the care home of a client of mine, a lady called Myrtle, so I decided to pop in and see her. It was during this time that... well, we prayed together. She asked me about myself and how I was, so I told her about the contents of the brown envelope I was carrying. I reckon Myrtle could tell that something was wrong.

"I didn't realise at the time that she was a devout Christian; she certainly had no qualms about pointing me in the right direction as you might say! I prayed to the Lord, and it came to mind—all that you used to tell me, Mary—and for the first time I realised you were right all along, and I had been blind! It was very real, and I know something happened to me at that moment as I prayed... like a peace came over me and a weight was taken off me.

"Mary, that is why I came over to see you just now; I wanted to apologise to you for all the ridiculing... and the hurt I put you through. I hope you will forgive me... well, for that anyway."

Mary excused herself at that moment, being overcome with emotion, and left the room under the pretext of visiting the bathroom. She had just heard words that were only dreamed of in times past but had never been forthcoming! Her prayers for him as her husband had seemingly bounced off the ceiling, and yet God had heard her cries all along; she had needed to wait for His timing, that's all!

How full Mary was at that moment! She could not help her continuous weeping; she sobbed and sobbed profusely! Dorothy felt it right to go to Mary, gathering how she would be feeling, and excused herself from Raymond's presence.

Raymond was unsure what to think. Was the outcome going to be good or bad? *It was relatively easy to apologise to Mary*, he thought to himself. But he realised that it couldn't have been easy for her throughout all those times when he had admonished her for her faith—and there were many! Raymond began to be concerned; should he stay or should he go?

Suddenly, both ladies returned to the room and his quandary ended. Instead, his eyes were now fixed upon those of Mary, observing her countenance and mood as she walked over to him. Her face looked flushed but was radiant, and as for her eyes, they seemed to shine like two new stars recently born in a galaxy. A smile emanated from her face, and instantly Raymond gathered that she seemed to be well and happy.

It was not obvious to Raymond that a woman's heart could be consoled by humility and contrition, the sort that he had just demonstrated with his reconciliatory words to her. Mary knew Raymond through and through, and never had she known him to be so genuinely apologetic towards her.

"Thank you, Raymond; I am pleased for you that you have had such an experience! According to what you have just described, you have clearly met with God, and… if He forgives you, then I certainly can also!"

This time it was Raymond who felt compelled to go over to Mary and embrace her with affection. It was a good feeling to be forgiven, so much so that teardrops welled up in his eyes. As Raymond stood back, they could not be withheld any more but trickled down his cheeks. Mary, unable to resist, hugged him again, shedding a few more tears of her own. Realising her actions, she withdrew and sat down again with Dorothy who had been the spectator throughout.

Raymond, not wishing to overstay his welcome and feeling that this was a good time to leave, stood to his feet to address Mary, indicating that he was about to go.

"I've finished what I came to do, and now I think I'd best be leaving you both."

Raymond politely shook Dorothy's hand; then, as he was about to do the same with Mary, she moved over to him and kissed him on the cheek. It was unexpected, and Raymond stood momentarily, staring into Mary's eyes with considerable interest before turning to head for the door. Mary called to him before he left and invited him to drop by the following afternoon when Julia would be present. In answer, he replied with a smile, "I most certainly will!"

After Raymond's departure, Dorothy and Mary talked together for a very long time; suddenly there had arisen much to talk about. Eventually, their conversation took a turn and became girly, if not frivolous. It had been obvious to Dorothy that something was in the air now regarding Mary's possible feelings for Raymond—and this as a direct result of that afternoon's meeting with him, so much so that she could no longer resist mentioning words to that effect to her friend.

"Mary, why do I get the feeling you are pulling at the strings of his heart?"

"I beg your pardon! What a notion, Dorothy!"

"Mary, you cannot play those tricks with me for I have known you far too long."

"I cannot imagine where you are getting these ideas from! How is it such things have entered your head, Dorothy? Hmm... you do surprise me!"

Dorothy took that comment from Mary as the closest she would get to a 'yes' from her!

"Say what you will, Mary Osborne, but you have invited him over tomorrow, and... well, I think you are in great danger of making him as much in love with you as ever!"

Chapter 35

A Very Special Day Arrives

Dorothy McGuire had come a long way through her life and its experiences, ever since the days when she would sit alone in her room suffering from her dreadful state of depression. She had been through thick and thin on a journey that all too many have suffered — and indeed still do.

Her story had been hidden away from all limelight and public knowledge. Few knew about her plight and circumstances in the beginning, and yet, as the ripples upon a calm lake moved outwards to the far and beyond caused only by a mere small disturbance, so Dorothy found a widening circle of friends and acquaintances on her journey in life as it progressed positively through the intervention of a loving and saving God.

While a lone figure in her private world of darkness, there had shone a light at an appointed time, lighting up her pathway and revealing a direction to follow. Even then, in her state of travail and anguish of spirit, Dorothy had considered that a loving, personal relationship with God was doable; there had been nothing to lose and it had given her a hope never experienced before.

She had once dreamed of seeing little sheep going astray, and in her dream she had cried out for help from the shepherd, only to be enlightened later that she had been the lost sheep stumbling by the wayside until she found the Good Shepherd.

Dorothy's first social contact in her remote and lonely existence had been Miriam, Pastor Peterson's wife, at whose dwelling she had resided this past year. Miriam had immediately realised that the call of God was upon Dorothy's life; indeed, she had once observed Dorothy's compassion, kindness and generosity in helping another young lady in distress at a coffee bar in town and thought to herself, *Surely, God has called this young lady for a purpose!*

God's purposes and plans for Dorothy's life were past finding out! The lady in distress, as it happened, had turned out to be none other than Mary Osborne — and it was her brother, David, that Dorothy was to marry this very day!

Dorothy's personality and life had changed from weakness to strength, from hopelessness to purpose. Her tenacity and resilience, which had helped her survive through her dark days, were suddenly channelled away from herself into helping others of similar plight. There was birthed within her a determination to help anyone who came across her pathway who was suffering, whether it was young people — like her wonderful friend, Maria Townsend, and Maria's boyfriend, Ian McPherson — or more elderly people such as Maria's father, Alfred, who in those days had been an alcoholic. As a result, God's plans and purposes had had a domino effect through the whole Townsend family in an unprecedented manner!

These had continued with the miraculous healing of Alfred's knee, leading to what he considered to be his Divinely appointed mission for the rest of his life — to speak his testimony in the open-air, which he faithfully carried out. Alfred's estranged wife, Jennifer, who had left him to live with her sister, Betty, had ironically turned to the Lord herself upon inadvertently hearing her husband in the far distance as he was preaching!

This book alone could not tell of every occasion where Dorothy influenced others for the better; it was a daily occurrence in her new life. Through her own personal experiences, she saw that God's love had no bounds!

Yet Dorothy had been very vulnerable in her condition due to suffering abuse since she was a child, and her depression had often been unbearable upon a daily basis, so that many of her acquaintances — who had also experienced similar conditions — often marvelled, saying, "How could you have come through all of that? There must be hope for me!"

Perhaps the greatest challenge Dorothy had had to face was that of a relationship with a man, and David Osborne was responsible for resurrecting that fear in a very real way, for

Dorothy had loved him from the very first time she had seen him—after she had been preaching in church! Fortunately, David had pursued her relentlessly and would not give up on her! His love for Dorothy had exceeded all her reservations and fears—fears that were not so much directed towards him, but rather were deeply entrenched within her scarred heart. David was the perfect example of the man she could not resist, someone who loved her for who she was as a person! It made no difference to him what her mood or condition was, especially when, after a short season in their relationship, she had learnt to communicate to him some things associated with it.

Now the special day had arrived! It was a day couples dreamed of for their wedding day— warm and sunny!

Pastor John and Miriam were, as usual, down at the church very early. John had been nervous every day leading up to this day; then he had suddenly become full of joy and confidence that morning upon getting out of bed. His only sadness about the day was personal; Dorothy had lived for so long now in the rooms once occupied by his daughter, Rebecca, and now they would be vacant once again. This was a circumstance John was not relishing, and he would miss Dorothy. However, Miriam assured her husband that Dorothy and her other half would be invited to have Sunday dinner with them very often, and he could then entertain her once again with his frivolity and conversation.

There was much activity taking place in Mary's home, which had been designated as the leaving place of all three bridesmaids! The home in question had been considered as the obvious choice given that Mary's daughter, Julia, was one of the three, the others being Maria Townsend and Sarah Manning. Now, Jennifer Townsend could be seen finishing the last details of their stunning light-blue dresses to perfection, but all attention to their hair was devoted to an outside hairdresser. The party were all to be taken to the church by limousine; excitement filled the air!

Robert Templeman had a very special job to do—that of best man—and these duties also entailed getting David to the church on time. Robert decided upon the strategy of picking up the bridegroom early and driving him around the block a few times until about thirty minutes before the ceremony was due to start; then he would transport him over to the church. After a few circuits, Robert—at the request of David – pulled over to park for a while, and they sat together relaxing. There was a good fifty minutes to go.

"Robert, thanks for being best man," said David.

"My pleasure, sir," replied Robert respectfully.

"You know, Robert, that is something about you I have always liked from the very beginning."

"And what would that be, may I ask?"

"Why! You always address me as sir… as if I were your teacher or something!"

"Well, you are; aren't you? You are my karate teacher!"

"Ha-ha! Very true. And a good student you are, I might add… black belt coming up, hey!

"But more seriously, Robert… forgive me for saying this, but in looking back to where you came from… I mean your past and all. From gangland in that notorious… Where is it? Damsonwood Estate? You are probably the most friendly and respectful young man I know! What exactly happened to you when you met with Alfred that day? I believe it was in the open-air; wasn't it?"

"David, I met up with Alfred in a café, yer know, after he had finished… but I also met with Jesus!"

"Robert, you sure did! I need ask no more. Your life has told me the rest! Good man, Robert… good man! I am about fourteen years older than you, but spiritually I am only a few months older. You have taught me a lot, Robert."

"Yeah, and so have you, David… and not just about karate!

"Come on now, David; it's time to go!"

The church was getting full. It was about twenty-five minutes before the ceremony was due to start, and Robert had got David in position very comfortably. A young couple, who Robert recognised as Clive Melham and Hannah Johnson, sat nearby. He had not seen them both for a good while, perhaps just once since that occasion at the *Blue Moon* when Sarah had collapsed and they had been the first to come to the rescue. That time seemed a long way away, and much water had passed under the bridge; Sarah Manning had since then succumbed to her feelings towards Robert — though not without much determination on his part — so that now they were very close and had what appeared to be a promising relationship together.

Jennifer had left the bridesmaid party in the good hands of Mary in order to pick up her sister, Betty, and now Jennifer and Betty were comfortably seated together as close to the front as possible. Jennifer was very proud of her husband's role of escorting Dorothy up the aisle and giving her away — a job which Dorothy had originally requested Pastor John do, before realising that he was marrying them!

At the back, an elderly lady was brought in in a wheelchair; it was Myrtle from the care home. However, her new convert — who had invited her to the wedding — was yet to be seen.

As time closed in — to within just a few minutes of the start — the organ began playing soft music, indicating to the congregation that Dorothy and her bridal party were soon to enter.

Then, two gentlemen came in hurriedly and sat down wherever there were available seats — which happened to be near the back of the church. They were Raymond and Maria's boyfriend, Ian. Raymond had been called upon to give Ian a lift, his vehicle having broken down, and he was the only person Ian could think of who was not otherwise engaged. Raymond had felt obliged to help, knowing full well that this diversion was sure to make him late. After all, it had been Ian and Robert who had come to his rescue one day when he had drowned his sorrows and staggered in to Damsonwood Green only to get himself mugged!

The music changed! It was the beginning of Mendelssohn's *Wedding March*! As was often the case, the initial herald of the music made a good number of the congregation jump with excitement; it pronounced the arrival of the bride!

Suddenly, Dorothy appeared! She was being escorted by Alfred who, on this occasion, was immaculately dressed, suited and booted; his old boots, having had a rest that day, were unusually cold under his easy chair.

Dorothy slowly walked down the aisle towards David as lady onlookers, who were dying to observe her wedding dress, turned their heads for a quick glance as soon as the opportunity arose. There seemed to be an audible sense of awe as Dorothy came into view!

Dorothy was wearing a beautiful, natural-waist, classic A-line dress that suited her figure to a treat and was complemented with elegant embellishments. A stunning feature of her dress was the sweetheart neckline; the bodice was made of delicate embroidered lace, and it had a dazzling, low back!

So, it was finally happening! David loved Dorothy dearly. And Dorothy loved David dearly!

Pastor John conducted the ceremony with a noticeable tear in his eyes as he uttered the words, "David, will you take Dorothy to be your wife?"

And later, "Dorothy, will you take David to be your husband?"

Suddenly, it had all finished!

~~~~~~

The two walked outside into the glorious sunshine to meet lots of clicking cameras and smiling faces.

Now, Mary was following close behind the party, proudly observing Julia in her pretty dress, when she observed Raymond standing by himself in the doorway looking in her direction. As Mary drew alongside Raymond, he stepped out to join her, and the two of them walked together, smiling at one another — their smiles seeming extra-special! No sooner had they walked a few yards, than suddenly they could be seen walking hand in hand.

Pastor John, with his wife, Miriam, stopped on the steps of the church entrance to gaze at the wonderful couple who had just been married. This gave them extra height to observe the couple in this their moment — their day!

"Rebecca's rooms will be empty yet again, Miriam," John commented to his wife.

"Oh no, they won't, my dear!" smiled Miriam.

John turned to look his wife in the eyes. "Good gracious! What on earth do you mean by that, my dear?"

"It looks like we have a new tenant... if that is, we both approve."

"Who would that be? Please tell me, my dear! Don't leave me in suspense!"

"It's Sarah Manning! David tells me she is looking out for an affordable flat, and... well, he suggested that she ask us as Dorothy is vacating her rooms. So, dear husband, what do you think of the proposal?"

John smiled at Miriam without saying a word, and the latter knew that it would most likely mean a 'yes' and had met with his approval.

Instead, John turned to gaze once again at the newly-wed couple. The proceedings had reached the stage were the bride was about to throw her bouquet of flowers over her head and eager bridesmaids stood waiting in anticipation, each one hoping to catch it.

The flowers flew through the air, and both Maria and Sarah dashed forward. Meanwhile, two young men stood nearby observing the scene nervously to see what the outcome would be. Now, as it happened, Maria and Sarah were of the same height, and they both took hold of the bouquet together.

Robert looked at Ian; Ian looked at Robert. "Looks like we got two more weddings…!"

Finally, someone in the crowd could be heard saying, "Kiss the bride! Kiss the bride!"

David gallantly responded without hesitation, and holding his wife closely, he kissed her affectionately upon the lips.

What followed next could only be understood by them alone; they smiled and whispered to one another as if saying,

At last we are together!

APPENDIX

Resume of characters from Dorothy McGuire
Books 1 and 2
(In alphabetical order)

Dorothy McGuire – a beautiful, 28-year-old who was born in a rural village in Dorset, the only child of a sea-faring man. A graduate at Oxford now working in market research, she lost her mother several years earlier, but more tragically lost her father in a recent accident at sea.

Dorothy, left scarred with the effects of sexual child abuse from her father, suffered intensely with depression amongst other things. She sought God's help and received a personal experience that turned her to a real, living faith.

After much struggle Dorothy succumbed to her feelings for 32-year-old, handsome David Osborne.

Ian McPherson – an 18-year-old drummer at Dorothy's church and boyfriend of Maria Townsend.

Mary Osborne – a Christian divorcee in her late twenties with a 3-year-old daughter, Julia.

Living alone, she also suffers from depression and is a close friend of Dorothy.

David Osborne – The caring 32-year-old brother of Mary Osborne who falls in love with Dorothy having had a shaky episode of conflict with her regarding matters of faith.

Miriam Peterson – wife of **pastor John Peterson** who supports and encourages Dorothy throughout her struggles.

Maria Townsend – 17-year-old daughter of Alfred and girlfriend of Ian McPherson who befriended Dorothy at the start with her warm, bubbly, down-to-earth personality

Alfred Townsend – alcoholic father of Maria in his sixties who had to retire early after 37 years as a farm worker, owing to a tractor accident which crippled him in one leg. Dorothy is instrumental in challenging him to consider his position before God which leads him to a surprising dramatic conversion as well as a Biblical-style healing of his leg.

NEW CHARACTERS IN BOOK 2

Jennifer Townsend – A strong-willed woman who initially is bitter about Alfred's past behaviour, and the fact that he has turned to the Lord—and been healed so that he can now walk—only rubs salt in the wound.

Robert Templeman – A young teenager from Damsonwood Estate—an area renowned for robbery and drugs—meets up with Alfred in the open air with life changing consequences.

Sarah Manning – who witnesses her friend, Maria Townsend, attacked in the street by The Duke—otherwise known as Robert Templman. Ian McPherson comes to the rescue with his karate skills.

Robert falls for Sarah but she is not a pushover.

Raymond (Littleton) (*Surname attributed, but not used*) – Ex-husband of Mary Osborne and consequently the father of Julia, Mary's three-year-old; now married to Susan

Miscellaneous Characters:

David's father **–Edward**
Dorothy's late Father – **Charles**
Robert Templeman's late mother – **Catherine**

NEW CHARACTERS/DEVELOPMENTS IN BOOK 3

Jerry Dickson – A suave-looking newspaper reporter who is not all he seems.

Raymond Littleton – A drama develops with his wife, Susan.

Miscellaneous Characters:

Betty – sister to Jennifer Townsend

Myrtle – resident of a care home who has an impact upon Raymond Littleton

Hannah Johnson & Clive Melham – young teenagers who help Sarah Manning out of a tight spot

Books by the Same Author
Published by Caracal Books

There is a Balm in Gilead – God's Healing Love, Grace and Compassion
A collection of short stories

Dorothy McGuire – Book 1
A novel

Dorothy McGuire – Book 2
A novel

Contact the Author

www.brianreddishbooks.uk
brian@brianreddishbooks.uk